SUNRISE TO SUNSET

Like *Canal Town*, this is another of Samuel Hopkins Adams' richly patterned romantic novels. Against a warm, colourful yet completely authentic background, Mr. Adams weaves the unusual love story of Obedience (Becky) Webb, a lovely and ambitious young factory girl, and Guy Roy, the handsome and wealthy manufacturer. The years between Becky and Guy's first meeting and the day when at last they find happiness together are marked by events both joyous and tragic —by suspense, murder, a gripping manhunt, and by Becky's strange marriage to the self-righteous millowner, Gurdon Stockwell. Not until Stockwell's violent end is the way paved to freedom for Becky and to a new era in an industry which had been notorious for the ruthless treatment of its workers.

The period and setting of this delightful novel is that of the young virile America of the 1830's, already in the fierce and sometimes bitter throes of the industrial expansion which were to make her the richest country in the world.

SAMUEL HOPKINS ADAMS

Sunrise to Sunset

JOHN LONG LIMITED

LONDON * NEW YORK * MELBOURNE
SYDNEY * CAPE TOWN

First published 1951

Printed in Great Britain
by The Anchor Press Ltd.,
Tiptree, Essex

PREFACE

WERE any Trojan—the York State variety—of the 1830's still living he could pick many flaws in my presentation of the Troy of his day. He might justifiably complain that, while his city did boast a Mansion House, a Harmonia Society, and the biggest waterwheel in the world, there was in the adjacent river no Sadler's Island so unvisited that a woman's body could lie for a week without discovery. He might well say, "Yes, I know the Fosmires and the Heartts, and Tim Freegle and Ike Leroy; but whoever heard of Gurdon Stockwell or Guy Roy, Prissy Stamm or Rebecca Webb?"

And his exceptions would be justified. Availing myself of the novelist's privilege, I have taken liberties with both the topography and the populace of the locality. While my principal characters are fictional, many minor members of the cast existed in the flesh and doubtless bred descendants whose names are to be found in the current directory.

No writer, for example, would have the temerity to invent a name such as Orlando Montague, much less append it to the town ironmonger. The Montagues, man and wife, lived and flourished and bequeathed to their community what was for a century its chiefest commercial distinction. Troy was for long the Collar City.

Possibly I should apologize for saddling upon the city of my literary choice a *cause célèbre* familiar to students of criminology, which took place in Rhode Island, and is still a legally unsolved mystery. But this transfer, too, I believe to be within the conceded license of fiction.

Why, since I have departed from the historical text, did I choose Troy for my locale? Mainly because it was a typical up-state industrial centre, controlled by the dominant "cottonocracy" of the period. And though I have disregarded factual accuracy, I have striven to keep my picture true to the essential character of early industrial America.

For essential and often obscure data on the early collar industry, I am indebted to Cluett, Peabody & Company, and in particular to Mr. Sanford L. Cluett and Russ W. Ziegler; and for information on historical Troy, to Prof. Donald L. McMurray

7

of Russell Sage College. Mr. William G. Roelker of the Rhode Island Historical Society and Mr. A. E. Noelte of Central Falls, R.I., supplied invaluable details of methods and conditions in the cotton-manufacturing trade of the 1830's. For various assistance I acknowledge with gratitude my indebtedness to the American Antiquarian Society and Mr. Clarence S. Brigham; to the New York City Historical Society and Mr. R. W. G. Vail; to Rev. Joseph D. Ibbotson, Col. Elliott White Springs and Mrs. Hannah Josephson; and special acknowledgment for editorial criticism and corrections to Miss Belle Becker of Random House and to Mrs. Robert S. Messenger of Auburn, N.Y.

SAMUEL HOPKINS ADAMS.

PART ONE

ONE

THROUGH the fresh, springtide morning of the Helderberg Hills, a lone horseman rode. The trail that he followed was half-choked in brush, but a promising plume of smoke rose above the flank of the hill. Towards this he pressed his mount. Where there was smoke there would be a house. Where there was a house there would be women. Amos Goodwilly could do business with women, particularly the women of the Helderbergs.

For this was the vast baronial estate of the Van Rensselaers whose rack-rents were driving all but the hardiest settlers away from their pioneer homesteads. Dispossessed females were readily persuadable to the city. And there, as he broke out of the underbrush, stood the token of dispossession, the sign manual of the "good patroon", staringly white and peremptory against the tarnished oak of the door, a notice of distraint signed by the Van Rensselaer factor. The rider gazed about him for signs of life. Perhaps he was too late. He hummed an old campaign-song whose prophesy had not been borne out by the result.

> Let Andy Jackson and his bucktails roar;
> It's John Quincy Adams for one term more.

A spare figure appeared at the corner of the house, half-carrying, half-dragging a mattock. Calm eyes peered at him from a thin little face.

"Good morning, little girl," he gave greeting.

She returned his salutation. "Did you come by the shunpike?" she asked.

"To be sure. Why not?"

She surveyed his obviously bespoken suit. "Aren't you rich?"

"Not rich enough to pay turnpike tolls when I can ride easy on a shunpike path."

"Oh!" she said. "Where did you leave your pack of notions?"

"Pack?" he repeated, puzzled for the moment. "Ha! You take me for a pedlar? That's a slick one!" He laughed.

"Aren't you?" she asked, disappointed, and turned away. "Nobody here but me," she added over her shoulder, and fell to upon a chokeberry root.

Mr. Goodwilly made a bid for her attention. "Listen, little girl. D'you know what I saw in that alder thicket?" He pointed with his whip.

"A bear," she said. "I saw him yesterday."

"No, sir-ree! Worse than a bear." As she evinced no interest but continued to hack at the root, he went on, "A striped goblin with green ears."

"I don't believe in goblins," the girl said calmly. "I'm not a child."

"Blight my soul! Not a child, says she. What are you?"

"I'm a paid skivvy and I earn my hire," she stated.

"Do you so! Perky as a chitterdiddle on a cockweed, ain't we! Where's your family?"

"They aren't my family and they've gone to the store for wolfbane."

"Hm! What's to eat in the house? I'll pay."

"How much?"

"According."

"I'll see."

Dropping her tool, she entered the house and presently returned with a pewter platter. He eyed it without enthusiasm.

"Hah!" he commented. "Skimmagig and a brace of cold boiled pritties. Thin fare for an empty belly; but it'll do, I expect." He took a bite of the larger potato and washed it down with a gulp of the fresh buttermilk, then finished the lot. "Here's a penny," he said. "Now we'll talk trade. Can you read, little girl?"

"Short words, yes, and some long ones."

He drew from his pocket a neatly printed broadside. "I'll read it for you," he offered, and pattered through the announcement:

" 'Wanted: Families from five to eight children capable of working in a cotton mill. Genteel employment. Moral surroundings. Superior lodgment and victualling. Light work, good pay, and humane treatment.

The Eureka Mills at Troy, N.Y.' "

She shook her head. "There aren't five and there aren't eight. There's only me."

His face fell. A homestead of this sort usually meant a large family and good business for him. The mills paid him a dollar a head for all the recruits sent in, and there was promise of a permanent job in the plant if he did well on his present quest.

"Would you like to work in the fine Eureka Mills?" he asked.

"Would they take me?"

"You're mortal little," he said disparagingly.

"I'm little but I'm nimble."

"Suppose there was a place? How much hire would you expect?"

"I don't know," she replied thoughtfully. "I aimed to be a schoolmarm some day."

"Pooh!" returned Mr. Goodwilly with a hearty laugh. "Who but a zany would teach school when elegant employ offers at the Eureka?"

"I'm not so sure I like mills," the child said.

"Blight my *immortal* soul! What do you know about mills, pinkling?"

"I worked in one. At Winchendon."

"Everybody knows those Massachusetts mills are no better than slave-marts," Mr. Goodwilly declared virtuously. "Not like ours. No, indeed! What was your employ there?"

"Bobbin-doffing."

"And you misliked it?"

"Who wouldn't?" she said composedly. "Work all day and no pay."

"What! No pay? Dotch me! Dotch me blind! No pay at all?" Mr. Goodwilly was shocked and grieved. "What kind of mill was that?"

"There was pay. But I never got mine."

"So you ran away," Mr. Goodwilly said shrewdly. "I say there's papers out on you."

She admitted it with a touch of pride.

One penny and a pail of sawdust for return of my errant daughter, Obedience Webb, evaded from her happy home in Winchendon, Mass. The undersigned will be responsible for no outlay on account of the ingrate.

"How long ago was that?" he asked.

"Five months."

"Then that's all right, I guess. Your father, eh?"

"He came every pay-day and took my envelope."

Mr. Goodwilly was a picture of righteous indignation. "What an old skinflint! You did right to make your evasion. A bobbin-girl, eh? How many bobbins could you doff in an hour?"

"I don't exactly know. I could always keep up with the loom."

"Could you, now!" He assessed with secret approval the sinewy form and her competent handling of the heavy mattock. "How old are you?"

She hesitated. She had heard that the York State factories preferred their help young.

"Short of my teens," she said.

"What would you say to nine shillings a week?"

She beamed upon him as if a halo had suddenly supplanted his woollen cap. "Nine shillings?" she said. "All my own?"

"Paid into your hand."

"And could I get to be a weaver some day?"

"Why not? A smartling like you. Mr. Stockwell believes in forwarding his help. He's the owner."

She said dreamily, "Has he got a sightly and pompous son?"

"Eh? Son? Who?"

"The rich and aristocratic owner," she murmured, still rapt.

"Well, damme!" said Mr. Goodwilly, pop-eyed. "What kind of a nitter has bit the child?"

"I read it in a book. A cruel, fine book. It's called *The Factory Girl*."[1]

Mr. Goodwilly cast a disparaging glance upon the coarse skirt which dangled below the wearer's knees.

"What fabric is that?"

"Hum-hum," she answered unhappily. "I've got a better."

"Our workers would scorn anything but silk. What do you have to eat?"

"Partridge, quail, teagle duck," she recited shamefacedly. "Sometimes a hog's harslett of a Sunday," she added, brightening.

---

[1] Which particular volume she possessed is indeterminable. Half a dozen romances of this identical title had been published since the war of 1812, by different authors and in various settings. All were alike in the glowing picture of factory life as enjoyed by the fortunate female employees, and in the gratifying hymeneal denouement.

"Our girls wouldn't look at such fare. Beef, mutton, lamb, pork; all they can eat every day. What do you do of an evening?"

"Go to bed and read."

Mr. Goodwilly launched into a panegyric of life as lived by the happy mill operatives of Troy, New York. Luxurious lodgings. Tasty victuals. Cultured associations. Churches, museums, lectures, baths, libraries (his hearer quivered); all the delights of modern progress. As for the factory:

"Lovely work!" the agent caroled. "The machines do it all; take care of themselves. The girls sing. They laugh. They exchange pleasant conversation like at a sewing-bee. They munch their sweets. They pattern their dresses. The owner likes his help to be happy. He insists on their being happy. You'll be happier than you ever were in your life in our mill. You couldn't help but be."

"Do they read?" the girl asked wistfully.

"Everything. Romances. Improving journals. Pious tracts. Everything."

Obedience pondered. She was not obliged to go back to mill-work. The dispossessed Ter Kuiles would take her with them to some other farm. They had treated her kindly enough. But they were dull folk, these Dutch. They spoke little English, and that unwillingly. Farm life was rugged, remote, monotonous. She longed for town diversions, independence. Money of her own. She could buy another book. Perhaps the kind-hearted factory people would allow her some schooling. She would wear a silk dress; the fat, jolly man had said so. There would be light, pleasant work and merry companions. Soon she would be a weaver, for she was deft of hand—and earn how much? Unthinkable sums. Maybe four shillings a day! She would grow tall and beautiful. She would be virtuous and diligent. And it would follow, as the night the day, that she would win and wed the owner's heir and they would live happy ever after.

"How do I get the employ?" she inquired.

Mr. Goodwilly exhaled a long breath and wiped his brow. He produced inkhorn, pen and contract-book.

"Sign here," he directed.

She set down "Obedience Webb" with a fine, compendium flourish.

"Report for work Eureka Mills, main entrance, Monday week."

"Yes, sir. Good-bye," said Obedience.

"Giddap," said Mr. Goodwilly.

He credited himself with one hard-earned dollar in advance and made an entry of ten cents for breakfast under the heading of "Necessary Expenditures".

TWO

TROY, New York, in the early 1830's was a city with a justifiable conceit of itself.

Its timber-lots, its malteries, its asheries, both pearl and pot, its blacksmiths and whitesmiths, its humming mills and factories formed a commercial structure of unshakable solidity. It boasted a hotel which charged a dollar a day for a single chamber. A reading-room, subsidized by the community at a nominal rental of one peppercorn per annum, dispensed culture to a public notably literate, since more than half its adult populace could read and write; and a handsome public bath encouraged it in cleanliness.

Its citizens were notoriously pious, patriotic and fashionable. That influential and authoritative journal, the *National Democrat*, had published this encomium:

> The enterprise of the Trojans is worthy of all imitation. We believe that they are, without exception, the most enterprising people in the United States.

Troy held every word of it for gospel.

Its most promising young citizen in the esteem of his fellow Trojans as well as in his own considered opinion, was Gurdon Stockwell. At twenty-eight he was universally accorded recognition as a solid man. A director of banks, a trustee of charities, a prop of the First Methodist Church, an earnest worker on committees for betterment, and an investor in any enterprise that guaranteed reliability with profit, he was already spoken of as a prospective mayor. He was a widower of three years' standing, grave to austerity, canny, slow-spoken, powerful of frame, dark and symmetrical in visage, and with no apparent propensity towards re-marriage.

Now Castle Hill, the Stockwell mansion, housed a guest. Gurdon Stockwell's cousin was there not from any community of interest or sympathy of temperament, but because he had recently come into a snug fortune and had further moneys in prospect. Young Guy Roy might be kindly disposed to put his fifteen-thousand-dollar inheritance into his kinsman's plant, the Eureka. The sum would be helpful in the projected conversion from water power to the new agency of steam. Hence the invitation for the visit.

In an upper chamber a gay baritone trolled out a lay of the licentious minstrel, Thomas Moore. Gurdon Stockwell frowned and then sighed. In his judicious view, Guy was a Corinthian, a wastethrift, a ruffleshirt, a young blade of fashion and frivolit without serious thought or purpose in life. Since his gradua from the classic shades of Hamilton College (with a higher gra Stockwell morosely recalled, than he himself, with all his indu and exemplary conduct had managed earlier to achieve) had done little but travel and enjoy himself. There were rumour of a romantic attachment for a lovely but unattainable Thespian which had kept him a bachelor to the unusual age of twenty three.

The trivial note of whistling on the staircase brought h his feet. One o'clock struck from the lower hall. The cousin down to their first meal together.

Foreseeing a dull day with his host, Guy asked across table, "What have you on hand for the present?"

Stockwell rose to consult a schedule on his desk.

" 'Fair grounds. Four-thirty,' " he read.

"Fair grounds? A bit of sport, eh?"

"Amusement is not my purpose."

"Then what takes you there?"

"I own the land. This entails a moral responsibility which I cannot in conscience evade."

Guy grinned. "Some things I've seen at those fairs would be hard on any conscience."

"Precisely. Hotbeds of impropriety, even downright vice not supervized. Also, I must look to my rentals."

"Fine!" said the irrepressible Guy. "I'll help you garner t wages of sin."

The fair had pitched in Gayn's Meadow at the foot of Mt. Ida. To reach it the cousins drove across town and along the turnpike in Stockwell's handsome gig. He spancelled out his blood mare and addressed his companion.

"I must leave you to your own pursuits for a time."

Nothing could have better suited Guy. He looked gustfully about him, sniffing the odour of trampled grass, wood smoke and animal effluvia with appreciative nostrils. On all sides sprawled the itinerant shows. It was a starveling, catchpenny outfit, travel-worn and weather-raddled, a sorry congeries of tents, Conestoga wagons and flimsy booths offering a variety of entertainment.

There were games and sports, a turkey shoot in one corner, a rat-pit in another. Fortune-tellers, palm-readers and an aged phrenologist set forth their rival solicitations. Indians jumped jerked and crowed in the electric grip of a penny shock machine, a device whose lure no aborigine could resist. A one-eyed gambler rattled dice and invited all and sundry to make their fortunes at his expense. A raucous-voiced hawker cried Russell's Itch Ointment, endorsed by Henry Clay and Governor Clinton.

Rough-planked drinking-bars dispensed whisky, peachy, peerie, killdivvle, callebogus, and scotchem, with here and there an authentic pipe of Hollands or Medford. Two medic shows addressed themselves respectively to men's digestive and women's reproductive apparatus. Sniggering customers surrounded a smiling quack who was vending a bottled invigorator to the accompaniment of a fresh line of lewd stories. Mme. de Brale proffered silver bullets, warranted effective against witches, whether broom or fork, at a cost less than the coinage that went into them. A stolid Tuscarora stood staring vacantly at the exploiter of a patent steam bed-bug machine, while his manager piped upon a whistle and announced that at six o'clock the Great Chief would run against all comers and endeavour to better his unequalled record of a mile in 6.44.

In the distance a melancholy mewing emanated from a cage wherein the Ferocious Tiger Cat of the Pampas (born an ordinary wood-lynx) was trying to lick the freshly painted stripes off its fur and being made sick in the process. A Striking Pictorial Representation of the Salem Murder held forth its lure, Admission twenty-five cents, children half price. Abruptly the air was filled with tooth-rasping stridency as Musical Backstein tuned up his saxomelodicon. The largest of several small crowds gathered before a booth where Mr. Stokes, the Celebrated Rope-Vaulter, was hanging himself in spangles. Guy Roy joined the excited onlookers. Having performed his feat and been cut down, apparently at the moment of dissolution, the showman exhorted the spectators to step within and witness a still more marvellous and death-defying phenomenon for the niggardly sum of tuh-hoo shu-hillings, two-henty-five cents, the qu-harter

B

part of a du-hollar. Guy was preparing to respond to the appeal when a female voice back of him exclaimed:

"Blarmy! If it ain't young Roy!"

An arm slipped through his and pivoted him round to confront a vivid, rounded wench of about his own age, with a face like a presentable fox, framed in rich red hair and a pair of shrewd and merry eyes.

"Gypsy!"

"At your honour's service."

"Are the Thalians playing this circuit?"

"The Thalians? Where have *you* been, cocky? The troupe busted up long since."

"What are you doing here?"

"The old game. Midding it. Belly-spottin'." She pointed back at a tent upon whose front a placard announced that Goodwives Browne & Hardwick offered expert midwifery at lowest rates. "Haven't got yourself a wife that needs a bit of birthin'?"

"Marriage is not for me," he said in a hollow tone.

"Huh! Still toosey-woosey over your singin' chambermaid?"[1]

He tried for the fashionable Byronic expression of heart-break. Gypsy was not impressed.

"Your pigsney's well out of reach," she observed. "She hooked her old moneybags and bred him twins before you could say 'marriage lines'. You're lookin' mighty macaroni," she continued, pinching his coat sleeve with appraising fingers. "Bottle-green velvet, no less, with silk facings. Swell!"

"How's trade, Gypsy?" he asked, in the conventional courtesy of the road.

"Lousy. My poor old womb-robbers don't book half a dozen jobs a week. No babies. What's the matter with you menfolks? A weak-backed lot. I'm quittin'."

"Got a better job?"

"I'm seekin' it. Mill work."

"Where?"

"Right here. The mills have got their paper out for hands."

"Not the Eureka?"

"Certes. What's amiss with the Eureka?"

"Nothing," he hastened to say.

"I've got a youngling working there now."

"*You've* got a youngling?"

---

[1] Generic stage term for a soubrette part.

"Oh, none of my makin'," she assured him. "The brat doffed bobbins in Winchendon when I was doin' a spell of honest work there."

Out of the corner of his eye, Guy had been peering across the breadth of the meadow, watching the progress of a black-clad figure as it passed on its inspections. Gypsy noted his interest.

"Who's that toff, and what's he snoopin' after?" she asked.

"Sin."

"Well, he can find it if he's got the dibbs to pay."

Guy chuckled. "He isn't in that market. Fact is, he's my cousin."

Gypsy took a long look. "He looks like money," she decided.

"Want to meet him?"

Gypsy arched her lithe back and regarded her questioner. "Has he got an eye to the gals, like?"

"I should gravely doubt it."

She pursed her lips to vent a modulated question. "How'd he get born kin to you, then?"

"He's the respectable strain in the blood," Guy explained. "He's the owner of the Eureka Mills."

The austere figure was approaching now.

"Business is business," Gypsy decided. "Lemme get a ribbon to my hair."

She whipped into the tent. When she emerged, in an incredibly short time, she was all dressed up, a saucy bow over one ear, her blouse tautened across the firm, neat breasts.

"So you think that will do it, eh?" he commented.

"He's a man, ain't he?"

"Try him and see."

Foreseeing amusement, Guy withdrew behind the tent flap. He watched his cousin pause before the nearby Egyptian fortune-telling booth. Gypsy's gay voice, modulated to demureness, said:

"Can I aid you, Mr. Stockwell?"

Stockwell whirled about. The girl stood, hands on hips, swaying as to some inner *tempo* of the blood.

"I do not know you, young woman."

"I'm Gypsy. Gypsy Vilas. Everybody knows me."

"What is the purpose of this accost?" he asked uneasily.

"You could do me a good turn—if you were kind." She gave him an insinuating smile.

He hastily averted his eyes. "I have no favours to accord."

"Your cousin, Mr. Guy Roy, said you have a kind heart."

"Not at all!" said Gurdon Stockwell in alarm. "How come you to be on terms with my cousin? To no good purport, I warrant."

"Do you call that Christian?" she protested. "To villainize a young female because she meets an old chum?"

"What do you want with me?" he asked coldly.

"A pay-envelope at the Eureker."

He scowled. "The Eureka employs no swingkettles, pikies or tramps."

"I'm an honest mechanic, Squire."

He observed her sceptically. "What's your trade?"

"Lady cordwainer in my time and got my card to prove it. Boots are pickish work for a female. I like the mills better."

"What can you do in a mill?"

"Spin, weave, card or finish," she rattled off glibly. "I'm a willing, strong hand. Look at me, Mister." She sidled nearer to him. "Look at me," she urged.

Fascinated, he stepped back from the danger.

"Apply to my overseer," he snapped.

"So said, so done," said Gypsy to the departing back. The mill-owner was almost running towards his gig.

Guy Roy sauntered forth into the open. "You've scared away the game."

"Men don't know much about other men," she said scornfully.

"And how do you estimate my kinsman from the lessons of your broad experience, Gypsy?"

"I can read him like a book," she said with conviction. "Mr. Pursymouth Stockwell may be powerful in prayer, but I wouldn't trust him in a thicket."

"Fah-doodle!" Guy said.

"Cold heart, hot eyes," said Gypsy. "I've as good as got the job."

THREE

Upon her first startled wakening to consciousness, the little girl on the floor-pallet shrank and quivered. It sounded exactly like the rattlesnake's warning, that bitter whirr in the darkness. Where was she? Then she remembered and buried her head. Around her in the dormitory rose a stir and a sighing. A plaintive voice said:

"Drat the contraption!" And another: "Choke it off!"

That newfangled invention, the alarm-clock, just installed, was muffled.

"Bohng-bohng! Bohng-bohng! Bohng-bohng!" boomed the factory bell.

Sparks crackled from a match. A lamp on the wall spewed out a reek of sperm oil. Eight beds, lined against the partitions, discharged their human content. The feminine figures stumbled and fumbled in the semi-darkness. The little form on the floor burrowed deeper, covering her eyes against the glimmer and ears against the metallic assault.

A door opened. The lanky form of the night-matron entered. She yawned prodigiously.

"Four-twenty. Gates open in thirty minutes."

By factory rules, the hands must be at the looms ten minutes before the sluice-gates set the ponderous wheel clacking and thundering.

"Fire up," a sleepy voice yawned.

Gypsy Vilas wobbled over to the stove and put a hand on it.

"Colder'n a witch's tit," she complained.

"You'll get no firing this day," the Widow Devroo snapped.

By Eureka rules, dormitory fires were not permitted when the mercury stood above forty degrees. For less-considerate factories, the mark was freezing-point.

Coughs and groans greeted the announcement.

"You want to freeze us?"

"I'll bet there's ice in the bucket."

"Hannah Boutwell's got a quinsy now."

"Let her choke," retorted the night-matron.

Moving to guard the wood-box, she stumbled over the form

on the floor and gave it a perfunctory kick. A squeak of protest responded.

"Get up, you little dawdle," the official commanded.

"Lemme alone," the figure whimpered.

"Hey? You won't?" Devroo passed to the corner and returned bearing a half-filled ewer. "You'll be mulcted," she said in final warning.

"I don't care! I don't care! I don't—wah!" Becky shrieked piercingly as the covers were wrenched off and a souse of icy water drenched her. She rolled out, naked, dabbling at her wet shoulders with a blanket end as she fumbled for her clothing.

Gypsy Vilas stepped up to the night-matron. "You want a clop in the face with a broom's end, Devroo?"

"What's the girl to you, and the devil take you, Vilas?"

"Godless speech. I'll report you to the pious owner," Gypsy returned, grinning.

"Enough to set anyone to swearing," the widow grumbled. She was responsible for having her charges at their posts on the dot. "Eight minutes to go." The metal voice in the tower had quickened its *tempo* to an insistent bing-bang. A hum of anxious voices sounded.

Gypsy raised her voice in song:

> "I am a simple working girl.
> Come, day; go, day;
> God send Sunday."

The procession of workers, dressed, half-dressed, struggling into their garments, shuffling nervously, filed through the door and toiled up the slope as the bell sounded in final urgency.

Becky, with a stifled shriek, made a dash for the open. Panting, she reached the summit and darted across the flat. The clamour from the tower died. She flung herself upon the door as it closed in her face. The bar within thudded into its rack. Becky beat desperately upon the oaken panels.

"Oh, please! Please!" she besought.

The door reopened, a grudging crack. Gypsy Vilas's calloused hand reached forth and dragged the child through.

"Couldn't you hurry, you little numbskull?"

"I couldn't button my shift."

Mr. Goodwilly stood before them, smiling his suety smile. He consulted a list.

"O. Webb, tardy. Sixpence!" he said, and made an entry.

"No, please, Mr. Goodwilly! They put me on the clean-up last night," she pleaded. "I wasn't in bed till ten."

"Give me no salvos,[1] little girl."

Her eyes became bitter and solemn. "I'll tell God on you."

"Tut, tut!" Mr. Goodwilly remonstrated, shocked at such blasphemy. "You're a wicked girl and an unprofitable worker in the vineyard."

He entered the penalty with quiet satisfaction. Every such item meant credit to him, as paymaster, in the esteem of his employer.

When Becky reached her place, Gypsy slipped a liquorice sucket into her hand.

"Chaw on that," she whispered. "Don't let 'em see you." There was a rule against eating in work hours.

She took the sweetmeat gratefully. It would be two long hours before breakfast. The loss of the sixpence burdened her spirits. The Eureka, she reflected, now that she had experienced a fortnight of it, fell far below Mr. Goodwilly's seductive representations. Mr. Goodwilly himself was no longer the genial gentleman who had signed her up.

Genteel ease was nowhere apparent. Nobody sat around in delicate silks, reading improving literature. Nor was the air full of merry song. If one so much as paused for breath, the overlooker was sure to be coming that way. Or the sharp call, "Bobbins off!" or "Foul spindle," would summon her on the jump. In these early hours, the cold numbed her fingers and made her liable to drop the abb on the dirty floor. Later, as the machinery stirred the air, the room would be filled with floating lint which tickled her throat and made her cough.

The two-hour stint before breakfast was interminable. Her knees fluttered from weakness. A dull pain gnawed at her insides. The most welcome sound of the day was the single stroke of the bell announcing the twenty-five-minute lay-off.

Gypsy shut off her loom with a clack.

The girls straggled away from the machines, waiting for the food which was presently brought in, steaming in wheeled carts.

---

[1] Salvo: an excuse: American College Dictionary.

They ate hastily and in silence. After finishing, some went out into the passage for fresher air or to exchange pleasantries with the mechanics from the men's side. A few curled up for a cat-nap on the littered floor. Others, restored by the hot porridge with milk and treacle for seasoning, the liberal chunks of corn and white bread, and the lavish supply of mock-coffee, lolled and talked. The favourite subject was pay-day. Imagination spent in advance at least three times the amount of the pay-roll. A hard voice acted the role of solvent to their luxurious dreams.

"Spend the dibbs when you get 'em, not before. That's my principle."

Clorinda Burgo, the oldest worker in the room, was a tramp spinner and a skilled one. It was her boast that she had been put to work on a Baxter at the age of five and had never lacked for a job since. What her present age was would be difficult to judge from her long, jawy, pallid face framed in colourless hair; but Becky suspected her of being an old woman, maybe of thirty or even more.

"Pay as you go," said Clorinda, and helped herself to a liberal noseful of Brown's Superior Maccaboy.

"Mr. Goodwilly told us we could draw on the store for any-thing we want," said Hannah Boutwell, a vacant-faced farm girl transplanted to a low-wage measurer's job.

"I think Mr. Goodwilly is a nice, sweet gentleman," fluted Priscilla Stamm.

"Mr. Goodwilly is a grasping bastard," Gypsy Vilas contribu-ted, and grinned at the gasp of dismay which so often rewarded her ribald vocabulary.

"The store has got some cruel fine garments," Rhuane Nichols, the sizer, said wistfully. She broke off in a fit of coughing. The others eyed her apprehensively. Lung fever was the scourge of the cotton-goods trade. All the best authorities agreed that it came from night air and particularly from sleeping with the windows open, and that it was not catching. Still, Rhuane's younger sister had been taken from the carding-room to die last fall.

"The garments may be good, but they do you out of two prices for 'em," the veteran Clorinda declared.

Gypsy backed her up. "You run up your buyin's and what do you get when pay-day comes? A bucket of shavin's and a thank-ye-ma'm. Hard come, easy go."

"It's best to trade in the company's store, though," said Mary Haynes. She was the best weaver in the room, a neat and comely girl of twenty-six who had passed over many a likely marriage because her earnings were devoted to putting a younger brother through divinity school. "Dealing outside gives a girl a bad name with the management."

"Handy, too," Mildred Hute, a gaunt, sallow spooler, pointed out. "It's all set down in the company book and all you have to do is sign opposite."

"Yeah! And who keeps the book?" Gypsy asked cynically.

"I don't think such ideas are proper," Priscilla Stamm protested. She was a piece-worker, a part-time girl on a six-mills-a-yard schedule, who was understood to put in her afternoons at churchly visitations and other devotional works. In a delicate, shy, impersonal way she was pretty, with large, liquid, gentle eyes and a fresh skin, quick to flush under stress of emotion or even of interest. Gypsy, who did not like her, had derisively dubbed her "Sweetie-pink".

"I saw you dealing in the store yourself last week, Gypsy Vilas." This from Hannah Boutwell.

"Buying two furlongs of rope," the other said. "D'you know what for?"

"What *do* you want it for?" gawked the Boutwell girl.

"A fourteen-foot drop, a dark night, and an open window," the other grinned.

"You wouldn't dast! The rules."

"That for the rules." Gypsy executed her most expressive gardaloo.

"What about your name on the paper?" Rhuane Nichols asked, disapproval in her tone. All employees were required to sign a form which bound them to observance of the rules, church attendance and moral conduct.

"Never put my name to it."

"Because you can't write your name," jeered Celia Sittser, a perky little brunette who stood high on Mr. Goodwilly's favours and was believed to be his spy, and perhaps more. "You made your mark, didn't you?"

"With my left hand, smarty-pie. Even Farmer Johnson's jackass knows that ain't bindin'." She tossed her head. "The rules ain't written that'll hold Gypsy Vilas. When I want a night out, I take a night out."

"Birds that do dark deeds fly by night," said Hepsabeth Parsons moralistically.

"What I do is *my* business." Gypsy winked at Clorinda. "I might rondyvoo the owner in a thicket."

A gasp passed through the group. "How can you say such awful things, Gypsy Vilas!" Priscilla Stamm protested. "Mr. Stockwell is a pious member of our Church."

"If you don't meet him anywhere but in church you'll come to no harm of him, Sweetie-pink," the irreverent Gypsy allowed.

"That's enough, Gypsy," Mary Haynes interposed quietly. "You've got no call to scandalize Mr. Stockwell's good name."

Gypsy's probable retort was shut off by the clang of the bell. The strollers hastened in. The sleepers awoke. The machinery clacked into motion. Work was resumed.

Becky Webb set to her bobbins. Doff—lay the abb by—clean the bobbin—return to the loom. Over and over again. Monotonous but demanding enough to keep her alert. Anyway, she would not remain long at that ignoble and inconspicuous labour. The owner's son, golden youth of her romantic dreams, would never as much as look at a humble doffer. A weaver she would be and earn her three-fifty a week.

Accordingly she lost no opportunity of familiarizing herself with the technique. If one or another of the expert weavers had to "go to the Andes", Becky was on hand to tend her machine while she made the round trip to the unpainted wooden shack overhanging the stream (which, incidentally, discharged into the city's water supply, but nobody minded a little thing like that). Thus she got the name of being a smart and serviceable youngling Even Mr. Goodwilly admitted it.

"She's spunky and self-willed," he reported to his principal, "but there isn't a more willing youngster in the plant."

Becky had no complaint of her job. To be sure, she did find herself pretty sleepy by evening. But that was mere weakness of the flesh and, as such, to be mortified by a more resolute application to the task. She remembered with shame having fallen asleep on her feet twice in the first week. The second time she toppled into a busy loom, fortunately Mary Haynes's. Too late to catch her, the nimble-witted Mary shut off the power and plucked the shaken body out with no damage wrought except to an end of the warp.

Nobody made much account of the mishap. It was too common an occurrence. If, however, a weaver or spinner fell asleep and jammed her own mechanism, the joke enriched the room for days.

"A good worker, but she goes to bed in her loom," was said of these.

The sore spot in Becky's workroom was Meg Shrink, the cleaning girl, a wheezy, snivelling little waif who had rheumy eyes and was always getting in people's way. When she was not scrabbling after rubbish or, with a futile broom, dispersing the lint and dust broadcast to set everyone hacking, she was furtively crying in a corner.

"Poor Tootsie!" she would gurgle to herself in self-commiseration.

Something usually ailed her. Now it was a sty on her eye, again a felon on her thumb, and always the small leprous knobs of the itch. In addition to her other griefs, she had fits at inopportune moments. She tucked her thumbs into her palms, foamed lightly and jerked upon the floor. Fines and threats of discharge had no curative effect. So her fellow-workers dashed water over her and set her outside to dry. In general esteem, it was considered a Christian charity on the part of the mill to keep her on at all, the more so in that she had a blackleg uncle who made lawless speeches at meetings and was dependent upon her when in jail.

She was such an unwholesome little starveling that the others, though a kindly enough lot, shunned her. Becky tried to do her small favours in a patronizing way, but the child only dribbled and wiped her nose with the back of her hand, and continued to weep, pustulate, have her fits, and complain in her private lamentation:

"Poor Tootsie!"

The presence of an inferior gave Becky a satisfactory sense of her own status. She needed it when the working day began to draw to its close. Those evening hours stretched out to infinity. Towards last-bell time she was likely to find herself staggering on her rounds. Bobbins slipped from her nerveless fingers. Her best hope was that the overlooker would not catch and penalize her by putting her with Meg on the final clean-up. That would mean an extra fifteen minutes after the gates closed. The booming note of release at varying minutes before nine was a blessed respite. Becky tossed her last bobbin into the creel and ran.

Supper was ready in the dormitory. She could hardly keep awake between bites. The others were more leisurely. Afterwards they would sit on the edge of their cots and gossip. The noise would not bother Becky. She shook up her floor-pallet, burrowed into it, and was instantly engulfed in sleep.

FOUR

Guy Roy had been at Castle Hill for nearly three weeks. He had not even inspected the plant, finding excuses to evade his cousin's frequent suggestions. Now Gurdon was after him with an invitation which he could not well dodge.

"Two factors from New York are arriving on Wednesday. I plan to make something of a gala of it. I shall personally conduct them through the buildings and shall take the occasion to address my assembled employees. The fact is, Cousin, my other interests have kept me away from the mills more than is desirable. I wish my employees to have opportunity of knowing their employer better."

"An excellent idea," Guy said politely.

"This will be a move in that direction. I trust that you will attend."

Guy said that he would be honoured and delighted.

What little he had seen of the plant hardly justified the latter part of his statement. What did he know about factories, anyway? He remembered a long and lavish supper-party in Utica, and, on the way back to his inn late at night, an encounter with a group of workers hurrying through the darkness. For them it was not late night, but early morning.

Those workers had not looked happy. The young lover of life felt a qualm as he recalled watching that slack and shuffling and machine-like parade. Would the Eureka work-people look like that? If so, he did not think that he would be comfortable, seeing them day after day.

Yet he felt that he should be doing something; he had idled long enough. Where would he find better economic opportunity?

To his help, Gurdon Stockwell was hardly more than an august name; a dignified presence, viewed from a distance. His authority, while accepted as absolute, was impersonal and vicarious, exercised through the paymaster-overlooker. "Mr. Stockwell wishes . . ." Mr. Goodwilly would say. "Mr. Stockwell is unwilling that . . ." "Mr. Stockwell regrets to learn . . ." Presently Mr. Stockwell's desires and forbiddances were embodied in a neatly printed formula, prominently displayed throughout the premises and signed formidably, "The Management".

Becky Webb put it to use by surreptitiously practising the art of reading on it.

The list of fines seemed exorbitant. There were mulcts for damage to or stoppage of machinery, for absences other than necessitous, for unsuitable apparel, for contumacy towards those in authority, and for conversation, singing, reading, or eating fruits or candies in work hours.[1] How different, the reader reflected sombrely, from the shining representations made by Mr. Goodwilly on the road. Damn Mr. Goodwilly! thought Becky in her rebellious heart. Wait till she married the owner's son! She'd fix Mr. Goodwilly.

The factory buzzed with excitement when word passed that a visitation from the owner was scheduled for Wednesday morning. There would be a half-hour lay-off without deductions, so Mr. Goodwilly announced. He hoped that all would show their appreciation by their bright and smiling faces. A meek deportment and a shining face betokened the willing workers. So eloquent did the overlooker become upon the topic that Becky, politely attentive, drew an inference: be contented or get sacked. She started practicing a meek smile.

How many, Mr. Goodwilly asked, knew the Eureka song?

There was a goodly show of hands.

"Why, very well, very well! We will take five minutes to rehearse it."

The machinery stopped. Hepsabeth Parsons stepped out on the floor and started the beat. She had written the song and been advanced from speeder to spinner immediately afterwards. Glad of the respite from monotony, the chorus sang lustily.

"Merry, girlish voices," the overseer commented appreciatively. "The effect will be best, I think, if you all burst spontaneously into song upon the appearance of Mr. Stockwell."

Gypsy Vilas nudged Becky. "There he is now," she whispered.

Out on the gravelled plaza the owner, hands clasped behind his back, was promenading in lonely dignity, giving a final, silent rendition of his forthcoming address which, with slight changes, had served him with signal success before the bible class of the First Methodist Church. Satisfied that he was letter-perfect, he now returned to the office where Guy Roy awaited him.

[1] The Eureka had adapted and improved upon the formula of Amasa Whitney's Winchendon, Mass., mill, for which see appendix.

There was time, Gurdon explained, to make a survey of the model dormitory before the guests arrived. Mr. Goodwilly would come along. Dutifully the newcomer admired the sleeping arrangements: a double bed for not more than two girls in each, except when a press of trade called in extra hands, with an ewer and a basin for washing. The walls were bedecked with inspirational prints in colour, depicting in the guise of female pulchritude those virtues most desirable in a manufacturing establishment: "Promptitude", "Fidelity", "Industry", "Cleanliness", "Honesty", "Prudence" and, for extras, "Purity" and "Science". The legend prescribing "Lights Out at 9.30" alone was un-illustrated.

Mr. Goodwilly, hovering at the owner's elbow, suggested that the hour of eleven was approaching and the hands would be eagerly awaiting the promised words from their respected employer. With Mr. Stockwell's kind permission, he would go and give the advices.

At his signal the water-wheel clacked into silence. He formed the girls up in a double line.

"Cheery faces, young ladies," he said. "Cheery faces."

Finding herself in the second row, Becky appropriated a spindle box to her needs and mounted upon it. She was between Clorinda Burgo and Gypsy.

The main door opened. Four gentlemen entered. At first sight of the youngest one, Becky lost interest in all else. To her witched eyes, he shone like a seraph in glorious raiment. A superb green jacket over a brocaded waistcoat set off his lithe figure. Fawn-hued trousers were strapped above the most elegant of morocco boots. A neck-cloth of flowered silk so jauntily set that it seemed to ripple in waves of lucent sheen, and a tall, shapely castor, delicately puce in hue, with a pale rose band, completed the costume.

A jog in the ribs from Clory Burgo brought the enraptured child back to actuality.

Around her, voices were raised in conscientious joyance.

> "O, sing me a song of the Factory Girl
> So merry and glad and free!
> The bloom on her cheeks, of health it speaks,
> O, a happy creature is she;
> A happy creature is she.
> She tends the loom, she watches the spindle,

And cheerfully talketh away.
Mid the din of the wheels her bright eyes kindle,
And her bosom is ever gay.
Her bosom is ever gay."

Now the great man was addressing them. It was all lost upon one of the audience. Her godling had moved over to lean gracefully upon the window sill with a smile of endurance. Never had she seen or imagined the like of him before. The most eloquent and stimulating descriptions in *The Factory Girl* were dim shadows compared to this reality.

Mr. Stockwell was developing the theme of Happy Faces. A Happy Face was the index to a Christian Soul. Everybody ought to have one. Yet it seemed to Becky, forcing herself to attention, that Mr. Stockwell's own face was not specially happy. That might be because of the heavy responsibility weighing upon him of making other people happy, particularly his hired hands. The Eureka mills, she gathered, were a haven of the blessed, where no one was ever unhappy, hungry or weary. How lucky they should deem themselves at a time when many an unfortunate young female was unable to find decent employment! Yet there were those who, through natural depravity, or misled by scheming and ambitious fomenters, demanded a wage beyond reason or justice and so were self-doomed to idleness and its unfavourable attendants, vice and guilt. Most earnestly did the speaker wish to warn them against the pernicious doctrine of the shorter working day which certain reckless and licentious agitators were advocating.

"The very harbouring of such a design," he warned, "would expose the entire labouring class to many improvident and temptational practices." (Long and vigorous applause.)

Continuing, the speaker referred with emotion to God's established calendar. None but an atheist would wilfully ignore the divinely ordained rising and setting of the sun, which the Almighty had set to mark the hours of man's fruitful toil. Becky wondered about winter and the lights on the looms, but suppressed the thought as unworthy and probably irreligious.

The speaker reached for a glass of water, amidst a respectful and admiring silence. It was slashed through by a wild and nasal falsetto from without penetrating to every corner of the room with its outrageous travesty.

"Oh, isn't it a pity
That such a pritty
Girl as I ,
Should be shut up in a fact-toe-ree
To pine away and die!"

Mr. Stockwell's face congested. A subdued giggling rose from nowhere in particular. Gypsy and Clorinda upset Becky from her perch, pressing to gain a view from the window back of them.

The courtyard below was empty. Keen-eyed Gypsy muttered to her companion:

"Look! In the crab-tree. Cash Barlow."

"What's he doing here?"

"Probably waiting on Prissy Stamm. He's dozened on her."

Gypsy leaned over to the row in front. "There's your spark, Sweetie-pink."

"I hate him!" poor Priscilla muttered.

"Hush up! The old cock's gabbing again," Gypsy warned.

They set Becky back on her box. But when she asked what they had seen, Clory squelched her.

"Clap your hands. Hooray for Mr. Stockwell!"

The speech was over. Beaming, Mr. Stockwell requested a second rendition of the Eureka Song. Once more the merry, girlish voices issued from bosoms always gay. It was then that the glory descended upon Becky.

The young man in the window embrasure had picked up his dicty hat and was smoothing down the nap with a careful sleeve. His idle glance roved along the dissolving ranks of the workers. It checked at Becky. He smiled. At her! A smile to turn one's heart to water. It was a flash of hot lightning, penetrating to the core of her being. She closed her eyes and let the current pulse through her nerves.

Thus happily she was spared disillusionment, as Gypsy Vilas, next to her, responded with a grin and a discreetly dropped eyelid, the slightest of winks to an old pal.

When Becky reopened her eyes, the godling was already on his way to the exit, following Mr. Stockwell. The workers straggled back to their jobs, all but one. As the lines opened up, little Meg Shink was revealed, fast asleep on the floor, with her frowsy head

C

pillowed upon a pile of waste, her emaciated body sprawled in the posture of exhaustion.

Mr. Goodwilly's sharp eye did not miss the disgraceful spectacle. He entered it in the company's fine book.

M. Shink—1 Shil.

FIVE

DORMITORY Four violated the rules that evening by prolonged conversation after lights out. Gurdon Stockwell's address was examined, analysed, dissected, and debated in its bearing upon their own concerns. General opinion approved it as an elevating exposition of Christian principles applied to the trade.

From this, the angle veered to the personal. Why had Mr. Stockwell not remarried? It quite startled Becky to hear him the subject of such speculation; he seemed too old. Nearly thirty, she supposed.

"Somebody'll be lucky to get him," Hepsabeth Parsons said.

Relief Lovejoy tossed her pretty head. "Who wants him for a husband! I wouldn't. I'll bet he's hairy all over."

A little, uncomprehending shiver went through Becky's nerves.

"His skin is so blue, too," added Malinda Prowitt.

"That's the mark of a real man," Mildred Hute giggled. "There's whiskers under that skin."

"Nobody'd want him except for his money," was Arvila Hopkins's opinion.

"Prissy would," Gypsy Vilas said maliciously. "Wouldn't you, Sweetie-pink?"

"You've no call to say that, Miss Vilas," Priscilla Stamm protested, palpitant with embarrassment. "I hope I know my place."

"Let her alone, Gypsy," Mary Haynes put in, seeing Priscilla on the verge of tears.

"I'll take that young feller that was with him," Hannah Boutwell declared.

Sagging to the verge of sleep, Becky's attention was alerted by the introduction of a new name.

"That's Mr. Guy Roy. He's mortal sightly."

"What fetched him to the mills?" someone asked.

"He's housed with Mr. Stockwell," another answered. "They're cousins, as I hear it."

"What does he do?"

"Nothing. He's a real macaroni."

"Does his pa own a factory?"

The question, in a high, eager pipe, quavered up from the

floor. Becky was sitting straight. She shrank from the cackle of surprised laughter, drawing the blanket up round her neck.

"What's that to you, you little scruff?" Clorinda demanded, not unkindly.

Becky made no reply. Another voice put the question which was surging in her heart.

"Is he married?"

"Nobody knows. No sign of a wife."

Gypsy offered a bet in the negative. "I know his kind. Quick to bed but slow to church."

Anyway, Becky knew his name now: a fine, proud name, gallant, like himself. Guy Roy. Guy Roy had smiled at her.

While it had mildly bored him, the ceremonial tour of the mills had also impressed Guy Roy quite favourably. The mechanics had evinced an unmistakable appreciation of their bounties. They had looked well conditioned and certainly not over-worked. Gurdon Stockwell's address had undertones of genuine concern for the well-being of his employees. Guy was inclined to explore the potentialities of the participation suggested by his cousin.

To this end, he called on the morrow at the Eurkea office where he found the two visiting factors making their farewells to the owner and his attendant paymaster. Upon Guy's explanation of his call, Gurdon drew down his ledgers and launched forth upon the active seas of finance.

"Twenty per centum," he concluded his lucid discourse, in the tone which distinguished his mention of money from lesser topics. "Twenty per centum on the investment."

"That seems satisfactory," Guy Roy said.

"And at a risk so slight that I can describe it only as contemptible."

Young Mr. Roy murmured that there was risk in everything. Otherwise where would be the fun in life?

Fun, Gurdon Stockwell said, was not the purpose of life. "Satisfaction, yes; the gratification of conducting this establishment as a model for the fabrics trade."

"I've heard of model factories," Guy Roy said with some interest.

His cousin's expression took on a slight strain. "A term too often malverted by reformers and agitators," he said. "The prime purpose of commerce is to turn out a sound product at the highest available profit. With due regard to the well-being of the employees, to be sure."

"I keep telling Mr. Stockwell," Goodwilly put in, "that he treats 'em too well. Asking your pardon, sir, you pay too high."

"Up to four dollars a week," the owner confirmed.

"And they fare too well. D'you know what our contract for victualling is, Mr. Roy? It would shock you, sir. A dollar eight per head per week. I could get it contracted for eighty-seven cents. Would you believe it, we give them a full meal Sunday evenings after their day of idleness when other mills serve no more than an ort-supper."

"No, no, Goodwilly," the owner said firmly but kindly. "No week's leavings for my people. Sound fare makes faithful work. I do not grudge it them."

The overlooker was not done with his pet grievance. "Look at the hours. Winter Saturdays, close at sunset. Gives 'em time to think. A good, long day's work is the thing. Keeps 'em tired; makes 'em sleep sound. When they're in bed they don't get into trouble."

Mr. Stockwell permitted himself a sly witticism: "Not when they're in *our* beds," he smiled. "Our bastardy rate is the lowest in Troy."

"They know how long the job'll last if *that* happens," Goodwilly said virtuously.

"Goodwilly's ideas are sound," his boss said, "though he may press them hard at times." He pointed a rhetorical finger at his cousin's chest. "What," he demanded, "is the curse of the mechanics class today?"

"Drink." Guy was confident of supplying the expected answer.

"Well—er—not among the females. I will inform you. Their curse is discontent, bred of money."

"Too little?" Guy suggested.

"Too much."

"Of course," Guy apologized. "I spoke without thinking."

"Money," Gurdon said, "is a wile of Satan for the female soul's destruction. They squander it upon gewgaws, they garb themselves in the flaunting colours of harlotry to seduce the souls of the unwary. The lusts of the eye which lead to the burning lusts of the flesh."

It occurred to Guy that his cousin dwelt upon the morals of his female help with an insistence not quite healthy.

"Yet they always want more," the employer went on, his tone changing to annoyance.

"They had the audacity to threaten a turn-out. The weavers headed it. They demanded more pay for tending two looms than one."

Guy said in his most reasonable manner, "But don't two looms produce more cloth than one?"

"They do. But they require no more labour on the part of the operative . . . Well, very little more."

"Nevertheless, they want more pay? That," Guy said brightly, "must be what our political leaders mean when they talk about the impudent encroachments of the proletariat."

"Exactly. There was no turn-out," Gurdon added grimly. "I did the turning-out when I took charge. A clean sweep of the malcontents. Have you ever heard of Cassius Barlow?"

"No."

"A pestilential fellow. A foul-minded, foul-tongued agitator," the financier said, showing signs of agitation himself. "He incited our mechanics to demand not only more pay but shorter hours. Shorter hours, mind you! And what becomes of our production? It's this cursed trades union influence."

"Was Barlow one of your hands?"

"Not he! He couldn't get a loom in town if he worked for a pistareen per day. It would be well if we could clear out all the men operatives," he continued thoughtfully. "That is my ambition for the Eureka. Females are less troublesome and far cheaper."

Guy nodded.

"My principle of management," Gurdon Stockwell pronounced, "is fair treatment for all, no matter how humble. To this you would be expected to adhere, Cousin, if you throw in your lot with the Eureka, as I hope you will."

"I shall give it my most careful consideration," Guy said in what he believed to be the best commercial usage.

Noon recess was on as Guy emerged upon the courtyard, into which a few of the workers were languidly seeping. A small and surprising figure rounded the corner of Factory No. 2. It was half dragging a heavy bucket and reciting in a conscientious monotone a lay whose burden was self instruction:

"Keep your frock and fixings clean
And never get them dirt-ty.
Five times five is twenty-five.
And five times six is thirt-ty."

At sight of the young man, she dropped the bucket and the heavy handle banged her on the calf of the leg. Guy contemplated with amused interest the elfish face beneath a wild mop of tawny hair. The greenish hazel eyes which she lifted to him were alight with eagerness. She pressed both hands to her meagre chest.

"Oh!" she breathed.

He swept off his tall hat with elaborate courtesy. "I trust, madam, that I have not startled you."

"Oh no. Is it truly *you*?"

He was puzzled by her identification. "You know me?"

"Yes. You're Mr. Guy Roy. You smiled."

"It's a foolish habit of mine."

"I think it's cruel pretty."

He laughed. "What's that bucket for?"

"Water to wash abbs."

"What's abbs?"

She stared, incredulous and grieved. "You don't know what an abbs is? Oh, deary me!"

"I'm sorry. Ought I to know?"

"I thought you had a mill," she faltered. "I mean—I thought you had a pa and your pa had a mill."

"No, I haven't any pa, let alone a mill. What made you think I had?"

"You're so seemly and pompous," she answered simply. "And if he did have a mill, like in my book . . ."

"Well?" he said encouragingly.

". . . You'd give me employ." She followed with a rush of words. "I'm a diligent and faithful worker. I'd work so hard that you'd have to notice me and your pa would be proud he'd hired me. But you said you haven't got any pa. Oh, deary, deary me!"

"Did you get all that out of your book?" he asked.

She nodded. "It's a romance. So lovely!"

"So you read romances," he commented, surprised and amused. It was a rare child indeed of the working class who could read. "Do you know all the words, minnikin?"

"All the common ones. And a lot of the big ones. Some of 'em," she continued confidentially, "seem mortal hard at first. But if you look at 'em long and kindly, they sort of tell you what they mean."

"Well, I'm damned!" said the young man. "And you work here in the mills?"

"Oh yes!" Becky gushed, mindful of Clorinda Burgo's instructions. "It's lovely, lovely work. Only, I get sleepy sometimes."

"Perhaps you get up too early."

"No—o—o. Not till nearly sunrise."

"And you work until dark?"

"Later sometimes," she replied placidly. "Not that I mind."

"Um!" said Mr. Guy Roy. "Would you like a shilling?"

"No, thank you kindly, sir."

"No? Sure?" He had an inspiration. "Would you like a book?"

"From you? Oh!" It was a long-drawn gasp of ecstasy.

"I'll send you one."

"A romance?"

"If that's your fancy."

She considered. "Maybe it would be better for me to have something improving."

"Well, I'm da—— What maggot have you got now, child?"

"I want to know things."

"What things?"

"Everything," she said. She recalled a useful phrase. "I wish to enhance my mind," she stated. "I'd like a Book of Knowledge. If it isn't too costly," she added with a touch of shyness.

"I dare say I can find one to fill the bill. What's your name, pinkling?"

She smoothed down the front of her skirt with as fine and free a stroke as if it were silk instead of fustian. "Miss Eudora Valencia St. Legerdemain," she pronounced distinctly.

"Good God! I beg your pardon. Shall I have the book addressed to you at the Eureka?"

Here was a predicament. Becky came back to earth, flushing painfully. "No, sir, please. I'm just Becky here. Obedience Webb."

"It's a very nice name," he said gravely.

"You won't forget, will you? About the book?"

"No, indeed."

Becky went to her bed that night dazed with such dreams as

the most romantic passage of *The Factory Girl* had never afforded her. The next day was one long, roseate anticipation.

No book came. Hope dwindled. By the end of the second day dark doubt supplanted it and was, in turn, displaced by wrath. On Saturday night Becky sobbed into her blanket. Her idol was destroyed. She hated Guy Roy. He had sworn. And he had abjured his pledged word.

SIX

ANOTHER and more immediate interest had supplanted Becky in the facile mind of her prince. Returning to the mansion after the episode of the water pail, Guy found his cousin pacing the floor.

"Anything wrong, Gurdon?" he asked.

"Yes. The redcaps are holding a powwow in Quaker Johnson's barn."

Guy had heard of these gatherings of labour sympathizers, dubbed "redcaps" because of their supposed affinity for the *sans-culottes* of the French Revolution, which was still a bugbear to America's ruling class.

"I thought they were supposed to be secret?" he said.

"So they are. To keep respectable folk from breaking them up. I've jest learned of this one."

"Are you going?"

"Yes. The gig will be around any moment."

"I'd like to go along."

The gig drew up at the door. They mounted to the high seat. Stockwell took the lines.

"You will see our proletary in their glory," he said bitterly.

"What is the purpose of the meeting?"

"Some folderol about child labour. It all derives from this cursed twelve-hour-day agitation."

"Is that so bad *per se*?"

"Bad?" Stockwell cried, his face suffusing. "You can ask whether the twelve-hour day is bad?"

"Never having worked twelve hours myself," Guy said pacifically, "I really don't know much about it."

"Then it is high time you did," declared the industrialist. "It means, if unchecked, the wreckage of our commerce and the downfall of our great nation. It is contrary to every law of God, nature, and man. This," he added darkly, "is some of Luther Simms's doing."

"I've heard that name. Who is he?"

"The most dangerous man in York State," Stockwell said positively.

"Sounds interesting. Will he be there?"

"I understand not. Cassius Barlow is his local henchman. Barlow is less intelligent, though equally malignant. He arranged the meeting, but Simms instigated it, as he does most of these lawless occasions."

Stockwell outlined the local miscreant's character and career. Once a skilled hand at a mule-spinner, Barlow had suffered a crippling accident. He had had the effrontery to bring an action at law against the Arbia Mills, where he worked. The suit was, of course, thrown out of court. Thereafter, no employer in Troy would hire him on any terms. Thus he was reduced to odd jobs about the taverns and taprooms as potboy, scullion, ostler, anything that would earn him a stray shilling. He had a little education, "just enough to unsettle his mind", eked out with much inflammatory reading. He would speak before any gathering that would listen to him, not without a certain rude eloquence, Stockwell admitted. The Eureka proprietor postulated the existence of a red revolutionary junta in the factory towns, perhaps financed by Luther Simms, with agents like Barlow to keep burning the fires of discontent and spies in every plant. The eventual object was to incite the proletariat to mob violence with a view to taking over the mills and even the government. It was a widespread if vague myth of the time.

Upon reaching the place on the outskirts of the town near the river, they found a crowd of some hundred ill-assorted people loosely clustered about a platform displaying the legend "SAVE OUR CHILDREN". A ministerial-looking man was droning out what seemed to be a set of resolutions in an insufficient voice. Guy caught a few key words, "proletary", "life-wage", "inadequate protection for youth", "heartless system"; it all sounded dull and mechanical. The speaker read from a newspaper clipping:

" 'If mechanics combine to raise their wages or protect their rights, the laws punish them as conspirators against the good of society and the dungeon awaits them as it does the robber. But the laws have made it a just and meritorious act that capitalists shall combine to strip the man of labour of his earnings and reduce him to a dry crust and a gourd of water. Thus does power invert justice and derange the order of nature.' "

Guy looked about him. The bulk of the crowd was made up
of working mechanics of both sexes, but there were present also
a number of rough and jovial-looking fellows of the taproom
guild. Guy guessed that they were there in the hope of "fun".
There was a sprinkling of young bloods, two of whom wandered
casually over to greet Stockwell. One of them said to him in a
low tone:

"Are the Halcyons coming out?"

"No," Stockwell answered. "Time lacked for a call."

He introduced the young man, a foppish fellow in an amber
coat and flaunting flowered neck-cloth, to Guy. "Mr. Jans
Urena."

Mr. Urena shook hands and waved a gesture about him.
"Tame, tame," he said in disparagement. "But there might be
some sport yet."

More interested in the audience than in the proceedings, Guy
strolled round the fringe. Two hearty-looking fellows of the
mechanics class, exchanging views on the outskirts of the gathering, attracted his notice. He stopped near them.

"Trouble-mongers," one said, scratching a patch of scabies
on his neck with the stained hand of the cordwainer. "That's
what they are—trouble-mongers."

His companion, a squat, dull-eyed man with a tobacco-
pouched cheek, asked incuriously, "What they after?"

"Want to stop the brats workin' in the mills."

"Whaffor?"

"Some ga-fooh about it's bein' bad for 'em."

"Good fer 'em," the chewer asserted, shifting his plug of
maccaboy and spitting liberally. "Keeps 'em outa mischief."

"I got three in the Eagle now and another comin' on when
she's six."

"My twins died last year, goddamit!" the shoe-worker said,
with feeling. "Lost me a good four dollar a week in wages."

The other clucked his sympathy. "After you had the cost of
raisin' 'em, too."

A woman was at the speaker's bar now: a mild-eyed, motherly
creature in the plain garb of the Society of Friends. She read
from a report on conditions among child-labourers.

" 'To look at the pale, dirty, and spiritless beings as they
pour out of the factory to their meagre meals at the clap of a

bell, stunted unfortunates of nine, ten or eleven years old; and, though inhumanly stinted as to time, to see the torpor of their jaded limbs and the blank expression of their woebegone visages—this is to foresee the existence of a populace in the approaching generation unfit to exercise the duties of freemen and citizens."

"That is untrue in every word."

Guy recognized his cousin's slow and weighty accents. A lanky scarecrow leapt to the front of the platform.

"Prove it! Prove it!" he challenged the factory head.

"She may come to the Eureka Mills and see for herself, Barlow," the proprietor retorted calmly.

"What would she see, with you at her elbow?" the agitator returned. "Nothing. Let *me* take her through your hell-hole. You wouldn't dare. You wouldn't let me in. You'd like to run me out of town."

"I shall," Mr. Stockwell said calmly.

A respectable-appearing workman near the platform addressed the Quakeress. "I'd like to ask you, ma'am, ain't our children better off in the mills than on the streets?"

"Thee has children?" she asked gently.

"Three. And no mother to look to 'em."

"And thee would see them grow up stunted and dwarfed?"

"Certes!" shouted the cordwainer from the rear. "The runts eat less."

Approving laughter followed the sally. A half-drunken man shouted at the speaker, "Why don't you go home and tend to your own brats?"

"Quaker! Quaker!
Mischief-maker!"

piped a boyish falsetto, and other voices took up the taunt.

A clod looped through the air, struck the Quakeress's loose dress, and rolled upon the boards, leaving her unharmed.

Scuffling broke out in half a dozen spots. It seemed silly and purposeless to Guy until the bereaved father of the late twins made a dash forward, seized upon the speaker's skirt and braced himself to drag her off the hustings. She clung to the rail, silent but looking piteously about her.

"Hang on!" Guy shouted, plunging down the cluttered aisle.

He laid hold on the assailant, plucked him loose and sent him whirling. Straightway he was in the midst of an extremely muddled row. He saw Cassius Barlow leap the railing and make for him, but his pressing concern was with a chunky, heavily-poxed man who was trying to throttle him with his own neck-cloth. He hit the would-be garroter a hearty clip on the ear. They grappled and the next moment creation collapsed upon Guy's defenceless head. A wooden bell clunked twice in his brain. He crumpled into unconsciousness.

When he opened his eyes, Gurdon Stockwell and young Urena were bending over him, and the Quakeress, with a most unbecoming black eye, was sponging his brow.

"Are you all right?" Stockwell asked anxiously.

"I guess so."

"Lie back," the Quakeress directed, rubbing camphor ice on his nose. "Thou art a godless and violent young man," she added gently.

"Eh?"

"Fighting thy fellows like a wild beast."

"Well, I'm damned!" said Guy faintly.

"I sorely fear it," she said.

Hurt in his somewhat muddled feelings by this rank injustice, he tried to explain that he had come to her rescue, but it all became confused and complicated with an outrageous headache that crossed his brain laterally, vertically, and in horizontal streaks of fire.

When he came to, he was surprised to find himself in bed.

"Lucky for you you have a thick skull, my boy," a friendly voice said.

"Who are you?" Guy asked stupidly.

"This is Dr. Saul Armitage," Gurdon Stockwell explained, advancing to the bedside. "A friend of mine."

"What hit me? Was it Barlow?"

"No. Barlow's in jail with a cracked head of his own."

"What for?"

Stockwell's deep and measured tones answered: "Breaching the peace and incitement to public riot. That will take care of him for a while."

Guy woke up in the morning with nothing worse than a tender scalp and a faint tightness across his forehead. But the jar to his brain had knocked clean out of his memory his promise to the small factory girl. The events of the meeting still filled his mind. He wondered about the Quakeress, hoped she was all right. Cash Barlow's face rose before him, gaunt, tragic, vengeful. Doubtless it was better for the general peace and welfare that the fellow should be in jail; nor could he quarrel with Gurdon Stockwell's intention to put and keep him there.

By Saturday the patient was sufficiently recovered to attend the trial. The prisoner sat glowering in a corner as Guy entered. He made little attempt to defend himself, probably, Guy thought, realizing from past experience the futility of any such endeavour. The sentence of the court was an indefinite jail sentence, "without bail or mainprize", and a fine on top of that for good measure. The purpose, Guy was informed, was to keep the culprit behind the bars until such time as he would see the light and promise to leave town.

The cause was good, but somehow the process did not strike Guy as being quite fair.

He subdued a rash and impolitic impulse to pay the fine himself as a gesture of dissent. But what purpose could that serve? Gurdon Stockwell would be justifiably annoyed. And the fellow would soon be in trouble again, anyway. A malcontent, a confirmed rebel against decency and order; what concern was it of Guy's to countenance him? Nevertheless, he could not wholly stifle the invincible and illogical sympathy for the underdog which had always been a flaw in his character. He got a side word with Barlow.

"Anything I can do for you?"

The prisoner turned upon him a look in which there was more surprise than gratitude.

"Huh? Oh! Do for me? Certes. Owl me in some baccy, if you like. Niggerhead's my chaw."

SEVEN

SUNDAY-EVENING supper in the Eureka Mills was something special. There would be true coffee or tea with buns and spice cake and a rich conglomeration of odds and ends to compose a meat chowder of inelegant but nourishing quality. Becky did full justice to her victualling.

Except for the inner gnawing of her mind, her life was satisfactory enough. The companionship was lively. The work was not too hard for a girl with a sturdy constitution and a sound appetite. Long hours, short sleep and dearth of sunshine notwithstanding, she burgeoned on it.

But shadow still lay over the secreted romance of life. She had not set eyes upon the beautiful young man since the evening of his broken faith. Resolutely she told herself that she didn't care.

Still nibbling delicately at crumbs on this Sunday evening, she went to her box and brought out a precious trove, a copy of the *Troy Gazette*, less than a week old, dropped in the millyard by a careless visitor. She was bent upon improving the added hour of lamplight allowed for the Sabbath. (Mr. Goodwilly would later prorate the cost of the extra oil against the dormitory occupants.) Gypsy Vilas approached.

"Got a journal, have you?" she said, keen-eyed with anticipation. "What's in it?"

It was a weekly exercise, improving to Becky's self-education, for her to read aloud as opportunity offered to Gypsy and the two or three other unlettered workwomen, usually from some pious work. A newspaper was a treat. She ran her eyes over the headlines.

"D'you know what happens this week?" Gypsy asked. "Pay."

"Oh, Gypsy! Do we really get our hire? What are you going to do with all your money?"

"Spend it. Aren't there any store advertisements in the paper?"

"Loads of 'em."

"Read 'em. Read 'em all. Begin at the top and go right down."

Several of the others gathered about with shining eyes as the girl began conscientiously:

" 'Help for the Ruptured and Gutsprung. Dr. Maripole can——' "

"No, not that," voices protested. "Read about garments."

Becky obliged, skipping from figs and nuts and pectoral gum jujubes to Valentia and Merino shawls and silken gloves, then further to milk-and-roses, lavender extract and odorous brown soap. Her audience greeted each item with fervid intentions of purchase. Obviously, such a rush upon the local shops as would strip their shelves was impending. Even the medicines were canvassed, with modest recital of interesting symptoms: cardamom powder for the grinding dyspepsy; summer savoury in leaf for the vapours; jalap berries to stir the torpid bowel; and Rolin Runaway, which was exploited as exercising mysterious properties of development for young females. Clorinda, who had a ribald streak in her make-up, evoked shocked giggles by warmly recommending to Gypsy camomile tea, potent in assuaging the unruly passions of youth.

"Maybe you wouldn't use that window-rope of yours so often," she cackled.

"Oh, go take some wormseed!" Gypsy retorted.

The Eureka Mills held to old ways and paid wages quarterly.

"It safeguards the help against wastethrift habits," Gurdon Stockwell explained to his cousin, anxious that his consideration for his employees should be understood. It also, though he did not specify, encouraged trade with the company store, since few of the hands enjoyed credit elsewhere.

On pay-day Becky could hardly wait to finish her dinner. Still secreting a chunk of hard pudding in her cheek, she trotted downstairs to the chin-high pay-window behind which Mr. Goodwilly sat on a tall stool, smiling like a benevolent gnome.

"Now, little girl?" He pawed at his ledger. "Name? Speak up!"

She did so in a confident, businesslike voice. "Obedience Webb—doffer."

Mr. Goodwilly set a long finger between two pages. "Nine weeks, four days. Right? Sign here."

She set her name to the form and grasped eagerly the thick paper envelope which he substituted for it.

"Thirteen dollars, three shillings and fourpence," he rattled off. "Right?"

D

Her jaw fell. "I—I thought it would be twenty dollars nearly," she faltered.

"Nineteen dollars, thirty-three cents, original accounting," he said. "Less fines, three shillings. Less purchases duly charged against buyer, five fifty-five."

"Oh no, sir! Five fifty-five at the store? I never."

"Move on, little girl. Next!"

Clutching her ravaged envelope to her breast, Becky crawled back to her job. She was not the only despoiled one. The workroom was seething with discontent. From loom to loom the indignant girls were exchanging grievances.

"He'd oughta let us see our own reckoning," Gypsy said.

"Why don't you go and ask him, Miss Vilas?" Priscilla Stamm suggested.

"Because I couldn't read the poxy figures if I saw 'em; that's why, Miss Smarty."

"Mary Haynes is the one to do it," said Arvila Hopkins. "She knows figures backwards."

"I'm willing to try," Mary said.

Mr. Goodwilly blinked incredulously when she presented herself at his office. "Never heard of such a thing in my life! Do you realize, girl, that those accounts are company property?"

"How can we tell whether they're right or not without seeing them?" Mary said reasonably.

"Right? Certainly they're right! Advise your companions that *I* am responsible for the books and that no hired hand will be permitted to inspect them. Mr. Stockwell would never approve it."

An indignation meeting was held in Dorm Four. Judged too young to take part, Becky Webb had discontentedly retired to her pallet.

"We can't do anything without the figures," Mary Haynes said.

"Then let's get 'em." This from Gypsy Vilas.

"What you got in your noggin, Gypsy?" Clorinda Burgo asked.

The other jerked her chin towards the corner. "Becky—she's skinny—that window . . ."

Clorinda walked across the room and bent over the sleeping bunch of humanity. "Hey, minnikin! Come to. We got a job for you."

"What is it?"

The other explained. As she spoke, the small face before her took on an expression of wide-awake excitement.

"Fetch out the rope," Becky said.

Equipped with a candle-end and some matches which she was instructed to use only if she could not locate the desired object in the dark, she was lowered to the ground. Getting between the curved iron bars was a tight squeeze, but she made it at the cost of a torn waist and a few abrasions on her firm-skinned body. Thanks to Mary's explicit directions, she was able to find the book, and up she went in the bight of Gypsy's love-rope (so termed by the sharp-tongued Corinda), to be hauled into the dormitory by eager hands.

Mary Haynes took over the booty for examination, while Relief Lovejoy, with a fresh-pointed goose quill and a cup of pokeberry-root ink, prepared to make fair copy of the items. Ominous mutterings rose in response to the details which Mary dictated for Relief's copying. For example, Hannah Boutwell was debited with a dollar's worth of flax seed.

"Where would I plant flax seed?" she protested. "And how would I find the time to raise it?"

"Mine's worse," Malinda Prowitt said. "Gunpowder, four shillings. Me, that can't abide the sight of a gun."

" 'One gallon prime rum, thirty cents,' " the reader proceeded. " 'Priscilla Stamm.' "

That proper young person uttered a maidenly scream. "I'm Father Matthew," she declared. "Liquor has never fouled these lips."

"What they got against me?" Gypsy Vilas queried.

Mary riffled the pages. "You'd be surprised," she warned. "Want me to read it out?"

"Certes."

" 'One pair embroidered suspenders, three shillings.' "

"Suspenders! Hell's cats! What would I want with suspenders?"

"To keep your drawers where they belong," Clorinda guffawed. "Good thing, too."

"You keep your tongue where it belongs, Miss Burgo," Mary Haynes advised severely.

"I won't pay it!" Gypsy exploded.

"You've paid it already."

Becky was again entrusted with the fateful ledger and lowered

on Gypsy's rope. When she returned, the copy of the false entries
had been secreted in Mary Haynes's box, for possible future use.
The fruitless discussion continued until midnight.

From that day the atmosphere of the factory deteriorated.
Workmanship fell off in quantity and quality. Negligence, viola-
tion of rules and breakage brought on more fines which, in turn,
bred further slackness. Trouble was plainly in prospect. Then,
one evening Mary Haynes made an announcement to Dormitory
Four.

"Goodwilly has smelt a rat. After this we get paid by the
month."

"How d'you know?" A dozen voices, eager with doubt and
anticipation, joined in the query.

Her information was well-founded. The notice, put up by
Mr. Goodwilly himself, read:

> Hereafter the Wages of Female Employees will
> be paid on the Last Day of Each Month.
>   By Order of Mr. Gurdon Stockwell, Owner.

The change in method had no connection with the lapse in
morale among the factory girls. Mary Haynes had misinterpreted.
It was the outcome of constructive thought on the part of the
proprietor.

Summoned to Castle Hill, Goodwilly had been conducted to
the Stockwell study, where he found his principal at a desk with
neatly columned figures before him.

"I have been examining our store accounts," Gurdon said,
"and it is plain that too many of our hands, particularly the
females, are trading elsewhere. How do you account for it?"

Goodwilly plucked up courage to reply that prices were lower
at other shops.

"This is disloyalty," his chief said severely. "It must be
checked. Are you familiar with the token system? It has been
operated with success in several of the New England plants. I
purpose to adopt it here."

"At the Eureka?" Goodwilly asked doubtfully.

"Yes. From now forward, wages will be paid monthly——"

"That will produce a favourable effect, Mr. Stockwell," the
official said, brightening.

"Be so good as not to interrupt me again, Mr. Goodwilly. All payments will be on a monthly basis, rendered in tokens which I am having prepared."

"Redeemable in cash, I suppose, sir?"

"Redeemable in goods at the company store."

"Asking your indulgence, Mr. Stockwell," the other said humbly, "there'll be dissatisfaction."

The owner made a gesture of dismissal. "Our females are well and suitably fed and lodged at no cost to themselves. What need have they of cash?"

"Do the token payments extend to the male employees also, sir?"

"Hm. Men are on a different basis. No. The females alone."

The ingenious Goodwilly mind conjured up a golden opportunity of personal profit in the proposed change. Officially, the tokens would not be exchangeable for cash. But what was to prevent him from accommodating the necessitous employees with money from his own pocket—at a certain discount, be it understood? Thus he would be performing a worthy Christian act and, in the same operation, touching a neat profit for himself.

The pace in the factory now accelerated. Discipline was eased. Shrewd Mr. Goodwilly anticipated trouble enough over the new pay plan without the exasperation of small fines. It was advisable to keep the hands contented. Those who were on piecework were accumulating nice credits, which remained practically intact as the girls were saving up for full envelopes on pay-day, and the paymaster had deemed it wise to omit, for the time, anyway, the imaginary items of purchase which had stirred up so much ill-feeling.

The four weeks passed without incident. Dormitory Four trooped happily down to the window where Mr. Goodwilly perched on his high schoolmaster's stool flanked by shelves. Neat piles of unfamiliar leather discs were ranged within his reach, each one based upon a slip of paper bearing a worker's name. The pious Hepsabeth Parsons, first in line, presented a smiling face. It was reflected in the beaming geniality of the paymaster's visage.

" 'Miss H. Parsons, carder,' " he read from his day-book. "No fines. No deductions. Eight full dollars and an extra five shillings over. Sign here, if you please, Miss P."

He carefully moved forward a tower of the discs. Each bore the figure of its denomination in dollars, shillings, or cents, and the legend, "Redeemable in Trade Unlimited, at the Eureka Mills Company Store." Hepsabeth stared.

"What are they?" she faltered.

"Tokens. Redeemable tokens."

"Where's my money? I don't know anything about tokens."

"Just as good," the paymaster assured her.

The meek Miss Parsons was for once aroused to protest. "Good for what?" she demanded.

"To buy goods with. You can take these tokens to the store and they will be honoured at face value for anything you choose to buy. Anything at all," he concluded, with a gesture so expansive that it threatened the stability of the ranged towers.

A silence of disappointment, doubt and indecision followed. It was ruptured by the high, clear pipe of Obedience Webb.

"I want my money that you promised me when I signed the paper to work here."

Mr. Goodwilly stretched his plump form to peer over the ledge.

"*I* promised, little girl? Oh no! I will show you the paper. It says value, not money nor specie. These are value." He tapped the leather circles.

"Can I pay my per centum with them at the bank?" Hannah Boutwell asked.

Mary Haynes pressed forward. "I'm putting my brother through college on my wages. Can I pay at Hamilton with a side of leather?"

Mild Malinda Prowitt summoned spunk enough to say, "How would that patch of shoe-top look in the contribution-box of a Sunday?"

"I owe my doctor money, not findings," Rhuane Nichols added.

"I want my money," Gypsy Vilas declared, "and I'm goin' to have it, you old scrounger."

"Shilling fine for contumacious language," the paymaster snapped.

"D'you want a taste of this in your guts?" She flashed the small scimitar-curved flax-knife which was her constant companion and protection, and added a surgical detail which fetched gasps of maidenly shock from her companions.

The time was come for diplomacy. Mr. Goodwilly made pacificatory noises.

"Be reasonable, ladies," he implored. "Comport yourselves like persons of discretion. You prefer money, cash, specie. Very good. It can be arranged."

"How?" It was a chorus.

"I shall be glad to convert your tokens into current money. At—er—a slight discount, naturally."

"What discount?" from Mary Haynes.

"A very amenable discount, ladies. Shall we say—er—forty per centum?"

"Sixty cents left out of every dollar," the accomplished Miss Haynes expounded.

"Lemme at him!" said Gypsy Vilas.

Mr. Goodwilly amended his hopeful mathematics. "It is notorious that I am a soft-hearted man. Shall we say thirty-five per centum? Oh, well, thirty! And I shall lose money at that. What does it matter? If it is a question of the happiness of our workers I willingly make the sacrifice. Those wishing to convert their tokens may apply to me personally, after hours. Deal with no other," he warned, "if you wish fair and generous treatment. Now pass on peaceably, young ladies, if you please."

He did a brisk and profitable evening's trade. In the glow of his successful deal, he paid little heed to Mary Haynes's quiet warning.

"You'll be lucky if you don't have a turn-out yet, Mr. Goodwilly," she said.

Dormitory Four drafted a respectful letter of protest to Mr. Gurdon Stockwell. He threw it into his waste-basket. He was busy with plans for a magnificent dinner to celebrate his cousin, Guy Roy's, entry into the Eureka Mills.

EIGHT

ALL Troy knew that Orlando Montague, the ironmonger, changed his shirt every day. It was incumbent upon him to do so if he was to maintain his social reputation. For though already ageing —he would never see thirty-five again—Mr. Montague was an approved maccaroni. His apparel set a pattern for the anxious imitation of the younger bloods.

The Orlandos lived in style on River Street in a house with a number of its own, like a business concern. Mrs. Orlando, born a Van Woggleum, of comely person and well thought of for dignity and thrift, was known to have a mind of her own and a tongue quite ready to speak it. It was her pride and complaint that she must always be at her tub, since her husband would allow no hand less skilled than her own upon his linen.

On this Wednesday afternoon of unseasonable autumn warmth, Mr. Montague walked home from the ironmongery humming a cheerful tune. He had hit the Literary Lottery lightly for twenty-five dollars and was meditating a new waist-coat of pale buff with a hand-painted floral design, and a pair of bespoken cossacks with special prunella tops. Doffing his broad-cloth coat in the hallway, he inspected it for wrinkles, and hung it on its peg.

"Wife," he called.

"Out here," a clear voice answered.

Passing through the kitchen to the rear, he observed with benign approval the activities of the trim, comely woman, busy above a steaming washtub.

"My shirt, wife."

She straightened her back and dried her arms. "What is it tonight, Orlando?"

"Harmonia Society practice." He contributed an earnest basso to the local choral.

"Can't you sing through the neckwear you have on?" she said discontentedly.

"My linen must befit a man of my condition and calling," he rebuked her.

"Then change your calling and follow a cleanly trade."

"Change!" he repeated, scandalized. "Change my trade? Me, the best b'dashed ironmonger in Troy!"

"Ironmonger, indeed! A sooty smith."

"What ails the woman?" He bent a stern regard upon her.

But Mrs. Montague was not easily awed. "A fresh shirt he must have, day upon day and another for the Sabbath. Look, you." She pointed to the streak of grime beneath her hand. "Wash, wash, wash! Nothing but wash, day in, day out. It's beyond reason. Must you always be gawking over your forge? Could you not set a towel to your neck?"

"Or a rope, you would say, to judge from your temper."

"Temper, says the man!" she cried. "You and your ale-guzzling, catch-singing cronies!" But her eyes were not unkindly as they rested upon him. "See to it that you wash your neck well with soap."

"Is that my best red cambric?" He scuffed into a pile on the floor with his foot. "I shall be needing it come Saturday evening."

"And what's my fine mister up to Saturday evening?"

"Mr. Gurdon Stockwell entertains," he said importantly. "Gentlemen only."

"And you must sport your best finery for that?"

"The supper is in honour of Mr. Guy Roy."

"The new-come cousin? They say he is a fine young blade."

"Oh, well enough, well enough. He plumes himself on the newest New York styles," he added selfconsciously.

Supper over and her husband departed upon his musical concerns, Mrs. Montague returned to her unending stint. Without special cause, she found herself suddenly loathing the tousled heap of fabric before her. Every piece would have been wearable at least a second time, but for the sullied space round the neck. She must wash and starch and iron a whole shirt because of a few hateful smudges on the collar. The wrist bands could be turned up out of harm's way by the wearer, but not the encircling neckpiece. In her father's day it was different. She conjured up the portrait of that respectable maltster, his long red neck protruding from a high circle of frilled paper which at a cost of sixpence the dozen could be worn once or twice and thrown away without undue infringement of economy.

A thought dawned in her active brain. If a detachable circlet of paper was feasible, why not a detachable circlet of cloth?

How much labour would be saved if she had to wash but a slim strip of linen instead of a whole cumbrous garment!

The hot passion of creativeness took form in action. She dashed out to her work-basket, selected her largest shears, rushed back and so to the attack. The wash-room became a scene of carnage.

Soon she was surrounded by decollated shirts. That finished, she darted upstairs, cleaned out her husband's tallboy of the reserve and brought them to judgment, resolved to make a clean sweep of it. Two garments only she set aside for the intervening days. Saturday would be the showdown. Until then she would conceal her revolutionary depredations. Then, let the heavens fall. . . . After all, if Orlando raised too much of a whoobub, what had been done could be undone; she could always restore the wreckage with needle and thread. The hope and pride of the pioneer encouraged and upheld her.

Saturday came and, at the usual five-o'clock hour, her husband appeared with the usual sooted smears and the usual demand for fresh apparel.

"Wash yourself well, dear," his wife requested with a sweetness which might have struck him as a trifle excessive had he not been absorbed in planning his toilet for the evening's festivities. He went upstairs humming the latest tune. His wife tiptoed out and waited at the stairway. Presently his complaint was heard.

"Can't find a b'dashed shirt."

"They're all down here."

"Then fetch 'em up and be spry."

"Come down and get 'em yourself."

"Huh?"

"I've got a little surprise for you." Still sweetly but with an undertone of decisiveness. When that note sounded, time was saved, as he had long since discovered, by meeting her wishes. He descended.

As he reached the stair foot, she was there with the required garment in her hands.

"The red cambric, you said. Here it is." She held out the fresh shirt towards him. "Arms."

Bowing his head and stretching out his arms, he felt the cool fabric slip into place. His fingers fumbled at the neckband. An expression of bewilderment clouded his features.

"What the devil's this?"

"Don't curse, dear."

"Wh-wh-where's the collar?"

"All ready." She held up the doubled and starched ring before his goggling eyes.

"What happened to it?"

"I cut it off."

"But it—b'dashed and b'damned! What for, woman?"

"To make the wash easier."

"Then you b'dashed and b'damned well put it back on again."

"*You* put it on," she returned, still mildly.

"How'll I put it on?"

"Tie it."

"Tie it to what, you—you puttering Jezabeel?"

The time had come for assertion and defiance. "Tie it to your ass's ears for all I care. And please not to use ignominious language to your lawfully wedded wife."

He snatched off the shirt, flung it into a corner and tossed the detached strip after it. "Fetch me another."

"Go into the washery and pick one out. They're all the same."

Mr. Montague uttered the roar of a goaded bull. "You've gone mad!"

"If you let your gorge rise like that you'll have a cachexy and I shall call Dr. Armitage to bleed you."

Retrieving the discarded garment, she smoothed out the two trips of tape appended at the rear, held the collar in place and deftly attached it through the accommodating apertures which he had failed to observe.

"Now come here," she coaxed.

Mr. Montague sidled and stamped and spluttered.

"It won't do a bit of good to prance," she told him placidly. "Turn around."

Slipping the shirt upon his indignantly panting torso again, she affixed the collar at the front and tied a neat bow.

"Look at yourself." She propelled him gently before the wall-glass. "There! Isn't that pompous!" she cooed.

"Um-mm-mm!" he grunted, craning. "Hah!" He waggled his head like a duck, easing his Adam's apple into place with a careful forefinger. Privately he was filled with admiration for her ingenuity. But too much praise was apt to set a woman above herself.

"I guess it'll do for this evening," he allowed.

He set forth to make sartorial history.

A loosely formed circle of Troy's solid men were wont to gather of an early evening at the International Inn where a special parlour was provided for their privacy. Thither Mr. Orlando Montague went for a drink, prefatory to the supper-party, assured of finding a number of his cronies. Discussion was well under way when the ironmonger arrived. Clarkson Crolius, the local printer and editor, at once appealed to him.

"Is it true this cousin of Gurdon Stockwell is investing in the Eureka Mills?"

"So I am led to believe."

"He'll get the skin scorched off his fundament if he deals with Gurdy Stockwell," said young Jans Urena with a giggle.

"How so?" Taylor Paulding, the up-and-coming young land factor, asked.

"When did anyone ever get anything but the worst of it in a dicker with Stockwell?" Franklin Wrench of Fortune's House lottery put in.

"*Nil tetigit quod nec profitavit*," Miles Tiggett, who was proud of his nickname of the Learned Tailor, contributed.

"What's that mean?" Timothy Freegle asked. He was mackerel inspector for the district, a well-thought-of man, but smelly by trade.

Michael Howland, son of the local ironmaster, obliged with a free translation: "He doesn't go into anything that he doesn't make money on."

"He'll be a prize for some smart damsel," Isaac Leroy, the whitesmith, stated.

"Once bit, twice shy," observed Freegle.

"Once froze, twice shyer," young Urena amended. "That wife of his! Brr-rr-rr!"

"*De mortuis nil nisi bonum*," the Learned Tailor pronounced, ever alert to seize upon opportunity. "The poor woman's three years cold in her grave."

"No colder than she was in his bed, I'll warrant," Wrench chuckled.

"He can warm himself with his hired hands," young Urena said. "Some of those factory girls have solicitous eyes."

"Stockwell's too cautious for that sort of thing," Elias Plum, newly admitted to the bar, gave opinion. "Prudence will guide him where conscience mightn't."

"Mr. Stockwell is a sincerely religious man," said Phineas Heartt, the bookseller, whose wife was Gurdon Stockwell's cousin.

"The religion of fear," Crolius jeered. "Every time old Hellfire Hoadley comes around with his flame-and-brimstone sermons, our Gurdon has the holy fidgets."

"They do say he's continent," from the tailor.

"You can't bottle up human nature for ever, though," Leroy grinned. "Some day the old Adam will bust his chains inside Mr. G. Stockwell. Ain't I right, Doc?" he appealed to the slender and handsome man of thirty who had just entered.

"Probably not," the newcomer returned. "What about?"

"Your patient, heaven almighty Stockwell."

"Since he is my patient, I suggest that the subject be changed."

"Score one for Doc Armitage," the lottery agent said. "Cold splashes for night sweats, and nothing further said. Eh, Doc?"

"I know what *I'd* prescribe," young Urena said, with his lewd smirk.

"A little decent reticence would not be amiss as a prescription for you," the physician said, fixing him with a chilly eye. "And the same for the rest who are about to profit by his hospitality."

Orlando Montague backed him up. "You gentlemen might be in better process, truly, than blackbird chatter about our leading Trojan. I propose that we join in one more drink and be on our way."

Though abstemious to the point of austerity, Gurdon Stockwell was known as a lavish host. He was always sensible of his social responsibilities, in which category he now reckoned his cousin and partner.

Everything about the event was on a scale of entertainment suitable to the Stockwell *éclat*. Steam heat, hardly a necessity in a temperature above seventy degrees, sputtered impressively in the gilded pipes. Genet's Patent Combustible Luminant Gas shed an aristocratic, if wavery, light from two overhead chandeliers and four wall sconces. Handsome brass-trimmed spit-boxes had been filled with fresh sand. Mr. Stockwell, his hands gently flapping the tails of his elegantly sober grey coat, viewed these accessories with pardonable pride. His pale and steady eyes shifted, in preliminary survey, to the handsome Savery sideboard

with its array of bottles and decanters. Rum from the Islands
of the Caribbean, choice Hollands from the Low Countries, corn
and rye spirits of Whiskey Johnnie's best, brandy from England,
wines both delicate and sturdy from France, Spain and Italy, and
a punch of his own brewing which exhaled the very aroma of
seduction. Not a man at that table should leave the place sober.
Except, of course, himself.

The supper hour was set for eight. The tower clock had not
done striking when the guests began to stream in. They were
not predominantly Gurdon Stockwell's chosen associates; those
would have been a selection of older, soberer, solider though not
more representative families. Most of those present bore the unmistakable Corinthian stamp, appropriate companions to the
newcomer. They were dressed to the nines; powdered and
perfumed to taste; ready to drink, to sing, or to fight as befitted
their tradition.

Each, as he approached the host, was presented with a frosty
mint julep of the most select Santa Cruz rum, garnished with
a segment of authentic pineapple, fresh-sliced. Therein each
pledged the guest of honour.

The feast proceeded with initial decorum. Toasts were offered.
Songs were proposed and sung. Amateur virtuosi performed upon
flute or fife or the Spanish guitar. Spirits soared with the passing
two hours, but were still well contained when the factory bell
sounded one clear, resonant peal. The guests looked at one
another.

"Fire!" a voice cried with lively anticipation.

"No, no," the host interposed. "Merely the ten-o'clock bell."

" 'Tain't nine yet," Tiggett objected.

Though Stockwell seemed unperturbed by the inexplicable
bell stroke, Roy noted that his brow was heavy, his attention
distracted.

"I wish to lead in song," Urena announced.

He climbed upon his chair and raised a strident voice in the
gross Scottish ditty beginning:

"Pintle, pintle, periwinkle."

With an expression of distaste upon his handsome features,
Gurdon Stockwell said:

"I will leave you to your harmonies temporarily."

Guy suspected that it was a pretext for him to resolve some worry. Stockwell mounted the staircase. After a moment, Guy slipped out into the hall and met his cousin descending.

"Anything amiss, Gurdon?"

"No, no. Pay no heed."

"Something going on in the factory?" Guy persisted.

"If there be, Goodwilly will look to it."

"Sure you don't want me to run down?"

"By no means. Kindly attend to our guests. I will rejoin you shortly."

Guy herded the crowd into the large parlour. There a curious diversion took place. Mr. Orlando Montague, lifting a taper to relight his choice cheroot, let it fall beneath his chin, irremediably besmirching his fine red-cambric neck-piece. This aroused some astonishment, since he was normally a deft-handed person.

"Oh, dear! Oh, dear!" the ironmonger bemoaned himself, examining the ruin in a wall mirror.

"Allow me," the Learned Tailor offered, producing a fine linen handkerchief and dabbing at the smears.

"Let be. It's past help. Thank you, nonetheless." He re-examined the damage. "Ah!" he ejaculated in well-feigned dismay. "I cannot remain in this respectable company thus."

Guy unwittingly played up to him. "You and I are much of a size, sir. May I offer you a selection from my wardrobe?"

"My recognizance, Mr. Roy. But—er—by happy chance I have a replacement with me."

"Brought an extra shirt, by Harry!" exclaimed Tiggett in admiring amazement.

"Not precisely." He looked about him with a deprecating eye. "Nothing so cumbrous. A little device of my wi—of my own."

From the tails of his capacious coat he brought forth a lightly starched circlet of the same delicate reddish hue as his cambric. The company crowded about him, staring and questioning.

The ironmonger put on his little show. Flanking the mirror with a pair of candles, he removed his greatcoat and proceeded to detach what in the world of fashion had hitherto been regarded as the undetachable, exposing an expanse of neck.

"Watsa mata, Mr. Montague?" queried young Urena, upon whom the potations had begun to tell. "Got a tetter under ya whiskers?"

Ignoring him, the subject of the inquiry laid aside the smutted fabric and substituted for it the circlet from his pocket. To tie it properly in the back involved some painful contortions; but he had put in a half-hour of practice before leaving home, and brought it off triumphantly. The attachment in front was simple. He adjusted his cravat, patted it into place, set it with a handsome intaglio, and flirted a handkerchief across the achieved task with a fine assumption of unselfconsciousness.

Gurdon Stockwell, re-entering, observed the process with interest.

"Your indulgence, mine host, for this interruption," Mr. Montague said.

Guy Roy picked up the discarded circlet and studied it. "Very ingenious," he said. "I've seen nothing like it in New York, nor yet in Philadelphia."

"Nor anywhere else," the other replied with modest satisfaction. "As I said, a little device of my own. . . . What ails our host?"

Gurdon Stockwell was edging over towards a partly open window, through which came strange and muffled sounds. A voice split the darkness in frantic anti-climax: "Murder! Help! *Owch!*"

"Sounds like our friend Goodwilly," Roy remarked, grinning at his cousin. "Could it be the dear soul is in trouble?"

"Remain where you are, gentlemen," the host said. "I shall look into this."

"Let's all look into it," cackled Urena.

A rock, fist-size, crashed through the garden window and rolled upon the floor.

"Halcyons out!" shouted a voice. There was a cheer.

Guy Roy crammed the Orlando Montague invention into his pocket and joined the rush for the door. The collar could wait. The fight would not.

NINE

DORMITORY Four, hotbed of trouble, had been in a slow simmer of inquietude since the introduction of the tokens. Open threat of rebellion, however, had died down. Distasteful though the leather coinage was, it did pass current at the company store where it was honoured at face value.

Furthermore, discipline in the work-rooms had been eased. Fines were fewer and rules not so rigorously interpreted. All of which was part of the Goodwilly tactics. The paymaster had an axe to grind. After some argument he had converted Mr. Stockwell to his theory that overfeeding bred contumacy in the help. A caterer had been found who would victual the female hands for one dollar her head per week.

"We'll cocker 'em up for a bit," said the paymaster. "Ease 'em off other ways, and they won't feel the change so much."

His policy of relaxation seemed to be working effectively after the first flurry of resentment over the tokens had passed. But wrath was stirred up again when the pinch of a restricted diet began to be felt. The Saturday evening conclave in Number Four, on the same night as Gurdon Stockwell's gala, was a heated one.

"Vittles, huh?" Clorinda Burgo said. "Swill!"

"Break my heart, but spare my belly," chanted Gypsy Vilas.

"And the boss up there in the mansion with his boon companions, battening on tasty viands and rich champagne wines," said Hester Smith, whose language was prone to reflect her avid reading of the elegant and profuse Mrs. Opie.

"We hadn't ought to stand it," Rhuane Nichols declared.

"What can we do?" the timorous Hepsabeth Parsons asked. "Jobs are scarce."

"We ought to have a union," Mildred Hute asserted.

Priscilla Stamm expressed a fear lest unions were unlady-like.

"The lady sempstresses got up a union in New York," Mary Haynes informed the assemblage, "and won a higher wage."

"How'd they do it? A turn-out?" Malinda Prowitt wanted to know.

"If that's the way, we better have one," Clorinda Burgo said.

"Young ladies! Young ladies! Go to your beds," Mr. Goodwilly admonished from below the open window.

Mildred Hute scrambled to her feet, laid hold on a familiar domestic convenience, and made for the window.

"D'you want a jorden dumped on your head?" she inquired.

The paymaster withdrew to a prudent distance. "I shall be on watch," he warned.

"You and your watch!" the girl jeered. "That fixed the yellow-belly," she gloated to the room in general. "Come on! Let's tell Stockwell what we want."

The sheer temerity of the notion excited them.

"Hooray!" Becky shrilled, scrambling for her jacket and skirt.

Gypsy turned upon her. "This ain't nursery play," she warned. "You stay where you won't be in mischief." Which Becky had no intention of doing.

One cot still remained occupied. A sad and earnest voice emanated from it.

"Oh, girls! You mustn't. It's very wrong."

"Hark to our Sweetie-pink, Pinkie-sweet," Gypsy jeered. "What's wrong about it?"

"Everything. It's—it's unscriptural to disobey those in authority over us. Mr. Stockwell is a kind employer."

"And we should all love him—just as much as you do, Miss Stamm. Hey?"

Priscilla's hysterically indignant disclaimer overrode the ripple of mirth. "I don't. How can you misspeak me so?" And the unhappy girl burst into maidenly tears.

"You just stay where you're safe and say your little prayers," Clorinda Burgo advised. "Come on, girls. Let's pull out the other rooms."

They poured out into the hallway, rousing the floors below. "Turn out. It's a turn out," they vociferated.

The Widow Devroo rushed from her cubicle, waving her arms. "Back to your beds. D'you want to lose your jobs?"

They chased her down to the landing and into a broom-closet where she barricaded herself.

Not all the groups were as revolutionary minded as Dormitory Four. Nevertheless the excitement carried its contagion and enough reinforcements joined to bring the total to almost fifty.

The little army, silent now under the caution of Mary Haynes, their natural leader, swarmed into the Castle Hill grounds and climbed the slope to the walled garden. There an alarmed Amos Goodwilly sought to check them with placatory words. They rushed him into the ornamental fountain and pelted him with clods. It was his lament that gave the first definite warning to the feasters.

With an attempt at formation, the females deployed on the broad gravelled semicircle before the mansion's main entrance, groping their way as best they could, for the night was pit-dark under a mantle of drizzling rain. There Clorinda, deepening her fine baritone to its most masculine pitch, called:

"We want Mr. Stockwell."

A side door opened. Three figures were revealed. Their arms were intertwined, their leads leaning forward in the concentric circle of harmonization. Messrs. Plum, Freegle and Urena were rendering a ballad:

> "At the close of the day
> I am off to the hay
> With my pretty young factory girl."

It was then that Gypsy, offended in her professional honour, flung her rock.

As the missile rolled across the floor several guests produced small silver implements from their pockets. The air vibrated with shrillness. It was the first time that Guy Roy had heard the whistles of the Halcyons.

"Rally!" a voice called.

Gurdon Stockwell moved briskly towards the entrance. The guests formed behind him. This promised to be a lark.

Stockwell was no coward. He flung the door wide and stood revealed in the broad wale of light. An indeterminate rumour greeted him. There was something uncertain and plaintive in it, like the sound of awakened birds.

From behind, Orlando Montague called out, "How many are there, Gurdon?"

"I can see nothing in this darkness."

"Let's rush 'em," said Guy Roy merrily.

"Wait!" the owner said. He projected his imperious voice into the blackness. "Now, then! What does this mean?"

"Justice." It was a thin pipe. As if a plug had been pulled, the clamour followed.

"Better victuals!"

"Shorter hours!"

"Quits on the tokens!"

"Stop Goodwilly's fines!"

"Give us the twelve-hour day!"

The rest merged into a soprano-also mishmash of protest and demand.

Guy Roy flung down the heavy cane he had seized and burst into a roar of laughter.

"Females, by gad!" he shouted. "All females."

"Ain't females got any rights, Mister?" the answer came back.

The blithe spirit of irresponsible fun now had full possession of Guy.

"Lanterns!" he called. "On to the hunt! Link arms! Round 'em up! And so back to their beds!"

The dark and crazy battle was joined. The female group, outnumbering the men by two to one, withstood the first onslaught without giving ground. The young bloods pushed and hauled with no special purpose. The factory contingent bucked and plunged and put up such resistance as they could, tooth and nail. There were shrieks, cries and wild laughter. A frantic female voice babbled: "Tear their eyes out! Tear their eyes out!" The dignified bookseller, Mr. Heartt, uttered a cry and leapt in the air. "Some bitch bit my leg!" he howled.

Soon the conflict resolved itself into a series of jumpled personal set-tos. Guy Roy found himself entangled with a vigorous combatant whose pungent language identified her.

"Quit it, Gypsy," he whispered, and administered a sharp but friendly smack upon the buttocks. "Go home and behave yourself."

"Lemme at that Goodwilly," she panted. "I'll kill him."

But the paymaster, emergent from the fountain into which the furies had driven him, had no stomach for further hostilities now that the battle had given him respite. He had fled the stricken field convinced that his once-docile charges had gone berserk. It was his project to make a roundabout course, reach the bell tower, and send forth a summons to the constables, the fire company, or anyone else who might restore law and order.

Lanterns began to flicker in the rear of battle. They contributed more confusion than illumination, until one was kicked over and the spreading oil ignited. In the flare, Guy, shaking himself loose from two Valkyries, saw Gurdon Stockwell nearby, involved in a hand-to-hand, breast-to-breast tussle with a tall fair maenad. Stockwell's face sent a shiver down the younger man's spine. It was a mask of blind and furious lust. Darkness blotted it out.

Soon the mêlée became a rout, a pursuit, shrieks mingled with hysterical laughter, nymph fleeing from satyr in the pall of the rain. A strange *finis* to strange strife, Guy thought, with amusement. And what about Stockwell? He called out:

"Hey, Gurdon!"

There was no response. Very well; Stockwell was well able to look after himself. Just the same, Guy would have been more comfortable in his mind had he not seen that ugly distortion of the other's features.

Afar down the slope, in the direction of the dormitory, a dispirited summons floated on the breeze.

"Back to the dorm, girls. It's all over."

"Sensible wench," the young man thought. "They'll be sorry in the morning."

He moved heedfully down towards the group of buildings on the lower level, feeling his way until an upspringing light in a hallway, almost instantly extinguished, gave him direction and confidence.

Idly, Guy leaned against the lintel of the entrance, suddenly and unaccountably dispirited. The gilded youth of Troy were acting like smutty little boys.

The night was silent now, except for the wind and the gusts of rain. Shuffling footsteps crossed the open space. Once or twice Guy heard a nervous cackle of laughter, followed by subdued speech. Somewhere beyond the factory corner rose a thin, disturbing wail, sharply checked. Impetuously he started in the general direction, but at once returned to his shelter. What was the use, in that blackness? A wild clamour burst out in the bell tower, shattering the quiet. That frightened fool, Goodwilly!

Becky Webb descended the slope and paused. Somebody was following her. She stumbled forward, broke into an uncertain run, rolled down a steep terrace and over a low wall and fetched up against a wooden building. It could not be the dormitory, she had not covered enough space. What was it? One of the storage sheds probably. She fumbled her way round the angle and found the door. Unlocked! Darting in, she leaned against the oaken panels. But when she felt for it there was no inside bar.

Slowly, remorselessly, the door was thrust open against her. She heard a light, thick panting. She heard herself squeak like a trapped mouse. Then the weight of the body was upon her, bearing her down beneath it.

She rolled, she fought, she twisted. Gathering breath, she yelled, a cry broken by the hands that gripped her throat. There was the pealing of a great, violent bell inside her head. Or *was* it inside? No. Outside! The murderous grip relaxed. There was a convulsion of the body above her. The weight was lifted. The door opened and swung on its hinges in the wild wind as the attacker plunged into the blackness.

Becky was alone. Sitting up, she tenderly felt herself all over. Her neck was sore, one knee was bruised; otherwise she appraised herself as undamaged. She limped to the door and closed it.

The saviour bell continued its mad assault upon the peace of the night.

Dormitory Four's lodgers sat about in various stages of dishevelment, discussing the evening's diversion.

"Farewell to my sweet job," Clorinda Burgo said, with a hard laugh.

"Farewell to all our jobs," Mary Haynes added gloomily.

"First-class weaver on the market," Gypsy Vilas chirped. "Who's for trying the Flag of Freedom Mills?"

"Starvation wages," was Mary Haynes's comment.

"Wasn't Ploesten Kill factory looking for hands a while back?" Rhuane Nichols inquired hopefully.

"Big fines and little vittles," some pessimist grunted.

"What about the Lark at Morn?" This was Hannah Boutwell's suggestion.

"Ever work there?" queried Clorinda. "I have. No dorm fires till the mercury touches freezing. Factory rule."

"There might be a chance in the asheries," Malinda Prowitt said.

"Choke to death on smoke and eat the cinders for breakfast," Rhuane Nichol coughed.

"There's always shirts," Relief Lovejoy pointed out.

"Shirts. Oh, yes, shirts," Mary Haynes came back. "Seven

cents a garment and find your own thread. Very genteel. Very ladylike. But how do you get to eat?"

"D'you know what I think?" This from Gypsy. "After tonight's towrow we'll all be listed. And then how'd you find a job? Whistle for it! Nobody'll hire you."

A loud wail rose from the floor. Little Meg Shink entered her disclaimer. "I didn't do anything. I did-*dunt*! What'll I do if I lose my job? I *gotta* work. Poor Tootsie!"

Gypsy rolled over to peer down at her. "Oh, shut up! Nobody's going to bother about firing you." A thought struck her. "What are you doing on Becky's mattress? Where's Becky?"

The question ran through the group. Nobody had an answer. The girl had not been seen since the ranks broke. Gypsy, with an oath, leapt to the floor, wrenched a lamp loose from its socket, and made for the open. Several voices volunteered help.

"I'll find her," she tossed back over her shoulder.

The darkness was as opaque as ever. Gypsy made her way through the shrubbery, calling Becky's name cautiously. She bumped into the shed. The door stood wide.

"Oh, Gypsy! Is that you?"

"Come out of there, you little skulk," the searcher commanded, wrath following her relieved apprehensions.

"I'm afraid."

"What of?"

"The man. Has he gone?"

"What man? Have you been in there with a man?" the other snarled.

"He came in after me."

"Ay-ah," Gypsy rasped. "Then what?"

Receiving no reply, she entered the low building, holding her lamp overhead. A tousled heap in the corner became a recognizable form as Becky crawled to her feet.

"Jee-hoshaphat and the holy prophets!" Gypsy gasped. "What happened to you?" For the girl was a mere wopse of ravaged clothing.

"He tried to kill me."

"Who?" the other asked stupidly.

"The man. I couldn't see who he was."

"Kill you, huh?" Gypsy grunted. "That's what you think, is it?"

"I started to yell and he choked me."

"Um-mm-mm-mm!" Gypsy muttered. "What else?"

"I don't know. I fought him."

"No," Gypsy said thoughtfully, "you wouldn't know. Maybe it's just as well. Tell me the whole thing. Begin at the beginning."

"I was right back of you when the gentlemen came rushing at us. Everybody began to push and shove, so I pushed and shoved, too. After somebody called out we'd better all run back, here comes the constables, I ran. You couldn't see a thing, it was so dark. I fell over the stone wall and bumped my knee mortal hard. I found the shed and somebody was following me, so I ran in and tried to shut the door, but he pushed in and grabbed me and we fought. D'you think he was crazy, Gypsy?"

"Crazy or drunk or—never mind. You never can tell what a gentleman will do," Gypsy said, drawing upon her wide observation of life. "Is that all, Becky?"

"Yes, of course it's all. I couldn't yell because when I tried, he choked my throat. Then the big bell went off and he got up and ran away."

"The man, now; was he big or little?"

"Oh, mortal big!"

That told the shrewd questioner pretty much nothing. Any mysterious assailant in the dark would seem mortal big to a terrified girl. Gypsy pondered, seeking a clue.

"What did he smell of?"

"Smell?"

"Yes, smell," the cross-examiner said impatiently. "Got a smeller, ain't you? All young bloods use scent. Come on! What was it? Lavender? Floral spice? Milk-of-roses? What?"

"I guess I was too scared to smell," the girl excused herself. "But I scratched his face," she added brightly.

"Good wench!" For the moment she forgot how little this was worth as a clue. Then she recalled that she herself had left nail-marks on several masculine visages, as had doubtless most of the others. "You didn't hear him speak?"

"I think he said a bad word when the bell rang. It sounded like it. He banged the door to, but the wind blew it open again. I thought he was coming back, and then I did yell, but nobody heard me. So I tried to hide till you came."

Gypsy thought it over. The event permitted of but one interpretation. She was not shocked. Things like that happened in a world of men and women. Nevertheless she was angrily determined to make what investigation she could.

After the victorious battle, Guy Roy had taken refuge from a wild burst of rain in a convenient factory doorway. The sound of heavily stumbling feet came to him. Gurdon Stockwell staggered into sight. His eyes were fixed in an unseeing stare. His mouth hung half-open. There was a splotch of blood on his chin. Guy caught at his elbow.

"Gurdon!"

"Who is it?"

"Me. Guy. What corner of Hell are you sprung from?"

Stockwell groaned and gagged.

"What's the matter with you?"

"Ruin!"

Guy shook him sharply. "Pull yourself together." His mind formed a quick conclusion. "You've been in the bushes with a wench," he said.

Stockwell made a despairing gesture.

"Who was it?"

"I'm not sure."

Guy laughed shortly. "You're not sure! Just any Jenny-come-jumping, eh?"

"It was dark inside," the other muttered.

"So there was a roof to your *amours*. Not the dormitory, I hope."

Stockwell stared at him in apparent incomprehension. He seemed vague, stunned. Guy guessed that his conscience was agonizing him beyond endurance. But there was something more. The man was frightened.

"Here!" Guy said. "Come inside. Let's get this straight."

He led the unresisting owner to the office. There he struck a light, but let it die. Darkness might make it easier for his cousin to talk.

"I ought to get back to the house," Stockwell muttered.

"Not looking the way you do."

The other tried to speak, but closed his teeth on what sounded like a sob.

"You do know who it was, don't you?"

"Not her name." The reply came after an effort. "She was small and—and young. Very strong, too."

"One of the factory children?" Guy spoke quietly, trying to suppress his shock and disgust.

"I saw her like a wisp of the darkness running for the tool-shed, and Satan took possession of me."

"You followed her in?"

Stockwell gulped.

"Did anybody see you?"

"Not that I know."

"Well! Come! Get it off your mind," Guy urged.

With agonized hesitancies, Stockwell told his story. Guy listened with mounting astonishment and relief.

"Is that the whole thing?" he asked at the close. "You haven't held back anything?"

"No."

"Then, so far as I can see, there's no great harm done. She's none the worse for you, if you're telling the truth."

"It's the truth. But don't you see?" Stockwell burst out. "The child will tell. It's ruin, black ruin."

"Use your headpiece," Guy sharply adjured him. "You knew her for a young girl when you got your hands on her, not from seeing. How is she to know who you were? Unless you spoke," he added. "Did you?"

"No. It—it was all silent."

A thought struck home to Guy. "Was the girl complaisant?"

"No. She struggled."

"Why didn't she cry out?"

"I choked her," he said dully.

Guy caught his breath. "You—you didn't kill her, Gurdon?"

"Oh no! I'm sure not." It sounded too much as if he were trying to assure himself.

"That isn't good enough," Guy said with vigour. "I'm going to make certain."

The location of the shed was known to him. He took a round-about way to it. A steep brow of the slope overhung the small building. As he was about picking his way down, he saw a flicker and heard voices, Gypsy Vilas's and a softer one. He craned cautiously forward until he commanded the upper window. Gypsy's companion, he was startled to see, was the child to whom he had promised a book.

In the uncertain gleam she did not look so much of a child

now. One vital fact he gleaned from what he could hear of the talk: she had no notion of who her assailant was.

Guy picked his way back to the office. Gurdon Stockwell was sitting where he had left him, his head sunk in his hands.

"It's all right, Gurdon," he said.

"How do you know?"

"I've been eavesdropping. The girl isn't hurt. Keep mum and all will be well. She doesn't know who it was."

"God be thanked!"

"I think you might leave God out of this," Guy commented, with a touch of grimness.

"You say that she is uninjured?"

"Yes. She thinks you were trying to kill her."

"So I might," Stockwell groaned. "Who—who is she, Guy?"

"Wouldn't you be better off, not knowing?"

The mill-owner writhed at the grimness of the tone. "For my own comfort, yes," he muttered. "But there are amends to be made."

"Conscience?"

"You may jeer at me . . ."

"I'm not in jeering mood, Gurdon. I want to know what you have in mind."

"Put it this way." Stockwell was regaining command of himself. "The girl is an employee of the Eureka. She has suffered mischance here. It is but right that it should be made up to her for the—the shock to her sensibility."

"I see. A matter of company policy."

"If you choose. But it must be so contrived as not to implicate me."

"Of course. Well, the girl's name is Webb. She is a bobbin-doffer."

Gurdon shook his head. "I don't know her."

"No. Why should you?"

"But Goodwilly will. I shall make inquiries. Cautiously, of course."

Guy looked him over. "Put yourself to rights, Gurdon. We must go back to the manor."

"Can I get to bed unobserved, do you think?"

"That won't do," Guy answered decisively. "If you evade, someone might smell a rat. Give the boys a nightcap and send 'em on their way. Can you go through with it?"

"Yes."

Most of the survivors of battle were inside, comparing abrasions and contusions, exchanging experiences. Pale to sallowness, the host was now sufficiently master of himself to perform his duties. Guy passed the word that his cousin had suffered a dunt on the head and that an early departure would be in order. The gala dissolved, the guests enthusiastically thanking Stockwell for the most entertaining evening of the year.

Before departure they organized themselves into an impromptu session, elected Mr. Guy Roy a member of the Halcyons by *viva voce* vote, and endowed him with the password and the silver whistle of their festive and honourable order.

TEN

To the incredulous relief of Dormitory Four there were no layoffs. Not even a fine was assessed. The phenomenon vied in local discussions with Obedience Webb's misadventure. A score of theories for the management's leniency were advanced, none of them approximating the facts.

The miscreants owed their immunity to Guy Roy. On the morning after the fracas, Gurdon Stockwell had come down to breakfast, his face heavy with determination. To his kinsman and guest he said:

"We shall have to look for female help."

"Why?" Guy inquired.

"Can you ask? All who took part in last night's disgraceful exhibition must be discharged."

"Do you think that wise?" Guy asked slowly.

"I regard it as a necessary measure of discipline."

"Gurdon, if I were you I shouldn't stir those muddy waters further."

"I do not take your meaning," the other returned with a frown.

"No? What of your own part in last night's little turn-up?"

"That is not at issue," the other said hastily. "Since none but you knows——"

"Knows who the assailant was," Guy broke in. "But you can't so easily quash an attempt at rape." Stockwell winced away from the word. "Do you deceive yourself that the whole plant isn't ringing with it?"

"I cannot silence idle tongues, but I can assure that they do not wag here."

"They'd wag worse elsewhere. The more ill-feeling you stir up, the more the story will spread and worsen. Hadn't it occurred to you that wholesale discharges might even direct suspicion? To the right quarters," he added pointedly.

Stockwell shot him a sharp and apprehensive glance. "There's been nothing yet, has there?"

"Not so far as I know. Let sleeping dogs lie, Gurdon. Wait long enough for the story to have reached you through natural channels, then bulletin a generous reward for the apprehension of the miscreant who attacked one of your female employees. The Eureka protects its own," he grinned.

Stockwell was impressed. "I will, myself, compose the announcement." He hesitated. "Cousin," he said, "I should be reluctant to have you think me insensible of the responsibilities of my—uh—my error."

Guy waited.

"I shall charge myself with the girl's future. She shall be sent away to school."

"Not immediately, though," Guy counselled. "That would certainly stir up the gossips."

"A point well taken." He reflected. "For the present, then, she shall be kept on at the mill with such schooling as can be arranged. Later, when this has blown over, she shall be sent to a school for young females. There is, I believe, an excellent one in Philadelphia."

The factory hands were favourably impressed by the fifty-dollar reward posted upon the board. Becky read it to Gypsy, who shook a shrewd head.

"Nobody fired? 'Tain't natural," she objected.

Some deep-rooted instinct within her was ill-content. There must be a clue somewhere in Becky's confused and shocked mind. But the child shrank from discussion of the episode with some dim, shamed sense which she did not fully comprehend.

"I don't *like* to talk about it, Gypsy."

"All I ask you is, ain't there something you didn't tell me? Didn't the dirty stinker say anything?"

"Only the swear word, 'Oh, my God!' I told you that. Please, Gypsy, don't make me talk about it any more. It gives me a funny feeling in my stomach."

Supper was called. The girls crowded forward with eager appetites. While they were still at it, Clorinda Burgo arose and made the rounds with a spindlebox in her arms. When she reached Becky she said:

"Come on, widget. Haffa that fat slice of cake."

"What for?"

"For the box. And your raisin bun, too."

Gypsy, sitting next, had already made her contribution, and now neatly transferred Becky's slice of cake. The girl huddled protectively over the other threatened dainty. Burgo cracked her over the knuckles. She uttered a dolorous protest.

"Why must I?"

"Oh, tell her!" Clory said. "Maybe she'll feel better about her raisin bun."

"It's Meg Shink," Gypsy said. "She's taking the prog to Cash Barlow. He's in clink again."

"What for?"

"The usual. Stirrin' up the mechanics."

"Won't Meg get caught? Why's she doing it?"

"He's her uncle."

"And you keep mum about it," Gypsy warned. "If old Hurdy-Gurdy or Goodwilly knew, she'd be shot out of her job quick's a wink."

Becky learned further that the food delivery would be a weekly operation. Without it the prisoner would have been starved into submission, which was the main purpose of his sentence. Though she understood little of the reasons for Barlow's plight, she did not begrudge the forced levy upon her rations thereafter.

It was Guy Roy's money, not himself, for which his cousin had angled on behalf of the Eureka. Nevertheless, there Guy was; some use must be made of him. His engaging personality might be an asset in disposing of the factory output. First, however, he must learn something of the goods themselves. Gurdon Stockwell advised that he spend some weeks observing the methods of manufacture before taking the road.

Guy was not averse. He would prefer travel to the plant work. Conscientiously enough he set about learning the details of production. Soon he evinced a bias of interest incomprehensible to the head of the business. He seemed quite as concerned with the producers as with the product. Day after day, he would come to his cousin with questions and suggestions that were wholly irrelevant. Could not benches be set up in the work-rooms? Was not the midday intermission too short? He had learned that the Rochester mills gave a full hour. What about safeguards for this mechanism or that, which could be put in at low cost? Would not sprinkling before sweeping stir up less dust? And so on to the point of exasperation. He could not be made to understand the proprietary point of view, which was simply and logically that the employees were part of the mechanism; to regard them in any other light made for confusion and disruption.

"Why should you concern yourself with these matters?"
Stockwell demanded. "Which of your ideas will fetch a better
price for the cloth?"

Guy could not have answered the first question. The best he
could have done would be to say that he was more interested
in people than in things, and his cousin would probably have
considered that answer unsatisfactory, if not worse.

For his part, Stockwell perceived that the sooner Guy was out
and away, the better for all concerned. He advanced the time of
his maiden trip. A few days before the date set for his departure
heavy orders had come in from the West, with a time limit on
them. Increased performance was decreed by Mr. Goodwilly.
The owner himself now visited the work-rooms to urge the
workers on. For the good repute of the Eureka they must quicken
the pace, speed the production, turn out more goods. Those who
fell behind in their stint would be fined. Laxity would be punished
by discharge. Unless the increased weekly quota were met, there
would be an extra hour in the evening without extra pay money
and the oil would be charged against them. The girls grumbled.
Some cried. Gypsy Vilas cursed. Clorinda Burgo called Mr.
Stockwell a bad name. Nobody dared to protest openly. The sore
lesson of the abortive riot after the dinner-party was too fresh
in memory.

A protest of a sort was lodged involuntarily by the pallid and
hollow-chested Rhuane Nichol. All the promises of the sure
cures, all the money spent upon lung balsams and cough emol-
lients, had not saved her from growing weaker and thinner.
There was one single week in which she had suffered two collapses
and three fines. She took to having nervous chills when the
overlooker approached. Her hand shook so that she could hardly
hold the cloth she was sizing. Mr. Goodwilly became impatient
with her. If she could not do the work, there were plenty others
who could.

As he left the room after one of his tirades, Guy Roy entered,
looking for Stockwell. A huddle of workers beneath one of the
narrow windows drew him to the spot.

"What's the matter?" he asked.

"Nothing," one of the group made haste to answer.

Guy pushed his way through the circle. A young woman lay
on the floor. Gypsy Vilas was holding to her bloodless lips a bottle
glaringly labelled, "Dr. Parker's Vitalizing Spark. $1.00 a Bottle."

"Who is it?" the young man inquired.

"Rhuane Nichols." It was Mary Haynes who answered him. "She'll be all right in a bit"

The figure on the floor echoed faintly, "I'll be all right." She tried to prove it by sitting up, but wavered back. A cruel cough racked her. The blood came and spread down her waistfront.

"Get a doctor," Guy directed sharply.

"Who'll pay him?"

"Call old Brockie," another voice said. "He'll come on tick."

Amos Goodwilly entered. "What's all this?" he blustered. "Back to your machines, all of you." He walked over to look at the sick girl. "You better go home," he said. "Ah, Mr. Roy! Didn't see you, sir."

"I'll take her home," Guy offered.

"Please, Mr. Goodwilly," Rhuane appealed to the over-looker. "I can work. It's been this way before. Don't take me away."

The doctor came. He was an ugly little man with a red nose and splay ears. Guy spoke a question into the nearest one. The man shook his head impatiently and bent over the patient. He gave her a stimulant from the small bag strapped to his waist.

"Let me up. I can work," she whispered dully.

Guy drew the little man aside and repeated his question. The physician nodded.

"Of course it is."

"What does it come from?"

"Too little food. Too little air. Too much dust. Too much work. Yours respectfully, Fitch Brockway, M.D. No fee for diagnosis."

"The other girls seem all right," Guy protested.

The doctor squinted at him. "Been here long?"

"A few months."

"And this is the first you've seen?"

"Are there others?"

The little man laughed unpleasantly.

"I suppose you can answer a civil question," Guy suggested.

"It's a crackpot question."

"Then there *are* others."

"Not right here in this lot maybe—yet."

"Elsewhere in the factory?" the young man persisted.

F

"Take a look on the next floor. Dust's worse there. There's two or three promising cases in the top storey. Probably more if you wanted to look for 'em."

The other girls had got Rhuane to her feet and were dabbing at her face and clothing with damp cloths. Amos Goodwilly made a note in his book.

"Oughtn't she to go home?" Guy asked Brockway.

"Certainly. But she won't."

"Couldn't you persuade her?"

"Might. But I wouldn't. She needs the money."

"What will happen to her?" He put the question apprehensively, knowing what the answer would be.

"Oh, she's got a couple more months' work in her."

"And then?"

"She'll die," Dr. Brockway said simply.

"Can't anything be done?"

"No."

"But that's awful."

"What would you expect? Wear 'em out and get another." The little man grinned impudently at his questioner. "How's dividends?" he asked.

Guy cursed him ardently. The doctor executed a mock salute and left.

At dinner Guy spoke to his kinsman. Stockwell listened with an impassive face.

"The consumption? Oh, well, yes. It's of common occurrence among young females."

"Factory workers?"

Stockwell's tone sharpened. "All women of that age. Factory work has nothing to do with it."

"That Brockway chap thinks different."

"Brockway? A pauper practitioner," said Gurdon severely. "An agitator. He is a friend of that fellow Cassius Barlow."

"No longer dangerous, I believe," Guy observed negligently.

"Not for the present. By the way"—he lifted his head to direct an inquiring regard upon his kinsman—"I learn that some person is supplying him with comfortables from the store."

"If you mean me, I have been sending him tobacco from time to time," Guy answered easily. "I'm sorry for the fellow. He got unfair treatment at the trial."

"Nothing of the sort. It must stop."

Guy stared at him in astonishment. "Are you undertaking to guide my personal conduct, Gurdon?"

"This is a factory matter, a question of policy."

"A plug of niggerhead," Guy said lightly. "You remind me that it is time I sent him another."

The other flushed. "Are you also victualling him?"

"Oh, come, Gurdon!" Guy replied, still with perfect good-humour, but also with decision. "I'm not in court."

"You may yet find yourself there," his cousin snapped, "if you consort with notorious law-breakers."

Guy's easy temper was due more to laziness than to self-discipline. Quarrelling seemed to him idle, wasteful of time, and a needless strain upon the nerves. When tension became too great, it was his practice to smile and walk away.

"I don't think this is profitable," he said. "Let's pass it."

Stockwell made an effort to control himself. In a calmer tone he said: "As for the furtive victualling of that scoundrel, Goodwilly thinks that he is on the track of the culprit. One of our own workers, he believes. It will go ill with the guilty one when apprehended."

Guy reflected that his cousin was never less tolerable than when he assumed the role of Justice personified.

ELEVEN

THE offer of fifty dollars reward was still on the factory wall when Guy Roy returned from a successful trip. Beside the notice appeared another announcing the arrival of the Rev. Harold Hoadley, who would conduct a series of revivals and soul-searchings at the First Methodist Church starting late in November.

"Hellfire Hoadley," Malinda Prowitt remarked in Dormitory Four. "That means we'll all have to go."

"*Have* to! I count it a privilege," declared Priscilla Stamm.

"I'd go, willing, if I was sure of getting the Rev. Hoadley's sermon on the Lusts of the Flesh," Hannah Boutwell said.

"That fetches 'em every time," Arvila Hopkins put in. "All the young bloods in town'll be there with their ears wagging."

Gypsy looked up sharply. "Will they?"

"Gypsy's got something on her mind," Relief Lovejoy said. "What is it, Gypsy?"

"Nothing," Gypsy said. "Not a thing."

This, of course, was a lie. Gypsy had plenty in her head. The scheme which she continued to ponder after they had all gone to bed had one flaw. It involved the despatch of a letter. Writing was not one of Miss Vilas' skills.

An earlier line of inquiry was still occupying her mind. There was something of the terrier in Gypsy. Once she had begun to dig for a bone she could not abandon it. Sundays afforded her the only time for this quest. She pursued it while the others were at church.

On this cloudy November Sabbath, Guy Roy, sauntering across the deserted mill yard, heard a noise in the old tool-house. Having nothing else to do, he investigated. Through the half-open door he saw a figure on hands and knees scuffing at the dirt floor. At the shutting off of the light from the door, the girl pushed her body up and squatted on her haunches.

"Who's there?" she said sharply. "Oh, it's you! Hey-o, feller-me-lad."

"Hello, Gypsy."

"How are you and Old Holy hittin' it off?"

"Well enough. What are you looking for?"

She stood up. "Fifty dibbs."

"Oh! The reward."

"That's it."

"Found any clues?"

"Not yet. I'll find out who it was if it takes me a year."

"Who what was?" he asked, yawning a little too obviously.

"The feller that tried it on little Becky, curse his guts!"

"Well, don't look so black about it. You don't think it was me, do you?"

"No. That ain't your style." She stepped into the open. An idea popped into her brain. Why not Guy Roy for her letter? "Would you help out a pal, lad?" she asked.

"Yes, if you're the pal."

"Do a letter for me?"

"With pleasure. To whom?"

"What you want to know that for?" she demanded suspiciously.

"I don't, but the postmaster might."

"Old Hankins? He's got no right to be nosy, either."

"You may be right in principle, Gypsy," Guy conceded; "but how is he to know who to deliver the letter to?"

"Oh!" said Gypsy. "I'll fix it so's my letter'll get where it's meant for without any postmaster messin' in."

"Very well. There's paper and ink in the office. Tell me what you want said."

He led the way, and sat down at the high desk, shaking up the muddy ink and looking to the nib of his pen.

"Mum's the word, lad. No names named."

Guy set down his pen. "You mean an anonymous letter? I don't like that, Gypsy."

"Who asked you to like it? Just do it."

Guy tried to explain his refusal. Anonymous letters were not the ticket. People did not write them, not decent people. Moreover, they made trouble.

"That's the idear," said the unimpressed Gypsy. "To scare the livin' whizzle out of the skunk that needs it."

"You'll have to find somebody else for the job, I'm afraid."

She wilfully caught at the last word. "Well, if you're afraid, that settles it. I could get Penmaster Robinson, I reckon," she reflected, naming the itinerant teacher of Elegant Chirography, Round Style or Fancy, whose advertisements had been appearing in the local paper. "But he'll charge me fourpence. Maybe six," she added gloomily. "Where would a workin' girl find sixpence, this far from payday?"

"You might negotiate a loan," he suggested.

"I might so. You wouldn't have a sixpence on you that ain't busy?"

Guy handed her the coin with a private grin directed at his own illogical principles.

"Take care it doesn't get you into jail," he warned.

"I'll have good company. Cash Barlow's a chum of mine."

"By the way, who's smuggling out food to him?"

"Now, how would I know?" retorted Gypsy with an innocent stare. "Ask the town pump."

"She'd better be careful, whoever it is. Goodwilly's on the watch."

"I'll pass the word," Gypsy said.

Anonymous letters were no novelty to the Rev. Harold Hoadley. Every revival conducted by him brought its teeming crop of suggestions, self-revelations, requests and accusations ranging from profanity to adultery. Often he found the information contained in these epistles valuable in scaring sinners into righteousness.

This present missive, in its beautifully symmetrical script, impressed him. "Bespoken" stood at the top of the sheet. It had been delivered in the dead of night at his place of temporary lodgment. He studied it with close attention.

Every town that he visited was, in his mind, an adjunct of Hell. If this letter could be believed, Troy was worse than most. There was, the missive stated, a cult of Corinthians, young and middle-aged, who gathered to indulge in strong liquors and profligate rites. As a climax to the gala described in convincing detail by the writer, a Violator of Womanhood had made a Dastardly Essay upon the Virtue of a Young and Beautiful Factory Girl. The criminal was not named, nor was the victim. But in one respect the letter was explicit. There was appended a list of participants of the orgy, as full as Gypsy's memory, abetted by discreet inquiries, could make it. After some consideration, Mr. Hoadley hit upon the inspired notion of sending a private notice to every name on the list, informing its owner that matter of special import to his soul would be brought out at the meeting.

If you were present (the Reverend gentleman wrote), *at a certain godless orgy at the mansion of a prominent citizen, you will be well advised to attend.*

The Sunday evening gathering filled the church. Foreseeing the press, Gypsy Vilas had come early with Clorinda Burgo and Becky Webb.

As the worshippers and those less worshipful than curious passed in, the three girls identified those who had participated in the Stockwell gala. Gypsy Vilas had told her companions of her hopes for the evening. They were to keep watch on all the suspects when the preaching began.

"There comes Tim Freegle," Gypsy whispered to Becky. "Did you smell fish that night?"

"No," Becky answered faintly.

"A couple of decent citizens, drunk or sober," Gypsy observed, when the Learned Tailor and Bookseller Heartt entered.

"So's young Taylor. He's sitting in by Lawyer Plum," Clory said.

"So ain't that Jans Urena." Gypsy took up the reckoning. "He'd be up to anything. Look at him now. Sweet Lard wouldn't melt on his tongue . . . What're you gawkin' at, spratlin'?"

"Nothing," Becky said, hastily averting her eyes from the Stockwell pew below. The owner and his cousin had just entered.

The Rev. Mr. Hoadley led in prayer and hymn. But when he announced his topic, Gypsy uttered a bad word. The subject was "Christmas Desecrated". She was not alone in her disillusion. A sigh of regret passed through the body of listeners.

Mr. Hoadley held up for inspection a broadside currently popular in town, showing a fat and jolly Santa Claus drawn by his plunging reindeer through a whirl of snow, above the title, "A Visit from St. Nicholas".

"Anonymous," he said in his deep, recriminatory tones. "The ditty is as lacking in sponsorship as in merit."

Sonorously he delivered the opening lines:

" 'Twas the night before Christmas, and all through the house
  Not a creature was stirring—not even a mouse."

Becky was charmed. What a lovely broadside! Why had she never seen it on the street corners where such prints were peddled

for twopence? She must lay aside a bit and buy a copy to pin
on her wall.

Gypsy's elbow jabbed painfully into Becky's midriff. The
girl had uttered an involuntary squeak of protest. There was
worse to come. This poem, scurrile and irreligious, the revivalist
asserted, was the keynote to a new and unholy Christmas spirit,
a spirit which manifested itself not in pious and solemn observ-
ances, but in levity of conduct and baubles upon a tree. Merry
Christmas indeed! Had a generation of vipers forgotten that other
tree on Calvary, that they should celebrate with unseemly merry-
makings and unchristian joyances, with libations and profligate
gifts? He caught up the offending broadside, cast it upon the
platform, and trampled it under foot.

Now he had returned to his place behind the pulpit. From
his pocket he took a sheet of pale-blue writing-paper which he
placed before him, smoothing it out with a careful hand. Quietly
he began:

"I am in receipt of an unsigned letter. It is written by a person
of some culture and pretensions to Scriptural learning. It may
be a wile of the Devil; I have little liking for anonymous poems
or letters. But the allegations herein are too specific to be lightly
set aside. It is laid upon me to probe to the bottom of this."

Speaking more deliberately now, and with eyes on the paper,
he added: "I have before me the roster of those who assisted at
a godless revel. Each and every one of them has been notified
to attend this service. I now call upon you, one and all, *stand
up*!"

The summons rang like a musket shot. A stir, a quiver of
unease and alarm trembled through the congregation. Men
peered sidelong at one another. Some stared straight before them.
Women rustled. In her eagerness, Gypsy leaned far over the
gallery rail, her questing gaze darting from face to face.

"Stand up, I bid you."

No man obeyed. The speaker drew a deep breath.

"Whoremongers, adulterers, strumpeteers, pimpers, panders,
and hucksters of the flesh that perisheth, perdition-bound, one
and all, in the frail craft of your profligacies! Ye have made a
covenant with death and with Hell are ye in agreement. Must I
summon ye to judgment, name by name?"

The hush was absolute. The Rev. Mr. Hoadley shook his head.

"Or shall I let remorseless time work upon you?"

A great sigh, in part relief, but chiefly disappointment, rustled faintly across the expanse of upturned faces.

"Yes," he continued weightily, "I leave you to the judgment of your own souls, for the present. *For the present.*" There was a minatory emphasis in the repetition. "One among you," he resumed in accents as measured as a tolling bell, "stands convicted before the Judgment Throne of a baser crime. Lecher, ravisher, batten upon innocence, would-be despoiler of virtue, I call upon you. Rise and face this congregation of the godly."

Again the impalpable wave of emotion and expectancy, again the quaver of controlled breathing. A female in a rear pew began to sob hysterically.

"Silence!" the preacher boomed. He swept the gathering with a slow circling of his eyes. Nobody rose.

"Damn!" Gypsy muttered to Clory. "Everybody tryin' to look innocent and *all* the bastards lookin' guilty."

Hellfire Hoadley strode to the edge of the platform.

"Shall I speak his name?" he shouted.

"Yes. Speak!" shrieked an old lady near the front, the spirit of induced hysteria welling up beyond control in her. "Do! Do! Do! Do! Do!" she tooted like a demented horn.

He silenced her with a flattened palm upraised.

"No!" he boomed.

Afraid to look at his cousin before, Guy Roy now felt Gurdon relax.

"No," the exhorter continued melodiously. "I can look into his soul. What do I see there? Amidst the filth and corruption I see budding the pure white flower of repentance. Not yet beyond salvation, that trembling soul. Hands off, Satan! Thou shall not possess him. Respite he shall have until conscience drives him to free and voluntary avowal. Let us all join in prayer for him."

It was a sorely disappointed congregation that passed out into night. The scattered Halcyons who had attended the dinner did not dare look at much less bespeak one another.

On the long walk home, shoulder to shoulder, the two cousins exchanged only commonplaces. At the mansion door Gurdon jerked out, "He knows."

"I doubt that he knows a thing. Old Hellfire is putting up a bluff. He hasn't a notion of whom he's aiming at with that sermonizing blunderbuss of his."

"Do you think so? I wish I could believe it."

"Go to bed and sleep it off," Guy advised him kindly.

"Sleep! When have I slept? I cannot remember." He turned away and went down the steps.

The Rev. Harold Hoadley sat over his dyspeptic's breakfast of weak though authentic tea and butterless toast. He was a tall, spare, sallow-complexioned man of sixty, with hypnotic eyes, a wide, firm mouth, and a chest like the smithy bellows. Formerly a tanner of rigorously pious life, he had been impelled to the pulpit by a conviction of righteousness and a mission to preach hell to the sinful. A profound persuasion of man's depravity was combined with a chronically rancid stomach to give him an unfavourable view of humanity and its prospects in the hereafter.

Pecking dispiritedly at his meagre meal, he heard voices at the entrance and his name spoken. Who would be calling upon him at six-thirty of a stormy morning? Some overburdened sinner, he surmised. This opinion he revised upon seeing Mr. Gurdon Stockwell appear. He rose, extending his hand with a smile.

"This is indeed a pleasure, Brother Stockwell."

The visitor's expression did not indicate agreement. "Can we be private, Brother Hoadley?" he asked.

The breakfaster cast an unregretful glance at the remaining sliver of toast. "Come into my chamber."

Gurdon Stockwell sat down before the Franklin stove and passed a shaking hand across his forehead. He had slept hardly at all.

"Are you unwell, Brother Stockwell?" the revivalist asked solicitously.

"Not in the body."

"Can I aid you?"

"Brother Hoadley, what should be the procedure of the guilty one whom you called to repentance last night?"

"Full and open avowal of his offence and true repentance. Do you come in his behalf?"

"You don't know his identity?"

Mr. Hoadley hesitated. "The power of the Lord will reveal him to me," he said.

"The power of the Lord has revealed him. I am the man."

The exhorter was shocked to the depths of his soul. A pillar of the Church! A model of conduct for the youth of Troy. Here, indeed, was a triumph for the powers of evil.

"You, Brother Stockwell!" he managed to get out. "I can hardly credit it."

"I was tempted and I fell," the other said.

The minister glanced up quickly. "The woman tempted you?"

"Satan tempted me."

Mr. Hoadley considered. "Why did you not free your soul of this at the meeting?"

"I longed to. Believe me, I longed to. Other considerations, consideration for others, I may say, restrained me."

"I fail to understand, Brother Stockwell."

"Consider my position in the community. I am, I say it humbly, held up as a pattern for the younger generation. My position in the Church, my importance in the world of commerce, my activities in public movements—all these impose upon me peculiar responsibilities." He spoke with a conviction which impressed the aging cleric.

"I will take it to the Lord in prayer," Mr. Hoadley said humbly.

"Any other amends within my power, you have but to impose. I undertake to accept any penance, any reparation."

"Ah, reparation." The evangelist mused. "There is the other to be considered."

"The other?"

"The woman. The victim."

"Not a woman. No more than a child."

"A child? The greater the sin," the clergyman said sternly. "To despoil a young maiden——"

"I did not despoil her."

"But you cannot deny the design."

"No," the penitent groaned.

"Allow that she is none the worse for you. But you yourself, are you none the worse?"

Stockwell gazed at him in mute anguish.

"You lusted in your heart for her," the relentless voice pursued. "So much you admit."

"Yes."

"Your purpose, though unfulfilled, was adulterous. Is it not true?"

"Yes, but . . ."

The other stopped him with upheld hand. "Who lusteth after a woman in his heart is an adulterer. For the salvation of your soul you have but one course open to you. Do you not perceive it?"

"No."

"You must marry her."

"Marry? That child?"

"She will grow to womanhood."

"But, sir—one of my mill-hands. A female mechanic. Hardly that. A chore-girl."

"Honourable labour is no disquality. Is the girl virtuous?"

"She is a child, I tell you!" Stockwell cried. "I doubt that she has attained to womanhood. She is not marriageable."

"Not with another than yourself, perhaps," the clergyman said thoughtfully. "It may well be that you have rendered marriage to any other man impossible for her. Who can assess the effect of shock and shame upon one so young? Do you owe her nothing?"

"I will send her away. I will pay her handsomely. I have already designed her education at no small cost. . . ."

"One cannot compound for sin with money."

"But have you thought of the conclusions that would be drawn? Would not such a step inevitably convict me?"

The revivalist reflected. "Perhaps. I shall not insist upon immediate action, which would be inadvisable in any case, because of the victim's youth. Send her away, if you will. Educate her to your station." Up to this point his speech had been mild. Now the implacable will of the fanatic shone in the deep eyes. "But you shall, when the time comes, make her your wife or I will, with my own tongue, publish abroad your shame, and cry upon Heaven for justice to the wronged and innocent. Gurdon Stockwell," he concluded triumphantly, "I shall save your soul from Hell in your own despite and Satan's."

Stockwell walked blindly out into the storm.

TWELVE

THAT pestilent peddler of turmoil (the phrase was Gurdon Stockwell's), Luther Simms, was in Troy.

"Would you like to see him?" Stockwell asked Guy Roy.

"You're going to receive him?" Guy asked in surprise.

"Matter of business," the businessman replied. "There are improvements pending on the mechanism he has invented. The Eureka," he added complacently, "keeps abreast of the times."

"I should assuredly like to see the most dangerous man in York State," Guy said.

"You will hardly credit it when you do. But don't be deceived by his seeming amenities. He is a man of property, thanks to the royalties derived from the very mills he denounces."

When they met at the mill office, Luther Simms did not present the picture of violence and rancour which Guy had been led to expect. It was a tall and bulky figure that heaved itself up from a chair to return the entrant's polite greeting. Simms looked to be short of fifty. His hair was grizzled, his pocked face heavy and thoughtful, based upon a massive jaw. His deep-set eyes were sleepy. A slow man, Guy estimated; slow of thought, slow of speech, slow to anger.

"Mr. Simms is not satisfied with our conduct of the Eureka," Gurdon Stockwell began, with a sardonic smile.

"Are *you*?" the agitator inquired of Guy.

"Why not?" Guy parried. The abruptness of the query had startled him.

The visitor thought for a moment before speaking again. (Whether or not his remark was in answer to the counter-question Guy could not make out.) "You had a turn-out some weeks since."

"You are kept well-informed, Mr. Simms," Stockwell observed. "Who is your spy in this plant?"

"A harsh word, 'spy', Mr. Stockwell."

"Informant, then, if you please."

"I have several friends among your mechanics. If you knew which ones, how long would their employ continue?"

The mill-head said, "Short shrift."

"As for the turn-out, it was ill-devised and ill-advised. I should never have countenanced it."

"Why not?" Guy asked, his interest in this strange person gaining.

"It lacked righteous cause."

"I am grateful for once to be able to agree with you," said Gurdon Stockwell.

"Victualling and lodging are of small concern. There are graver issues."

"What would you consider fair justification for a strike?" Guy used the new term, which, however, the agitator had no difficulty in interpreting.

"Wages. Hours of work," Luther Simms replied promptly.

"Simms is a proponent of the twelve-hour day," Stockwell said.

"What chance for leisure has the worker under the present system?" Simms demanded.

"For that matter," said Guy, "what leisure would they have in a twelve-hour day?"

Simms glanced at him in faint surprise. "One must make a start some——"

"What these people are really agitating for," Stockwell broke in, "is the iniquitous ten-hour day. The twelve-hour is no better than a lying pretext."

His rudeness, plainly designed for provocation, failed to ruffle the visitor. "Substantially true," he said. "From six to six with two hours for meals."

"Do you really expect that?" Guy asked curiously.

"Why not? New York has it. Promising start has been made in Albany, Utica, Rochester. Smaller places like Seneca Falls and Batavia are coming to it. Do you think Troy can hold out against the trend?"

"Yes, as long as I live here," Stockwell cried. "I'd rather see every wheel in the city stopped than yield to that abominable anarchy."

"It will come," Simms asserted with invincible placidity. "Even here."

"*None sine sanguine*," the mill man muttered.

"Not without blood? Perhaps not." Simms spoke sadly now. "Take heed that your own hands be not reddened with it, Gurdon Stockwell."

"I should accept even that terrible responsibility," the other returned with profound conviction.

"Or that the blood be not your own," Simms continued, unmoved.

"Do you threaten me, Luther Simms?" Stockwell's powerful muscles were twitching.

"Steady, Gurdon," Guy warned.

"No, no. I am no advocate of violence," the labour man protested.

"I hear you say so. And yet"—the owner leaned far forward, his lips taut, his eyes alight—"I verily believe that there is no excess to which you would not go in order to gain your ends."

"Not my ends. God's ends. The ends of humanity."

"You see!" Stockwell turned to Guy, who was intent upon his visitor. "As I told you. The man is possessed. For his fanatic cause he would stop at nothing. *Nothing!* Is not that true?" he challenged.

"Nothing," Luther Simms confirmed gravely.

Guy had already revised his opinion of the man. He saw him to be, in his way, as convinced, as devoted, as religious, for example, as Hellfire Hoadley. An odd comparison, but the likeness of the two men had suddenly flashed into his mind. Luther Simms might indeed be a dangerous man.

"I see no occasion for continuing this interview," Stockwell now said stonily.

Simms did not move. "A moment's indulgence," he requested. "There was, I believe, no aftermath to the outbreak of the female mechanics."

"What of it?"

"It is hardly in character with the Eureka policies under the Stockwell regime to let so gross a breach of discipline go unpunished."

"That is wholly the concern of the management."

"The same night there was an assault upon one of the female hands." Guy shot a startled glance at his cousin. Stockwell's face was impassive.

"Ah, well!" the visitor continued. "Such occurrences are only too frequent in our mills."

"Not in the Eureka," said its owner warmly.

Simms nodded, made his farewells, and left. Stockwell turned to Guy.

"Do you think he suspects?"

"No. How could he?"

"I don't know. He has sources of information. An ugly customer."

"Ugly, perhaps, but interesting. I'd like to talk with him further."

"More of your strange tastes. You could overtake him now if you make haste."

"I think, if you don't mind, I will."

He caught up with Luther Simms at the gate and fell into step beside him.

"A model mill," Simms said.

"What's wrong with it?" Guy asked, not contentiously, the other noted, but as if he would like to know. Something might be done with this young fellow.

"Nothing that isn't as bad or worse in other plants," he admitted.

"Then why set upon my cousin?"

"Oh! Is Gurdon Stockwell kin to you?" Guy nodded. "Then there is nothing further to be said between us."

"There might be. I am too new here to be committed to all the commercial standards of the mill or the town. I should really like to know why you select the Eureka for your target."

Simms reflected. "Because Gurdon Stockwell is the most influential mill-owner in Troy. He is a man of principle."

"You admit that?" said Guy, mildly surprised.

"And his principles are inspired by Hell."

"That's what he thinks of yours."

"Doubtless. But for his opposition the twelve-hour day—aye, and the ten—would prevail here within a year. He is the head and front of the obstruction."

"On principle," Guy smiled.

"Always on principle," the other agreed. "That is what makes him so formidable. We shall beat him yet," he muttered.

"By strikes?"

The agitator shook his head gloomily. "No. The day of successful turn-outs is past. Unemployment is rife. Mostly our attempts fail. There is too much force against us, too much fear in us. And here there are too many females. Women make poor material for the battle."

"My cousin's ideal—this is no secret or I should not be telling you—is machinery which can be operated wholly by women."

"And children."

"And children, of course."

"You endorse that, young sir?"

"I'm not sure that I do."

"Then there may be hope of you yet."

"But not of the ten-hour day, I fear," Guy said, with his ready smile.

"No. The Eureka women won't starve for a cause. We must look to a change in the heart of man. Even such as Mr. Gurdon Stockwell."

"My cousin is firm in the faith that God is on the side of the propertied men."

"Doubtless. And he turns his faith to the Devil's ends. The world would be better rid of his kind."

"Precisely what he thinks of you," Guy observed with amusement. "You two knights of principle should meet, armed to the teeth, in a single combat to determine the issue. The ten-hour day or death! Shall I make the arrangements?"

The other did not respond to his levity. "My bullet would fly true," he asserted, with a conviction that startled his hearer.

Guy stopped in his tracks. "Do you mean that you would really kill Gurdon if you could?"

"He kills women and children in his mill."

"Oh, come!" Guy protested, revolted by such excess. "That's going too far."

"I acquit him of the intent," the fanatic said, "but not of the result."

"I don't think you're fair," Guy said uneasily. "But I'd like to talk with you again some time."

"To what purpose?"

"To hear more of your ideas. You must not think me inhumane," he added, with his charming smile.

"No. Only misguided," Simms said mildly.

"There again you echo my respected cousin," Guy said. "*Au revoir*."

THIRTEEN

On a Monday morning in December, Becky Webb, pulsating with excitement, received a packet-parcel from New York. The beribboned and scented mystery, being unwrapped in the presence of her curious fellow-workers of Dormitory Four revealed a copy of the *Book of Knowledge: a Compendium of Useful, Valuable, and Improving Information on All Subjects* It was inscribed with graceful flourishes:

To
Miss Obedience Webb
with the Respectful
Homage of a Friend and
Well Wisher

The other girls did everything but beat her because she stoutly disclaimed any certainty as to the identity of the donor Her proud bearing implied that there were numerous cultivated noblemen of her acquaintance, any one of whom might have bestowed the gift. To Gypsy she owned up; also to Mary Haynes. But this latter was of necessity. She needed Mary's aid in composing a letter of thanks couched in sufficiently lofty phraseology.

The letter was sent, and in due time Guy Roy received it with mild amusement and forgot it. Meantime, Becky pored over her treasure every night until lights-out, and slept with it cuddled against her rounding body.

Guy returned in time for Christmas with a growing interest in the business which he had at first found dull. His work as a sales-factor took him to New York, Philadelphia, Boston, and other pleasant places where he knew pleasant people. Gurdon Stockwell was well satisfied with the orders which he sent in and privately glad to have him away from the plant.

The looms were going full-time when Guy reported to his principal and received, in turn, a brief bulletin of conditions in the factory. Gurdon mentioned with satisfaction that the miscreant who owled in the clandestine food to Cassius Barlow had been found.

"It was a wretched little cleaning-girl in Dormitory Four."

"Not Meg Shink?" Guy said.

"How do you know so much about our help?" Gurdon asked discontentedly. "*I* do not even know their names."

"I suppose it's because I am more interested in people than you are, Gurdon."

"You need have no further interest in this particular one."

"Are you sending her to jail, too?"

"I should, if I were not a merciful man."

"What form does your mercy take?"

"I shall discharge her."

"I suppose that is only fair," Guy admitted.

"But not until her month is up. She will then be sent away without a recommendation and," he concluded with the self-contented air of the just man convinced of his righteousness, "without a wage."

"Let me understand this, Gurdon. You mean to let the child work the rest of the month without pay?"

"I do. In satisfaction of the food she has stolen. And fortunate enough she may think herself."

There was little Yuletide gaiety in the Eureka. The great mansion on the hill was dark except for the study where the young magnate figured the year's balance. He, it seemed, had taken to heart the Rev. Hellfire Hoadley's strictures upon the impiety of a merry Christmas. As dogma, it appealed to the puritan in him. Besides, it saved money.

No such inhibition cramped the Orlando Montagues. They hospitably included Guy Roy in their Christmas party. There was good cheer, many-voiced harmony, and a glittering haw-thorn tree with a gift for everyone present. Guy's was a box of fresh Montague collars in no less than three designs: the high turnover, the low turnover, and the open throat. The gratified recipient tried them all on the next day, studying the effect in his mirror. This was not vanity, though indeed he was pleased with the effect. A business scheme had formed in his brain.

There followed a long conversation with the inventive-wifed ironmonger, attended with consultation of textile price lists—muslin, linen and gingham—and much figuring on many sheets of paper.

"I'll talk with my cousin," Guy said.

"I have already approached him on the matter without success."

"You tried to interest him in George Jones's work-room, didn't you?"

"Yes. He could see no per centum in it. Said if Jones wanted to sell it couldn't be worth buying."

"Those collars you gave me—are they Jones's work?"

"My—our design, Jones's workmanship."

"They're an excellent product."

"George Jones is a fool," the ironmonger said warmly. "Fairly launched in an affording trade with me behind him, and he drops it all. And for what? To go to New York and embark on a catchpenny journalistic junket that will never make a cent for him or anyone else."[1]

"I think," Guy Roy said slowly, "that something may come of this. I'll see what can be done with my cousin."

It was his plan, sometime during the year, to have a room set aside in the Eureka for the facture of the new neckwear, on a semi-independent basis under his operational management. He had theories about the handling of labour, which he meant to try out if Gurdon Stockwell could be persuaded to give him free rein for the experiment. As to help, he could consult Gypsy Vilas.

Opportunity of talking with the factory hands in working hours was infrequent. But a breakage of ice clogged the water-wheel two days after Christmas, stopping the machinery, and the girls took advantage of the respite to scatter to their dormitories. Guy intercepted Gypsy Vilas.

"Hello, Gypsy! Haven't seen you for a spider's age."

"Hey-o, lad! How do you like your little job as far as you've gone?"

"How do you like yours?"

She cocked her head to look at him sidewise.

"Who'm I talkin' to? A boss or a pal?"

"This is between friends."

Gypsy nodded. "All right. I don't favour my sweet employer. I think he's a mean son of a bitch."

"That's not nice talk, Gypsy."

"You asked me. You got it."

"Is that your only objection to the place?"

"Spring'll be along one of these days. Come April, I get road-itch in my feet."

---

[1] The catchpenny journalistic junket upon which George Jones had embarked was the germ of the *New York Times*.

"You've stuck to this job quite a while, though."

"Because of young Becky. Somebody has to look after her."

"She'll be getting her loom soon. Then she won't have so much need of you."

"Maybe so, maybe not."

"But I may."

She turned upon him her wide grin. "Why, Mis-tur Roy! Which side of the blanket? Marry me or keep me?"

"Hire you, maybe."

She reflected. "Any place would be better than this andy-hole. Tell me something, lad: is it true that little Shink got found out?"

"I'm afraid it is, Gypsy."

"Does she get the boot?"

He nodded.

"For the jail trick?"

"Yes"

"How'll Cash Barlow get fed now?"

"On county rations, I suppose."

Gypsy's ready laugh burbled richly from her lips. "A doodle-bug would starve on the county." She spat out an oath. "Cash won't. I'll see to that, if I have to fetch the prog to the jail myself."

"Down the rope?"

She stared. "You know too much for a boss, lad. Where do you get it?"

"Oh, I pick it up around the place," he answered carelessly.

Her estimating gaze had a new respect in it. "Who'd 'a' thought it! I guess you see more than you say. Maybe I would like to work for you."

Guy adjusted his rich-hued neck-scarf with its intaglio pin holding it in the fashionable folds, and touched the circlet into which it was snugged.

"What do you think of this collar?"

"Smart."

"Do you know how it works?"

"I know a flash drummer that's got one. He bought it off Montague, the ironmonger."

"Did you ever see him take it off?"

"What damn' business is that of yours? You ain't payin' my rent."

"No offence, Gypsy. I merely wanted to find out how much you know about it. Look."

Easing the neckpiece, he exhibited the strings. The girl walked round him, studying the contrivance with an expert eye.

"Clever," she approved.

"Do you think you could make one?"

"Certes, I could make one. Better than that one you got on."

"What's wrong with mine?"

"It's muslin. I could make one of cambric that wouldn't wrinkle."

"That's a notion."

"Or I could make a finer one of linen with grosgrain in the fold. When do we begin?"

Guy laughed. "These things take time. I'll have to have other girls. And I'll have to consult my cousin on it."

She drew back with a grimace. "Does old Stuffygut have a hand in it?"

"Not in the running of it. I'll handle that myself if the plan works out. Could I get Mary Haynes, do you think?"

"Mary's nimble. She'd come, I reckon, if you made it worth while. Clory Burgo is handy. Hepsy Parsons is brisk. Hannah Boutwell is dumb, but she's steady."

"Pick me out the right lot and I'll make you forewoman."

"Jeez!" the girl breathed.

"I hope to start production by summer."

It proved unnecessary for Gypsy to act as delivery agent for the imprisoned Barlow. Custom ordained that from Christmas to New Year's the town jailor and his assistant should get and, as far as might be, stay drunk. Casual prisoners, not in for any heinous offence could, by a tacit understanding, slip out for a few hours of liberty on their implied faith that they would honourably return by morning.

Cassius Barlow availed himself of the privilege by surreptitiously visiting the Eureka plant. His errand, however, was not food but a long-cherished and hopeless passion for the pious Priscilla Stamm. On the chance of a sight of her, he skirted the millstream, came up through the shelter of the woods and secreted himself in a thicket at dusk.

Three of the factory girls, out for their Sunday stroll, passed that way. They were halted by a sharp:

"Psst!"

Becky Webb jumped. "Snakes!" she quavered.

"Shut up!" Gypsy Vilas ordered. "There ain't any snakes abroad in wintertime."

"It's down the bank," Mary Haynes said. "Over there."

A cautious head protruded. Barlow said hoarsely, "Where's Prissy?"

"Prob'ly up reading her catechism," Gypsy answered.

"I've got to see her."

"There's a hamper of grub all ready for you."

"I don't want the grub. I want Prissy Stamm."

"I'll tell her," Becky chirped and bustled upstairs to bear the message.

At first Prissy demurred, but on second thoughts decided to go. "If only to forbid him to repeat the visit," she said upon joining the others. "I wish you girls to remain within hearing."

"That's a fine way to treat a swain," said the disgusted Gypsy.

"Cassius Barlow is no swain of mine," the girl disclaimed. "He is an evil fellow without respect for authority."

Becky wanted nothing better than to remain within hearing. As Priscilla trod daintily through the snow to Barlow's place of concealment, Becky edged as close to the scene as she could decently get. Only the dull rumble of the male voice with an infrequent response in Prissy's delicate soprano reached the listener's ears at first. She could not make out much of it. But Barlow seemed to be making an impassioned appeal and then to grow angry. His words of upbraiding and threat became audible. He was denouncing his *inamorata* as faithless for not having joined the turn-out, calling her a scab, a dung, and other injurious names.

Priscilla was stung to resentment.

"Don't you put your filthy words on me, Cash Barlow."

"And I love you so," he groaned.

"I don't want your love. I want your quittance. Stop following me."

"What are you afraid I'll find out? About you and your precious Mr. Stockwell?"

She flamed out: "How do you dare! He—he wouldn't look at me."

"Oh, wouldn't he! I've seen him, damn his guts!"

"You are a low, vulgar fellow."

There was a mutter in the man's voice, a thin scream, and the girl came scuttling up the slope like an outraged hen.

"Protect me," she twittered, cowering between Mary and Gypsy. "He's crazy."

"You'd better go back," Gypsy said into the gathering darkness. "Wait a minute. Here's the grub. I've made a packet of it."

He thanked her in a desolate voice. "She treats me like a dog," he complained. "Not so much as a decent word. She'll tell Stockwell, and then I'll have her life."

"Get out of here," Mary Haynes urged.

They heard the rustle of his progress, which died away in the sound of the stream.

As the four girls walked back, Gypsy said to her charge:

"You can have my bed tonight, younglin'."

"Oh, Gypsy! Are you going out?"

"By the pale—moon—light," Gypsy sang lyrically. "There's a debt-drummer in town with a Yankee-doodle-dandy-fine whisker and a fetchin' way. He's got a horse for tonight and a firkin of gin punch. Out-a-twinder and in-at-winder, and the clock strikes the hour."

On the stroke of ten, with Dormitory Four sunk in slumber, Gypsy tiptoed across the floor to her box. She groped and fumbled. She heaved the contents of the box out upon the floor. Her voice cut through the darkness like the rasp of an angered hornet.

"Who took my rope?"

Sleepy plaints and protests responded.

"If I find the dirty trollop I'll tear every inch of skin off her buttocks."

"Oh, go to bed."

"Shut it off, can't you?"

"Clam up and let us sleep."

"Nobody's got your poxy rope."

"Go and ask Devroo about it."

"Jump and break your neck!"

Growling in her throat like an enraged cat, the girl contrived a makeshift out of her bedclothing. It was far short of the ground. She would never be able to return by it. What of it? She wasn't going to be cheated of her flash drummer with his horse and his firkin. Let the Widow Devroo report her if she liked. Let 'em fine her! Let 'em fire her! To hell with all of 'em. To hell with the job, too. She'd have her night and take what came of it next day.

Only a head as drink-resistant as Gypsy Vilas' experienced

one would have enabled her to return to work that morning. The bell had ceased its final racketing when she pushed open the door, five minutes late. Five minutes or five hours, Gypsy didn't much care. It was no fault of hers that she had been unable to get back into Dormitory Four. If she could lay hands on the lallock that broke into her box, she'd make a holy mess of her.

The big wheel groaned and clacked into activity. Her looms would be waiting for her. The very thought of throwing a lever and seeing the mechanism move made the pit of her stomach writhe.

Just to make her feel worse, the Widow Devroo appeared, letting the door slam behind her. Most likely carrying her sneaking, tell-tale report to Goodwilly. The belief was held among the girls that she touched a per centum on every fine that was laid, as a result of her snooperies.

Gypsy felt belligerent enough to punch Devroo's sour face. She turned and set her arms akimbo. The night matron reached the spot, unseeing. Her eyes stared; her twitching mouth drooled a little at the corners. Gypsy did not like the looks of her and was prepared to say so.

"Hey, you!" she hailed.

The widow paid no heed. She walked into the other's outstretched arm.

"Where's my rope?"

"Oh!" said the night matron under her breath. "Oh!"

"You drunk, or what?"

Devroo eluded her grasp and broke into a stumbling run, which terminated at the office door. She threw it open without knocking and staggered in.

"Well, damn my giblets!" said Gypsy thoughtfully.

Something was up. She hurried after Devroo. She was hardly within the hallway when the office door burst open, and the overlooker hurtled out, turning in the direction away from her. The night matron followed part way, but swerved and scuttled up the stairs to the work-room.

At the top of the flight she recovered coherence. With appalling clearness, she shrieked:

"She's hung herself! Meg Shink's hung herself!"

Answering cries came from within. A torrent of girls swept out through the door and down the stairs, shrieking, sobbing, praying. The human flood poured along the hallway and round the far turn, still exuding the hideous, meaningless clamour of infectious hysteria.

Gypsy started to run after the rest, when a heavy impact from behind hurled her against the wall. Gurdon Stockwell was already two rods past her, running like a steam locomotivator. Gypsy scrambled to her feet and set out in pursuit. She saw him leap like a deer over Relief Lovejoy, who had fallen to the floor, and seize the quaking Amos Goodwilly by the shoulder.

"Where?" he snapped. The voice, sharp, imperative, controlled, cut through the frantic babble.

The overlooker gulped and pointed to the door which obviously he had not dared to open. It led to the small storeroom for cleaning apparatus at the end of the passage.

"Stand aside."

Stockwell wrenched the door open.

Gypsy saw her rope. Meg Shink, small as a doll, dangled in the loop.

Stockwell lifted the body and released the noose. He touched the face, shook his head, gently lowered the corpse.

The cries among the massed workers mounted again. The employer strode amongst his help, lifting one here, shaking reason back into another there, speaking in the calm voice of authority until a semblance of order was restored.

"Go to your rooms. Work is dismissed for the morning."

Gypsy thought—I hate his tripes, but, by hookey, he can act the man when the pinch comes.

A silence fell. The wheel-tender had thrown off the power.

The Eureka was to have an unscheduled holiday.

FOURTEEN

A SHIPMENT of No. 5 weave had gone astray and Guy Roy went to Schenectady to trace it, staying there overnight. When he got back the next afternoon an ominously silent mill yard stretched before him. Could there have been a turn-out without warning? The only sign of activity seemed to be in the office. There he found Amos Goodwilly. The paymaster-overlooker told him the news. There followed a colloquy which left Goodwilly limp.

"He took it hard, sir," he reported to his employer. "You'd have thought it was the fault of the mills. A heady young man, Mr. Stockwell. A plunger." He wiped his brow with a shaky finger.

Gurdon Stockwell was thus prepared for the visit from Guy, though not for Guy's appearance, which shocked him.

"Are you indisposed, Cousin?" he asked in genuine concern.

"I've just heard about the Shink girl."

"Ah, yes! Very unfortunate. Accidents will happen."

"Do you call it an accident?"

Stockwell laid down his pen. "I do not take your meaning, Guy. What have you in mind?"

Guy yielded to a swift, injurious impulse. The taunt of the malignant little doctor had come back upon him; he passed it on.

"How's dividends?"

"What is the purport of that question?" the mill-owner asked coldly. In a more amiable tone, he added: "This has been a shock. Don't let it unman you, Guy. It happens everywhere."

Guy bit his lip. "There's a matter I want to put to you. Little Shink's pay should go to Cash Barlow. There were deductions. I have directed Goodwilly to strike them out."

Stockwell frowned heavily. "As a matter of principle, I cannot permit——"

"Oh, I give you all credit for your principles. They're too damned correct for me. I want no more Eureka money, made up of suicide's shillings. I'm quitting."

Gurdon rose from his chair. "You mean that you wish to withdraw from the Eureka? Surely you will not act so hastily?" Upon second thought, he perceived that this might not be so unfavourable. Guy had evinced troublesome tendencies, which apparently were enhanced by every untoward occurrence in the plant. The Eureka would be better off without him. The owner sat down again. "That is your privilege," he said quietly.

"Of which I wish to avail myself as soon as possible."

"*You* can withdraw. Your capital remains. That is understood, I trust."

"I'm not sure that it is."

"Read over our contract," Stockwell said quietly. "Terminable at the end of seven years, on notice. No capital to be withdrawn before then."

"I need that money," Guy said.

"So does the Eureka. We shall be under heavy cost, changing to steam. All our avails will be needed. For what do you need it?"

"To start the collar business of which I spoke to you."

"In which we were to join in a limited partnership."

"I've signed no contract for that, at least," Guy retorted savagely. "I don't want you for a partner. And I am leaving your house this day."

"Is this a quarrel, Cousin?"

Guy recovered himself. "No. I should be foolish to quarrel with you. Unfair, too, I dare say. You are acting according to your lights. Allow that they are as good as mine. Still, I can never again touch a cent of the money made that way." He went on more quietly: "We're better apart, Gurdon. You would never accede to some of my plans. I must work them out alone."

Stockwell shrugged. "As you choose."

It was arranged without too much difficulty of detail that at the end of sixty days Guy was to abandon his official position in the Eureka. An agreement was reached whereby the factory was to supply the projected firm of Roy & Montague with cloth at prices regulated by the market. But Guy's original intention of renting space and buying power from the Eureka was abandoned. The farther away he got from that ill-omened mill, the better for his peace of mind; the farther from the evening shift, staggering with exhaustion as they plodded across the mill yard to the crowded dormitory; from the imagined echo of Rhuane Nichol's strangled coughing—from the phantom of the childish body swinging in the rope—from the rancid jeer of the little doctor, "How's dividends?"—from Mr. Goodwilly's careful accounting and the clamour of the early morning bell.

One point remained to be cleared up. He wanted to be scrupulously fair to his ex-partner.

"Gurdon," he said, "some of your help may want to come to me."

Stockwell's regard was severe. "Have you been soliciting my labour?"

Guy flushed. This was a cardinal sin in industry. "Certainly not. But I have had inquiries."

"From what quarters?"

"Dormitory Four girls."

Unexpectedly, Stockwell's expression mollified.

"To tell the truth," he said quite affably, "I should deem myself well rid of them. A hotbed of turbulence."

What he had in mind was the future marriage to which the overhanging threat of exposure at the hands of the Rev. Horace Hoadley rather than his own conscience compelled him. If he must go through with that, it was most undesirable that his future wife's fellow workers should be employed in the Eureka. He would take measures to discourage any associations of that sort.

Wild rumours began to fly in the excited atmosphere of the mill about Becky Webb. It was known that she had been summoned into the presence of Mr. Goodwilly and put on half-time at a special rate, so that her afternoons would be free for schooling. She was to get a loom. What could be the explanation of such favouritism?

Arvila Hopkins, who was a sentimentalist, guessed that the girl's budding charms had infatuated some rich and ardent stranger who planned to educate her secretly with a view to making her his bride, in the current tradition of the romances.

"She's growing up fast enough," said Clorinda Burgo.

"She'll live to trouble the hearts of men," Mary Haynes prophesied.

"I don't know where you see it," cried Priscilla Stamm. She was quite peevish about it. "A poor little urchin with a snubbed nose and freckles." Priscilla's skin was pure rose and white.

"But look at the eyes," Mildred insisted. "Hazel velvet with a touch of Jezebel green. And she walks like a thistledown in a breath of air."

Gypsy agreed. "She's got the makin's of a men-pleaser, give her a couple years and two stone meat on her frame."

Mildred Hute proffered a theory which was received with some respect. "Maybe she's Goodwilly's by-blow daughter."

Discussion of the fascinating possibility was checked by Becky's arrival. She had no solution of the mystery of her good fortune to contribute. All that she knew was what Mr. Goodwilly had told her. He had been quite slick and pleasant about it.

"What are you goin' to do with all that spare time?" Gypsy asked.

There was no difficulty about that. "Go to school."

"What for?"

"To learn. Do you think I want to grow up an ignorama?" said Becky.

Becky would have had reason to be set up had she known of her employer's personal concern with her. If he must marry this little mechanic—and he had small hope of the Rev. Mr. Hoadley relenting in his determination to force the marriage upon him— he would acquire what information was available about her. Discreet inquiry in the factory apprised him that she was a brisk hand, clever and ambitious for her years, though, in Amos Goodwilly's opinion, inclined to be unruly. Young though she was, she had her loom.

After much self-debate, Gurdon Stockwell hinted to his cousin and nearest female relative, Bookseller Heartt's wife, his possible intentions, and received a surprising response.

"You might fare farther and do worse, Gurdon."

"Do you know the girl, then?"

"I know of her family in Winchendon. They are most respectable folk."

Mrs. Heartt, a confirmed romantic by virtue of much sentimental reading in her husband's shop, had heard of the mysterious favours accorded to the mill child and had quietly investigated for herself. Becky's ripening beauty and intelligence had not only astonished her, but had enlisted her sympathy. Why should not Gurdon marry her, if he was interested, as she assumed? It was high time that he took a wife; there had been suggestive whispers about another Eureka girl of whom Mrs. Heartt did not approve. The inquiry in Winchendon had so satisfied the investigator that she had bidden Obedience Webb in for a private cup of tea on pretence of some Sabbath-school interests, and was charmed with her.

Gurdon was further informed that Deacon Webb, who had

remarried, took no further interest in his runaway daughter. So far, so good. There would be no family entanglements.

"Of course, nothing is settled," Gurdon warned. "This is most private."

"Does the girl know anything of it?"

"Nothing. Whether or not it comes to anything, I shall see that she receives a ladylike education."

"I should be glad to see you settled, Cousin," Mrs. Heartt said judicially. "The girl is said to be virtuous. Any eye can see that she is beautiful."

"Eh?" Gurdon Stockwell jerked out. "What's that you say?"

Mrs. Heartt smiled. "Don't tell me that you haven't noted it."

"I haven't set eyes on her since . . . I haven't seen her for three months."

In that three months Becky had burgeoned beyond her own consciousness. Contentment with her lot was a maturing influence. The work was light, the schooling delightful, and life, though tinted with mystery and therefore uncertainty, was all that could be desired except for the gnawings of unsatisfied romance. She saw no more of Guy Roy who, she understood, was much absent on his own affairs.

It was with some apprehension that she received a summons to report at the mansion on Castle Hill. Was she in fault somewhere? What could she have done? Her fears were assuaged by the gravely pleasant greeting from her employer. He informed her at once that she was to be sent away to school at the beginning of the fall term.

"Away?" she said, wide-eyed. "Why? Where?"

"Philadelphia. An excellent and refined academy."

"Isn't that cruel far, sir?"

"The farther, the better." She did not understand that.

"But I shan't see Gypsy," she said dolorously. "Or Clory. Or Miss Mary Haynes. Or anybody."

"You will form new associations better befitting your prospects."

"Please, sir, I don't understand about my prospects—about anything."

"The Eureka Mills feel a duty towards you," he explained benevolently. "A responsibility for the—er—indignities suffered by you on an—er—unfortunate occasion. We seek to make restitution."

"Yes, sir. It's mortal kind. But—but I like it here."

"Do you not wish to augment your education?"

"Oh yes, sir!"

"Then you should be glad to go to where you will have opportunity of improving yourself in all departments of science and ladyhood."

Becky sighed. "I shall endeavour to profit by your condescension," a line lifted bodily from Mr. Guy Roy's precious gift-book. Becky lost herself in melancholy reflections about Mr. Guy Roy.

Perceiving that the conversation was coming to a halt, Mr. Stockwell drew out a large and rich bandanna handkerchief, preparatory to the austere ceremony of blowing his nose. The permeating odour of Bunting's Milk of Roses spread on the air.

Everything went black behind Becky's eyes. She slumped, felt herself caught, and was lost to the world.

A sharp stab of smoke in her nostrils supplanted the cloying perfume. Mr. Stockwell was waving a burning feather rhythmically beneath her nose. His arm was stricture about her shoulders. She wiggled hastily out of the tightening embrace.

"Better now?"

"Yes, sir." She caught the rose smell again and all but disgraced herself upon the carpet.

Air was what she wanted, lungsful of it. She staggered towards the door, thrust it open before her employer could intervene and ran like a deer for the mill yard, driven by a panic which she did not comprehend.

Gurdon Stockwell sat back in his chair and gave himself over to an unexpectedly pleasurable review of what had just taken place. This was not the raw factory stripling of his reluctant anticipations, but a fresh young maiden, demure and desirable. The form which he had briefly supported and encircled was that of womanhood. That beauty of which Amanda Heartt had spoken, stirred his blood. With the proper education and guidance the girl would develop into a wife for any man's pride and delight. He discovered in himself an impatience over the long period of waiting before she could be his. Yet respect for appearances dictated patience and restraint.

Until the lay-off bell, Becky had no chance to tell her astonishing news. Gypsy and Clory were the recipients of her confidence.

"The boss himself, huh?" Gypsy was properly impressed. "What did you say to him?"

"I sank to the floor in a ladylike swoon," Becky answered with pride.

"What call has a young squirt like you to have the vapours?" Gypsy rebuked her.

"Playing the fancy on us already," Clory commented.

"I didn't mean to. Honestly. I don't know what made me. He waved his bandanna at me and I went all queer. It smelt like something I'd smelt before, but I couldn't remember where. While I was trying, everything got black."

An amazing, a wildly exciting, suspicion blazed in Gypsy's brain. "Try again," she said urgently.

The girl shook her head. "All I can think of is how scared I was."

"What happened when you keeled over?" Clory demanded.

"Mr. Stockwell fetched me to with a burnt feather. I smelt the roses again and almost threw up on the carpet."

"What were you so scared of?" Gypsy insisted. "Mr. Stockwell? Did he try to do anything?"

"Do what?" Becky gaped.

"Anything, you little blockhead," said the exasperated Gypsy.

"I do remember he was looking at me kind of funny. It made me feel queer all over again."

"Didn't he say something?"

"He said I was to go to a genteel school. But that was before."

Gypsy considered the situation. "Does anybody know about you and old Hurdy-Gurdy?"

"Oh no."

"Then don't you breathe a word to a livin'. Promise?"

"Yes. But I don't know why."

"You don't hafta know. When are you startin' on your tol-lol schoolin'?"

"In the fall." Becky fingered the rough fabric of her skirt. "I'd rather make collars with you and Clory," she murmured.

"*What?*" Both women shouted it. Gypsy laid hurtful hands upon her protégé's shoulders.

Becky made no further protest. Privately she determined to seek an interview with Mr. Guy Roy before committing herself to the desperate step of a far-distant lady's academy.

Gypsy, also, wished to see Guy Roy and caution him not to take the girl on in case she did apply. Learning that he was

H

about to leave on an extended trip, she called on him that evening. She delivered her warning and got his ready assent. The other object of her visit demanded a more cautious approach.

"I want to ask you a question, lad."

"Ask your fill, Gypsy."

"If I wanted to give a feller a bottle of scent, what'd be the grandest kind?"

"Why, I hardly know. I don't go in for it much, myself. Soap is good enough for me."

"What kind does a dandy man like Mr. Stockwell use?"

"Milk of Roses, I believe."

"Always?"

"Never knew him to use any other brand."

"Did he wear it the night of the big gala at Castle Hill?" Gypsy was quivering.

"I suppose so. What ails the girl?"

She abandoned strategy for open dealing. "He's the man."

"Who? What man?"

"The man that tried it on little Becky. In the shed."

Guy successfully concealed his perturbation. "Balderdash!" he said stoutly. "You're crazy, Gypsy."

"Crazy I may be," she retorted. "But the spratling ain't. The minute she smelt it on him, she knew." (What was a small lie in so good a cause?) "And that's the reason he's sendin' her away to school. You can't fool me, Mr. Guy Roy, so don't try."

"Look, Gypsy." He spoke earnestly. "You're going to get your neck between the fence rails if you're not careful. The prudent course for you is to forget these baseless suspicions and keep your tongue between your teeth."

"Baseless, huh?" she jeered. "You'd stand up for him, wouldn't you! You young bloods all hang together like bugs on a beggar."

"And warn that child to keep her mouth shut, too," Guy went on steadily.

"She'll be mum till the time comes."

"And when, in your wise judgment, will that be?"

Gypsy was maturing grand plans, but she was not yet ready to reveal them to her old friend. "Day before yesterday and wait till it comes," she said impudently.

Fateful autumn was almost upon Becky when she heard that the new firm of Montague & Roy had set up a temporary office over the tinsmith's shop on Elbow Street, and that Mr. Guy Roy, as managing head, had returned to take up quarters there.

Becky arranged her lustrous hair after an adult pattern, sewed three pale-blue flounces upon the sixpenny cloth of her skirt, and climbed the stairs to a door which bore the firm's name in gilt lettering.

"Come in," called an abstracted voice.

The managing proprietor was sitting with his back towards her, bent over his desk in the study of some papers.

"Could I have the privilege of speaking to you about employment, sir?" she began in her most grown-up voice.

He did not so much as lift his head. "We are not taking on any hands at present," he said mechanically. "Sorry."

Becky drooped. There was finality in his tone. But she would not so readily give up. She abandoned the book formula.

"*Please*," she said in a desperate squeak.

He turned in annoyance and, in the same movement, came to his feet. "Good lord!" he said, staring. "What's this?"

"Don't you know me, Mr. Guy Roy?" she faltered.

"Do I?" He scanned the anxious and lovely face. "You're never . . . By Granny, it *is*!" He swept her a magnificent bow. "Welcome, Miss Eudora Valencia St. Legerdemain, to our humble premises."

"Now you're making fun of me," she complained.

"Far from it. I am delighted to see you."

Reassured, she reverted to formula. "I wish to apply for employment. It is my ambition to forward my worldly fortunes." If he recognized the excerpt from the *Book of Knowledge* he gave no sign. He simply stared and smiled. "I am a competent mechanic," she added.

The irrelevance of his next remark threw her quite off the track of commercial approach. "I wonder if you know how beautiful you are," he said.

"Oh, dear!" said poor, flustered Becky.

"You really are the little bobbin-doffer?" he said, still incredulous. There was nothing left of the wild-haired, eager-eyed mopsy of the mill yard in this alluring apparition.

"Yes, sir. I'm Obedience Webb. And you gave me the improving-book. And I want to thank you from the heart." It all came out in a rush of words. "But I'm not a little girl any more. I'm a weaver now; I've got my own loom. And I'd be cruel proud to work for you."

Now he remembered his promise to Gypsy—and regretted it. But for the girl's own sake he must not encourage this strange whim of hers.

"I'm afraid we have no place for a weaver," he said.

She gazed at him piteously. "You don't want me?"

Guy was puzzled. Did this girl know nothing of what was in store for her? How much would he be justified in revealing? Cautiously he said:

"I have heard that you are to be sent away to school. This will be very advantageous to you, much more so than any employ I could give you. You must study hard and prepare yourself." (He sounded to himself dismally schoolmasterish, but it was the best he could do offhand.)

"Yes," she said. "Far away where I shan't see you any more. You'll forget me."

To his astonishment he heard himself say fervently, "I can think of nothing more unlikely." He added hastily: "You will find many new interests there. More than you ever dreamed of."

"How can you know what I dream of?" sighed Becky. "A long farewell, Mr. Roy."

She went out with her nose proudly in the air and a small tear trickling down either side of it.

"Well, I'm damned!" said Guy Roy, and stared after her, bemused. A long farewell, eh? Not if he could help it!

The date of Becky's departure was close at hand. Time to put a flea in the wench's ear, Gypsy decided. Over a roast frankfurter sausage in a secluded corner, she led the conversation round to the interview in Mr. Stockwell's study. Becky's innocent replies satisfied her that the girl had not recognized the association of ideas, evoked by the scent of Milk of Roses, which had brought on her collapse. For the furtherance of the Great Scheme, it was better that way. Anything that inspired fear or dislike of Gurdon Stockwell might spoil all.

"When you came out of your faint, Mr. Stockwell was tendin' you?" she asked.

"Yes. He was very kind."

"Mr. Stockwell is always kind," Gypsy declared without so much as a gulp over the outrageous reversal of her opinion. "And I bet you didn't so much as give him thank you."

"I—I'm afraid I didn't. Was that awful of me, Gypsy?"

"Listen to me, brat. How'd you like to be Mrs. Gurdon Stockwell?"

Becky gaped and goggled.

"If you play your cards right, you might get Mr. Stockwell to marry you."

"Mr. Stockwell? Marry *me*? Why would he?"

"Never you mind why."

"You're making fun of me. I don't believe it. What makes you think so?"

"A piebald fox with a scab on his tail told me."

"If he did want to, would I *have* to marry him, Gypsy?"

"Have to! Gawdamighty, wench! You'd live in the big house on the hill. You'd have a coach and horses. You'd have shillin's to fill your purse. You'd wear a new gown every week, silk and satin, and velvet and sarsanet. You'd have education and know how to speak like a lady on the stage, and you'd eat off plate and everything." Gypsy paused only because she was out of breath with the headlong recital of glory.

"Well—but—Mr. Stockwell! Do I have to sleep in the same room with him?"

"That and more." Gypsy became more explicit until Becky gasped and begged her to stop. "And see you don't do it with anybody else beforehand," she admonished.

"Goodness gracious me! Why should I?" demanded the puzzled girl.

Gypsy's answer added nothing to her enlightenment. "You're growin' up," she said.

Becky reflected, striving to adjust this development to the dreams and ambitions inspired by rapt readings of *The Factory Girl*.

"I suppose he *is* rich," she mused.

"Rich as a maggot."

"And pious."

"As a prayer-meetin'."

"And learned."

"So will you be if you mind your p's and q's."

The other side now presented itself to Becky's logical mind. "But he isn't young."

"He might surprise you," said Gypsy sagely.

"Or handsome."

"Prissy Stamm thinks so, and plenty of other girls."

Becky sighed for dreams foregone. Guy Roy, the young, the fashionable, was not for her.

"Well," she said, with as worldly an air as she could muster, "I suppose a girl might do worse."

A week later she took the canal packet, *Chief Engineer*, for New York, *en route* for Philadelphia and the unreckonable adventure of life.

PART TWO

ALTHOUGH it had been running for a month, the Rensselaer & Saratoga Railway train was still a nine-day wonder to the citizenry of Ballston, its terminal. Never did it depart without the respectful godspeed of an admiring crowd. It was a social event; the fashion of the town attended. Children were brought to the spectacle as a reward for meritorious behaviour. Daily the platform outside the Haverstraw-brick edifice, rented as a depot, began to fill as early as nine o'clock, an hour in advance of the scheduled departure.

The two passenger cars stood, a little aloof, waiting to be backed down. They were exhibits of decorative art on a groundwork of delicate fawn colour with buff shading, each displaying a pictorial design. Crimson morocco seats trimmed with coach-lace lent distinction to the interiors.

A young female gazed from the station window, observing the pictures with a languidly critical eye. She was something of a work of art herself, slender and poised, with that grace which is erroneously connected with fragility but which actually derives from robust health. She was arrayed in a silk-and-crêpe gown, an elaborately be-laced bonnet, a multi-patterned kerseymere shawl, and dainty morocco bootees. One gloved hand dandled an umbrella of Mr. Goodyear's strong-smelling caoutchouc, the other was buried in an ermine muff. Back of her a full-length surtout of seal's fur richly draped a bench.

A grizzled old man entered, sloughed off a mangy bearskin, and delivered a philippic against the railway. Those who were so foolhardy as to travel by it, he asserted, took their lives in their hands. The locomotivator was fabricated in the nether regions, was operated by atheists, and spewed out the foul fumes of hell. He enumerated the manifold perils of rail traffic and cited horrid instances. A little old lady in respectable black timidly approached the elegant stranger.

"Young ma'am!"

"Yes?" The smile in the hazel-greenish eyes encouraged the

old lady to believe that this superb creature was not so un-
approachable as she appeared.

"Have you ever travelled behind the locomotivator?"

"Oh yes! At Charleston, where I have visited. On the
Santee Road—the famous locomotive engine, Friend of the
People."

"You are young and beautiful," pursued the other anxiously.
"You would not risk your precious life unless—unless you
deemed it reasonably safe?"

The girl smiled again. "Have you never travelled by rail?"

"Never. And would not now but that illness of my grandchild
calls me back."

"You need have no fear. The conductor will reassure you."
She indicated a tall man in brass-buttoned uniform who was
approaching.

"Miss Obedience Webb?" he inquired deferentially.

"Yes."

"Conductor Amasa Wood, at your service, ma'am. I am
instructed by prepaid post from Mr. Gurdon Stockwell that you
have been paying a visit at the Mineral Springs, and that you
would proceed to Troy by our road. Proud to serve you, ma'am.
May I procure your ticket?"

"Thank you. I am conversant with travel by rail." She spoke
with the hauteur of the worldling.

Pointing out to him the timorous old lady, Miss Webb purchased her ticket and emerged upon the platform with her chin
at the angle prescribed for impressing the public with maidenly
unapproachability. Having assuaged the granddam's fears,
Conductor Wood rejoined the girl and escorted her forward where
the model locomotive engine was breathing gustily. There he
presented her to the engineer, an honour reserved for distinguished patrons of the road.

Mr. Peter Hoag was a gentleman of position and prestige,
who wore the tallest and glossiest of castors while engaged in
his arduous duties. He was now directing the efforts of an overgrown hobbledehoy in a leather jacket to keep the blazing oven
supplied with scrub-oak faggots. He acknowledged the introduction with professional courtesy.

"Fine weather," he observed with a glance aloft. "We shall
make a good head of steam."

The two men then put their heads together in private consultation, after which the conductor set a small horn to his lips and produced therefrom a metallic bleat.

"Five minutes to departure," he announced.

Mr. Guy Roy, who was in Ballston at the time to drum up trade for his collars, had naturally taken half an hour from the cares of business to help speed the daily train. At this scene of festivity he would meet the young bloods of the town. They would cheer the hard-working locomotivator on its way and then repair to the inn for a drink.

From his high seat in a commercial friend's gig he looked out upon a scene of animation. The crowd on the platform milled and chattered.

Passengers were bidding friends good-bye, some with ill-suppressed emotion. Factors were instructing their roadsmen. A small group of churchly folk stood with bared heads while their pastor invoked the protection of Heaven upon them during the voyage. A sporting character in a bottle-green broadcoat was offering wagers on the duration of the trip. Who'd lay a bet on four hours? Who on three and a half? Anybody want to bet on three? He'd offer odds.

Baa-haa-haa! blared the little horn. "Passengers will kindly assume their seats," Mr. Wood announced.

He established Miss Webb in the middle of the front car and counselled her to mind her headgear. "We shall make speed this morning," he said confidently.

Again the horn bleated. Mr. Hoag swung to his place, inspected his mechanism and made some adjustments. Mr. Wood waved his castor and took a graceful pose on the sidestep. "Ca*hoot*!" the engine snorted, and belched a gobbet of smoke into the crystal air.

The wheels spun. The cars jerked into motion. Small boys pranced alongside. The crowd raised a huzza. They were off.

At this moment the normally fashionable and restrained Mr. Guy Roy astonished his companion in the gig by going demented. With no more explanation than a gasped-out and ungrammatical, "Good lord! It's her!" he made a wild leap to the ground, vaulted the fence, and set out at full speed after the cars. He overtook the escort of galloping urchins, plunged through their lines, scattering them to all sides, lost his costly beaver in the contact and, all unheeding, launched himself at the last car's sidestep and was hauled aboard by helpful hands, conscious of an unreckonable damage.

At the very moment of departure, he had seen an unforgettable face peering out from the front car. The rest was automatic.

Obedience, who had withdrawn to the central part of her bench where the wind of swift motion would not derange her toilet, did not witness the desperate and successful pursuit. She set herself to enjoy the adventure. She was conversant enough with this mode of travel to recognize that the locomotive engine which she had just inspected was a superior mechanism to the old Santee puff-and-grunt. The voice of its progress was more authoritative; its traction more potent. Proceeding along the level ground, it gathered headway with impressive power and rhythm.

Now it was entering the forest. The pace slackened at each curve so that the hard-worked fireman might run ahead and make sure that no trees had fallen across the track. At one point they came to a sharp stop. The lookout was making gestures and shouting excitedly. Men left their seats, descended to the right-of-way and set to gathering rocks. Led by Mr. Wood, they moved forward, deploying as they advanced. The girl passenger leaned out and descried on the track a mother bear with two cubs frisking about her.

Disturbed by the shouts, she reared up and threatened the locomotive. A stone hit her in the belly, another on the snout. She dropped to her paws, weeping. The cubs made for the shelter of the forest, and she presently lumbered after, pausing only to show her fangs to the violators of her domain. The engine gave an important cough and resumed progress.

Here had been Guy's chance to shift to the forward coach where sat the lady of his quest. He was unable to avail himself of it. Furtive investigation showed that his last wild lunge for the speeding train had sadly disrupted his smallclothes. He was in no condition to face a lady or even turn his back upon her. He must remain, wretchedly seatbound, under such scant protection as could be derived from a careful disposal of his bandanna eked out by his neck-cloth. And there, a few miserable rods in front of him, was lovely Fate!

Obedience was enjoying the trip. The train had been ascending by a gentle gradient. Now a long declivity stretched before it. It gathered speed with shocking momentum. An old gentleman in the seat back of Obedience shouted excitedly in her ear that they were making all of twenty miles an hour, he'd bet.

Faster, still faster, they sped. Panic spread. Men swore, children bawled. Ladies with escorts shrieked and fainted on their shoulders. Ladies without, merely shrieked. Obedience was impelled to join the chorus, from excitement, not fear, but her ladylike training forbade. Up front was Engineer Hoag, the imperturbable, the undaunted. He would fetch them through.

Now they approached a hill formidably long, formidably steep. Was it possible that the brave little locomotive could surmount it, with the ponderous weight of the two cars to drag? Insensibly the experienced traveller leaned forward on her bench, making herself light, straining with every muscle to help the difficult traction. The engine, too, was straining, feverishly calling on its reserve. The power had given out. The cars stopped, reversed their motion, ingloriously slumped back all the way to the level whence they had toiled.

Mr. Hoag popped out as if blown by the expiring gasp of steam. The fire-boy rolled out after him. He seemed to be trying to explain, to palliate. The engine-driver kicked him soundly. He howled. The conductor ran forward with pacificatory gestures. His fellow addressed him with passion, pointing to the boiler. Mr. Wood walked slowly along the line, calling dejectedly:

"All out, if you please. Lady and gentleman patrons will please leave the cars."

Everybody got out but Guy Roy. Conductor Wood approached him.

"Now, young sir, if you please!"

Guy spoke in his ear. A twenty-dollar note on "Emperor" Biddle's Bank of the United States, good as gold anywhere in the nation, passed. The conductor grinned, nodded, and went away. He returned with the gambler's bottle-green broadcoat and three dollars in change. Guy put on the garment and descended, not quite the perfect maccaroni as before, but still presentable. But he still kept his distance from the object of his adventure. He was figuring upon the best approach. At worst, he could probably find a seat a near her when they climbed aboard again.

The passengers now fringed the right-of-way. The crew resumed their official positions. The engine set forth sturdily enough with the lightened cars. Half-way to the top it lost headway. This time the train did not coast back. Volunteers had rushed forward to block the wheels.

The abandoned passengers hoofed it up to where the stalled cars stood. An impromptu indignation meeting was held. Everybody started talking and shouting at once, and the conductor sat down on a fallen tree-trunk and took his head between his hands.

Guy Roy walked over to him and spoke in his ear. Mr. Wood shook his head despondently. Mr. Roy spoke further. Mr. Wood rose and pushed his way through the throng until he reached the other official.

"Mr. Hoag, can your locomotive haul one car to the summit?"

"She can haul one empty, I guess."

"Uncouple and snake it up, then."

"How will that advantage us?" the engine driver demanded.

"You get one car up and I'll take care of the rest."

"With what?"

"Brains," replied the conductor disparagingly. "Locomotives are your business. Cars are mine."

Mr. Hoag grunted suspiciously. Nevertheless he stamped across to his loutish aide and set him to work. The train was parted and the front coach drawn upward without too much strain.

"There you are," the engineer said complacently. "Now what?"

"Now, we'll double up the passengers into the one coach and run 'em into Troy."

Mr. Hoag's jaw set. "And do what with the other?"

"Leave it."

"And you're figuring on *me* to do that?"

"Certes. You're the engineer, ain't you?"

"Yes, I'm an engineer. I ain't half an engineer," the outraged official bellowed. "And I don't figure to finish no run with half a train. I wouldn't drive my locomotive engine through the pearly gates of Heaven with the other half of my train sleepin' on a back-track. What'd the coachees say? What'd the canawlers say? What'd the dod-swiggled, brass-bellied, cinder-eatin' Skenekers[1] for Gawdsakes say? Not me, Mr. Wood, not me! I'd be laughed plum off'n the rails if I done it."

"You refuse orders?"

"I dad-blamed, blast-your-guts-and-be-damned-to-you do."

The conductor turned away and addressed the young man at his elbow. "It's your innings. Go ahead."

[1] Railwaymen of the Albany to Schenectady route.

Guy Roy summoned the urchin. There was a passage of coin.

The fire-boy vanished around the curve ahead at full run. The conductor came back to impart the bad news to his passengers.

"He's gone to fetch Farmer Cluyn's ox-team. It'll be a couple of hours."

The sky had greyed over. Light snow began to fall, thickening swiftly. Switching into the north, the wind whistled drearily through the boughs. Enterprising spirits gathered brush and lighted fires for the comfort of the ladies. Several of the young blades produced wicker-covered flasks, looking hopefully at the sightly young passenger who evinced no interest in them. She had seen and recognized Guy Roy.

All her two years' training in rigorous ladyhood was no more than sufficient to preserve her decorum when his eager look crossed hers. She turned her head away, her heart beating uncontrollably. Happily for her self-command, he did not approach at once but stood, taking in every detail of the picture.

It was a charming memory that he had carried these two years. But it was pale and vague beside this reality. He had remembered a girl, lovely, appealing but immature. Now he beheld womanhood, vital and gracious. He read in her face the potential joyousness of one fitted to get the most out of life; one who could take joy and give it. Beyond and above any beauty of feature was the sweet, pervasive warmth of her femininity.

With an effort, he broke from the spell and advanced to address her.

"Miss Webb? May I recall myself?"

"How do you do, Mr. Guy Roy? I was not aware that you were on this train."

"I nearly wasn't. Then I saw you. I recall Gypsy Vilas saying that one day little Becky Webb would grow up to trouble the hearts of men. A very prophetess!"

"Gypsy?" she said eagerly. "Does she work for you?"

He nodded. "We couldn't get along without Gypsy."

"You've nothing to do with the Eureka any more?"

"No. That split is permanent," he said gravely.

She hesitated. "And personal as well?"

"Oh no. My cousin and I speak kindly," he smiled.

"But you still don't like his way with his hired hands," she murmured.

"Well, he doesn't like my way with mine. So that makes us quits."

Her vivid face grew sombre. "I was thinking of little Meg Shink," she said. "Old memories, old sentiments, if you will."

"For which there is no cure," he said so significantly that she flushed.

They had strolled insensibly back along the track and were alone in a darkening world of snow.

"Two years," he mused. "I knew that I should see you again. But I thought it would be sooner."

"I wanted to come. But Mr. Stockwell didn't think it best."

"Ah, yes, Gurdon. What does he design for you now?" She was silent. "Have you seen him in these years?"

"Yes. He has visited the school. He addressed the pupils."

"I'll wager he did," Guy said with a grin.

There was another silence. Then she said, "You don't like Mr. Stockwell, do you?"

"Like him? He is my kinsman. I respect him. There's a sincerity about him that one must admire. His standards are so important to him that he believes them equally important to the world." He shrugged.

"Let's not talk of it. Tell me about Troy."

"You speak as if you were homesick."

"Why shouldn't I be? I missed the girls so much that I almost ran away."

"What would you have done? Come back?"

"Yes, and asked you for employ again. Even though you were so mean to me." For a moment she was the child of the mill yard. Guy's heart turned over.

"I wouldn't have given it to you. Not the employ you asked for. There would have been another place for you, if you would take it."

She gazed at him uneasily.

"Becky," he said, "I've never married. Do you know why?"

She would not meet his eyes. "Yes," she answered. "Gypsy told me. It was an unrequited passion for a singing chambermaid."

He laughed. "Did you know that I came to the school to see you?"

"No! Did you, truly? When?"

"Twice. Miss Lever would not admit me. She reported to my

cousin and he exacted a promise that I would make no further attempt."

"And you promised? Oh!" It was a sigh of deepest reproach.

He shrugged. "What else could I do? He was within his rights. You must have known that he was paying for your education."

She was deaf to the words. "You came to see me," she murmured. "And I never knew!"

"Now you know. And you may as well know the rest," he went on recklessly. "I love you, Becky."

"Oh *no*!" she breathed.

She was being drawn into his arms. With a powerful effort she thrust herself away.

"Don't," she pleaded in a muffled groan. "We mustn't, Guy."

"Why?" he said gently. "I know I could bring you to love me. Couldn't I, Becky?"

"It isn't that." She was oblivious to the implied admission.

"If it isn't that, it isn't anything," he retorted triumphantly.

"Don't," she said again. She drew a deep breath. "Oh, Guy! It's too late. Guy, I'm married."

"Married? . . . I don't believe it."

"I can hardly believe it myself. I'd—I'd almost forgotten it."

"Married! When? How? To whom?"

"Oh, *don't* look like that," she begged. "I couldn't help it. How could I know?"

"To whom?" he repeated dully.

"To your cousin. I'm Mrs. Gurdon Stockwell."

He still stared at her. His expression changed, hardened. "You didn't tell me."

She was mute.

"You led me on."

"That isn't fair," she cried. "That isn't true."

"Why not the truth at once?" he went on inexorably. "Why did you wait so long?"

"I didn't know," she whispered. "How could I know? That you hadn't forgotten me?"

He turned away but came back to her at once. He lifted one nerveless hand and kissed the palm gently. She made no sign, but stood, statue-still, until he had vanished in a whorl of snow. Then she stumbled blindly back to the others.

Two oxen appeared on the crest of the hill. A chain was

clamped to the front of the blocked car. A score of passengers set willing shoulders to the task. The coach shook itself, moved, and made the ascent at a slow, steady, uninterrupted pace until it was joined to its companion. The train then proceeded at a sulky eight-miles-an-hour rate until the city was reached.

The elapsed time was a little more than five hours.

TWO

SHE was married. Snug and safe between the sheets of Mrs. Heartt's massive sleigh-bed, Becky could hardly believe it. Indeed, she had actually forgotten it for a dangerous space, in the excitation of the encounter with Guy Roy. She was Mrs. Gurdon Stockwell. But not in thought or conviction. There had been so little to give reality to the change.

Married at high noon by a New York City magistrate, she had been aboard the Albany boat at 2 p.m., in charge of the captain, who was known to Mr. Gurdon Stockwell. It all seemed phantasmal: the hurried farewells, the austere injunctions to secrecy by Mr. Stockwell, who was obliged to remain in the metropolis on business, the confusion of mind, and the—eyes, the relief. For her husband had made it plain that he would not regard the marriage as effectual (his own word) before it had been sanctified by a church ceremony. Until then she would remain in maiden separation at the Heartt mansion in Troy.

It had all been so sudden and unexpected. True, she and Mr. Stockwell were formally though privately betrothed since the previous spring, when he had visited his "ward" at the school and developed a surprising and daunting ardour. No announcement was to be made until she should return to Troy; the wedding would follow within a month.

The circumstances of her debarking at the Battery from the Philadelphia packet had knocked that decorous procedure into a cocked hat.

Gurdon Stockwell sighted his affianced bride first at the rail of the boat, lovely and joyous and glowing, the centre of a group of young gallants. Light and, to Gurdon's austere mind, unseemly persiflage was passing to and fro. Obedience bore her full part. Seeing her thus surrounded by attentions and solicitations, he was seized upon by a hot and proprietary jealousy.

Suppose she should escape him! Who could tell but that her untried affections might already be engaged by one of the zealous young flitterwits who pressed about her? He must take precautions.

She was still in their midst when she tripped down the gang-

I

plank. Gurdon strode forward, shouldering his way through the pack.

"Welcome home, Obedience. I trust you had a favourable journey."

She put her small hand into his. "Very favourable, thank you, Mr. Stockwell."

The vivacity had gone from her bearing. She regarded him with suppressed dismay. She had half-forgotten how dark he was, how solemn, how elderly. He must be almost thirty, she thought with a qualm.

He escorted her to a waiting equipage. Gurdon Stockwell was a man of decision and action. There should be no more such risky associations as the voyage with the attractive ship-mates.

The rest was a daze to Becky. There was an interview with an elderly and smiling lawyer, a visit to a magistrate, papers to sign, and she was a wedded wife by legal enactment. Next the boat for Albany, the drive to Saratoga, where she was to spend some days with relatives of her husband; then Troy by the rail. Unreal, all of it.

Most unreal of all was her being Mrs. Gurdon Stockwell. Even her presence in the Heartt household did not lend conviction to that strange fact. She fell asleep, resolutely thrusting thoughts of Guy Roy out of her mind.

"You must see our fair city, my dear," motherly Mrs. Heartt said to her over the breakfast coffee. "You will find it greatly enlarged and improved." She would order out the carriage and take her on a tour.

"I'd rather walk," Becky said.

"My dear! In your position. You will soon be the wife of Troy's foremost citizen."

"Foremost?" Becky echoed.

"Gurdon Stockwell is president of our Mill Employers Association. He is already an alderman and magistrate; he will one day be mayor. When the new bank is opened, he will head it. In all public weal and religious endeavour ..." She went on to enumerate the many functions in which Gurdon Stockwell was pre-eminent.

The city looked dull as they drove through its streets. None of her old friends was to be seen. They were all at work, she supposed. For a mutinous moment she wished that she were, too. Only once was she roused to interest and inquiry, and that was by a name on a street sign. Her companion repeated the name, shaking her head.

"Montague & Roy? A sore spot of our local commerce, my dear."

Strangers passing along Elbow Street stopped in front of Number 37 to stare and wonder. Through the broad windows they could make out a workroom occupied by a dozen busy females. Indubitably the females were labouring. What aroused attention and, often, unfavourable comment, was that they appeared to be enjoying themselves at their work. There was animated chatter. There was laughter. Sometimes there was song. Such goings-on in a factory had never been heard of in Troy before. It was all the doings of a crazy young man who came of good people and ought to know better. And they would point to a placard, wafered against a central pane:

TWELVE HOURS' PAY
for a
TEN-HOUR DAY
Skilled Sempstresses Interviewed.
MONTAGUE & ROY COLLAR FACTORY
Guy Roy; M'g'r & Prop'r.

Nine young women and two smallish girls were occupied in the comfortable, well-lighted room, most of them plying needle and thread. Two or three others came and went from rear and side. At a broad table, a fattish cutter with a vacantly happy expression worked from pattern, humming monotonously to herself. Bolts of linen, muslin, satin, bombazine and lesser materials flanked her, from which she selected cloth for cutting.

A door at the back was thrown open, emitting a puff of thin steam, through which loomed the face of Mildred Hute.

"Starch-o!" she bawled with professional vigour. "Think I can keep my water hot all day?"

Mary Haynes stood up from her measuring-stand and moved over to a blackboard. "Tally," she called, brandishing a length of chalk. Mildred reached for her collecting-basket and started her rounds of gathering the finished collars for the wash-room.

"Dozen Fashion Flares," she called to the tallier. "Eighteen Wavies. Even dozen Board Fences. Arvila, you're doing fine.

Corries, doz—— Hey, Hepsy!'' She dangled a design in fortified satin between thumb and forefinger. "Call this a Corinthian? It'll never pass Gypsy.''

"No fault of mine,'' Hepsabeth Parsons returned defensively. '' 'Twasn't cut to pattern. Marty must have slipped her shears.''

Martha Mull, the cutter, dropped her implement with a thud. "You're a nasty fib!'' she shouted, sorely wounded in her professional pride.

A hall door opened and slammed. Gypsy Vilas stood with her fists on her hip-bones.

"What are you hellcats up to now?'' she demanded without rancour.

"They pointed at me and said I didn't cut to pattern,'' wailed the offended one.

"Just because she's a natural, you don't have to pick on her,'' the forewoman chided. "She's worth any two of you as a worker.'' She strode over to the table. "Here's a pep-mint sucket for you, Marty. Don't you mind 'em. They're jealous 'cause you make good money.'' The half-wit who, by virtue of an inborn knack of pattern, was well paid, seized upon the red-striped gob of sweet stickiness and crammed it into her mouth. "Pick up your shears, dearie. What about those shams, Hannah?''

Hannah Boutwell, who had been working on linen dickeys, yawned loudly. "They'll be ready come closing-time,'' she said.

"And the sooner the better for you, huh!'' commented Gypsy. "Whatsa matter? Oversleep between your silk coverlets? Trouble with you ninnywits, you don't know when you're well off.''

They did, and Gypsy well knew they did. She also knew that girls, working in a group, turn petulant about once in so often, and there is nothing to do but let them grouse it out. Cora Sprague, a cripple, complained about the bombazine. Clorinda Burgo, who laboured under the disadvantage of being unable to add two and two, and was consequently suspicious of all figuring, questioned Mary Haynes's tally. Arvila Hopkins claimed that her last batch of muslin was scamped. Everybody seemed bent on trouble. Gypsy flapped her powerful arms.

"Are you paid to gab or are you paid to work?'' she snapped. "Get into it or I'll fire the lot of you.''

"You couldn't fire *me*,'' the natural chirped happily. "Mr. Roy wouldn't letcha.''

Gypsy glared round the room. "There you git it! He's too good to you. Treated like a lot of princesses. Don't start work till six o'clock; long after sun-up half the year. Haffa nour for my lady's breakfast. Another for dinner. 'Nour for your supper. How'd you like to be back in Dorm Four at the old Eureker? Forgot about those days, haven't you, you lily-fingered lollipops!"

"Lily-fingered yourself, Gypsy Vilas!" Mildred Hute retorted. "We turn out more work than Stark's girls. And he's working a sixteen-hour stretch."

"You do so," the forewoman admitted. Independence Stark ran the competitive factory round the corner on River Street. "And you better!" she added ferociously. "If you couldn't beat those fat-rumped cows, I'd slash your pay-envelopes and let 'em bleed to death."

"I wouldn't cut for 'em," asserted Marty virtuously. "Not if they was to pay me ever so."

"I guess we don't do so badly," Hannah Boutwell offered contentedly. "Three dollars is a good week's pay for any girl any day."

The booming of a distant bell announced the hour. Everybody stood up and stretched. "What's for grub?" Clorinda inquired avidly.

"Champagne and oysters, whaddayeh think?" Gypsy answered. "Could I have the honour of serving your ladyship with a delicate ice-cream and a dollop of vanilla cake?"

"Make mine bee-ah," Relief Lovejoy chanted. She had come in from the packing-room. "Orders piling up," she said. "Our Mr. Roy's been gallivanting at some fancy rout in New York, wearing his new Corinthian, and all the young bloods there are crying for 'em. Recorders by every post. New store in Ballston, another in Saratoga and two in Albany. Rochester buying. Boston asking. Mr. Roy'll be a millionaire-man."

"Not with cloth prices rising," Mary corrected. "Cotton's up to sixteen and going higher. That means trouble."

"You think that's trouble?" Hepsabeth Parsons interpolated. "The half of it hath not been told." She was given to quoting Scripture, usually to some gloomy purpose.

"What's that fat owl hootin' about?"

"How'd you like to go back to 4.30 call? That's what's liable to happen."

"Who says so?"

"Mr. Gurdon Stockwell."

"That's all right for them as works at the Eureka. What's it got to do with us?" Mildred Hute wished to know.

"Mr. Stockwell's head of the cottonocracy,[1] ain't he?"

"What if he is?"

"I guess he makes the rules for this town."

"I guess he don't make 'em for Montague & Roy," said Gypsy Vilas, thrusting out her chin.

"He and the other mill-owners are going to hold a public meeting to stop the short work-day. Mr. Crolius, the printer, told me so. Printers know everything."

Guy Roy entered, with a sheaf of letters in his hand. He looked cheery, alert and businesslike. Glancing at his watch, he said: "Three minutes to go. Everything moving well? Gypsy? Mary?"

They answered in the affirmative. He waved the letters before them. "We'll all have to work harder to keep up with the trade. The more work, the more pay, eh?"

Clorinda washed down the heel of a raisin-bun with a huge gulp of hot tea. "Could I ask you a question, Mr. Roy?"

"If you don't choke to death first, Clorinda."

"Are we going back to the old trick?"

"What trick?"

"Sunrise to sunset."

"Not here."

"Not if they made a law?"

"Who's going to make a law?"

"I dunno. The mill-owners, I guess."

"Let 'em make all the law they like for their own mills," Mr. Roy said amiably. "They can't make it for us."

"There's going to be a meeting," Hepsabeth insisted.

"So I hear," the owner said. "Though they forgot to invite me. Maybe I'll go anyway."

There was a rumble of masculine voices on the low steps outside. Gypsy went into the hallway and reported back:

"Couple of mechanics to see you, Mr. Roy."

"We're not taking on any mechanics."

"These ain't real mechanics," the forewoman qualified without troubling to abate her voice. "If you was to ask me—loafers."

"Little matter of business, Mr. Roy," a hearty voice boomed from the hallway.

[1] Factory-town slang for the employers' associations.

"Take them into the office, Miss Vilas," Mr. Roy directed. "I will be in shortly."

The two visitors sat, furry caps in hand, in the small cubbyhole which hardly sufficed for the concern's growing business. One of them, a florid fellow with whitish eyebrows, greeted him as he came in with some effusiveness.

"Remember me, Mr. Roy? I'm Josh Loach."

"Yes, I remember you," the proprietor replied without enthusiasm. Loach was a notorious casual, drifting from one factory to another; never to be relied upon when the fish were biting.

"This here is Eli Dobby."

Dobby touched his forehead clumsily. He was a damp, limp creature in his late twenties, with a snuff-mottled upper lip.

"He's a steady churchgoer, Eli is," the other continued. "But I guess the collection-plate don't get no heavier for that." His guffaw rang out in wholesome appreciation of his own humour. Dobby grunted.

"What is your errand, men?" Roy asked.

"Little matter of employment wanted," Loach answered. "Jobs, Mr. Roy."

"None here."

"What's your paper in the winder mean?"

"That is for female help."

"Like I mean. It's for my younglings. They need work."

"What can they do?"

"One's been a cleaner at the Ida. That's Mary. Martha, she was a bleacher's help up on the Kill till work run short. Milly Ann tended a Baxter in the Lark at Morn mill. Now there's no more Baxters and what's a poor girl to do when she ain't tall enough to reach a loom?"

"It's hard times for the deservin' poor," added Dobby in a sepulchral tone.

"How old is this girl of yours?" the prospective employer inquired.

"Milly Ann? Well, she's nigh on to six now."

Experience of the cotton fabric trade had pretty well shockproofed Guy Roy, but the outmoded Baxter machines, heritage of the early New England mills, primitive enough to be operated by any child above infancy, had not come under his immediate observation.

"And the others?" he asked.

"Mary's goin' on for eight, and Martha's past nine."

"They've been working?"

"Well, they have, but they ain't."

"Why not?" Guy was curious.

"There's something wrong with the brats," the father said plaintively. "They can't make out to keep awake over the machines. Mary fell into a press last summer and lost two fingers. Not but what she can work just as good," he added hastily. "She's prime with a mop."

"So you want to put them here," Guy said slowly. "Why?"

"Well, Mister, I thought as how you work 'em short hours, they could tend the house aftertimes."

"Girls of that age don't belong in workshops, Loach."

"Why not?" the man grinned. "If you can get 'em cheap."

"They belong at home. Or in school."

"And who's to keep 'em?" propounded Mr. Loach reasonably. "Eatin' their young heads off. Not that you'd have to feed 'em too good," he qualified. "Martha don't eat no more than a squirrel hardly. You can have the three of 'em for twenty-five shillings a week and their prog and they can sleep home."

"I'm not employing children."

"You mean you won't take 'em on? Not any of 'em?"

"Precisely. Twelve years is our limit here."

"Now, listen, Mr. Roy," the visitor said earnestly. "You don't understand. You ain't got any of your own, or you'd show more feelin's for a father. I brung up those children. I fed 'em and lodged 'em. I worked my fingers to the bone for 'em, I did. And now they're growin' into—into"—he groped for a telling phrase—"into useful members of the community, they can't get no job. Is that reasonable? Is that Christian? Is that the way to treat an honest American working man?"

Gypsy put in her word. "Histin' a mug to your ugly phiz is the nearest honest work you ever done, Josh Loach," she said.

"I'll crack you one in the teeth, you huzzy," the outraged proletarian cried.

"Be still, both of you," Guy ordered sharply. He turned to the other caller. "What's *your* offer?" he inquired. "Have you any slaves to farm out?"

"I dunno what you mean, Mister. Slaves? Who's sayin' anything about slaves? I got a sister wants work."

"How long has *she* been out of the cradle?"

The irony was lost on its target. "She's eighteen years old," the man answered.

"Then why doesn't she apply, herself?"

Disregarding a wigwagged caution by his companion, Dobby said, "She ain't feelin' so good today."

Gypsy interposed. "Is that Katie Dobby? I know her. She's got a lung fever from breathin' lint."

"Who says so?" the brother challenged sullenly.

"The doctor."

"He's a liar. She ain't bleedin' beyond what a bottle or two of Gawdle's Expectorant'll clear up. How's she to get 'em if she don't earn a wage?"

"I'm sorry," Guy said, "but I can't have a consumptive among my healthy hands."

"Then Gawd help her," Eli Dobby said. "Poor Katie'll have to go on the county."

Josh Loach rose. He pointed a recriminatory finger at Guy. The purplish red of a righteous indignation flushed his features. "See what you're doin'!" he boomed. "Doomin' the helpless pore to be an almshouse charge. Turnin' the children of the workin' class in sorrer and shame from your doors. D'you know what Cash Barlow is sayin', young mister?"

"No, I don't," Guy said, interested.

"He says that now you've started the ten-hour day, the other workers'll demand it."

"I hope so."

"He says there's a time comin' when our children—our young that we bore in pain and raised in trile and tribulation—he says they won't be allowed to work no more."

"And that means that you'll have to yourself, eh, Loach?"

"And it'll be your fault, young mister," charged Loach. "Look out for the day when you'll have to answer to the fathers and mothers of our city."

Guy stood up. "Are you through?"

The orator picked up his cap. "Come on, Eli " he said. "I guess we ain't wanted here. Good day, Mr. Roy."

"That," remarked Guy pleasantly, "is the first sensible observation I have heard from you."

"A brace of polecats," Gypsy said as the pair shambled out. "There's plenty like 'em, though, in town. They could make trouble for you, lad. Not but what you ain't able to make plenty for yourself."

He shrugged it off. "Where's that Utica consignment list?"

He worked until after nine that evening. No ten- or twelve- or fourteen-hour day for Mr. Roy of the up-and-coming collar works.

The rock lay in the middle of the floor when the manager-proprietor, who was always first on the job, opened up the next morning. Shards of glass from the shattered window glinted in the lantern's beam. He picked up the missile, hefting it thoughtfully.

He had a suspicion that it might be the opening gun of war.

THREE

THE assemblage gathered in the high, dim parlour represented the industrial might of the city. There hung, impalpable in the atmosphere, a solemnity accorded only to religion and business. With a neat blending of the two, the Reverend Simon Bortle invoked the blessing of Heaven upon the commerce of Troy.

Although the official summons was to the Mill Owners Association, non-members had been invited because of the importance of the occasion. More than forty representative citizens were present. The Hon. Gurdon Stockwell was in the chair.

Having called the meeting to order, he suggested that no record be kept of the proceedings. Nobody objected.

"Gentlemen," Gurdon Stockwell addressed the meeting, "you need not, out of consideration for my sensibilities, be chary of naming names. The ties of kin have no claim where the public interest is threatened. I warned you two years ago, when the twelve-hour day was broached by my headstrong young cousin. That was the time to take action. You blinded yourselves to the danger. His system would fall of its own weight, you believed. It has not fallen. It prospers. He has proved his point. Now the rest of us face a demand for the twelve-hour day in Troy, which is no more than a preliminary to the ten-hour. Presently it will be eight—and then we may as well hand over our commerce to the proletariat and be done with it."

"Isn't there a law?" Gideon Beebe, the pinmaker (Sixty Perfect Pins Per Minute by Mr. Hoe's Patent Machine), was on his feet. "Can't Lawyer Dorr advise us?"

"There was." The lawyer unfolded himself to the height of six feet four. "My friend doubtless has in mind the trial of the Albany cordwainers. The honourable court entertained a charge of conspiracy to raise wages against the defendants and, in an eminently just and righteous decision, convicted and punished all six."

"Hah!" trumpeted Ironmaster Howland. "There's the point. Isn't a reduction of hours tantamount to a raise of wages?"

"That," replied the legal light, "is a point upon which I should prefer to give an opinion after receiving a retainer."

"What about the Lowell case?" Peter Osband of the Arbia Mill asked hopefully.

"That was a turn-out against reduction of wages," Mr. Smith of the Shot Tower said.

"Same principle," Howland snapped.

"Wages must come down," Mr. Paulding of the Rivermen's Bank declared. "Otherwise I tremble for the future of the nation."

"We are running at a loss at the Eagle," stated the proprietor of that profitable enterprise.

"And we at the Paragon, rather than discharge our help. And what reward do we reap? Threats of a turn-out if we suggest a cut. Such is the recalcitrant spirit of labour today."

"They'd better take warning by the Tariffville case," Le Grand Cannon, the builder, said darkly.

"What was that?" Several questioners joined in the query.

"Tariffville, Connecticut. Haven't you read of it in the journals?" The builder took the floor. "Three contumacious carpet weavers have been indicted there on charge of combination, conspiracy, and confederacy to raise wages. They are also laid by the heels on a fifteen-thousand-dollar damage suit advanced by the employing factory."

"Make a notation of that, Mister Lawyer," Howland crowed.

"According to my best information," Cannon continued with immense satisfaction, "they are well on their way to a long jail term."

"Then you haven't read today's news," Lawyer Dorr said tartly. "They were acquitted. I *don't* know what the law is coming to."

"Was it the twelve-hour day that was at issue there?" someone asked.

"Worse. The ten-hour day."

"Nor is that the only place," Banker Paulding put in. "I direct your attention to factory conditions in New England. How many looms are prostrated in stricken Lowell, no man knows. Seventy thousand spindles are stilled in and around Fall River. At Easthampton, in our own Empire State, the button factories have laid off fifteen hundred hands, mostly females. The short-work-day heresy is being pushed in Pennsylvania. Yet, through the northern mill towns female workers are glad—yes, are *grateful*—

for employ at five shillings per week. I should have said *were* grateful until the agitators unsettled their minds. Now, I am informed, there are graceless grumblings against the sixteen hours of work per day which keeps them from the streets."

"The working classes," interposed the Rev. Mr. Bortle gloomily, "have lost all sense of God's infinite mercies."

"I have advice from Pottsville, Pa.," the speaker continued. "There two thousand men are roaming the roads, seeking work. They wanted the ten-hour day. Now," he let his tone sink ominously, "they would be thankful for sixteen, eighteen, twenty hours, I dare affirm. My banking correspondent there writes me, 'Hands may now be had for the boarding'."

Mr. Fosmire popped up. "May I have a word? The wiser of our working folk here are sensible that hard times impend. They would, I conceive, accept without too much demur an equitable reduction of wages. They know, too, that we have them at our mercy. And at this propitious juncture there appears in our midst the upstart, Roy, with his subvertisements and agitations. Down with all such traitors, say I."

"I am gratified to have the gentleman's support," the banker acknowledged. "Upon this same subject of agitators who incite and mislead the honest American working man, I have here"— he reached into his breast pocket and fetched out a clipping neatly wafered to a square of white paper—"an editorial utterance from that high-toned and truly representative journal, the *Commercial Advertiser*, of New York City."

He adjusted his glasses, suppled his throat with a prefatory hawk, looked about for the parlour cuspidor which an obliging foot propelled within range, and, having discharged this preliminary, read with slow emphasis:

" 'Lost to society, to earth, and to heaven, godless and hopeless, clothed and fed in iniquity by theft and blasphemy —such are the infidel apostles of this new and destructive onset upon our institutions by this band miscalling themselves friends of the mechanic. Let them go to prison and have the mark of Cain branded upon them, these practitioners of incest, robbery and murder; let them die like ravenous wild beasts, hunted down without pity, and go to render their account before a God whom they blaspheme in their ignorant, snivelling and puerile speculations. Such is

too true a picture, in all its parts, of this slime of our respectable community.' "

"Amen! Amen! Amen!" The confirmation rose in solemn
cadence.

"It should be embossed and a copy affixed to the walls of every
plant in our city," Mr. Bortle said.

"And another copy sent, with a noose of rope, to that vile
fomenter, Cassius Barlow," Mr. Cannon supplemented.

An imposing-looking patriarch stood up and smoothed his
great spread of beard as he looked inquiringly towards Mr.
Stockwell. Mr. Stockwell nodded and announced, "Mr. Gilead
Hall has a word for us."

"I had not purposed," Mr. Hall began in a deep, warm voice,
"to inflict my personal aggrievances upon this respectable con-
sortium." Encouraged by polite murmurs, he continued: "But
the matter is pertinent to the purport of this meeting. Two of
our well-esteemed mechanics paid me an early call—Ephraim
Loach and Eli Dobby."

"Were they sober?" The speaker was young Ralph Miller, of
the Excelsior Works. He was there representing his father, who
sat painfully at home on a boil.

Mr. Hall turned a pained face towards young Miller. "I have
said that it was morning," he returned in mild rebuke. "They
related to me the shameful treatment accorded to them by Mr.
Guy Roy when they applied at his establishment in respect to
employment for their womenfolk." He gave a touching account
of two meek proletarians being brutalized by an irresponsible
young aristocrat. "He even hinted at bodily violence," he
averred.

"What!" broke in the irrepressible Miller. "All by himself?
And only two of them?"

The complainant passed it over in Christian forbearance.
"As a paterfamilias who has raised four daughters," he pursued,
"I deemed myself justified in instituting a personal inquiry. I
trust that you gentlemen will recognize my competence in the
premises."   •

All of those present knew of, though perhaps some did not
sympathize with, the speaker's method of raising a family. For
many years that dignified figure had been a familiar spectacle
on factory pay-days as, arrayed in his puke-hued coat with tall

castor to match and a flowered neck-cloth, he made the mill rounds, collecting his daughters' wages in a flannel bag. The fact that one of the girls had escaped by marrying a county pauper and another had eloped with a lame tenker, while possibly germane, did not seem appropriate for the occasion, so nobody mentioned it. A courteous murmur of assent helped him on his narrative way.

"I subsequently called upon Mr. Roy at his collar establishment," he informed his hearers.

"Did he offer *you* bodily violence?" Miller asked hopefully.

"He did not, sir. He received me with due courtesy. As I neared the Elbow Street corner, my ears were met by sounds of music. Gentlemen, at ten o'clock in the morning the employed females were singing!"

"At their work?" someone asked in scandalized accents.

"Was Mr. Roy present?"

"He was. He even hummed the measure as he came forward to meet me."

"Can't you give us a rendition of it, Mr. Hall? Do try," young Miller urged.

"I have no mind of it," the other disclaimed with a sour face. "One stanza was some ribaldry about a bag of beans.[1] I inquired about Mr. Roy's colloquy with Loach and Dobby and he readily admitted his part in it. He wanted no children in his place, he asserted. Mr. Dorr"—he appealed to the lawyer—"is that a defensible position?"

"The premises are his," the man of law gave opinion. "I presume that he can determine whom he chooses to employ."

"Then I denounce it as an impious trespass upon parental rights," cried the father of four wage-earners.

"Mr. Hall is right," Mr. Howland declared. "Consider the vicious example set by this miscreant."

"And he proposes to advance the example," the patriarch stated. "He admitted it. He boasted of it. He had the temerariousness to tell me to my face that every factory should adopt the proposed English law."

---

[1] Perhaps the popular and guileless fair-booth ditty:

> Was a body met a body
> In a bag of beans
> Can a body tell a body
> What a body means?

"Vhat's dot?" Sweer Van Velsen of the pearl ashery asked.

"Gentlemen, you positively would not credit it. I made a note of it, lest there should arise a question of error." He appealed to the chair. "May I present it, Mr. Chairman?"

"Do so," said the Chairman graciously.

"*Primus:* children under eighteen years of age may not work more than twelve hours a day."

"The opening wedge," Mr. Howland barked.

"*Secundus:* persons under eleven, eight hours only . . ."

"Scandalous!"

"Unbelievable!"

". . . with schooling to be provided *in factory hours.*"

"Commerce would never survive such an impost," Mr. Paulding said solemnly.

"And *tertius*"—Mr. Hall lifted his chin and fairly bayed the portentous words—"no employment permitted of persons under nine years of age."

There was a heavy silence. Mr. Osband broke it. "That comes out of England?"

"It does."

"Then England is a doomed nation. And I, for one, should not be sorry to see it."

"Those revolutionary regulations," the bearer of the dread news continued, "are posted on the wall of the Montague & Roy Company."

The ironmaster came out of his seat like a rocket. "He ought to be run out of town!" he yelled.

"On a rail," snarled Mr. Smith.

"With Cassius Barlow for balance," suggested Mr. Cannon.

"Who's this that's to be run out of town?" a mellifluous baritone asked.

The portly and elegant figure of Mr. Orlando Montague stood in the doorway. He apologized courteously to the chairman for his tardiness. There was an awkward pause. Mr. Montague was not only a substantial citizen, but was known for his independent spirit and caustic tongue. He repeated his question. Gurdon Stockwell gave an indirect answer.

"I have already stated as chairman of the meeting that I deprecate violence."

"I agree," Mr. Hall said. "I agree fully, in principle. But this I will make bold to say: if the presence of a certain young mal

feasant should be determined to threaten the best interests of
our fair city, then"—his voice sank into the ripples of his beard,
but not to extinction—"then I can call to mind fifty respectable
heads of families—yes, one hundred, if need be—who will rise
in defence of home and fatherland as our forebears rose at
Lexington and Bunker Hill."

When the cheers had died down, Mr. Smith said quietly: "I
think we should form a Committee for Patriotic Action. A secret
committee."

"Is there any contrary opinion among us?" Mr. Howland
demanded, glaring formidably about him.

"Action against whom?" Mr. Montague inquired blandly.
Receiving no response, he added, "And why all this secrecy?"

Nobody seemed inclined to be specific. Mr. Hall took refuge
in a generality. "Protection to the best interests of our commerce."

"Nothing to do with Mr. Smith's fence rail, then?" young
Miller insinuated.

Mr. Fosmire ruffled up to him like a plump fighting cock.
"How does it concern you, young man?"

"Yes," Mr. Cannon supported him. "Do you set yourself up
in opposition to the sense of this meeting?"

"Who? Me? Heaven forbid," the young man said sweetly. "I
should merely admire to know more precisely what the sense of
the meeting is."

"And I should like to know," said Mr. Montague, still bland,
"whether this is in reference to my partner, Mr. Guy Roy."

"We propose to stop this revolutionary nonsense of Roy's
without further ado," Banker Paulding said sternly.

"And if there be any attempt to stay the hand of justice," the
ironmaster warned, "someone is going to get hurt."

"Several people are likely to get hurt," Montague assented.

"What precisely are we to understand by that, sir?" Mr.
Cannon challenged.

"I was no more than agreeing with Mr. Howland," was the
placid reply.

"In the measure of a threat, if I take your meaning."

"Is there no threat implicit in the Committee for Patriotic
Action?"

"Gentlemen! Gentlemen!" protested the Rev. Mr. Bortle.

"I have in mind another organization," Montague said, with

K

a mildness not intended to deceive, "which also resorts to action
upon occasion."

"The Halcyons," Gideon Beebe interpreted. He turned to
Miller, Jun. "Is Mr. Guy Roy a member?"

Young Miller's smile was suavity itself. "That, sir, is private."

"A lawless band of young rufflers and ne'erdoweels," Mr.
Howland rumbled.

"Of which your son and heir is reputed to be an ornament,"
Montague said.

"Is not the avowed purpose lawlessness?" the Rev. Mr. Bortle
inquired.

"Ask Gurdon Stockwell," Miller returned. "*Polyphloisboios
kai oinos*, eh, Gurdy?"

The chairman turned red. "I have no knowledge of your
bastard Greek," he said.

"Once for Argos, ever for Argos," returned the other. "Remember the fight with the Highkettles at Mark's Hill? And the head
tenker who tried to knife you? And the canawlers at Lock
Fifteen? Give him footroom and a good oaken cudgel," said
young Mr. Miller, addressing his scandalized audience with ill-
conceived enthusiasm, "and there are mortal few heartier
fighters than our honoured chairman."

A frosty twinkle briefly lit the Stockwell visage. "All in the
past, all in the past," he deprecated.

"*Evoe Bacchus!*" the irrepressible one chanted. "Hey, Mr.
Montague? Ah, well! Having said this much I may as well proceed. The Halcyons, gentlemen, are not a band of rufflers and
wastrels as charged, but a social confederation of gentlemen and
Corinthians, Troy's best blood, conjoined for mutual improvement and enjoyment. Harmless as the fabled dove, we—that is to
say, they—are animated by a spirit of fellowship which inspires
them to support a menaced member. I say no more except to
endorse again the prudential warning of Mr. Howland that, in
the event of an overt act, somebody is going to get hurt."

"Do we understand, then, that this precious organization of
yours supports the iniquitous twelve-hour day?"

"God of Olympus forbid!" the defender piously disclaimed.
"Down with the rabble! To hell with Andy Jackson! Perish the
honest working man and all that! No politics for us. We only
uphold our own fellows."

An uneasy silence followed. Ironmaster Howland shook out his neck-cloth. "Bluster and brag," he snapped.

"Do not rely upon any such assumption," Mr. Osband warned. "I was a boat passenger at the Lock Fifteen *fracas*. The Erie was shoulder-deep in humanity at the end, and most of 'em were canawlers."

"*Forsan et haec olim meminisse juvabit*," Gurdon Stockwell murmured absently, his eyes, for the moment, alight with memories. He brought himself back to the respectable present with a jerk. "Better measures than force can surely be devised," he said.

"Will Mr. Stockwell name a committee?" Mr. Smith suggested.

"Put Mr. Montague on it," the irresponsible Miller suggested.

"I should be delighted to serve," said the accommodating ironmonger.

"The committee will be named in due course," Gurdon Stockwell announced, frowning. "The chair will now entertain a motion to adjourn."

Mr. Orlando Montague and young Miller went out, arm in arm.

FOUR

THE Italian marble fountain in front of the Mansion House pulsed with iridescent colours in the wintry sunlight. Gypsy Vilas, pausing to admire its play, took note of a fashionably clad young lady who picked a dainty way across the cluttered street. Furs and furbelows, thought Gypsy, but without envy. Was she not, herself, earning an abundant wage of six dollars a week? She need envy nobody.

The rich figure turned in at the Troy Reading-Room. Now Gypsy did feel a mild touch of jealousy. There were times when she regretted that a life too full of other and more pressing interests had left her no time for learning her letters. It must be, she reflected, very nice to be able to walk unabashed into that literary sanctum, plank down twopence and select a volume from the laden shelves, as this young aristocrat was doing when Gypsy, coming opposite, gazed through the window.

Except for the attendant, the young person was alone in the room. With a proficient whisk of her heavy silk skirt, she settled into a languid pose at the table, her volume open before her. Slowly her head turned, giving the onlooker a fair view of her profile. Gypsy uttered a word of amazement, darted up the steps and pushed through the door.

"Becky!" she cried.

"Gypsy!" The elegant creature seized the newcomer and hugged her ecstatically.

The attendant advanced with hand extended. "The fee for non-members," she announced, "is tuppence."

"I don't want to read your poxy books," Gypsy began, when Becky interrupted her by thrusting a crisp note into the official's hand.

"Change, if you please," she said haughtily.

"Biddle bills, too," Gypsy said, gazing admiringly and lustfully at the roll within her friend's porte-monnaie.

"Oh, Gypsy! Gypsy! How joyed I am to see you! Sit down. Let me look at you. Have a comfit. We'll go out and partake of tea when I'm through my reading."

"Tea?" Gypsy repeated. "You mean boughten tea?"

"At the Palladium Tea Rooms. With cakes."

"Me?" said Gypsy. "In a tea-room? I'm no lady and you needn't think it."

"I wish I didn't have to be," the younger girl sighed. "But one can't have everything."

Her friend bent a distrustful look upon the illustrated page of the volume. "Is that about being a lady?" she demanded, pointing a finger at it.

"No-o," Becky answered. "It isn't." She read the title. "*Physiology of the Human Frame; with Faithful Illustrations.*" Her cleanly marked brows drew down. "Only," she qualified, "they aren't so faithful."

The attendant, returning with the change, supplied an interruption. Becky closed the book with a snap.

"I ought to claim my money back," she said to her friend. "It doesn't tell anything that a girl wants to know."

"Maybe," Gypsy suggested with a shrewd look, "you want to know too much."

Becky pondered. "Gypsy, I wonder if I dare tell you a secret."

"Secret? You ain't in trouble, are you? Ain't gone and broke your leg above the knee, have you?"[1]

"Certainly *not!*" Her indignation was convincing. "Gypsy, I'm—I'm going to be married."

"Married? Who to?"

"I mean, I am married. I guess I am."

"Well, for cripesake-and-a-coat-with-brass-buttons! Don't you know if you're married or not, you little ninny?"

"I'm married in court but not in church."

"How about bed?" asked the ever-practical Gypsy.

"*No!*"

"Well, don't get rambunctious about it. It's usual. And you ain't told me the man yet."

"Mr. Stockwell."

"Holy!" Gypsy ejaculated. "What'd I tell you! What'd Gypsy say would come of it if you played your cards right?"

"I didn't play any cards," the girl disclaimed. "It just sort of happened."

"Mrs. Gur-don Stock-well," Gypsy mouthed with relish and admiration. "Like the book you used to tell me about, huh?"

"No-o-o. Not like the story. I didn't want to marry Mr. Stockwell."

[1] A current vulgarism for an unfortunate feminine predicament.

"The more fool you. You didn't have to marry him, did you?"
She was still suspicious.

"I guess I did," Becky giggled. She was, for the moment, like
a small girl again. "There was a lawyer and bailiffs and the
magistrate told me, 'Say yes,' and I thought they'd put me in
jail if I didn't, so I did."

"Then what?"

"I took the steamboat for Albany and Mr. Stockwell bade me
not to tell a soul because we'd be married in church with a
preacher and bells and an organ as soon as he got back from
New York."

"When'll that be?"

"He's here now," Becky answered lugubriously. "I kind of
wish I hadn't done it, Gypsy. I don't see why I had to be married.
I don't see what Mr. Stockwell wanted to marry me for."

"That ain't your worry. Play your luck while your luck's
in, gal."

"Am I lucky? I suppose I am," Becky said wistfully. "I'll be
rich when I'm Mrs. Gurdon Stockwell."

"Rich! Oh, my eye! You won't know what to do with all
the dibbs."

"I shall give parties. Gala ones. And invite all you girls."

"Ay-yah? And what will Mr. Gurdon Stockwell be doin'?"

"He'll be standing at the doorway of the mansion with a
nosegay in his velvet coat and saying, 'Welcome, young ladies.' "

" 'Welcome, young ladies,' huh?" the other broke in. "More
likely, 'What's that scum doin' in my house?' " She chuckled.
"D'you remember the last party we went to at the mansion?
We was outside, wasn't we? That's where mechanics belong.
Outside. Mechanics are low."

"Are you low, Gypsy?"

"Lower'n a snake's belly button, by Stockwell reckonin'."

"Then so am I."

"Look, your ladyship, slick's your game till you can say, 'Mrs.
Gurdon Stockwell' with your visiting-card between your pinky
and your thumb."

"Then I won't marry him. Oh, dear! I am married to him."
She became thoughtful. "Gypsy, that explains something.
Has somebody passed word to the girls about not coming to
see me? Why haven't *you* been? You must have known I was
back."

"I did know," Gypsy admitted. "I was comin' but I got an advisement not to."

"Who from?" asked Becky indignantly. But her heart misgave her. Was Mr. Stockwell going to start obstructing her life so soon? Gypsy's answer was a shock.

"Mr. Guy Roy."

Becky shrank back. "Oh no! I don't believe it. He wouldn't."

"He had it from Mrs. Heartt. And Mrs. Heartt had it from old Hurdy-Gurdy himself, I reckon. Mr. Guy just passed it along. He said that might be the easiest way, but that we could do as we'd a mind to. He sorta smiled when he said it, but he looked like he wasn't too pleased. You said it explained something. What does it explain?"

"Prissy Stamm."

"Miss Owly-eye? What about her?"

"I saw her this morning. She was coming out of the side door of the First Methodist Church."

"She's piouser than ever," Gypsy commented. "Was Mr. Stockwell with her?"

Becky stared. "No. Why should he be?"

"No. Accourse not. I misspoke myself."

"Prissy was as near to me as you. She didn't so much as give me how-d'ye-do."

"Likely she didn't know you in all your hifalutins."

"She did so. She looked at me as if she hated me."

"Why not?" Gypsy said.

"Hate me? Why should she?"

Gypsy regarded her thoughtfully. "Now you're going to be Mrs. Gurdon Stockwell, you might as well find out a few things."

"What kind of things?" Becky asked uneasily.

"You knew old Hurdy-Gurdy was married before."

"Yes."

"To a pickled icicle. Well, what happens?"

"What did?" asked the young wife, as Gypsy paused for effect.

"Just what you'd think. There was Prissy, makin' sheep's eyes at him every Sunday and some weekdays. After all, he's a man. The cuckoo that couldn't nest with the robin roosted with the crow."

"Gypsy! You don't mean they did *that*!" said Becky, horrified.

"Well, I didn't see 'em. But they got the name for it. All on the quiet, though. Everything was hushed up."

Becky became thoughtful. "Even so, why should she hate me? She couldn't know about—about what's happened. Nobody does except you and Mr. Roy."

"Mr. Roy? Hey-o! What's this? Who told him?"

Colour flushed up into Becky's face. "I did."

"Where'd you see Guy Roy? You been randyin'[1] with him already?"

"I don't know what you mean by 'already'," Becky retorted with dignity. "I met him on the train and—and—well, I—I let it out. It has no importance," she stated loftily. She changed the topic. "Why didn't Mr. Stockwell marry *her*?"

"Why should he? He didn't have to, if what they say is true."

"And I always thought she was such a good girl." Becky's expression was properly prim.

"That's it. Too good. They're both good together. All swiggered up in church work. Hymn-singin'. Campground meetin's. Missionary doin's for the poor, hungry cannibals. Love-feasts. Queer things happen when gentlemen and work-gals get to bein' good together."

"Gypsy Vilas, you've got a nasty mind."

"Oh, I ain't sayin' that anything's goin' on now. But it's just as well the Big Bug should get him a wife to keep him busy nights."

The girl's face flamed. "I think you're horrid and beastly and low."

"Told you I was," Gypsy answered comfortably. "Six months from now you won't be speakin' to me on the street."

"Who'll stop me?" Becky demanded.

"Your lord and master."

Becky attempted the only response that seemed sufficient to the occasion. She pursed her lips for the raspberry. Only a feeble burble resulted. Gypsy laughed consumedly. "Save it for old Hurdy-Gurdy," she said. "He'd have a cachexy."

Becky wished to know all about her friend's job. From this, she switched the talk by a natural gradation to the girl's employer.

"Is his business prospering?"

---

[1] Probably a contraction of rendezvousing, rather than the commoner meaning of skylarking.

"We're full of orders. The money's comin' in faster'n it goes out. *If* it keeps up."

"Why shouldn't it keep up?"

"There's certain parties," the working girl said, "that would liker see Guy Roy in Hell than in Troy."

Becky tried to look wise. "The other collar-makers?"

Gypsy's snort dismissed them. "As fast as they copy our models, Mr. Roy gets out a newer and more fashionable one. It's the big bugs. They'd like to drive us out of town."

"Why? I thought the more businesses a city had, the better for all businesses. I read that in a learned book," Becky said importantly.

"It's the ten-hour day. They're all gall-sour against it."

"I remember how angry Mr. Stockwell and Mr. Goodwilly used to get," the girl said. "Are you going to have the ten-hour day in the collar factory?"

"We've got it now. And the others want to stop it."

"They don't have to have it in their factories, do they?"

"That's what they're afraid of: that the other mechanics will ask for it. That's why they're all against Guy Roy."

"I think it's paltry. Is Mr. Stockwell against him?"

"He's the deadest-set of any of 'em. He says Roy is no better than an agitator and the town must be rid of him."

"But they're cousins," Becky said, puzzled.

"Gal," Gypsy said impressively, "kin don't count in business. When you goin' to be churched?"

"The day after New Year's," the bride answered dispiritedly.

Though habitually negligent of local news, as being beneath its journalistic standards, the *Atlas* relaxed its dignity to the extent of a quarter column in reporting the Stockwell nuptials. The item set forth approvingly that the wedding was an *élite* and pompous event. Owner-printer Clarkson Crolius, himself, penned the account. The bride, he stated, looked "fair as a rose", which was true, and "happy as a sunbeam", which was not. "The wealth and fashion of our fair city attended. A sumptuous banquet followed upon the ceremony, after which the fortunate couple set forth upon their hymeneal tour in the bridegroom's new and elegant cutter."

Privately the printer thought that the bride looked pale and the groom grumpish. He noticed that she cast a glance about the church, as if in quest of someone not there, and spoke under

her breath to her attendant. Though well-informed upon much
that could not be printed, Mr. Crolius did not learn until later
of a difference of opinion between the couple, a few days previous
to the wedding. Mr. Stockwell had intercepted a sheaf of personally inscribed invitations from his betrothed to several undesirable persons—including Miss Gypsy Vilas, and, it was said had
spoken firmly to her on the subject.

The only person present in the church below top social level
was Miss Priscilla Stamm. By virtue of her good works, a seat in
the gallery was assigned to her, where she sat and wept throughout the proceedings. Between tears, she prayed with bitter piety
for the happiness of the wedded pair.

Mr. Guy Roy was an absentee. As a near kinsman of the
groom, he had been invited to sit in the family pew, but had
unaccountably declined. Gypsy, who was on easy terms with her
employer, expressed astonishment at this, and received a reply so
churlish that it amazed her. What was wrong with the normally
sunny-tempered Guy Roy? Gypsy tucked that question into a
corner of her brain for future examination.

"The happy couple," Printer Crolius informed his public,
"will perform a tour of points of interest."

They visited Trenton Falls, which was not only nearer than
the more voluminous Niagara, but was also held in higher
esteem as a spectacle. They were escorted through the thriving
city of Utica and drove out to Clinton where the alumnus introduced his bride to the campus of his Alma Mater. Thence they
sleighed it to Rome and, the weather holding phenomenally clear,
on to Syracuse.

Young Mrs. Stockwell docilely received instruction in the
operation of the salt-beds which were the rising city's prosperity,
and learned that her husband owned shares in one of them. In
Auburn they attended a lecture at the Theological Seminary.
Mrs. Stockwell was bored. She vastly preferred the visit to the
State Prison at sixpence admittance, with its lugubrious spectacle
of the convicts shuffling in lockstep to their meal of thin soup,
dark bread, and salt pork. And she was favourably impressed
with the vast Exchange Hotel which boasted nearly three hundred
beds and a stationary bathtub lined with tin, said to be the first
installation of the sort in the nation.

Rochester was to be the terminus of the journey. To the
bride, not the least of the hardships was the Stockwell insistence

upon examining into every industrial establishment and explaining in detail its operation. As a dutiful helpmeet she was expected to attend with interest to the long discussions between the escorting owners and the visitor about prices of raw materials, the relative advantages of rail or canal traffic, the most favourable system of trade discounts, and always the baseless and unrighteous discontent of labour with the divinely constituted order.

At meals and between times she was treated to endless discourses of an educational and improving nature upon commerce. Mr. Stockwell was unendurably well informed. A genuine zeal for the enlightenment of others fired his brain. While sensible of the sterling quality of his discourses, his wife found them dull.

They were at Little Falls on the return trip when, at breakfast, she gave voice to a question which had formulated itself as a result of many conversations between Mr. Stockwell and his business friends. She had been preparing his tea in accordance with carefully detailed instructions.

"Mr. Stockwell," she began, "I have wanted to ask you . . ."

He held up an admonitory finger. "I observe that you eat but little," he said. "A good breakfast is the foundation of a useful and profitable day."

"I satisfy myself."

"Too little, I doubt. That is the mark of the vapours. Upon our arrival I shall consult Dr. Armitage on your behalf."

"I don't need any doctor, Mr. Stockwell. I do very well."

"Let me be the judge of that," he returned, not ungently. "I trust, Obedience, that your mind has been enlarged by the opportunities afforded you on this excursion."

"I hope so," she answered listlessly. "Your tea, Mr. Stockwell." She poured it with nicety and passed the cup.

Inhaling the aroma, he regarded her thoughtfully. "It is proper and fitting that in the presence of others you should address me as Mr. Stockwell," he said genially. "When we are alone, as now, I prefer the more familiar form."

"Thank you, Mr. Stockwell."

"Gurdon," he prompted softly.

"Gurdon," she repeated like a lesson.

"And now, Obedience, what have you wanted to ask me?"

"Why do you hate your work-people?"

He all but dropped the saucer into which he had turned his tea for cooler drinking. "Hate my—what absurdity is this?"

She was looking at him with level attention. "You do, you know."

"I never heard such folderol in my life!"

"You may not realize it. I don't believe you do realize it."

"Hate my work-people?" He echoed the incredible charge to assure himself that it had been advanced. "It is notorious that the Eureka hands are the best fed and lodged in all Troy."

"The same is true of your horses, isn't it?"

"Certainly. I should think shame to do less."

"And for the same reason in both cases."

"What maggot has bitten your brain?" he cried. "Am I to be criticized for my consideration of man and beast?"

She paid no heed to this but continued, half-dreamily, to follow her thought. "I suppose you are no different from other employers."

"God give me patience! Wherein have I failed?" he asked coldly.

"You repel every attempt at betterment. You resent it."

"Ah! There's the nub of it. Now we have it. What betterment do they need?"

"Shorter hours. Fewer rules."

"The hours are as God set them. The rules are as wisdom established them. Let the workers do their duty and take their wages and leave the rest to their superiors in whom an all-seeing Providence has imposed this responsibility. Or," he shouted, "take the consequences."

"Hatred." She nodded in confirmation of the word. "I believe I know why you hate us. It's because if we better our wage, it means money out of your pocket. It's a question of balance, isn't it? That's why you must think of us as enemies."

He glared at her, thunderstruck. 'Us'? Think of 'us'? Are you aware of what you are saying, woman?"

"Moderate your voice, Mr. Stockwell."

Gurdon Stockwell prided himself on his self-control, among many other carefully cultivated qualities. He said, in quieter tones: "Let us have this clear, Obedience. Are you thinking of yourself as of the proletariat?"

"Yes, I suppose I was."

"I forbid you. Do you understand? As your husband, I forbid you to harbour such wicked, disloyal thoughts."

"How can you forbid thought, Mr. Stockwell?"

He essayed a swallow of his beverage and half-strangled over it. "I shall have a dyspepsy," he lamented. "With whom have you been consorting? What damnable doctrines have you been absorbing and where? How do you come by such desperate notions? Has the schooling upon which I ungrudgingly expended large sums to make you a lady, fomented rebellion in your once-innocent mind?"

"I'm sorry" she said. "If you don't like my having been a mill-hand you should have told me. But I don't see why you should speak so wildly."

"Enough of this," he said sternly. "I wish to hear no more of this. The subject is closed."

"You will hear no more from me, Mr. Stockwell," his wife replied. "Never again."

The words were docile. Conciliation was implicit in them. He suspected uneasily that reservations lurked back of her apparent amenability. He was not sure that he understood her.

On one point, however, his resolution was settled. Enamoured though he was of her beauty, her freshness, her abounding and sweet vitality, he must conceal his sentiments. To betray the depth of his passion would be to place a weapon in her hands which, he more than suspected, she would be quite unprincipled enough to employ.

For the remainder of the trip he found her circumspect.

Though it was not within his competence to realize it, the pattern of their marriage was set.

FIVE

THE bride returned from her wedding journey haggard. Something of the sweet lustre of youth was gone from her. Dr. Armitage, called in by Gurdon Stockwell, said it was only natural and to be expected. Nevertheless he administered a routine leeching and purging. When her appetite returned, as was inevitable in a young and healthy animal, he gave himself credit for a cure. Stockwell, a solicitous spouse, cockered her up with undesired attentions and well-appreciated luxuries, to an extent which caused some brow-lifting among the ladies of his circle. They said that he fairly doted on her.

Within a month it was all over town that young Mrs. Gurdon Stockwell was "sleeping cold". She had her own chamber, across the hall from her husband's. Female Troy was agog with the scandal. What did it mean? Had the bridal pair quarrelled already to the point of sundering? There was no outward sign of it in their behaviour when in public.

Medical orders, some said; it was known that Dr. Armitage Rad been called in. Others had heard that she was too restless a bedmate for Mr. Stockwell, talked and kicked in her sleep. There was even speculation as to whether the separation might be at the disappointed husband's wish. How complete was it? That is what curious Troy would have liked to know.

"Every sewing bee in town has got the itch over it," Gypsy Vilas said.

Gypsy firmly intended to put it straight to Becky at the first opportunity. But she had not yet seen the young wife. Could there be somebody else in the case, she wondered—Guy Roy, perhaps? She would much have liked to query him, to find out whether he knew anything of these peculiar proceedings. But there were lengths to which one did not go with that young man.

Moreover, this was not the time to be bothering him. Business was booming for Montague & Roy. Other and greater industries were bewailing hard times; not their line of trade. The detached collar had caught the fancy of America's young bloods. Housewives approved it as lessening their burden of washery. Grave and important men had taken it up. Edward Livingston had

discarded his tall and strangulated stock in favour of the new
fashion, and it was rumoured that the massive chin of Daniel
Webster, from above which so much leonine oratory gushed,
had been measured for a bespoken straightaround. The Mendels-
sohn Society of New York gave a concert at which every voca-
list wore one of the Guy Roy open-throats, thus giving free
musical play to the Adam's apple. Collar jokes appeared in
the newspapers, sure sign of popular recognition. Yankee Hill
included a hilariously risible jest on the subject in one of his
monologues.

Presently an expanded plant would be needed. The proprietor
must look about for more commodious quarters. Le Grand
Cannon, the builder, was putting up a three-floor building on
Madison Street; Montague & Roy might take over a floor. Guy
was covering a paper with figures of square footage one noon
when a double tap on the door interrupted.

Forewoman Vilas entered. Her eyes were snapping between
the rufous bristle of her brows. Through the open door back of
her came a sound of wailing in a childish voice.

"Who's that?" the owner demanded.

"It's that damn' natural."

"Marty Mull? What ails her?"

"I gave her a slap across her silly face."

"None of that in my shop, Gypsy," he said sharply.

"How else you goin' to handle a ninnywit like her?"

"Fetch her in."

The overgrown and dim-minded cutter shambled into the
office, dragged, rather than led, by Gypsy.

"You lemme be! You lemme bee-ee-ee!" she wept.

"What's the matter, Marty?" her employer asked.

"I c-c-can't work here no more," she quavered.

"Why not?"

"I'm scairt."

"Nonsense! Nobody's going to hurt you."

"They looked at me through the glass."

"She's been all a-flitter since she checked in this morning.
Peekin' and peerin' across at the window," Gypsy explained.

"Who frightened you, Marty?" Guy inquired kindly.

A look of cunning came into the weak eyes. "I dunno. I didn't
see nobody. I wanta quit."

"She's scared spitless at something," Gypsy put in, an

inaccurate characterization since the unfortunate was drooling at the mouth with fear. "Won't tell me who, what, or whysoever."

The prospect of losing his best-skilled cutter, whose instinctive talent for faithfully following design had been discovered by Guy himself, was little to his liking.

"She says she's got another job," Gypsy said. "I think she's a liar."

"At a better wage?" Guy asked.

"I guess so," the girl said.

He had lost several hands in the last two weeks, and he thought he knew through what agency. "How much are you going to get, Marty?"

She palpated her blubbery lower lip with her forefinger. "A lot. Fifteen shillin's."

"Why, you foozlebrain, you're gettin' twenty here!" Gypsy cried.

"Now, Marty," Guy said gently, "tell me why you want to leave."

"I'm scairt they'll do me a hurt."

"Who?"

"Two gentlemen. They'll make all my teeth fall out. They said so. They made me promuss I wouldn't tell. Now you made me tell and they'll hire a witch to put a hex on to me," she wailed.

"It's that Loach and another of his breed," Gypsy said. "I saw 'em hooverin' around here like a coupla nitters over a dungpile."

"Please let me go, Mr. Roy," the natural begged. Her features writhed in an effort of memory. "I ain't a slave," she got out at length.

"We can't keep you against your wishes, Marty. See that she gets her pay, Gypsy."

The forewoman was scandalized. "Ain't you goin' to mulk her for breakin' her week?" she demanded. Receiving no answer, she grumblingly led her captive away.

Guy Roy rose, carefully set his collar, swathed it in an elaborately patterned neck-cloth, got into his fur coat and dark castor, and took up his heavy imported cane. Upon a moment's reflection he restored it to its corner. His present errand might put a strain upon his self-control.

His initial survey from the front stoop revealed nothing but the normal traffic. But, as he walked down Elbow Street towards the river, two figures ambled out of a pothouse door, sighted him, and turned in the opposite direction. Guy had some difficulty in catching up with them. He touched the larger man on the shoulder.

"A word with you, Loach."

Loach turned. "What you want with me, Mr. Roy?" he said defensively.

"You and your friend, Dobby, are too much around here lately."

The second man interposed. "I guess the street's free."

Guy ignored him. "Don't tamper further with my hands," he said to Loach. "I'm giving you fair notice."

"You can't threaten us honest working men, mister," Dobby protested.

"That's all." Guy was still addressing Loach. "Wait! On second thoughts, it isn't. Who's hiring you?"

"No job right now," Loach answered sadly.

"Who hired you for the dirty work?" Guy insisted, quite pleasantly. "It wouldn't be the Mill Owners Association, would it?"

"Don't know what you're talking of, Mr. Roy."

The young man slipped off his glove, delved into his pocket and extracted a shining coin. Spinning it high in the air, he caught it on the flat of his palm.

"A shilling," he said. "A minted shilling. More money than you've earned by honest work in a year, I'll warrant. All yours if you'll name me your employer."

"I tell you, Mr. Roy, I'm a poor man, out of employ," the aggrieved Loach began.

"Yes, yes," the other cut in, spinning the coin once more. "I don't wish to hear the sad story of your unmerited afflictions. I want only to know who hires you and your fellow rum guzzler to frighten halfwits. . . . Don't care to earn an easy two bits? Very good. I'll try elsewhere."

He pocketed the piece, took a cross street, and made his way to the Eureka Mills where he found Gurdon Stockwell in the office of a depleted factory. The local fabric industry was running low. Stockwell's greeting was dimly illumined by the smile of pained uncertainty which was his habitual and usually inadequate defence against the eccentricities of the younger man.

"This is cousinly of you, Guy," he said, rising and extending a limp hand.

"I'm afraid it isn't, Gurdon," the caller responded cheerfully. "It's official, in a sense."

"In any event, I am gratified to see you here. The first time in several weeks, if I mistake not."

"I've been much occupied with my own business concerns," Guy said. "I'm wondering how far you have been occupied with them." He spoke with a smile, but the emphasis was not to be mistaken.

"With *your* business concerns? My dear Guy!"

"Am I correct in assuming that I speak to the chairman of the Mill Owners Association?"

"I have been selected for that honour," the other replied stiffly.

"Honour, eh?" Guy said. "Your association is putting a severe strain on the term."

Gurdon Stockwell bridled. "Are you charging the Mill Owners Association with dishonourable practice?"

"Well, somebody is up to devilment around my place. I've lost some good hands in the last fortnight."

Gurdon leaned forward in his chair and spoke with an earnestness that did not lack appeal. "Cousin, why must you pursue this destructive course?"

"Meaning the ten-hour day?"

"Yes. Is this a time to advance such a measure?"

"A very favourable time, so far as our company is concerned."

"You think only of yourself," Stockwell pursued, more in sadness than accusation. "Consider the state of trade. Raw materials are up. Prime cotton may yet touch twenty cents the pound. Sales are torpid. We have been compelled to lay off help. Every plant in town is doing the same."

"Except ours."

Stockwell flushed, but controlled his temper. "Nothing can come of it but ruin for you and harm to commerce. Yet this is the time you choose to instil further unrest among the labourers by your wilful and impracticable effort to upset an established system."

"What's impracticable about operating at a profit?"

Stockwell shook his head. "I ask myself what motive inspires your course."

"You may answer yourself," said Guy, leaning easily back in his chair, "that my experiences with the long workday at the Eureka had much to do with it."

Stockwell abandoned this line. He said coldly, "Has it occurred to you that by your insistence upon your Utopian projects you are giving aid and comfort to the enemy?"

"You regard your work-people as the enemy?"

Stockwell set his strong teeth. "When they move for unrighteous measures like this damnable ten-hour day, they are enemies of the common weal. I give you fair warning, Guy Roy, if this goes further, the substantial men of Troy will be forced to stern measures. The matter is under consideration now. If this were not a confidential conversation I should report it to the Association."

"By all means report it. I shall be delighted to explain my position at any time."

"Guy," his cousin said hopelessly, "you are inveterately light-minded and frivolous"

"That's as may be," Guy replied pleasantly. "My blessing to the Mill Owners Association, and tell 'em this from me, Gurdy: you run your factories to suit yourselves. I'll run mine to suit myself. And if I want to reduce the hours to twelve or ten or two per day and let my help drink tea and twiddle their fingers in work hours, that is my affair and not theirs. And the only way they can stop me is to run me out of town."

"It may yet come to that," Gurdon Stockwell retorted.

"To quote a respected authority," Guy chuckled, "*non sine sanguine*."

"If there be bloodshed, who will have caused it?" Stockwell said sternly. He drummed on his desk-top. "Guy, is it you who have sent for Luther Simms to come to Troy?"

"No."

"Someone has."

"Is he coming? When?"

"We shall not know until he gets here."

"Well, if you see him," Guy proceeded, with flagrant intent to annoy, "ask him to call at Montague & Roy. I'd enjoy a word with him. Good-bye, cousin."

He shut the door lightly after him.

At his desk again, Guy set down to think things over. He felt
more resentment than alarm. While he did not underestimate
the power wielded by the group round Stockwell, he did not
see how they could seriously harm him.

Guy was not, himself, so much concerned with the implications of the shorter workday as with its application. In his view, it
made for a satisfied work force. His establishment turned out
more and better collars in ten hours of actual working time—
two hours being allotted to recesses for meals and rest—than
either of his two rather feeble competitors in thirteen or fourteen
hours. Thus it justified itself commercially, which was always a
satisfaction to his pride. Besides, fighting for a principle was
something new. He would much have preferred to be let alone
to work out the problems of a developing trade. Like a great
contemporary statesman, he was "a little hard to coax; but as
for compulsion, that is out of the question."

He summoned Mary Haynes and Gypsy Vilas to the small
and cluttered cubbyhole which he used as an office.

"How many girls have asked for their time?" he inquired
of Mary.

"Six since the first of the month," the timekeeper answered.

"There'll be more," Gypsy prophesied. "They're all sidlin
around and whisperin' in corners. That means trouble."

"We know about Marty," the employer said. "Have Loach
and Dobby been threatening the other girls?"

"It's Sweetie-pink, the Pride of the Eureker, if it's anyone,"
Gypsy said in her most venomous manner.

"Priscilla Stamm?" Guy asked in surprise. "I wouldn't think
she'd frighten anyone."

"She was around here Tuesday noon, with her little mealy
mouth so prissed up you couldn't hardly hear her speak. I told
her she'd better watch out if she didn't want to catch what
Paddy gave the drum across her skinny shoulders."

Guy frowned. "Priscilla wouldn't be hiring for the Eureka
would she?"

"Prissy would be doing whatever her deah employah damn
well told her," Gypsy said.

"Nobody's hiring for the Eureka," Mary stated. "They're
letting out, not taking on."

"I understand that's true of all the mills," Guy said. "Then
she isn't trying to win our help away."

"Did you ever hear of the Paterson ban,[1] Mr. Roy?" Mary inquired.

"Of course. But that's to scotch a strike, isn't it?"

"It works like this," Mary explained. "Take our Susan Grimes. She's on the boxes. She's got two sisters, still working. One's in Lark at Morn and the other in Arbia. Her father works half-time in Mr. Saltmarsh's soapery. Somebody comes to Susan —might be Prissy Stamm, might be someone else—and tells her she'd better quit here and find herself another job or the rest of the family will lose theirs. Maybe they'll have a job ready for her."

"As good as her present one?" Guy asked.

"It wouldn't have to be, sir. You see, they've got her scared. The Grimes are bone-poor. He's part crippled. Mrs. Grimes has got yearling twins and can't work steady. They need all their wages. The two factory hands come home crying, because they've heard something. Then Mr. Saltmarsh sends for John Grimes and says to him: 'John, I hear you've got a girl working in that ten-hour place. Better get her out if you know what's good for her—and you.' So Susan quits."

Guy thought it over. "You can fill her place, I suppose?"

"Ten times over, as things are now," Mary Haynes assured him. "The streets are full of 'em looking for places. But it means training a new girl. That's time and trouble."

"Let me know of any other cases," Guy directed. "That's all, girls."

The timekeeper left, but Gypsy lingered. Before others she was propriety personified in her address towards her employer. It was a respectful "Boss" or "Mr. Roy" always. But in private they were on more familiar terms. She now turned her foxy grin upon him.

Guy responded in kind: "Well, let's have it. What's on your mind?"

"Gurdon Stockwell and the rest of his clique. You don't know what you're up against, young feller."

"I've just had an inkling of it, but I can't say that I'm specially alarmed."

---

[1] By the terms of the employers' agreement, every member of a striker's family was declared unemployable for a year. This device broke the Paterson silk strike, wrecked the union, and established a reign of quiet terror which lasted for years in the silk industry.

"You oughta talk with Cash Barlow."

He laughed. "Then my esteemed cousin *would* have reason to call me an agitator and fomenter."

"Guy, nobody's ever licked that lot yet nor ever will," the girl said earnestly. "What makes you think you can?"

"Bless you. I don't want to lick 'em," he cried. "I only want to be let alone."

"There's never been a turn-out in this city that they didn't smash," she continued. "There's never been a troublemaker that they haven't hunted out or jailed. This ten-hour business is catching like pox, by their reckons, and they're just as scairt of it. They're goin' to stop you."

He turned upon her his slow smile. "Gypsy, pull yourself together. I'm going to give you more of a shock than you ever got from the Patent Penny Electric at the fair. As soon as I can find space, we're going to double our work force."

She tossed her hands, fingers splayed, in the air. "You're crackers."

"It may be so."

"They'll gutch you before the year is out."

"Want to quit me, Gypsy?"

She glared at him. "You ask me that again and I'll fetch you such a kerchunkus alongside your cho—oh, Gawd!" she exclaimed, clapping a hand across her disrespectful mouth. "I forgot. Well, don't say I didn't warn you, lad."

"I've had all the warnings I want," Guy laughed.

"So said, so done," Gypsy assented. The door slammed resentfully behind her exit.

SIX

To exhibit his new possession, in whom he took an unconfessed pride, the master of Castle Hill arranged a series of ceremonial suppers. He wished Mrs. Gurdon Stockwell to become better acquainted with Troy and Troy to become better acquainted with her.

Three months after marriage he was still enamoured of her with an ardour that ill befitted his years and his position. That his feeling was in no measure returned added to his sense of indignity. To betray his infatuation to the object of it would be a perilous confession of weakness. Already he had given ground in permitting Mrs. Stockwell a separate room. In vain did he tell himself that the concession grew out of their mutual comfort; it remained a sore spot in his consciousness. There should be no more such surrenders of principle.

Wedded life had given him no comprehension of this irritating, elusive and bewitching young creature. She managed his household efficiently. She acceded to any explicit wish of his. Since that one outbreak on their bridal tour, she had not questioned his standards nor challenged his opinions.

If only there were to be a child! To every intimation of his hope, Obedience presented a blank and inscrutable front. It was the duty of woman to bear children; he tried to impress that upon her, only to encounter her invincible silence. Was she barren? How should she know? she replied. Some women were that way, weren't they? The indifference in her tone dismayed him.

"Should you not consult Dr. Armitage?" he suggested.

She could not tell him that she did not wish a child—not of his fathering.

"I fear I am a disappointment to you, Mr. Stockwell," she said with a touch of remorse.

Gurdon Stockwell reflected bitterly that he little deserved the unjust fate of having married two cold wives. Obedience was, at least, submissive, where the former Mrs. Stockwell had been mutinous. He sighed and changed the subject.

It was the tradition of the house, the master of it informed his wife, that the Castle Hill galas should be held on Saturday evenings in the spring. April being here, they would start the following week. As was proper to the head of the household, he made out the lists without consulting her.

The fourteen guests represented the *élite* families of Troy, both in commercial and social status. The table talk touched lightly upon taxes, the crimes of the Jacksonian clique at Washington, the increasing traffic of the Erie Canal, the recent visit of a touring Britisher who had gladdened the hearts of his hosts by comprehensively damning American manners, morals and speech, the business expansion of the city, and so on to the more engrossing topics of the Missionary Society meeting movingly exhorted by an ex-cannibal, and the forced resignation of the Rev. Mr. Callender from the First Particular Baptist Church because of his heretical denial of the doctrine of eternal damnation.

Her table neighbours found their young hostess a model of decorum. She laughed genteelly when Mr. Cannon related a humorous story which she had already read in *Niles's Register* (but how could he have foreseen that, ladies not being supposed to peruse the press?). She exhibited a praiseworthy knowledge of last Sunday's sermon, and was properly interested in the plans for the great camp meeting at Thompson's Grove in July.

The dinner was approved a success.

Nine o'clock rang from the Eureka bell-tower in double clangs, dismissing the hands for the night. Some surprise was expressed. Mr. Stockwell explained that, as the working force was depleted owing to the vicissitudes of trade, it had been found expedient to extend working hours for the remaining employees.

"Has there been any cavil, Mr. Stockwell?" one of the men asked.

"Nothing to signify," the owner replied. He addressed his wife across the length of the table. "Mrs. Stockwell, if you will conduct the ladies to the parlour, we will rejoin you in due course."

Rising, the hostess led the way out. Having disposed themselves in the parlour, the ladies settled to their coffee. The subject introduced for masculine discussion immediately before their departure lingered in mind, and the conversation presently took the form of that eternal grievance of the rich, the contumacy of the poor in disliking to be poor.

"Pampered," Mrs. Beebe said vigorously. "That's what I always tell my husband. He pampers his mechanics."

"No good can come of it," wheezed old Mrs. Curry, who was on a visit to her daughter, Mrs. Waring. "My father was a sea captain. Sailed out of Portsmouth. He used to say, 'Spoil fo'c'sle hands, make devils!' It's the same in the mills."

"The more is given them, the more they ask," Mrs. Heartt confirmed.

"Is it true that the Arbia mill-hands have petitioned for butter on their breakfast bread?" Mrs. Paulding asked.

"What! With butter eleven cents a pound?" Mrs. Miller cried. "They wouldn't dare."

"They dare talk about the ten-hour day," Mrs. Cannon pointed out.

"That'll never come to anything," Mrs. Osband said comfortably.

"Why?" The clear, calm voice had a note of challenge. Coffee cups were set down as heads turned towards the speaker. Old Mrs. Curry peered at her.

"Is that Gurdon Stockwell's wife?" she queried.

"Yes. Hush, Mother!"

"Why?" repeated the quiet voice.

"Wh-wh-why," Mrs. Osband stammered, "what would they do with all their spare time?"

"Spend it on gin and lechery," Mrs. Smith said hollowly. She was echoing a passage from Hellfire Hoadley's sermon on Discontent, the Signpost to Damnation.

"The joiners' manifesto states that they want the time for education and association with their families," the hostess said.

"What's the joiners' manifesto?" someone asked.

"I'd admire to know how she knows so much about it," Mrs. Curry said in a hoarse whisper which, in that hush, might as well have been a yell.

Obedience Stockwell obliged her. "I used to be a mill-hand, myself, Mrs. Curry," she answered with shameless explicitude. "I worked in my husband's factory, just below on the flat."

Every Troy woman there was, of course, conversant with their hostess's detrimental past. But the dictates of good taste and respect for Gurdon Stockwell—fear, also, in a measure—had relegated that delicate bit of history to private whispers. To have it thus nakedly paraded was a shock.

A buzz of meaningless and disjointed chatter immediately broke out to cover, so far as might be, the scandal. It was not loud enough to drown out Mrs. Stockwell's next and incredibly provocative statement.

"I think the ten-hour day would be a very good thing."

Mrs. Heartt slipped out of the room. As a family connection, she felt herself charged with duty. Gurdon Stockwell must be informed before his wife involved the household in further disgrace. Finding a servant, she had the host summoned from the dining-room, and poured into his ear in a distracted mutter a version of Obedience's avowal which lost nothing in the telling. A heavy frown set itself deep into Stockwell's forehead.

"I will deal with it," he said.

He appeared at the parlour door, his face a chill mask. "Your pardon, ladies," he said. "Mrs. Stockwell, I wish a word with you."

Obedience rose, composedly made her excuses, and joined him in the hallway. He closed the door behind her. "What is this foolery I hear of?" he said, his voice a thin wafer of wrath.

"I couldn't help it; I truly couldn't," she pleaded.

"You have committed a grave breach of the proprieties. I shall expect you to return to the room and retract your wicked follies."

Her eyes widened. "Take back what I said to the ladies?"

"At once."

"But it was all true."

"Will you do as I tell you, Obedience?"

"How can I? I should feel like a fool."

He opened the door. "Mrs. Stockwell is indisposed, ladies," he announced on a toneless level. "She begs to be excused for the balance of the evening."

"Never felt more hale in my life," his wife called past his shoulder, and ran upstairs with a trill of defiant laughter.

Having reached her room, the young wife sat down to wait. Cautiously opening her window, she could presently hear the subdued noises of departure. The party was breaking up at an unwonted hour. That was her doing. For a moment she experienced a stab of contrition. It was not quite fair to Mr. Stockwell to scandalize his friends with her heresies.

Below her, the last of the carriages was spattering through the April mud. Gurdon Stockwell would be locking up, a routine he confided to no other member of the household. She listened for his deliberate tread on the stairway and along the upper hall.

It paused at her door. She stepped forward to open to him. He strode in, his expression heavy and judicial.

"You have been a sore disappointment to me, Obedience."

"I'm sorry."

"That, I believe, is untrue."

"Not for what I said to those ladies. I'd say it again. What do they know about mill life?" she concluded contemptuously.

"Need you flaunt your vulgar knowledge in their faces?"

"Do you expect me to forget that I was a factory girl?"

"Yes," he said violently.

"Dismiss the hope. I neither can nor wish to. Sometimes," she added with cold deliberation, "I would give anything to be back in Dorm Four."

He locked his hands behind him and walked the length of the chamber and back, his chin dropped on his chest. Presently he raised his head and nodded, as one who has reached a decision. "You have writing materials here." He indicated the desk between the windows.

Her brows went up. "Yes."

"Seat yourself. Prepare to write."

She drew in the chair, but did not sit down. "What am I to write?"

"A letter. Six letters. One to each lady who was present tonight."

"What am I to say?" she asked suspiciously.

"I will dictate. Be seated."

She shook her head. "It is useless. You expect me to apologize, I presume."

"I direct it."

"I won't."

"Obedience, I am your husband. Do you refuse to accept my authority?"

"Yes, in this."

He pointed a rigid finger at her. "Obedience Stockwell, I could have continued to endure your frivolity. I could have condoned your flouting of the responsibilities of your position. I could have suffered with patience your frequent and indefensible denials of the marital status. But this—this passes Christian tolerance. I shall leave you to ponder in solitude your wicked contumacy."

He stalked through the door and drew it strongly to. She

heard the great key creak in the lock. She threw herself against the panelling.

"Let me out! Let me out!"

His voice outside adjured her hollowly: "Pray, Obedience. Pray for pardon. Until you manifest repentance you shall remain locked in your chamber."

She cried brokenly, "Do you think, if I hadn't dreaded locked doors, I wouldn't have barred you out long since?"

The words did not reach his ear. He had shut himself into his chamber. He was content with his handling of a difficult problem. In the morning, he made no doubt, her spirit would have been properly chastened.

Left to herself, Becky fought down the terror which overwhelmed her. Fortunately, her well-supplied work-basket was at hand. Stripping the heavy linen sheets from her bed, she cut them into two-inch breadths. For a manually deft cotton worker it was no task to plait two serviceable ropes from the stout fabric which, spliced together, were a good eleven feet in length. The drop from the window she estimated at fifteen feet. Allow half a yard for the anchor-knot and she could still reach ground without difficulty.

Noiselessly she edged the ponderous four-poster bed across the room until the curve of one post touched the sill. She attached her cord firmly to the post, tested her knot with all her weight, blew out the candle and accomplished the descent without mishap. A prowling dog yelped and took to his heels, barking distractedly as he ran. Becky cowered into a leafless bush, but there was no movement within the house. Her husband's windows remained dark.

She gathered her skirts about her and fled lightly down the slope.

Gurdon Stockwell spent a fitful night. In his waking spells he considered his actions dispassionately. It was not enough; his wife must be brought to perceive and admit the justice of his course.

At seven o'clock, having dressed himself, he took the massive key and stepped across the hallway. He heard no movement within. She was sleeping until this late hour—another cause for reproof.

Under his pressure the door opened, and upon a scene of astonishment. He noted first the displaced bed.

"Mrs. Stockwell!" he cried sharply. "Obed——" His utterance was checked in his gullet. He had spied the plaited linen dangling from the post. For an instant he was convulsed with horror. Memory set forth in grisly detail another opened door, and back of it a rope, stretched taut with its dreadful burden. Gathering his forces, he strode to the window.

This cord was not taut. It swayed, limp in the morning breeze. Thank God, then; this was only an evasion, nothing worse. Yet it was bad enough. The scandal! What black ingratitude from one whom he had elevated and cherished! Mingled with his just resentment was the cruel pang of his loss: the young, fresh, vital loveliness which was abandoning him. For something told him that this might be the end.

He stood in thought, biting a grievous lip. Obedience must be found and fetched back. There was just a possibility that it might be managed in secret. She could hardly have left the city —not alone and by night. Where could she have sheltered? Who would dare to afford sanctuary to the fugitive wife of Gurdon Stockwell?

A note! Surely she would have left a note. He made a feverish search. Nothing! Incongruously an advertisement shaped itself in his frenetic brain: "My wife, Obedience Stockwell, having left my bed and board without due occasion, I offer one penny and a bucket of ashes for her safe return and warn all and sundry to allow her no monies against my credit."

He went out, carefully locking the door of the vacant chamber. For as long as possible he must maintain the pretence of her presence. Mrs. Stockwell was unfortunately indisposed.

Returning to his room, he shaved with a firm hand. He descended the stairway and spoke to old Jeshurun, busy with the dishes.

"Mrs. Stockwell will not be down to breakfast. You may prepare a tray for me to take to her."

The Negro regarded him with a fallen jaw. Gurdon Stockwell's restraint broke.

"What ails you, you fool?" he snapped.

"Miss' Stockwell, she a-settin' at table now," Jeshurun said.

What most discomposed Gurdon Stockwell as he entered the dining-room was his wife's calm. As he seated himself, she looked up from tempering his coffee with hot milk.

"Good morning, Mr. Stockwell."

"Good morning."

"Jeshurun, Mr. Stockwell's cup."

"Yessum."

"The milk is thin this morning," she informed her husband.

"Instruct Whiting to change cows, Jeshurun."

"Yassuh."

"Have you any instructions for the day?" his wife asked. This was formula.

"None."

Silence settled upon the meal. Gurdon Stockwell did not even glance at the morning journal, a bad sign. Worse, he ate but a light meal. As soon as the servant retired, he gave his directions.

"Come to my study," he said, and strode out.

She entered the room after him.

"Close the door," he said.

He seated himself at his desk, without bidding her to a chair. She took one and waited. He turned to confront her with a formidable visage.

"You absented yourself from my roof last night."

"I cannot sleep in a locked room."

"Where did you pass the night?"

"With Gypsy Vilas."

"You make a low choice of associates," he replied grimly. "There will be no place for such as she in this town presently." He pondered. "I shall compose a set of rules for your future observance, day *and* night."

"It will be nothing new, Mr. Stockwell. I have lived under your rules before."

He winced, touched in his pride as always by any reference to her factory days. "These will regulate the conduct of a wife," he said, with stress upon the final word.

"Or a slave?" She regretted the taunt as soon as it had passed her lips. She had not meant to give him needless provocation.

"That reply," he said, "proves how ill you appreciate your privileges and accept your responsibilities."

He launched upon a disquisition on the subject of the mutual relation of husband and wife and the duties inherent therein. Since the head of the family was responsible for his spouse's behaviour, it followed that he must be endowed with the authority to control it. Such authority was enforceable by any reasonable method at the husband's choice. With what he intended for a happy touch of humour, he quoted the decision of a Delaware court upholding wife-beating with a rod not exceeding a half-inch in diameter.

Obedience did not laugh. In fact she hardly knew what he was saying.

She reflected that she was glad there would be no children of their union. Not if she could help it! Gurdon Stockwell was sealing the fate of their marriage with every righteous word that he uttered.

Now he said, claiming her attention, "How am I to be sure that you will not repeat your evasion?"

"I have a horror of being shut in," Becky said. "If you lock my door there are still the windows."

"You remind me. They shall be cross-barred. A six-inch mesh may check your purpose."

"I think you would hardly do that." What was this! The minx was actually smiling at him.

"Do not deceive yourself," he said. "I shall put it in hand today."

"Invisible bars?" she asked slyly.

"What is this jest?" he demanded.

"A jest, indeed, when visiting Troy observes that the Hon. Gurdon Stockwell finds it needful to keep his wife behind bars. What a tidbit for the next Halcyon supper!"

He must not show his discomfiture. "I shall find a way," he asserted impressively. It was the best that he could do at the moment.

She was no longer smiling, but was regarding him with a look which seemed surprisingly to have in it an element of pity.

"I am truly sorry to have proven so unsatisfactory a wife, Mr. Stockwell," she said in a low voice. "May I go now?"

He made no answer. She left the room.

SEVEN

A QUARTER of a million years before Becky Webb hired out to the Eureka, the ice demon who was then in charge of the continent, thrust his glacial fingers southward, playfully pried out a chunk of mountain from what is now Canada and tossed it into the river above what became Troy when man had crawled upon the scene.

There it remained, a bit of alien geology, with plants and trees of its own, quite distinct from the vegetation of the adjoining terrain. The transplanted landscape was picturesque but too rugged for easy farming. The one house ever to rise from its soil had been built by the proprietor of a gravel pit of superior quality. When it burned down, Mr. Sadler moved away leaving nothing behind him on the deserted island but his name.

Opposite the western end of the island, a swift, bright stream issued from the mainland and poured into the broader current. Salmon lurked there. It was a favourite resort of Guy Roy when he had problems on his mind.

On this clear May day the fish were not biting. In an hour of casting he had taken but one, and that an undersized grilse. He reeled in his line, settled himself comfortably in the stern of the buoyant periauger and left the rest to the whim of wind and eddy. A flaw of the offshore breeze propelled the light dugout towards midstream and the island. When the shadow of the bluff was already over him, the boatman caught up his paddle and sheered off.

The change of direction brought into view a trickle of smoke issuing from the screen of underbrush on the cliff's face. Guy recalled hearing that there were secret caves on the island. Probably some water-gypsy or fugitive swingkettle, having stolen a boat, was harbouring there to cook his meal. Guy was paddling back into the current when the shrubbery parted and a man emerged. He was carrying a leather bucket. Sliding down the short declivity, he edged out upon a dead tree-trunk to dip up a pailful. Only then did he catch sight of the craft nearby. He started sharply and at first made as if to conceal himself, but perceived the futility of any such attempt.

"Hullo," he said guardedly.

"Hullo, Barlow," Guy returned.

"What you doing here?"

"If it comes to that," Guy returned, with smiling amenity, "what are you? I thought you were in jail."

"Leave of absence," the agitator grinned.

"No business of mine," Guy said. "If you want it that way, I haven't even seen you today."

Barlow replied cheerfully: "Oh, that don't matter. I'll be back by locking-in time. What *are* you doing here, though?" He answered himself, on sudden thought, "Looking for your horse, I bet."

"No," Guy replied in some surprise. "My horse is in the stable."

"Somebody's ain't. It's gallivanting around the other side of the island."

"Riderless?"

"Couldn't rightly tell at this distance."

"Not very safe around there, is it?"

"What ain't safe about it?"

"The abandoned gravel-pit."

Cash shrugged. "Nothing to me. It ain't my horse."

"I'll take a look when I round the point," the canoeist said. "A man who didn't know the ground might go into that pit and not be found for weeks."

A voice issued in hollow cadence from the cave. "Where's that water, Barlow?"

"Couple of friends of mine inside," Cash explained hastily. "Sort of a picnic."

A bulky form appeared above, and now Guy knew why the voice had seemed familiar. It was Luther Simms. He greeted the intruder soberly.

"This is a private occasion."

"I was about to move on."

"Private and to be kept private," the big man added significantly. "Some friends stepped in for a bite."

"Blackamoors?" Guy asked quickly. It would be quite in the Simms line to be aiding fugitives to Canada.

"No. But just as quiet for the present."

Guy smiled. "It wouldn't have any connection with the Amsterdam turn-out and riot last week, I presume?"

M

"What you don't hear'll never give you the earache," Cash
Barlow grunted.

"It's safe with me," Guy assured the two men. "I'm not
interested in reward money."

"I'm sure you're not," Simms said gently. "He's staunch,
Cassius."

"He's a good judge of plug," Barlow admitted more amiably,
mindful of the young man's earlier benefactions.

Guy resumed his paddle, waved them a farewell and put his
shoulders into the stroke. The periauger surged forward, rounded
the point, and fought the swifter current on the far side. He might
have been sixty or seventy yards out when he saw the horse and
with a great leap of the heart, recognized the rider.

She was mounted crosswise, loping freely and jauntily away
from him and towards the brush which masked the brink of the
treacherous chasm. He stood up and shouted through cupped
hands. If she heard, she made no sign. To his vast relief, she
turned her mount short of the danger. But on the next turn—for
she was evidently coursing up and down the stretch—what
guarantee was there that she might not push too near? He waited
for her to reach the point nearest him, and called again. Pressing
close to the cliff, she headed her eyes to gaze out over the stream.

"Danger!" he shouted, and again, "danger!" He made
energetic and dissuasive signals.

She shook an uncomprehending head. Uncertain as to
whether he had made any impression, he caught up his paddle
and impelled the dugout towards the shore.

The soft cliffs at the turn of the island, mined with burrows
of kingfishers and sand swallows, descended in a bold slope to
the ribbon of strand. Guy made the turn, checked his progress
hailed and listened. His quick eye had noted a fissure in the wall
Driving towards it, he beached his boat and set himself to the
ascent. Small trees and shrubs aided him. When he emerged
upon the meadow, she was sitting her mount, idly waiting.

"Don't you know any better than that?" he panted.

She gazed at him mutely.

"Plunging back and forth like a mad woman."

"Why! You're angry with me," she breathed wonderingly.

"Do you want to be killed?" he demanded.

She looked about her, then down at the high grass. "I don't
see anything. Is it snakes?"

"There are snakes, too. But you might have ridden over into the pit."

"Where? I see no pit."

"That's the danger. The brink is beneath the undergrowth yonder. It's treacherous soil. You were close upon it, that last turn."

"Thank you for your officiousness,[1] Mr. Roy," she said, with courteous formality.

A moment of silence followed. "How did you get here?" he asked.

"The ford."

"You've been here before?"

"Yes."

"Why do you come?"

She stared out over the river. "I don't know. I saw the island. It looked lonely. I wanted to get where I could breathe. Don't you ever long to be alone?"

He smiled. "I might take the hint and leave you, except that you wouldn't be alone on the island."

"Who?" Her brows arched upward.

He shook his head. "Not that I think there is any danger from them. But you might have been frightened."

"I'm not easy to frighten," she said indifferently.

Another silence fell. The roan whickered softly. Guy made an effort to establish an easy status between them. "How do you like Troy?" he inquired conversationally.

"Oh, very well," she said briskly, catching the cue and relieved to have the insensibly growing strain relaxed.

"You doubtless find plenty of occupation for your days."

"Indeed, yes. My household. My church duties. The Ladies' Circle. My—my friends. Troy is a very affording society."

Another hiatus. Then, "Did you attend last week's dramatic performance?"

"No. Mr. Stockwell does not approve playgoing."

The talk went dead again. She felt that it was her turn to restore it.

"I trust your business is prospering, Mr. Roy."

"Business? Oh yes. Very kind of you to inquire."

That led no further. Becky gazed out over the river. Guy examined the turf at their feet. Pegasus whisked at the flies

[1] Helpfulness.

which had discovered his welcome presence. Again Becky took up the burden.

"You warned me of a pitfall. Will you show it to me? I shall be coming here again."

"When?" he questioned eagerly.

"Oh!" she said, startled by the swiftness of the return. "Any time. I don't know."

"Sadler's gravel-bed is yonder. Shall I lead the way?"

He strode ahead of the horse until they reached the fringe of maythorn concealing the long-abandoned excavation. The thickly set and stunted trees were in full flower. Still making conversation, he said, "This is the only place hereabouts where this giant thorn grows."

She made little account of the information at the moment, her mind being too intent upon other matters. Later she was to remember it.

"It's cruel pretty," she said, and leaned out with grasping fingers.

"Mind the thorns," he cried. "They're like scimitars."

He spoke too late. Two thin weals of welling scarlet streaked the back of her hand. With a little ejaculation of pain she set the warm curve of her mouth to the scratches. At that gesture of instinct Guy's self-control broke.

"Becky!" It was a cry of longing.

She twisted in her seat to look down at him with wondering, troubled eyes.

He reached up and drew her down into his arms. She lifted to him a mouth that was at first unresistant, then eager, then a clinging fire.

"Becky," he said. "My love. My little love."

She had known man's passion and revolted from it with an instinct that was still virgin. Now it kindled her to her nerve-ends. The blood pulsed in her temples, in her lips, behind her closed lids. When she drew away to take gasping breath, the faint, wild fragrance of the thorn plucked at her heart as if it were part of the swooning enchantment engulfing her senses. She thought, I shall never forget this, not as long as I live; not a glint of the sun, not a breath of the wind, not a ripple on the river; never, never, never. She closed her eyes again, as if to hold the print indelibly on her brain, and again yielded wholly to his kisses.

At length she leaned back from him, pushing a bright wisp of her hair into place.

He said fiercely: "You can't go back to him. You don't love him."

"No."

"Do you love me?"

"Yes," she said, unhesitant.

"Then . . . ?" he said.

"But I'm married—married—married!" she cried. "I'm trapped."

"Marriages have been broken before." He held out his arms to her. "Since we love each other," he pleaded.

She thought, "If I go to him now, I'm lost—and I wouldn't care."

Something within her resisted the urge upon her passion. She said: "Guy, I'm frightened. I've never felt like this before."

"All the more reason," he said. "Will you go away with me, my love?"

"Where?"

"Anywhere together."

"To live in sin?"

"I don't know the word," he said recklessly. "Not with you."

She said slowly: "Guy, I've been faithless to him in every other way. Don't ask me to do this."

"What else is there for us?" he persisted. "He'd have to divorce you."

"Don't think it. Did you ever know him to give up anything he once held?"

"Let me go to him and tell him how it is with us."

"No, Guy. No, love. Not yet. Wait," she pleaded.

"For what?"

"How can I tell? Give me time to think. Oh!" she cried piteously. "Can't you see? My whole world has changed around me between a breath and a breath. And you ask me to choose my way."

He bent and pressed his lips to the palm of her hand. "For me, all is a plain path. You are the core and centre of my life. I knew it from the moment when I saw you at the train."

"I am a wife," she said soberly. "Bound by a vow." He gave a gesture of revolt. "Oh, you are asking me to do nothing but what I long to do with every drop of blood in my veins. I am asking you only to wait."

He said sadly, "What else can I do?"

Heedful of injury, she broke a spray from the nearest dwarf tree to fix it in his coat. "A memento and a symbol," she murmured.

"Too pat to our occasion," he returned sombrely. "Are there to be more thorns than flowers in our love?"

She smiled and turned the scarified back of her hand to him. "I am the first to be wounded, Guy."

"No hurt nor shame shall come to you through me, my darling," he said passionately. "But I must see you again. Give me that much, Becky."

She considered. "A week from today. Here. Now catch Pegasus for me." Her last word as she rode away was, "Don't make it too hard for me, Guy."

EIGHT

"Look, wench," Gypsy Vilas protested, "this is a factory. It's eleven o'clock. I'm a workin' gal."

"I don't care," Becky said desperately. "I've got to have somebody to talk to."

"What pebble's stickin' in your crop?"

"I can't tell you here."

"Meet me outside at noon."

Before the church clock had finished its slow recital, Gypsy was on the pavement with her friend. They walked to the water-front and sat down on the step of a vacant mill.

Becky drew a quick, broken breath. "Gypsy, I can't live with my husband any more."

"Hullo! What nonsense's bit the brat now?"

"Now that I know what it is," the young wife went on, hardly conscious, in her self-absorption, of the purport of her words. "What it might be."

Gypsy studied the rapt face. "That night you roped out and bunked with me. Where did you go before?" she demanded abruptly.

"Nowhere."

"Look at me, wench. If it wasn't then, it was some time. Something has happened to you. You ain't the same gal. And I reckon I know what it was that happened."

"You don't! It didn't! I scarcely know myself. It was all so—so chancewise."

"That's what they always say," returned the derisive Gypsy. "And it wasn't that night?"

"No. Yesterday afternoon."

The other gave an exclamation. "Guy Roy! The dirty dungeon!"[1]

"He isn't! It wasn't his fault. It wasn't what you think, either," she finished defensively.

"Jumpin' Jabez! When he came in yesterday so late, I knew there was something. His boots were all sandy, and he hadn't so much as cleaned 'em. Where had you two been? Down the river?"

---

[1] Jon Juan, presumptively. Gypsy may have attended the current performance of *The Faithless Suitor*.

"Yes," Becky broke. "Oh, Gypsy! I love him so cruel much!"

"Mmph! Whenja find that out?"

"I always have, I expect. Since I was a child."

"Ay-yah," the other confirmed thoughtfully. "I kinda remember how you had a crush on him when you was in the mill. Well, you ain't a child any more. You're a woman. Hell, you're a lady!"

Becky muttered something of mutinous import.

"All right. Tell me about your meet-up."

Becky gave a fragmentary, excited and emotionally confused report of the *rencontre* with Guy Roy.

"Uh-huh," her friend commented. "Not that I believe all of it. Sadler's gravel pit, huh? You keep away from there, wench."

Becky made no response. Her friend leaned forward to peer into her face. "Are you figurin' to meet him again?"

"Oh, Gypsy! How can I help it!"

The older girl wagged a sagacious head. "I know how that'll end."

"I hate you when you talk that way, Gypsy," Becky flamed.

"Hate away. But mind what I tell you and you'll get over this," Gypsy prophecied.

Becky stared out across the shining river to where Sadler's Island formed a smudged outline against the far blue. Gypsy rose.

"Don't go yet." Becky picked a stalk of ladybedstraw and began to shred it. Hardly above her breath she said, "He—he tried to get into my room last night."

Gypsy fairly jumped. "Who? Guy Roy?"

"*No!* Mr. Stockwell."

"Well, who's got a better right?"

Becky's whole face quivered. "Gypsy, won't you understand? I can't go on with it."

The other considered the situation and put a sly question. "He'll go to other women. How'd you like that?"

"I don't care what he does, if only he'd let me alone," the wife said passionately.

Gypsy gave her small comfort. "Here's my word to you. You made your bed. You made it soft and easy. Now lie quiet. And let no outsider share it. Gotta get back to my collars now."

Becky changed colour, but said, "I'll walk back with you."

They parted at the near corner. The forewoman got back with two minutes to spare. Mary Haynes was waiting for her in the hallway.

"What ails the boss?" Mary asked anxiously.

"How would I know?" Gypsy answered.

"He's barred himself in and I can't get anything out of him.'

"What d'you want to get out of him?"

"New hands. And quickly."

"Where'll you put 'em?" the other asked in surprise. "We're jammed in already like a stink of salt mackerel."

Mary whistled. "Haven't you heard? About the big turn-out at Amsterdam?"

"What's that got to do with us?"

"They've taken eight of our best workers and shipped them up there by canal packet."

"Who has?"

"The cottonocracy. All expenses paid."

Gypsy whistled in turn. "And new orders comin' in every post."

"We're running behind now. We'll lose our trade if we don't look sharp."

"Put an advertisement in Printer Crolius's journal."

"He wouldn't print it."

"The streets are full of hands."

"They're afraid of the ban."

Gypsy delivered herself of a powerful expletive. "I'll find some that aint."

"You can't hire without Mr. Roy's say-so."

"I'll get his say-so."

Gypsy knocked discreetly on the office door. "What do you want? I'm busy," Guy called.

She entered and explained about the raid on their workrooms. To her relief, he listened with frowning interest.

"When did this happen?"

"They didn't check their time this morning, Mary says. It's those bastards on the committee."

He shook himself like a terrier. "We'll give 'em a fight, if that's what they want."

She brightened. "I hoped that was the way you'd feel about it. I'll bet I can round up a dozen gals."

"Get all there's room for." He waved a hand towards the heaped-up desk. "There are orders enough there to keep us going, full head, through the summer. Too many orders for this small plant. I'm negotiating now for roomier quarters."

"When's our rent-time up here?"

"July. I'm considering a floor in the new Cannon Block."

She regarded him uncertainly before inquiring, "Have you spoken to Mr. Cannon?"

"No. I'm leaving that to Taylor Paulding, the land factor. He's working up a business in local rentals. Something new."

"It's gettin' on towards July," she said significantly. "If I was you, I'd get it settled."

Such was her earnestness that he pushed the piled-up papers to one side, wrote a note, and despatched it to the real-estate man by a temporarily idle clean-up girl.

Taylor Paulding answered the summons promptly in his suicide gig, so termed because the high wheels made it top heavy, hence fashionably dangerous, hence again favoured by true-blue Corinthian youth. He hitched his horse to the ringed block provided for the purpose, and strode into the office, flicking his morocco boot with his whippety cane. Stiffening his back, he gave the Halcyon salute: chin up and three fingers to the brow. Guy responded in due form.

"What's Cannon's price?" he asked.

"No price. No space," the factor answered laconically. Producing an enamelled box, he offered the other snuff which was declined.

"But I read his advertisements in the prints no later than yesterday," Guy protested.

"Better try some of this," the caller invited, waving the box. "It's a fine old custom; very much the thing." He inhaled, sneezed heartily, and repeated, "No space."

"Look further, then," Guy directed.

"I have. Same thing."

"We can't stay here." With an impatient gesture he indicated the cramped quarters.

"You never spoke a truer word. You can't, not if you wanted to."

Guy stared.

"The premises are rented out from under you as of July 1st."

"That's their game, is it? Well, busy yourself and get something better."

"There's nothing to be had. Not for your business. Plain fact is, Guy, you're an undesirable tenant. This ten-hour game of yours doesn't commend itself to the respectable citizenry of Troy."

"You won't believe it, Taylor, but what the respectable citizenry of Troy thinks will never keep me awake of nights."

"That's your trouble," the other complained. "You take up with such scalawags as Cassius Barlow and his strikers in preference."

"When and where have I taken up with Cash Barlow?"

"He and the rest of the short-day fomenters are bragging around town that all the factories will have to follow the lead of the Montague & Roy Company."

"I can't help what they say. They're not running my business any more than my esteemed fellow citizens of the Mill Owners Association. And be damned to 'em, one and all," he concluded gaily.

"They'll run you out of town before snowfall," Paulding predicted. "Consider what you're doing, Guy. All your respectable friends oppose you on this. Haven't you had some trade difficulties lately?"

"Several. Slow deliveries. Material held up in the warehouses. Misunderstandings with the factors. They might be accidents. And then, again, they might not."

"What about your bank loans?"

"They've raised my interest to twelve-and-a-half per centum. Money has tightened, they claim."

"It hasn't. Your own cousin, too. Would you be surprised if it went to fifteen on the next loan?"

"Is that your opinion?"

"I think it highly probable."

Guy consulted his watch. "I may as well have that settled at once. Will you give me a lift? Or do you think my company might compromise you?"

"Don't be a damned fool," his friend adjured him.

Equipping himself with certain essential papers from his desk, Guy mounted into the gig and was set down at the bank.

The Merchants & Manufacturers Deposit & Savings Bank was the largest financial institution short of Albany. Its location was central, on the ground floor between Heartt Brothers' book store and Harmon Teale's human hair emporium. Due to press of patronage, it had recently taken on an extra room, making two in all. The front windows were reinforced with wire mesh and the door was iron-sheathed against possible malefaction. In one corner stood a large desk liberally perforated with pigeon holes. The other was occupied by a No. 2 Herring Safe whose massive construction served mainly to reassure the eye, since it could have been cracked by any reasonably accomplished burglar with a bent hairpin. There was a stove designed for burning costly anthracite coal, a chair at the desk and another for any patron of sufficient importance to be seated.

The bank was open to the public on Wednesdays and Saturdays. It received and safeguarded deposits but paid no interest on them. Mr. Gurdon Stockwell took a modest pride in being its head, the youngest bank president, it was said, in the State of New York.

Into this sedate atmosphere Guy Roy entered with a cheerful insouciance which accorded ill with the prevailing hush. Gurdon Stockwell rose to greet his caller with precise courtesy. "I am glad to see you here, Cousin. How can I serve you?"

"I need a further accommodation, Gurdon. Will you look over these orders?"

He took the papers from his pocket and laid them before the banker.

It was the custom of the trade for a manufacturer, upon receiving an order for his product, to present it at the bank as a guaranty of his capacity to pay, and draw what money he needed to meet the cost of his materials. The process was so well established as to be practically automatic if the orders were from recognized firms. Several of Guy's were from first-class establishments.

The banker scrutinized them carefully. If he was surprised at the magnitude of the figures, he showed no sign of it. "I see that your trade is increasing," he said.

"Yes, we're not doing badly," Guy said modestly.

"But, as to the character of the security, that is another matter."

"Character! Bramhall and Stokes! Whitehall's Ladies Emporium? The State Street Fair? Good Heavens, man! What do you want? A lien on the Federal Treasury?"

"Payable in sixty to ninety days. These orders are revocable," Stockwell pointed out.

"Have you ever known these firms to default?"

"No-o-o."

"Six thousand, four hundred and fifty dollars of trade there, and I need fifteen hundred dollars at most. Where can you hire out your money more safely?"

"We might consider it." Stockwell assumed the banker's plural, which, quite as often as the editorial "we", affords a convenient impersonality. "I do not affirm it positively, but we might consider such a loan at twenty-five per centum."

"Say that again," Guy requested.

The other obliged. "Twenty-five per centum," he repeated, and supplemented it with, "in advance of loan, you understand."

"I'll see you in hell," Guy said.

Gurdon Stockwell retracted his chin. "This is not the language of commerce," he protested.

"Purely personal," Guy assured him. "All in good fellowship."

The banker riffled through the papers again, before stacking and binding them in a neat packet. "If the security were more desirable——" he began, when his cousin cut in.

"Are you sure, Gurdy, that the desirability of the applicant is not more in question?"

Gurdon winced, as always, at the diminutive which comported, so ill with his dignity of position. "Character is always a factor," he admitted cautiously.

Guy restored the papers to his pocket. "There are banks in Albany," he remarked.

"There are," Stockwell agreed. "I have friends in financial circles there." He paused, and added with his evasive half-smile, "They might question why a Troy man of business feels obligated to go beyond his own city to secure credit."

"I see." The effect of casual and friendly conversation was admirably maintained in Guy's manner. "And as for the Rivermen's down the street, I suppose . . . Eh?"

Stockwell nodded. "President Paulding and I see eye to eye in this affair."

"Putting it bluntly, I may whistle for my loan."

Gurdon Stockwell leaned forward. His manner became almost pleading. "It is not for me to dictate your conduct, Cousin, but I wish from my heart that you could be brought to see the folly of your ways."

"Referring to the management of Montague & Roy, I presume?"

"This labour-pandering policy of yours can lead to but one

end," Gurdon said. "I make no threat, you understand. I warn you in all friendliness that your present course will involve you in certain catastrophe."

"By your procurement and that of your fellows."

"We shall adopt such measures as are necessary to protect the best interests of our community."

"All from the highest motives! Always from the highest motives! It must be a strain to be so consistently high-minded."

"I disclaim any such pretence," the banker said with some heat.

"Pretence? Far from it. The strange thing about you, Hurdy-Gurdy, is that you mean so damned well. You're so eternally sure that you're right."

"In this matter I am."

"Let it rest. I didn't mean to be offensively personal."

Stockwell took the opening. "I trust that we are both gentlemen and can discuss these questions without injurious implications. Do you appreciate, Cousin, that you have not crossed my threshold since my marriage?"

"Haven't I?" Guy murmured. He was about to conjure up some lame excuse in connection with stress of business when he changed his mind. "Do you wish me to come to your house? Are you quite sure, Gurdon?"

"That is a strange question. You are my nearest male kin in town. Your absence becomes notable."

The visitor took up his castor and cane. "I will come," he promised, "when invited by you and Mrs. Stockwell."

Considering the casual nature of the social interchange, Gurdon Stockwell failed to understand the tone of levity, almost of recklessness, which characterized the other's acceptance.

Guy Roy had all but laughed in his face.

NINE

LUTHER SIMMS was in town and Cassius Barlow was out of jail. This, in the minds of the mill-owners, boded ill for the public weal of Troy. Certainly the trouble-mongering Simms had not brought in a lawyer to free Barlow without some malign purpose.

In jail, Barlow was not subject to militia regulations. Freed, he was. The military authorities at once laid him by the heels, following a well established practice. With the exception of a few exempted classes, every mechanic was liable for three days' service in the year with full military equipment to be provided at his own expense. Failing this, he must pay a fine or go to prison. This civic duty was commonly winked at by the authorities. Nobody wished to interfere with a workman who was faithful to his job and submissive to his employer. But let a man play truant or manifest seditious sentiments, and the majesty of the law was invoked; he was summoned to the service. He must now buy a musket and uniform. Rarely could he command the ready money. Upon presenting himself without proper accessories, he might expect a term in debtor's jail where he must maintain himself or go hungry.

It was an admirable system; simple, expeditious and effectual, operating to the discomfiture of the unruly and the edification of all good citizens.

Barlow rested his defence mainly upon an aggrieved repetition of the query, "And where would *I* get twenty dollars to pay for a musket and uniform?"

The fine was twelve dollars, in default of which the delinquent must go to debtor's jail. To the discomfiture of the court martial, the accused confidently thrust his hand into his pocket, but withdrew it.

"The law says I got to get me a musket?" he said, addressing the presiding colonel.

"It does."

"Will the law learn me to shoot?"

"You will receive the regulation instruction in gunnery."

"I'll buy a musket," Barlow said. "I'll find the money somehow. I'll learn to shoot." He turned to stare thoughtfully at Major Gurdon Stockwell who was present. "Straight," he added.

Colonel Howland, presiding, leaned forward. "Is this a covert threat, my man?" he demanded sternly. "If not, what is its purport?"

"I might want to shoot a didapper duck for my breakfast," Barlow explained mildly.

Luther Simms, who had attended the session, loaned Barlow the money for the required equipment.

"Quiet does it, my boy," he warned. "You talk too much."

"I thought you wanted me to talk."

"So I do. In the right place. At the right time. To your fellow workers."

"With the mill-owners running the town? They'll have me back in jail quick-o."

"I'll get you out again. Go forth and preach the message."

Cash Barlow's message was vehement to the verge of violence. He haunted the factory exits, button-holing the mechanics, male and female, delivering inflammatory harangues, instilling discontent. The burden of his preachments was shorter hours. Shorter hours or a general turn-out!

When Barlow, arrested again as he expected to be, found himself facing a Magistrates' Bench of three, with Alderman Gurdon Stockwell presiding, he resigned himself to martyrdom in the cause. The complainant was Owner Fosmire of the Lark at Morn where the prisoner had delivered one of his most passionate harangues, and the charge, incitement to riot. The full influence of the Mill Owners Association was understood to be back of the action.

To the distress and scandal of his colleagues, the president of the Association and leading proprietor of them all deserted the cause. Magistrate Stockwell thus addressed the prisoner at the bar:

"It were better for the city of Troy, which you dishonour, for the commerce of the community, which you seek to disrupt, for the cause of labour, which you distort and misrepresent—it were better for all of these, I say, that you were safely hanged and out of the way. This is not the last time we shall have you before us. Let me warn you, Cassius Barlow, that the smallest incitement to violence on your part will meet with the sternest reprisals. On the present count I am constrained to acquit you. Malign though your influence is, false and corrupt your doctrines, vile though your character and conduct, nevertheless you are a citizen of the great State of New York and entitled to the protection of its laws. This court will abridge no privilege of free speech in your case which any other citizen enjoys. You are discharged."

By virtue of this decision Cash Barlow became something of a hero to the local working class. Appreciating his usefulness to the cause, Luther Simms, canniest and most devoted of leaders, briefed him on how far he could go within the limits of the law.

"That is a just man, Stockwell," he told his disciple; "a man of principle who will live up to his duty as he sees it. And now I have requested the mill-owners to accord the workers' committee a hearing before their body."

"They'll never do it," Barlow asserted.

"Appoint your committee and see."

The memorial from the labourers was received by the Mill Owners Association with an outburst of wrath. Hear the representatives of a lawless and rootless union? To what heights of insolence would these scurvy fellows go next?

The younger element, however, were for receiving the agitators and hearing what they had to say. Gurdon Stockwell supported this view.

"Let these fellows hang themselves with their own rope," he said grimly.

After heated debate a motion permitting, not inviting, the committee to come at a certain hour on a specified day prevailed. It was stipulated that only Troy mechanics would be acceptable. Luther Simms would not be admitted. A limit of three was set to the deputation.

Gurdon Stockwell, in the chair, took the initiative upon the appearance of the trio.

"Stand here." He indicated a space to the side of the rostrum where he sat. "Who speaks for you?"

Two of the men nudged the third to step forward. Barlow, attempting an air of independence, said, "I'm the chairman."

"You are petitioning for a twelve-hour day?"

"Yes."

"What good end can be served by so radical an abbreviation?"

"To allow us more time in the evenings for moral and intellectual improvement." The speaker had returned the conventional answer.

"Doubtless your next demand will be for an improved wage," Banker Paulding said.

"Stick to our point, Cash," the second delegate advised. He

N

was an unemployed "blackie", the factory furnace which he stoked being cold. "Don't let 'em put you off. Even a ox won't work sixteen hours of the day."

"It's the hours, not the pay," Barlow insisted.

The chairman continued to address Barlow directly. "Can you cut down hours and not cut down product? No. Can you cut down product and not reduce receipts? No, again. And when you cut down receipts, do you not impair the avails which go to pay your wages?" Chairman Stockwell spoke with the confidence of relentless logic. "That is simple mathematics. Can you refute it?"

"Mr. Guy Roy pays standard or better," the hautboy driver said stoutly.

"On a ten-hour day," the blackie supported him.

Magistrate Strong pointed a weighted finger at Barlow. "Is this Mr. Guy Roy implicated in your purposes?"

The mechanic blinked. "I dunno what you mean, Mister."

"I will be explicit. Is he incriminated in this conspiracy? For such I must term it, if concerted action be proven to undermine our system of employment."

"Mr. Guy Roy's got no this-or-that with us."

"Your honours," the cartman advanced timidly, "our petition lies before you."

"Leave it and get out," Fosmire directed.

"And don't come back unless you crave lodgings at county expense," the magistrate warned.

"That's the way the honest working man gets treated when he tries to stand for his rights," Cash Barlow protested.

The meeting adjourned.

The collar firm's enforced change of base to the Mansion House, the only available quarters, had been costly. In the cramped hotel nook which was now his office, Guy Roy conferred with his two trusted aides.

"We lost a hundred and eighty dollars and forty-four cents last month," said Mary Haynes, ruefully contemplating a neat and forbidding array of figures.

"We're still doing business," Guy said.

"How long can we keep on?" Mary inquired.

It was a question which Guy had been putting to himself frequently. His income, which was ample to maintain him as a youth of fashion and even of luxury, was being pretty well exhausted by the recurrent trade demands for ready money. Moreover, his receipts were dwindling. Dividends had been reduced or intermitted. The Eureka had passed its quarterly for two dates. This was probably a justified measure, due to the stringency in the cotton fabric market. On the other hand, it might be one of Gurdon Stockwell's measures of strategy directed against Guy with a view to crippling him.

The two employees left him to his consideration of the inexorable figures. Compute them as he would, they summed up to the same disheartening purport: take your loss and quit while there is yet time. The Montague & Roy Company was more than a deficit for its head; it was a drain upon his last resource, or bade fair to be.

All right; he could meet the strain for a while. If matters grew no worse he could hold out for at least six months. Yes, for eight or nine months by cutting his personal expenditure to the bone. By that time there should be a turn in his favour; just how he did not know, but it was in his fibre to stick and hope. He would go out himself and drum up new accounts. He would present a balance sheet so convincing that Emperor Nick Biddle himself would be glad to advance money from the nearest branch of his Bank of the United States.

A few months of grace. Not enough. Not nearly enough! For better or worse, he could not, by the most elastic mathematics, stretch out those dollars-and-cents, debit-and-credit columns, to cover three years. And it would be more than three years before he would come into his trusteed funds: twenty-five thousand dollars plus accumulations. A very pretty little fortune. If only by some financial legerdemain the business could survive the long interval, he could cock the snook of triumph at Gurdon Stockwell and his fellow connivers.

Conditions were more likely to worsen than improve in the local collar trade. What then? Move to a less-hostile environment? Rochester, for instance, a city of prosperity and progress, hospitable to new ventures. Intimation had reached him that he and his collars would be welcome there. But—leave Troy? Quit under fire? Let the Mill Owners Association point him out as a horrible example of what happened to an upstart who defied their will? Not by a damned sight! Nobody was going to drive him out of the city of his choice, not while he had a sixpence left to fight with.

Besides, there was Becky.

TEN

OBEDIENT to her husband's instructions, Becky wrote an elegant and formal invitation for supper to Guy Roy, Esq. Would he accept? She told herself that she hoped not. Hungry though she was for the sight of him, she felt that such an encounter would be gallingly unsatisfying, a harsh emotional strain upon both of them. Notwithstanding, her heart leapt when she received his affirmative reply, couched in terms as conventional as her own.

On the Saturday set for the event, her husband sent for her to attend him in the dining-room where he was composing the rum juleps with his own careful hand.

He looked her over critically and vouchsafed a word of compliment for her costume. Had he known, she reflected grimly, for whom she had so carefully arrayed herself, he might have been more chary of his approval. She was happily conscious of looking her best. And, indeed, in her crimson sarsanet slashed with green and with true-lace ruffles at wrist and throat, she was an apparition to stir the blood of men.

For her the supper was an ordeal. Except for her polite and cool greeting upon his arrival, she had exchanged no word with Guy. He sat mid-table, too far away for communication. To all appearances he was enjoying himself thoroughly. How could he be so animated and easy, she thought enviously. Not only was he entertaining his partner (whom Becky at once disliked for a forward little hussy), but he was taking full part in the general conversation which held to the high level of trade conditions, the advent of Monsieur Darré, instructor in French and Social Manners; the programme of Improving Discourses by President Sereno Dwight, of the Hamilton College faculty, and the plans for the great camp meeting projected for July at Thompson's Grove.

Try as she might to bear her appointed part in the sparkling exchanges, the hostess found her attention wandering to the place where Guy Roy sat. She maintained with increasing effort the necessary responses to her neighbours.

At the far end of the table her husband delivered his oracular dicta in well-modulated discourse. Immersed in his own performance, he did not note her preoccupation, for which she was duly grateful.

Guy Roy maintained his flow of amiable talk which she resentfully surmised to be mere parroting.

Chatterer! she thought.

The intolerable processes of the meal drew to an end. Mrs. Stockwell, at a signal from opposite, rose and led the ladies to their temporary retirement over elderberry cup and Isabella, while the men were left to their Oporto, brandy, or, for the Dutch element, schnapps. Some of them, Becky knew, would make their adieux before the masculine and feminine elements coalesced in the parlour; Guy Roy along with them, very likely. She wished with all her heart that it might be so, hoped with all her heart that it would not.

After an hour of conventional feminine interchange in the parlour, the men entered. Guy Roy came straight to his hostess.

"Cousin," he said.

She had summoned her self-possession. The form of address unsettled her. "What?" she murmured.

"Must I remind you of my privilege of kinship?" he said gaily.

"You have taken small advantage of it," she returned, in a tone of equally light raillery. She had recovered her poise.

"Gurdon has been telling me of a family album," he said smoothly. "Perhaps you would be so good as to substantiate my claims to relationship by sharing a view of it with me."

"What—where——" she began when he cut her short.

"On the Bible-stand in the window bay yonder." He offered a formal arm to conduct her to the spot.

Once in the embrasure, they were comparatively remote though not concealed from the company. He turned over the leaves of the collection, which was made up of records, clippings from various journals, and a scattering of camera obscura drawings of the kind turned out by itinerant portraitists.

She said under her breath, "Why did you come?"

"You asked me," he reminded her.

"I thought you would decline."

"Did you want me to, Becky?"

"You make it so difficult for me," she complained.

"I never want to do that. But—do you know how long it is since we have seen each other?"

"No . . . Yes."

"How much longer do you think this can go on?"

"What can I do?" she pleaded.

He startled her by replying urgently, "Smile." He bent over the stand. "This must be my Great-Aunt Mehitable. She was an old tartar by all accounts." With unchanged intonation he warned, "There are cat's eyes in the room."

"Yes," she responded, and laughed lightly and falsely.

His eyes were sombre. "You have not been to the island," he charged.

"Do you think I didn't *want* to come?" she whispered.

"I love you," he said.

"Don't!" she begged. "Don't say it." She closed her eyes until the tumult of her pulses quieted. "I couldn't come," she said. "My husband is having me watched."

"Does he suspect anything? How could he?"

"Not about us. It's Gypsy Vilas. He forbids me to see her."

"But you do see her?"

"Yes."

"And not me."

"I've nothing to fear from Gypsy," she whispered.

"Nor from me, my beloved."

"From myself."

At that avowal he touched her hand. She drew a quick, hard breath. "I'll write you," she said. Then quickly: "Now, do *you* smile. My husband is approaching."

Gurdon Stockwell appeared at the opening of the bay. "Still engrossed in family pursuits?" he commented not unamiably. "Obedience, Mrs. Howland has consented to oblige the company with a vocal selection. She desires that you assist her upon our new pianoforte. It cost me," he said to his cousin with smiling pride, "two hundred and fifty dollars."

"I will do my possible," the wife agreed.

As he turned away she had barely opportunity to mutter a cryptic message to Guy.

"Camp meeting." Noting his look of frowning incomprehension, she repeated, "I will write."

Hoping against hope for a private word later, Guy sat patiently through the trills of "Roon's Bride", the afflicting quavers of "The Link is Broken", and the arch merriment of "The Origin of Gunpowder" rendered in a peep bird soprano. Becky set him an example of distasteful prudence by a determined devotion to her other guests until eleven o'clock broke up the gathering.

The collar firm's enforced change of base to the Mansion House, the only available quarters, had been costly. In the cramped hotel nook which was now his office, the head of the firm was vague in his replies to inquiries, impatient and inattentive when any problem was set before him. Twice a day he called in person for the post, and came away with the look of a man for whom the world had forfeited all interest. Gypsy Vilas could not understand it. She resolved to wait until Saturday and make a final appeal for attention.

She couldn't have picked a luckier day. Guy came back from his morning visit to the post office with a flagging pace and a lack-lustre eye. He was about to dispose of the meaningless mail which had come in by canal packet, when a small and dainty wafered square, placed in the exact middle of his desk, gave him a start so violent that the letters fluttered to the floor. Only once before had he seen Becky's mature handwriting, yet he knew at first glance from whom the missive came. But how had it got there? With burning impatience he tore it open and read the few words:

Mr. S. will be at camp meeting Wednesday. The island, between two and three.

That was all. It was enough. With a face transfigured, he greeted Gypsy when she entered.

"How came this here, Gypsy?" He held up the wafered square.

She stared with assumed stupidity. "Somebody must have left it."

Plainly there was nothing to be had from her. Nevertheless Guy was well satisfied of the agency of delivery.

It was the longest week-end Guy had ever known. Two hours before the rendezvous, he was afloat in a blessed mist rising from the river, which cloaked observation and so minimized the risk for Becky. No smoke issued from the cave mouth as he drifted past it. They would be alone on the island; aloof from the outer world in an inner world which they might transform into a paradise at their will. At her will, he swore to himself; for, in the humility and the gratitude for love returned, he was resolved to exert no pressure, no matter how imperative his yearning. Let her be the arbiter of destiny for both.

He clambered up the steep past the tunnelled homes of the cliff birds and set himself to wait. She would come from the lower end of the island, taking the gradual slope of the old wagon-trail leading to the high grassland. The minutes passed, grew interminable; brought no relief to his impatience, his apprehensions. He conceived of a thousand reasons why she had not come, why she might not come.

The hour of appointment passed. Despair was closing in about him like the mist. . . . He heard the whinny of a horse, and his name called softly through the grey blindness. He ran to her and would have lifted her to earth, but she resisted his arms with gentle firmness.

"No, Guy, please! You mustn't touch me. It makes me feel— I can't tell you. I don't know, myself."

"That you are a woman," he interpreted gently.

"Yes," she admitted, very low.

"Were you spied on today?" he asked.

"I saw nobody. I'd have come, anyway. There's something I have to tell you, something I overheard. Mr. Fosmire said to my husband, 'We must so arrange it that any mechanic who has once worked the ten-hour day shall be debarred from any further employ in this town.' They were speaking of your factory, Guy?"

He nodded. "The Paterson Ban with Troy improvements."

"You knew of it before?"

"Substantially."

"You and Mr. Stockwell seem on easy terms personally," she went on.

"It simplifies my seeing you. And, after all, why not?"

"When he is trying to ruin you?"

"That is purely a business matter. It's nothing personal with him. I'm sorry for him, in a way."

"I'm not," she said impetuously. "I hate him. I can't help it. I hate my husband. Is that a sin, Guy?"

"It is probably an injustice." He was striving to be fair. "You hate him because he loves you. How could he help it? How could anyone help it?"

"Love," she retorted contemptuously. "He has never so much as said so."

"Very well. You hate him because he has you." he amended.

"He hasn't," she murmured. "Not any more." She doubted that he had heard her.

"Gurdon has his principles," Guy went on, "and lives up to them."

"Always?" she queried.

He gave her a quick, startled glance. What did she know or suspect? Could anyone have told her of Stockwell's past surrenders to his hot blood? Of his night-runnings, of the wench who had left town with a pocketful of dollars three years before, of the whispers about Priscilla Stamm?

"Must we talk of him?" Guy changed the subject. "When shall I see you again?"

"Next week, if I can contrive it."

"You must," he urged. "I ask so little of you, my love. But that little is my life to me. I must and will see you. If you love me . . ."

"Next week. I promise," she said recklessly. "I will let you know what day."

"Through Gypsy?"

"Yes. As before. The fog is thinning, Guy. I must go. Good-bye."

"Good-bye, my love."

He stood with lifted hat until she turned and waved farewell at the far dip of the hill.

ELEVEN

HEAVEN and hell waged annual warfare for supremacy at Thompson's Grove. The inner fortress, the camp-ground proper, was held by the legions of the godly. Beyond its immediate boundaries, the forces of Satan rioted and revelled.

Up to the very limits of the church's soil and sometimes encroaching upon it there was commercial license. Gaudily bedecked booths offered gin, rum, whisky, brandy, and such compounded diabolisms as scotchem, whipbelly-vengeance, killdivvle and gumption. Marketable lust was represented by the local bawds from Troy, draggletail Cyprians from Schenectady, and bed-for-two-bits giglets from Albany. Bowkers hawked their prints openly, lewd ballads and outrageous travesties upon Scripture. Pox-doctors cried their cures. Aborters offered thinly veiled promises to the unwary. Charms both of the white and the black magic were for sale, together with amulets and potions. The scum of town, turnpike and towpath thronged the approaches.

The infection of evil spread even into the religious fastness, itself. Sinners were welcome, but their sin entered with them.

Gurdon Stockwell, had counted upon his wife to accompany him to the meeting. But in the morning she was white and wrung with one of the headaches which had recently become a recurrent affliction.

"Megrims! Vapours!" said the angry husband.

Against her protests, he called in the doctor to back up his diagnosis. Dr. Armitage failed to do so. As a preliminary and before examination he bled, purged and vomicated her. Thereafter there was no question of her going anywhere but to bed. Gurdon Stockwell set out alone and in a grim humour.

A committee of escort met him at the approach to the grove.

"There is a threat of turbulence," one of them warned.

In the mood that possessed him, Stockwell would have welcomed a measure of turbulence. Indeed, he was quite ready to contribute his share in the cause of righteousness.

"Who threatens it?" he asked.

A group of half a dozen evil-looking fellows lounged beneath a sign inscribed, "Superior Hollands in the Pipe: Fresh Rec'd by Canal Packet." One of them, a lanky chap with pockpits checkering his face from brow to chin, was known as a bruiser and brawler with a minor criminal record. About to address himself to the man, Stockwell felt his arm caught. Priscilla Stamm's delicate face was raised to his. She was palpitating. "Do not approach them," she pleaded. "They will do you a mischief, Mr. Stockwell."

He put her gently aside. "Have no fear, Sister," he said. "I am on the Lord's business."

"Give 'er a kiss, Elder," one of the group suggested with a snigger.

"Or pass her along to some as will," another supplemented.

Gurdon Stockwell walked up to the pocked man. "You are Long Gib Darrow," he said.

"What if I be?"

"I hope to see you and your companions at the service this evening."

"To listen to a lot o' your pious gibble-gabble?"

Gurdon Stockwell's lips tightened. "I come to you with a heart filled with loving-kindness," he began ominously, when a voice interrupted.

"Ah, spit up his nose, Gib."

The bully shifted his cud. His long jaw worked. Stockwell moved forward a single step on the balls of his feet. His churchly, black broadcoat tightened across a pair of shoulders of impressive construction. Darrow, a man experienced in trouble, knew potential murder when he saw it, and was in no mind to tempt it. The accumulated spittle dissipated harmlessly against a tree-bole. Stockwell's glance swept the group.

"You are all bidden to the worship of your God," he grated, and went on his way.

Priscilla was by his side, her eyes adoring. "Oh, Gurd . . . Oh, Brother Stockwell! You were wonderful."

Gurdon would have been less than human had he not felt a glow. "It was nothing, Sister Stamm," he deprecated. His voice lowered. "Walk with me," he said.

For a moment she hesitated. Her eyes were frightened and hungry. She fell into step beside him.

"You have been shunning me," he said.

"You know why."

"I must talk with you."

"What's the use?" she said dispiritedly.

"There are things that you don't know," he muttered.

"What difference can it make—now?"

Another worshipper joined them, and the three fell into pious discourse which was continued until they came in view of the platform. This was of raw wood, lighted by flares and torches. Mottoes painted on boards were fastened to the rails. They exhorted to repentance, praised the Lord in words of the Psalms, and exalted the spirit of Christian unity among all present. Backless benches were ranged in a crescent about the rostrum.

As evening fell, the torches blazed; the benches were semi-lighted by lanterns swung from the trees. In the darkened outskirts young people of both sexes huddled together, already excited and giggling. The seats were rapidly filling up. There was a tensity, an emotional expectancy in the atmosphere.

Priscilla found a seat at the far end of a forward bench and closed her eyes in silent prayer. She opened them to see Gurdon Stockwell mount the platform and seat himself back of the Presiding Elder. The opening hymn was announced. Priscilla lifted a small, clear soprano in the beginning of a religious and sensual ecstasy which was to mount with overwhelming force as the ceremonies proceeded.

The exhorter of the evening, Deacon Daniel G. Stopes, was a natural orator; his magnetic presence fortified by an ascetically handsome visage and a deeply musical voice. His hearers were composed mostly of church folk and camp-ground followers: seekers after the sensual exaltations which were defined as salvation. But there was more than the usual sprinkling of the lawless element.

Deacon Stopes began on the note of loving-kindness. He was sincere and moving. Sinners were welcome to repentance; the grace of God was broad enough to cover all: rum-sellers, gamesters, whoremongers—let them abandon their evil ways and beg forgiveness before the throne. He stopped to sip from the glass of water set on the pulpit. As at a signal, a loud, concerted raspberry burbled from the lips of a group in the background. Yelps of derisive mirth followed.

With uplifted hand, the Deacon stepped from behind the stand and advanced to the rail. He had foreseen this and prepared for it with his most telling passage. Now the stage was set for him. His voice deepened.

"I hear the mirth of demons," he declaimed. "The challenge of the Tempter. The crackling of thorns under a pot. Stand forth!" he thundered.

The answer came in a wavering chorus of jeers. It sounded ill-assured, as if the speaker's eloquence had already daunted the disturbers. Nobody moved to respond to the summons. The Deacon launched with pleasurable fervour upon his prepared diatribe.

"Who are these contaminators of the spirit, these church-despisers, these truth-betrayers? Since they dare not stand forth and avow themselves, I will tell you. They are hirelings of Satan, human caterpillars, Pharisees of the slime of the spirit, hypocrites, varlets, seed of the serpent, foolish builders with sand for stone and weedsap for mortar; dead dogs that dare not bark, blind men, rotten souls, womb-fruit of devils, death's playmates and boon companions of hell. Let them avow themselves now or for ever hold their peace, these girders at God and traitors to their fellow man. Let them deny if they dare that their goal is the destruction of religion; their destination, the bottomless pit."

This was more than Long Gib Darrow and his mongrel crowd of gutter-knights had bargained for. They had come there for the purpose of picking up a few easy dollars. To hear themselves denounced in theological terms of such range and fury was disconcerting. Angry mutters rose around them. Still, they were a score strong, and church people could not be much in the way of rough-and-tumble fighting. They held a hasty consultation, and started forward with uncertain purpose.

Women began to cry. Benches were overturned. The younger and lustier men of the churchgoers poured into the aisles. There was every prospect of lively doings.

From the fringe of the seating space, where a growth of saplings afforded a thin cover, there sounded a gay voice.

"Up, Halcyons!"

Half a dozen of the Corinthians of the city had come un-obtrusively to the meeting for sport and conquest. The over-strained atmosphere of these gatherings offered rich pickings to the careless young libertines. Religion was no part of their pro-gramme, but if the turn of events called upon them to become defenders of the faith, that was quite all right. Anything for a good ruckus!

The rallying cry rattled out:

> "Brek-kek-kek-kex;
> Co-ax! Co-ax!"

At the summons, Brother Stockwell reverted to his youthful days of Halcyonship. Vaulting the rail, he landed upon Long Gib Darrow's shoulders and bore him to the ground. On his feet instantly, he fought his way to the embattled youths and put himself at the head of the wedge which ploughed through the crowd, scattering men and women to right and left, and formed up round the stairs mounting to the platform, a formidable line of defence. The ill-formed mob of disturbers at once decided that they were better off elsewhere. They dissolved into the convenient darkness of the thickets.

Gurdon Stockwell was a figure of glory. The throng swept forward upon him. Men pressed his hand. Women wept upon his shoulders. There were cries of, "Praise the Lord!", "Blessed be His name!", "Jesus, our fortress and our might!", "Who shall stand against His Power?" With difficulty the meeting was restored to order. With further difficulty, Gurdon Stockwell rescued himself from his admirers and sought respite in a retired spot.

Through all the excitement, he had kept one object in mind. Escaped into the shrubbery, he made a roundabout turn and emerged to seat himself beside Priscilla Stamm on the far end of the bench. Her face was flushed and provocative with animation, her eyes heavy with religious abandonment. From the platform a hymn was being announced. She held out the little book to him. Her fingers trembled against his powerful hand. Her shoulder insensibly pressed his. Their voices, soprano and basso, blended in the pulsing, hammering rhythm of the Salvation Hymn:

> "We are saved—saved—saved
> By the blood—blood—blood,
> We are saved by the blood of the Lamb!"

Warmth and passion pulsed between them from the urgent contact. Their bodies remembered forbidden ecstasies, their pulses throbbed to a rhythm more compelling than that of the hymnal. Priscilla was white and panting. Under cover of the thunderous refrain his low voice entered her like an enchantment, a possessing.

"Meet me after hornblow."

"Oh no! We mustn't."

"Back of the Bible Booth."

"It isn't safe. We'd be seen."

"Go into the willow copse," he urged. "Nobody will be there."

"No, Gurdon," she quavered.

"I must talk with you."

"I know your talk," she muttered. "Please, Gurdon, don't press me."

"Once more," he went on in his urgent whisper. "What can it matter?"

She said brokenly, "We swore—last time—that we never would again."

"We can't help it. It's stronger than we. You'll come. You'll wait." His hand touched hers. She quivered all over. "Ten minutes after hornblow," he said and, by the deep-lit desire in her eyes, knew that she would be there.

The horn sounded, signalling the brief intermission before the final hymn, the announcements for the morrow, and the invocation. Priscilla slipped away into the shadows. The lights were out in the Bible Booth. Driven by her irresistible longing, she threaded the vague footpath which lost itself in the thickness of the willow growth. There she stood, tremulous, gathering her forces for final, despairing defence. It seemed to her that she had hardly drawn breath when she heard him shouldering his way through the boughs from the opposite direction. Even as he seized her she made her pitiful protest.

"Oh, my dear! Let me go!"

"You're mine again," he said in hoarse triumph.

"It isn't the same," she pleaded. "We swore. It is deadly sin. Your wife!"

"What kind of wife is she to me?" he said furiously. "You are my wife in better truth."

His mouth closed down upon hers. Desperate, she tried to wrestle away from him. "I want to be saved—saved—saved," she panted, as her last resistance broke to the rhythm of the music, heard faint and far and deadly across the darkness and the distance.

Afterwards she wept softly, clinging to him. "We broke our oath, Gurdon."

"I know," he answered gloomily. "I meant to keep it. But when I saw you so sweet and warm, when I felt your breath, Satan shook me."

"We shall lose our souls."

"God will judge her, not us," he muttered.

She composed her clothing to decency. "I must go."

"You were not seen coming here?"

"No, I don't think so."

"We must be more prudent in future."

She gasped. "What future?"

"I must see you again."

"Oh, Gurdon!" Then, "Do you love me?"

He thinned his lips. "I have never said so."

"No, you haven't." She began to sob quietly. "That makes it worse. That makes my sin the greater. Oh, what shall I *do*? What shall I *do*?"

"There, there," he soothed her. "I have an esteem for you, Sister Stamm," he added lamely. With renewed ardour he pressed against her. "We can arrange so that no suspicion will attach to us," he urged. "As we did before."

She said with a breath-catch, "Cash Barlow suspects."

"What! How? What can he know?"

"He knows nothing. But he warned me against you. It's his mad jealousy. If he knew, he might kill us both."

Gurdon Stockwell frowned. "Has he offered threats?"

"Against me. Not against you."

"What did he say?"

"That he'd strangle me with his own hands if I yielded to any man."

"Before witnesses?"

"Clory Burgo heard him once. And Hannah Boutwell, only last month."

"Then he must be bound over," Stockwell asserted with vigour. "Go to a lawyer. I will find the money for the costs. Bring your witnesses and swear Barlow into bond."

"I will," she agreed, docile and sweet. Her prudent self-restraint gave way before her infatuation. "I love you so, Gurdon," she murmured.

Within the week she had left the window of her ground-floor

lodging open to his midnight access. Lying in his arms, she told him that the magistrate had been most obliging. Cash Barlow was held in 100 dollars bond to keep the peace and refrain from molesting the said Priscilla Stamm, spinster, by word or deed.

Since at no time in his life had Barlow been possessed of such a sum, his friends in the labour movement raised the money. His help was needed to forward the twelve-hour campaign.

TWELVE

THROUGH that August Becky and Guy met on the island twice, sometimes thrice, a week. Immunity had lulled Becky's fears. It seemed to her that her husband was paying little heed to her comings and goings. Always aloof and forbidding, he had become distrait. Often he would sit late over his concerns, burning the lamp in his private room on the ground floor until after eleven o'clock.

There is no indifference more cruel and unreflecting than the insensitiveness of a woman in love towards the suffering of an unloved man. Yet the wife of Gurdon Stockwell felt a pang at her heart when sometimes as late as midnight she heard the light, unexpectant tap at her door, and the formal, "Good night, Obedience."

With something like contrition she answered: "Good night, Mr. Stockwell. A peaceable sleep to you."

She reported to her friend and confidante:

"He's a changed man, Gypsy. I doubt that he's having me watched any longer."

"I wouldn't stake my luck on that," the other said dryly.

"He's got something on his mind. Would it be business worriment, do you think?"

"Might be business. Might be women trouble," the ever-suspicious Gypsy pronounced.

"Mr. Stockwell? Fah-doodle!" Mrs. Stockwell was scornful.

"You cheat a man of his bed rights and he'll look further," the wiseacre pronounced.

"Not Mr. Stockwell. His conscience wouldn't let him."

To this Gypsy returned a pungent version of a proverb dealing with the limitations of the male conscience, which was familiar to respectable ears only in its Latin form. Shocked, Becky laughed.

"What's more," Gypsy proceeded, "I'll bet a fip I can put a name on his little bit o' stuff."

"I don't want to know," Becky said, and meant it.

Gypsy did want to know. For all her confident assertions, she had only vague hearsay and random observation to go on. If her suspicions could be supported, something might be made of it in behalf of Becky or even of the Montague & Roy Company.

A bit of useful blackmail was not beyond Gypsy's scope in a good cause. She sought out Clorinda Burgo.

"You go to the Thompson's Camp Ground meetin', Clory?"

"Yes. It was a beautiful love feast."

"Yay-ah. More love in the bushes than on the benches, I guess."

"I wasn't in the bushes," Clorinda said virtuously.

"Did you hear Deacon Stopes's exhortation?"

"Did I so!" Clorinda lifted ecstatic eyes. "It nigh to h'isted me right out on to the sinner's bench."

"You'd-a had plenty company, I reckon," Gypsy said. "Was Prissy Stamm there?"

"Certes. She rode over in the carryall with us."

"Come back, too?"

"Now that you say the word, I don't know as she did. Why?"

"Nothing," Gypsy returned carelessly. "Nothing at-all."

"Sa-ay! You don't think there's any toosey-woosey going on there, do you? Why, Prissy's in his Sunday School class."

"And the heifer quoted Scripture to the bull," Gypsy scoffed. "I'm sayin' naught and you'd better do the same."

Clorinda rubbed her large pale nose. "She's quit her hire."

Gypsy straightened up. "Left the Eureker?"

"Ay-up. Left town, too. Mildred Hute had a letter from her. Said she'd been sick or something."

At the first opportunity Gypsy sought out the spooler. "I hear Prissy Stamm's quit her hire."

"Ay-up."

"Where'd she go?"

"Lawrence Mills."

Gypsy whistled. "She can't make a doffer's wage there."

"I guess she couldn't. That's why she's coming back."

"To the Eureker?"

Mildred nodded. "She's got her old job promised."

"What made her quit in the first place? Did she get the boot?"

"Don't believe so. Got something on her mind about her religion. She was always a one for church and suchlike. I'll fetch her letter."

Priscilla had written to her friend:

I do not enjoy any religion attall. I have not seen a well or happy day since I left Thompson Camp Ground. The Methodists

are my people. To them I am indebted, under God, for my spiritual
birth. I once knew what it was to love God with all my heart, once
felt that God was my father, Jesus my friend, and Heaven my home,
but have awfully departed and sometimes fear I shall lose my soul
forever.

"I always did think Sweetie-pink was a chucklehead, but that
makes you kinda sorry for her," Gypsy said.

Although hands were being laid off daily at the Eureka, Mr.
Goodwilly had a loom for Priscilla Stamm. Such was the owner's
order, and who was he to question high authority? As the girl
resumed her work, it was glaringly evident to the overlooker that
her listless and sloppy performance did not justify the wage paid
to her. That was no concern of his, either. He set down Mr.
Stockwell's interest in the weaver to the fact of her churchly
activities. Once, indeed, he asked himself with aroused curiosity
whether there might be some other bond between employer and
employee. That was one morning when, approaching the office on
noiseless feet, as was his custom in making his rounds, he heard
his employer's crisp accents addressing someone unseen.

"This is the height of imprudence."

Some murmured and indistinguishable reply followed. Then
the impatient rejoinder: "Yes, yes. I will let you know in due
time."

Priscilla Stamm emerged and hurried down the corridor,
fortunately in the other direction from the overseer, who had
flattened himself hastily into a broom-closet. He could not see
her face, but her shoulders were twitching.

Had he been close enough to hear the girl's part of the conver-
tion in Mr. Stockwell's office, his doubts would have been resolved
into near certainties. For she had risked the august displeasure by
going there to urge upon her employer the necessity for a private
talk at length. Where it should take place she left to him. Her
convenient ground-floor chamber was no longer available to his
access. In her absence it had been rented to another lodger and,
on her return, she had been taken into old Miss Stamm's room on
the second floor. She would sneak out and come to him whenever
he said the word.

Reluctantly he had given her rendezvous for the following
Monday night in the mansion grounds.

The night was moonless when they met. She was there first,

and he found her cowering in the interior darkness of the toolshed
at the upper end of the garden. He said hoarsely and without
preliminary, "Are you *sure*?"

"Yes, oh yes!"

"How can you be sure this soon?"

"It's nearly three months. The lady doctress in Lawrence said
it was certain," she whimpered.

"Did you take the medicine as I advised you?"

"Nn-no."

Stockwell uttered an oath and at once privately besought his
Maker's forgiveness.

"I was afraid," she quavered.

"What of?" he demanded harshly. "Didn't I give you full
instructions?"

"The doctress said it might have killed me. Oh, Gurdon!
Didn't you *care* whether it killed me?" she wailed.

"Silence! Do you think me a murderer?"

"Wouldn't it be murder to kill the child in my body?" she
asked timidly.

"Do you want to let it be born to live to shame you and ruin
me?"

"Oh, I don't know! Oh, Gurdon, why did we do it? I knew it
meant disaster."

"Then why did you yield?" he retorted savagely. "No, I don't
mean it," he muttered, as she burst into sobs. "Leave it to me. I
will contrive."

"How? What?"

"I don't know yet. I must have time to think. How much
longer can you go without suspicion attaching itself to you?"

"Nothing shows yet," she murmured. "I haven't so much as
loosed my stays. Another two months, I think."

"I will contrive," he repeated with more assurance. "Meantime, the less risk we take of being surprised, the better. As for
money . . ."

She interrupted with an ejaculation of pained protest.

". . . you shall have no reason to complain of my generosity,"
he concluded.

"Gurdon!" she breathed.

"Yes? What is it?"

"Shall I lose my soul? Shall I go to hell?"

"No, no!" he exclaimed, thinking that if she went to hell, he must go, too. "Our sin was forced upon us. Pray, Priscilla, pray nightly as I do. Pray for my soul as well as your own. God help us both!" Gurdon Stockwell entreated in unwonted humility.

So powerful was his revulsion from sin that he put her firmly away when she lifted her face in farewell.

Phineas Heartt, the bookseller, was a man of genial spirit and plenteous speech. His appetite for gossip was voracious, but, having acquired a morsel, he was generous about sharing it with the wife of his bosom. On this bright autumn afternoon he came home to dinner, rubbing his hands.

"Prepare to welcome a new cousin, my dear," he said.

"Which branch this time?" asked comfortable Mrs. Heartt, who was kin to half the respectable families in Troy.

"What would you say to the mansion on Castle Hill?"

"Not Gurdon Stockwell!" she cried. "Well, it's high time."

"Yes. There will be a young Stockwell scion, please God, to carry on the honoured name."

"When? Are you sure? How do you know? Did he tell you?"

Mr. Heartt chuckled. "When a young husband comes to my place and purchases a volume entitled *Obstetrics for the Home, the Care and Protection of the Expectant Mother*, one may be reasonably certain of what is in prospect for that household."

Kindly Mrs. Heartt took the first occasion of felicitating the young matron on the blessed event impending. She reported back to her husband: "You would have thought her still a school-girl. Such flushes and blushes and fidgets. She pretended not to know what I was talking about. I think she would have denied it to my face."

"Did you tell her of the book?"

"That fossicked her," Mrs. Heartt giggled. "She opened and shut her mouth like a fish. But she wouldn't tell me when. Said she didn't know. Such silliness!"

Home after the puzzling interview with the gratulatory Mrs. Heartt, Becky made a survey of the library. No such volume was there. Had the bookseller's wife been making sport of her, then? She extended her search to the study. There in her husband's private desk, she brought the book to light. Several chapters were marked with slips. Chapter VI on "Care of the Expectant Mother"; Chapter VIII on "Miscarriages, Their Cause and

Prevention"; Chapter X on "Case Histories". Did Gurdon Stockwell still hope? she wondered in contemptuous pity.

Her thoughts turned to Guy Roy.

In every unfulfilled love relationship there comes a time when one or the other says, "We can't go on this way." If it be the woman, it means withdrawal, "We must break it off." If the man, it takes the form of the demand imperative, "Leave everything and come to me." Inevitably Becky and Guy were approaching that crisis.

What was there left in life for Becky but those meetings with Guy Roy? Once a week now they kept tryst on the lonely island. She did not minimize the danger of discovery. If that were to be the event, let scandal do its worst. Gurdon Stockwell might take what measures his righteous wrath dictated. So long as she felt herself guiltless in the major degree, she could face him with fortitude.

Matters might have drifted had it not been for Amos Goodwilly playing truant and going fishing on a warm autumn morning. While engaged with a brisk river trout, he caught sight of a distant horsewoman fording the stream towards Sadler's Island. Inspired by curiosity, after landing his fish he cautiously rounded the island and, on the opposite side, made out a male figure climbing the cliff to the upland. The distance was too far for recognition of the man. But the woman he knew and did not like. In his opinion, his employer's young wife was a pernickety upstart.

It would not do for him to admit having been fishing in work hours. He went home and wrote an anonymous letter, which he prudently left by hand and at dead of night on the Stockwell mansion doorstep, rather than entrust it to the post.

Obedience Stockwell had become aware of an increased watchfulness on her husband's part. She was not unprepared for his inquisition when, one evening after supper, she was summoned to the private room. Gurdon Stockwell began on a coldly judicial note.

"Mrs. Stockwell, what is your destination when you ride abroad in the morning?"

"Now here, now there," she replied cautiously.

"Sadler's Island?"

Her heart leapt to her throat. "Sometimes."

"I, too, have visited Sadler's Island," he said. "It is a lonely and forsaken spot. What takes you there?"

"I like the loneliness."

"Lonely and exempt from observation," he continued. "An appropriate location for secret crime."

"Are you accusing me of crime, Mr. Stockwell?"

His voice took on an edge. "Can you deny that you go there to keep an illicit assignation?"

She was silent.

"Is it he whom you met the night you made your evasion from my house by rope?"

"I met no one but Gypsy Vilas."

"You will hardly claim that your encounter on the island is with the Vilas wench."

Again he took angry note of those obdurately compressed lips. He said with deadly quiet, "I believe you to be an adulteress."

Strangely she felt a surge of relief. At least this was in the open. "Then why don't you divorce me?" she said calmly.

"Divorce!" He was incredulous. "You would abide a divorce?"

"I should welcome it."

"At the cost of your good name?"

"I should welcome it," she repeated.

"Are you aware that harlotry is a crime punishable by imprisonment in this state?"

"I am not a harlot."

"Do you remember our visit to the States Prison in Auburn?" he continued with still ferocity. "The female occupants, the degraded and depraved Cyprians among others?"

Becky's lids twitched.

"The filth. The stench. The squalor," he went on in a deadly monotony of utterance. "The roaches on the floors. The blankets acrawl with bugs. The lice, creeping on the walls. The crazed voices, foul with obscenity . . ."

"Don't!" she gasped.

"Pay good heed to this, woman," he adjured her with bitter solemnity. "If I hear of you privily consorting with any man, though it were only to pass the time of day, I swear before God on high that I will pen you behind those reeking bars to rot there. Do you believe me?"

"Yes," she answered dully.

"The interview is over."

"Not yet," she said. "Not yet, Mr. Stockwell. I have my word to say. If you ever enter my chamber again, seeking me, I shall fling myself from the window." There was deep malice in her smile. "Do *you* believe *me*?"

"No," he said. But she knew from the deadened skin about his lips that he did.

Meeting Guy on the following tryst day was now out of the question. But two days later Stockwell was called out of town on business. Becky got word to Guy and they met in the garden. It was a risk which must be taken, she felt. As soon as he set eyes on her he cried out:

"Something has happened."

"I can't come to the island again, Guy."

"Does he know?"

"He knows that I go there, but not that it is you I meet."

"Then . . ."

"He is half-mad with jealousy and suspicion. I believe he would kill you, Guy."

"Never mind me," he said impatiently. "Did he threaten you? He did!" he cried as she refused to meet his eyes. "What did he say? Tell me."

"That he would jail me as—as an adulteress. I'm not an adulteress, Guy. I—I don't think I could be, not even for you. Can a husband swear his wife into jail, Guy?"

He had grown haggard as she spoke. "How should I know? The law—it gives a husband terrible power. By God, I'll kill him!" he said under his breath.

She shuddered all over. "There is too much talk of killing."

"How can you go on living with him on such terms?" he demanded.

"I can't. I'm not. I never will again."

"Becky!" he whispered. He stretched his arms out to her. She leaned back from the long kiss. He said hoarsely, "It can't go on this way."

"No," she whispered.

"Will you come away with me?"

"Yes," she said. There was not the slightest doubt, the briefest hesitancy. She must have known from the first that when the issue was made plain, this would be her answer.

"When?"

"Whenever you bid me."

"We shall have to go beyond his reach—to leave the State."

"What does it matter? Anywhere with you," she breathed, reckless with passion.

"I shall have to tell Gurdon."

She drew back from him with wide eyes. "That we are going away together?"

"That we have gone. I shall write him. Then he must divorce you and we can marry."

"He never will. You don't know him."

"And you are willing to go away with me anyway?"

"What else is there for me in the world? I love you, Guy."

He said: "We must plan carefully. How shall I reach you in case of need?"

"Through Gypsy Vilas."

"Are you going to tell her?"

"I must. I shall need someone to help me plan."

"When is Gurdon going away again?"

"How should I know? He never admits me to his plans. If he did go, he might well insist upon my accompanying him."

"If he does, we will take that for the signal. Otherwise—my darling, it checks my heart to wait. But, for your sake, I must be able to take care of you. It will require two months or even three to settle my business affairs. But if you are truly mine, must we wait for that?"

Her eyes were clouded and heavy, her breath quick. "Oh, Guy!" she murmured. "Bear with me. I can leave everything for you and go to hell for my sin if I must. But I can't stay here under his roof and play the smooth and secret masquerader in his house. Don't ask me . . . Kiss me now and let me go."

She sought out Gypsy the next day.

"Gypsy, I can't stand it any longer. I'm going away."

"With Guy Roy?"

"Yes."

"You thought it all over, gal?"

"Yes, till I'm wearied of thinking. Oh, Gypsy! Haven't I a right to happiness? I've never known what it was before."

"Maybe. But I think you're a fool."

"I'm a woman," Becky said vehemently. "I've never known what that was before, either."

"Come over here to the light and lemme look at you." She conned the lovely and quivering face. She sighed. "All right, gal.

If it's like that, it's like that. I know your kind. It's one man in all the world or nobody."

"Yes," Becky agreed.

Gypsy gave herself over to concentrated thought. This, she foresaw with chill certainty, would mark the end of the Montague & Roy Company, if it were permitted to fulfil itself. Guy would withdraw his funds while there was still available money. The workrooms would close. The hands would be thrown out into the street with no chance of further employ. Couldn't Becky, who had been a working girl, herself, see that?

Should she put it to her straight? Better not, the sapient Gypsy decided. What was the use of arguing with a lovesick girl in the throes of an unslaked passion? But if that passion could be assuaged? It was worth trying. If Becky balked at it, the shrewd mechanic had another plan at the back of her busy brain.

Becky was appealing to her. "You'll help me when the time comes, won't you, Gypsy?"

"You're a fool and I'm another. I s'pose I will. When'll it be?"

"Not for a few months, I'm afraid."

"That long?" This was encouraging news. Gypsy had feared that the lovers were planning a quicker escape. She took it for a sign that Guy was not wholly unmindful of his responsibilities towards the firm. That might be something to build on. Anything to keep the company going and the girls off the street.

Something might be done with Becky, too. It was worth trying. Gypsy tried.

"Listen, wench. You got where you are by takin' Gypsy's advice, didn't you? Take it again."

"What is it?"

"Stick to what you've got tighter'n a leech to a fat man's rump."

"And give up Guy?"

"Who said anything about givin' up Guy?" Gypsy mocked. "There's other ways for a smart wench."

"You've changed your tune, Gypsy. You've always said, 'don't'."

"I'd say it now if it'd do any good. It wouldn't. I know that look in a wench's eyes. You're goin' to play the fool one way or the other. So said, so done. Play it so's you can get the most out of it."

"You mean for me to stay here in *his* house and . . ."

"That's it. It's risky. But I'll help. It might work. The other's sure deuces and pass the dice."

The wife shook her head. "I can be a wanton for Guy, but not a cheat."

"So you're goin' to bust up the whole show, huh? Have you figured what this'll mean to other folks?"

"Who? Mr. Stockwell? He'll get over it," Becky replied vaguely.

Gypsy regarded her strangely. "I wasn't thinkin' of him. Never mind," she said.

THIRTEEN

SADLER'S ISLAND, that strange geographical excrescence, was by no means the unfrequented spot which Gurdon Stockwell supposed it to be. Nor did the lovers know all that went on there. Both Becky and Guy would have been vastly surprised to know that Gypsy was familiar with one portion of it. She made her cautious way after closing hours, from the workrooms to the riverside, appropriated a dugout, paddled across to the west end of the island and climbed the few feet to the same cave which Guy had accidentally discovered, cursing under her breath as the spiked branches of the exotic thorn growth snatched at her.

A light twinkled at the cave mouth. A man's quiet voice said, "Is that you, Gypsy?"

"Yes, sir. Anybody inside?"

"No. I am alone."

She entered. Luther Simms had been writing at a rough desk. He motioned her to a bench, the only seat in the place, thrust his quill into the sand-box to dry, pushed aside his paper and turned to her.

"Is this true about Montague & Roy closing down?"

"Mr. Roy's set on it. I got an idear, but I dunno how it'll work out."

He did not then ask her what it was. Association with her of more than a year had taught him that Gypsy's "idears", generally secret and often devious, were best left to her own development.

"The only ten-hour shop in Troy," he said. "To have it fail now would be a disaster to the cause."

"Was you goin' to pull the turn-out against the Eureker?" she asked.

"Yes. In the next month."

"Mr. Simms, the turn-out can't win."

"You think not?"

"How can it? Look at the other mills. Shortenin' their help every week. Look at the streets. Full of hands beggin' for hire. Look at the wages. Goin' down, down, down, and the more they drop, the more folks are fightin' to get 'em. Amos Goodwilly is struttin' the sidewalks, braggin' he can get mechanics for bed and board. What kind of a time is that to be callin' a strike?"

Luther Simms's face was heavy with gloom. "If we don't best Gurdon Stockwell now, we never shall. He'll be king of the town and the long workday will be fixed on Troy for God knows how long."

"Cock o' the dungheap," she confirmed. "And don't he know it! We might get Cash Barlow to shoot him," she added hopefully.

He raised the lanthorn to scan her face. "Why should Barlow wish to kill Gurdon Stockwell more than Fosmire or Smith or Osband or any one of a dozen others who have maltreated him?"

Gypsy thought for a time before saying, "Female reasons."

"The Stamm girl?" he asked.

She nearly fell off her bench, so sharp was her start. "You must have three ears. What do you know about Prissy Stamm?"

"Little enough. Idle talk, very likely. Something about a camp meeting."

Gypsy nodded. "I wasn't there. But others was."

"Do you credit the gossip connecting her name with Gurdon Stockwell's?"

"Well, I dunno," she answered thoughtfully. "She's a pretty pious piece. If she did get herself seduced, it'd likely be in the name of the Lord."

"No impiety in my hearing, Gypsy!" he sternly admonished her. "Have you any reason for supposing that Miss Stamm has been seduced?"

"That's accordin' as you look at it," was the judicial reply. "She's back here now——"

"Then she did leave town?" he interrupted. "I had heard so."

"Took a job in Lawrence. When she comes back to Troy she gets her old hire at the Eureker. And at this very time," she added impressively, "they're layin' off help instead of takin' it on. What d'you make of that, Mr. Simms?"

"Continue."

"Now the talk is that Cash Barlow is tryin' to marry her and she ain't sayin' no. She hates the sight of him. So what do you make of that? S'pose she does marry him and give him a family surprise in a few months?"

He gave a start in his turn. "Do you think that likely?"

"She looks pretty pale and pindly."

"But Gurdon Stockwell," he broke out. "That man of known piety and rectitude. Why, Gypsy, it's monstrous."

"I got no proof," she admitted. "But if it ain't him, who is it? She never looked at any other man."

"What mill did she work in at Lawrence?"

"The Happy Toiler."

He made a note. "I have a confidential informant there. Have you told anyone else of your suspicions?"

"Only Mary Haynes."

"Keep a tight tongue. This may alter our plans. If Gurdon Stockwell should be publicly discredited . . . Gypsy, do you think I might profitably interview Miss Stamm?"

"No, I don't," she said bluntly. "You leave the woman end to them that understands it, Mr. Simms."

"Very well. Now as to young Roy. I presume he is to be left to you also."

"I reckon so. Till we see how it comes out, anyway." Complete as was her faith and trust in Luther Simms, she was not going to betray her friend's love secret to him. "Likely it'll come to naught. I'll let you know."

"Do the other hands know of the impending closing?"

"Not from me. What's the good of worryin' the poor wenches?"

Paddling back, Gypsy heard the oars of a larger craft passing in the darkness. Other workers in the working man's cause, she guessed. They and Luther Simms would be talking and planning far into the night in their retreat.

In assuming that the impending collapse could long be concealed from her fellow workers, Gypsy had reckoned without Mary Haynes. The shrewd accountant sensed something ominous in prospect when she was instructed to decline incoming orders for delivery after the end of November. She laid the problem before Gypsy.

"What does it mean? We can meet the orders."

"Ask the boss."

"I did. He said we were running short on supply goods. Why," she said indignantly, "the market's flooded."

"Oh, well! What the skunk told the weasel gets around the barnyard. We're shuttin' down."

"Shutting down?" the other said breathlessly. "With all the trade that's coming in by every post? Why, it's crazy! For how long?"

"For good."

"I don't believe it!" Mary cried.

"It's true. But mum's the word. No good lettin' the girls know till they have to."

"When's the date?"

"A coupla months, at best."

"I can't believe it of Mr. Roy," Mary cried vehemently. "He wouldn't do that to us. Did he tell you himself?"

"Not yet."

"How do you know, then?" with a gleam of hope.

"I know. That's all."

Mary began to cry quietly. "What'll they do? What'll become of our girls?"

"Quit your blubberin'," Gypsy bade her, the more ferociously in that she was near to it herself. "The old hoss ain't dead till the blowflies come. As long as the notice ain't up, the less said the better."

Mary nodded, rubbing reddened eyes.

"By my reckonin' he can't hold off notifyin' the help much longer. Likely he'll have us do it."

"I won't," Mary declared, rebellious for once in her docile life.

Gypsy's preference was always for direct action. With Guy Roy, she reflected, one did not need the indirect approach. She went to the office.

"When you goin' to put the paper up?" she asked bluntly.

He studied her sombre face. "How much do you know, Gypsy?"

"Plenty."

"The others?"

"Only Mary."

He stirred restlessly. "I suppose it's only fair to the hands to give them as long notice as possible."

"What good is notice when there's no jobs open?"

He winced. "Would it be better if you told them?"

"No. Might as well make it official. Lad, will you meet a committee of your mechanics?"

He nodded dispiritedly. "It won't avail anything. But I'll see them."

"Just me and Mary and Clory Burgo and Mildred Hute," she said encouragingly. "And another," she added to herself, "if I have to bust my girdle gettin' her."

The time was set for the following evening at nine. The place, Guy's office.

On the stroke of closing-bell, Gypsy was out of the door and on her way to Castle Hill. She made a cautious approach, found Becky alone in the sewing-room, and tapped on the window-pane for admittance.

"Where's old Grumblegut?"

"In the study."

"Can you rope out tomorrow evening?"

"What for?"

"To see a friend."

Becky began to tremble. "Oh, Gypsy!"

"It ain't what you think. I'll be along, and some others. Can you make it?"

"Yes, if it isn't too late. He doesn't come upstairs till after ten, usually."

Gypsy gave directions. Becky was to be at the Mansion House side door at 8.25. Better wear a calash to be drawn about her face in the event of meeting anyone she knew.

Mary, Clory and Mildred were rounded up and carefully instructed in their parts. The cast was now ready, the stage set. Only the two principals were unversed in their roles.

The five young women were seated in a stiff row when Guy Roy entered. At sight of Becky, he stopped as if a flame had reared itself before him.

"Good evening, Mr. Roy," she said composedly.

In his perturbation he ignored the others. "I did not expect to see you here."

"If I am *de trop*," said Becky, very much the lady, "I can take my leave."

"No, no," he returned. "No doubt you are here for a purpose, though"—with a sharp glance at Gypsy—"I cannot conceive what it might be."

"You'll find out soon enough, my bucko," Gypsy said inwardly. To her fellows she said, "Mr. Roy's got something to tell us."

Thus prompted, Guy said stiffly, "I regret to inform you that the Montague & Roy Company is obliged to close its trade."

"Then it's true," Mary Haynes said.

"Till empty?" Clory Burgo asked.

"Wages will be paid for a supplementary week after closure."

"That's fair enough," Mildred Hute admitted, "as far as it goes."

"Don't go very far, though," Gypsy grunted.

"It's the best that I—that the company can do," he said. Becky could have cried out in pity for the shame and misery in the utterance.

"Kinda sudden-like," Clory remarked.

"Twenty-two gals," Gypsy said. "Out on their behinds."

"Twenty-four," Mary corrected.

"Oh! If you're countin' you and me."

"We've got to eat, too," Mary murmured.

"Nobody's got to worry about me," Gypsy declared cheerfully. "I can hit the road. But the others, they took a chance of it, stickin' to Mr. Roy."

Guy said harshly: "Here is the notice. Make the copies, Mary."

Gypsy turned to Roy. "Look, Boss. We've seen the time when trade was slacker'n a witch's britches and there was no talk of quittin'. Now that the orders are pilin' in . . ."

"The more orders, the more loss," Guy said sullenly.

". . . it's you that wants to quit. The hands didn't quit when they was bid away."

Guy made a despairing gesture.

"What's to become of 'em? Anything about *that* on this paper?"

"Oh, Gypsy! Don't!" Becky pleaded in a whisper.

"There are other employs," Guy muttered.

"For our girls? With the ban on 'em?"

"There's Albany," Mary Haynes said. "That's not so far to walk, and they've opened the soup-cellars, so I hear."

"One ticket a day. Nobody gets fat, but you can keep alive," Mildred said. "Might be just as good to stay here on the county."

"Town for me," Clory said. "They only allow fifty-three cents a week to feed a county pauper. Town pauper allowance is sixty-five."

"I never tried it—yet." Gypsy gave her accomplice a wink of approval over Guy Roy's head which was gripped between his hands. The girls were playing up in fine shape.

"You have to apply to the board. Likely a Montague & Roy girl wouldn't have a very good chance."

"Accourse, there's *one* trade there's no ban in. The madams like 'em young."

Becky cried out suddenly. Guy Roy lifted his head from his hands.

"Get out!" he said clearly. "Damn you, get out!"

Gypsy got to her feet with alacrity. "Come on, gals," she chirped.

Becky rose with the others.

"Not you, wench," Gypsy whispered vehemently. "You stay." She thrust the girl back and closed the door between them.

The lovers stood in haggard silence. Becky spoke first.

"Guy!"

"Yes?"

"You're going on with the factory, aren't you?"

He said helplessly: "You know what it means for us. It's the end."

"Nothing is the end for us," she said passionately. "You will go on?"

"Yes," he said. "What else can I do?"

She touched his cheek with light, tremulous fingers. "I'd have gone away with you," she said, "and we never would have been happy again."

She left him and hurried down to the darkness of the street.

A few moments later Guy came out into the hallway. He approached the waiting group.

"Tear up the notice," he said to Mary Haynes, and passed on.

FOURTEEN

"ONE can stand so much and no more," Becky complained fiercely.

"How long since you've seen him?" Gypsy asked.

"Nearly three weeks."

"Whose fault is that?"

"I did tell him that I couldn't meet him any more," Becky admitted. "But I didn't expect him to believe it," she added morosely.

"Shall I tell him you want to see him?"

"I ought not to."

"Is that goin' to stop you?"

"No," the wife answered on an indrawn breath.

"He's been away a coupla weeks drummin' up trade."

"Is the business prospering?" Becky's inquiry was formal and listless.

"Doin' likely enough, but the hotel's throwin' us out."

"He won't move away?" Becky asked in quick alarm.

"You don't know Guy Roy."

"But what other place can he find in Troy?"

"Quaker Johnson is rentin' us his extra house, out Miller's Hill way."

Becky's eyes widened. "I thought he was a moneyed man."

"All Quakers are moneyed men."

"Mr. Stockwell says there isn't a respectable man of means in all Troy who would rent an unused shed to be used for the ten-hour day. They wouldn't dare."

"Them Quakers," said Gypsy, "ain't scared of Old Scratch with his tail afire. We stand to better eighty dollars a month by the change." She shifted the subject. "Look, gal. Guy Roy'll be back Wednesday. When d'you want to see him?"

"Thursday," said Becky.

"At my room?"

"No. Bring him to the shed at the top of the garden."

"Want I should be there to see fair play?" Gypsy grinned. "All right. Ten o'clock."

The meeting between the lovers was sober and restrained.

One point of caution they mutually surrendered: they must find ways to continue to meet either there or at Gypsy's.

"And if he surprises us?" Guy said.

"So long as we are guiltless," she murmured.

"Will he believe that?"

"I don't know, Guy. With every week that passes I think I know less about him. Last night I heard him groaning."

"In his room?"

"Yes. It was nearly midnight."

"Did you speak to him?"

"I feared he was ill. I knocked at his door but he said it was only a hollow tooth and bade me go back to bed. Oh, Guy! He sounded so mournful, so—so lost."

"Don't think about it, my darling," he said. With a change of tone he added: "I want it to be clear to you how matters stand with me. The Montague & Roy Company can last out through the winter and perhaps·into spring. After that, I see nothing but ruin. If I could only hold out for three years . . ."

"Why that?"

"I shall come into my patrimony. Then, if matters come to a crisis with you, I can take care of you. Will you wait for me?"

"For ever," she said.

"I have to see Gurdon soon," he said. "Probably tomorrow."

"Oh, Guy! Do be careful."

"It is only a matter of business," he said, surprised at her apprehension.

"He's been so strange lately." She laughed a little. "He's taken to wearing gloves in the house. Guy, you don't think he's going mad, do you?"

"Pss-sst!" Gypsy signalled from the bush where she had posted herself as sentry.

They moved cautiously towards the door.

"Somebody on the prowl," the watcher warned. "Down below. By the wall."

Through the dimness a bulky figure could be seen, pacing the walk that led to the lower gate, to and fro, to and fro.

"That's Mr. Stockwell," Becky said. There was no alarm in her voice. "He's been doing that every night for the last week."

"Poor devil!" Guy muttered involuntarily.

"Witch-ridden," said Gypsy, and crossed her two forefingers over her thumbs.

"You'd better go, darling," Becky sighed.

"Good night, my love."

Guy called at the Eureka Mills office the next day. Gurdon Stockwell's face was pasty. His hard black eyes, restless and lustreless, stared at the visitor for a moment and roved away. He did not rise nor offer to shake hands. Guy asked quickly, "Are you sick, Gurdon?"

"No. I am hale enough. Why should I be sick?" Then, conquering his petulance: "How d'you do, Cousin. How can I serve you?"

"I have come to inquire about the Eureka statement. When may I expect it?"

The magnate leaned forward. "You are in need of money?"

"Oh, well! You know how trade is." Guy was elaborately casual.

"There will be no dividend."

"Then," said Guy jauntily, "we must make do without."

"Guy, when will you be done with this wastethrift enterprise of yours—this ten-hour chimera?"

"Hardly wastethrift, Gurdon. Montague & Roy is doing famously."

Gurdon Stockwell's right hand came up, clutched a pencil, and drummed a tattoo with it on the desk top. "That," he said, "is not current report. If you are prepared to be reasonable, the differences between you and the representative commercialists of the city may still be composed."

Guy hardly heard him. His eyes were fixed upon the back of his cousin's hand. Beneath the gross black hairs the flesh was streaked in parallel weals, still angry on the recently healed edges. He said involuntarily, "What ails your hand, Gurdon?"

"My hand? Nothing, nothing." He dropped the pencil and thrust his hand into his pocket. Guy remembered Becky's comment on the gloves, worn indoors. Then he recalled in a flash of surmise and perturbation where he had seen just such scarifications before. On Becky's tender skin where it had encountered the taloned thorn bush!

Gurdon Stockwell, then, had been on Sadler's Island, and recently. Had he hoped to surprise his wife there? Hardly, after giving her warning by informing her that he knew of her earlier visits. What could he have been seeking in that lonely spot? Guy's brain buzzed with conjecture.

He commanded his voice sufficiently to say with an effect of natural concern: "You should have those wounds dressed, Gurdon. They may be envenomed."

"Nonsense," the other snapped. "A mere claw scratch. I was playing with the old tom and the creature turned on me."

Well, it might be. Yet he remembered that, as a boy, Gurdon had always had an aversion for cats.

As he came out, after bidding his cousin good-bye, he brushed against Amos Goodwilly, who expressed effusive pleasure at the sight of him. Two of his former employees, passing that way, greeted him with smiling welcome. Pausing to answer them, and before the office door closed, he heard the overseer inquire: "What about Loom Four, Mr. Stockwell, sir? It's been vacant a week now."

"Loom Four?" the proprietor queried irritably.

"Priscilla Stamm's loom."

"Don't pester me with such trivia! Double one of the other hands on it."

Loom Four had been an annoyance to Goodwilly ever since the Stamm girl returned to it. Her output was scanty and poor, full of flaws and overlaps, typical of the sluttish standards of the half-timer. She kept her job, the overlooker figured, by virtue of her reputation for piety and her association with the boss as a church worker.

As shown in the hire-book, the girl had failed to report on the morning of 14 October. No explanation was forthcoming, either that day or on the succeeding days. Probably she was ailing. That was no worry of the overlooker's.

Old Miss Stamm, Priscilla's spinster aunt, came to him on the third day to make reluctant inquiries; he could tell her nothing. As he offered her no place to sit, she went out and perched patiently on the steps, awaiting the half-hour lunch-recess when she could talk with some of Priscilla's fellows. Little help was to be had from them, though they were kind and willing enough.

"When did you last see her?" a speeder asked the old lady.

"On Wednesday. She came home at closing-time very tired and wouldn't take her tea before she went to bed."

"That was the night the fire-ball fell," a corder put in.

There was a chorus of eager comment among those who had seen the flaming marvel of the meteor.

"She never slept in her bed," the old lady said in frightened tones. "It woke me and I went to tell her of it and she wasn't there."

"Maybe the devil came for Prissy on it," a small bobbin-doffer giggled.

The head weaver hit her a resounding clap across the jaw. "You clam up, you little chatterbox!"

Above the sobs of the assaulted one, Miss Stamm said indignantly: "My girl Prissy is a good girl. I defy anyone to call her out of her name." A long and strained pause followed. "Can anyone here say different?" she challenged in a tremulous voice.

Scattering "No's" responded.

Several remembered—or thought they did—hearing Prissy refer to a better job elsewhere. One girl, a measurer, was sure that Prissy didn't like her hire at the Eureka, didn't seem to take any interest in her work, no vim. Another opined that she didn't eat enough to keep a humming-bird alive.

A spinner spoke up. "I saw Cash Barlow waiting on her at the gate. That was Wednesday, too," she added excitedly.

"I seen the two of 'em, a-walkin' down the street," a little cleaner put in. "Only I didn't think nothin' of it then. She was cryin', like."

"Mightn't Cash know something about it?" the spinner asked the visitor.

"I've been to see him. He cursed me foully," the old lady replied. "He said Prissy had thrown him over and she could go to the Bad Place for all of him."

"Nobody ever got any good out of companying with that fellow," the speeder said darkly.

The old lady burst into tears and withdrew, dabbing at her eyes.

Strange happenings were remembered of that October Wednesday. The meteor lit the night with horrid fires. There was dim, unexplained movement by land and water. The middle air stirred with tainted breezes and unholy traffic; witches were reported, both broom and fork. Voices, not of this earth, sounded through the darkness, one raised in mortal agony and quenched with frightening abruptness. Gracie's Ladies' Emporium, which carried a sideline of charms, did a record trade next day in protective devices: old horseshoes for doorways, used brooms for roof peaks. It was wasted money, the phenomena did not recur.

Item by item, more detailed rumours circulated. Little Marty Mull, the cutter, being a "natural" and therefore unafraid of the dark, was gigging for fish in a backwater that evening. Presbyterian time had struck nine from the church tower when a tall figure, cloaked in some garment blacker than the enshrouding night, appeared noiselessly from the shadows and busied itself casting off the moorings of a small boat. It was the Devil. She knew it because, being down-wind from him, she caught a whiff of brimstone. Terrified, she dropped her catch and hid under an old wharf. The boat put out, heading crosscurrent, she thought. She waited until the sound of the oars was lost. When she came back to her place, her whole string, five sticklebacks, a bass, and an eel, were gone: further proof of the dark figure's identity. Every good Catholic knew that Satan ate meat on Fridays and fish on other days.

Tipsy Turner, the First Ward drunkard, added his bit. A little after nine he had seen, so help him, God!, a young witch tripping it lightly across the water. The moon had pushed aside the clouds for a few brief, bright moments and he sighted her as plain's the nose on your face. Headed towards Sadler's Island, she was. Certes, there was a ford there, everybody knew that, and the water was uncommon low this fall. But this female wasn't wading, she was dancing on the little waves. The clouds closed in and he saw her no more. Not so long after that, the big fireball fell out of the sky and then, of course, he knew what *she* was up to. Trysting it with Old Nick. Well, he might have had a pint in him at the time, and what of it? He was sober enough to know what he saw, and it was all true and he'd swear it on the Book.

Further tidings came a few days later from below Albany. Three river gypsies had been laid by the heels at Beckman's Landing in the matter of a small, half-rotted ark, for the possession of which they could not satisfactorily account. Contrary to tribal custom, one of them proved garrulous. Stimulated by a gratis potation of killdivvle at a waterside inn, he related a strange tale. On the night of the falling star, their craft was passing Troy. It was pitch dark. The current drew them in towards a longish island on their right. It was out-poles for them. As they were fending off he noticed a light flickering through the low growth on the heights. Knowing the place to be uninhabited, he would have taken it for a bob-o-light and thought little of it, but for what followed.

They were clear of the shadows and out in the main current when a man's hoarse cry brought them up short.

"Where are you? Where are you?" it called.

They rested on their sweeps. It might have been a quarter of a minute later or even less when the sound of crackling brush came to their ears, as of some body pushing urgently through undergrowth, followed by a single, high shriek. Silence fell. They could see nothing in the murk.

It is the gypsy principle never to meddle gratuitously with what does not concern you. Thus one escapes needless troubles in a Gentile world which is hard enough, at best, for the Romany. The trio conferred in whispers and reached agreement: the prudent course was to set broad water between their craft and the scene of such questionable doings. They put their sturdy backs into the stroke, and were well past the downstream point when the shooting star scared them almost witless. It confirmed their opinion that they had done well to leave the unchancy spot.

The tale travelled, mouth to ear, and reached Gypsy Vilas. She went to her employer with it.

"A week ago last Wednesday?" he said thoughtfully. "Isn't that when Priscilla Stamm was last seen?"

"That's what I was thinkin'."

"Can you believe what those fellows say?"

"The Gyppos? Not on oath. It's generally all gobbledygotch."

"Just the same, Gypsy, no other news of the Stamm girl has turned up. I'm wondering whether this shouldn't be a magistrate's information."

Gypsy had the distaste of her kind for legal involvements. "It's no scab off our itch," she pointed out. "Prissy ain't one of our girls."

"No. It's the Eureka's concern." Guy meditated. "Gurdon Stockwell ought to be notified. Then, if he chooses to take cognizance of it as a magistrate, he can do so. I'll give you a note to take over to him, Gypsy."

The emissary was not admitted to the Eureka office. Mr. Stockwell accepted the note, but sent out word that he was busy.

FIFTEEN

THE Stockwells were seated at their silent dinner-table at two o'clock when Amos Goodwilly came rushing up the hill from the factory and burst in upon them.

"They've found her," he panted. "Mr. Stockwell, sir, they've found her."

Gurdon Stockwell's face became a stony mask. "Compose yourself, Mr. Goodwilly. Who is 'they' and whom have they found?"

"Priscilla Stamm. She's dead."

Becky gave a little cry of consternation. "Oh, Mr. Goodwilly! How?"

"They found her in the gravel pit on Sadler's Island, ma'am."

Gurdon Stockwell said:

"A perilous spot. Or so I hear. The unfortunate girl fell over the brink?"

"She may have thrown herself over."

"Suicide? Why should she commit that rash act?"

Mr. Goodwilly coughed discreetly behind his hand. He cast a sidelong glance at the mistress of the household. He was a man of sensibility. "She was discovered to be in a state of domestic solicitude," he explained delicately.

"Do you mean she was pregnant?" Gurdon Stockwell was painfully affected, as could be told from his intonation. "I cannot believe it. Let me have the details, please."

Two eleven-year-old brothers, as the overlooker told it, had paddled across to the island that morning to gather edible fuzzballs on the heights. On a mutual dare as to which would approach nearer to the dangerous pit brink, they had espied the crumpled body below. Horrified, they rowed back to spread the news. Dr. Fitch Brockway hastened to the spot, made an examination and recognized both the girl and her condition.

"This is doubly shocking," Gurdon Stockwell said. "How long had the poor young woman been lying there?"

"Several days, they think."

"Were there any marks of violence?"

Again Goodwilly hesitated, glancing in the direction of the intent wife. "Dr. Brockway found evidence of an attempt at a criminal operation," he said. "He thinks that the girl may have resisted?"

"How so?"

"There is a fracture of the skull. That may have been caused by the fall, which also broke her neck. Or her assailant may have hit her over the head and dragged her through the brush to pitch her down the cliff. Her hands are badly lacerated."

Gurdon Stockwell's own hands twitched beneath the damask tablecloth. "Is anyone suspected?"

"There's talk about Cash Barlow."

"I thought that Barlow was in again."

"Being in jail don't bother him. You know our jailer. If it happened Wednesday night—and they think it did—Cash was seen outside." He paused for effect. "With Priscilla Stamm, too," he added.

Becky uttered a shocked exclamation. Gurdon Stockwell said thoughtfully, "Is it true that they were keeping company?"

"He was after her, sir. No doubt about that. If it should turn out to be murder—well, Judge Lynch might be called in."

"That cannot be allowed." Gurdon Stockwell spoke with vigour. "Has the sheriff been vigilated?"

Goodwilly's lip curled. "You know our sheriff."

"An extra-legal hanging in York State?" Stockwell pursued. "It would be a blot upon Troy. Judge Lynch may hold court in the lawless West, but not in this community."

"Would the community be any the worse for it if that rabbler of a Barlow was out of the way, Mr. Stockwell, sir?"

"That is not the question. An innocent man—a man who may be innocent," he corrected himself, "must not suffer mob violence. Our respectable citizenry . . ." His voice became a mutter and died away.

"Our most respected citizens, if I may make bold to say so, sir," the other filled in the pause, "would look the other way and whistle upsy-daisy if they saw the loop around that scoundrel's weazand."

"Well, well! Keep me advised. That is all for the present, Goodwilly."

For a long quarter-hour after Becky left him, he sat at the table, his face contorted with thought. When he rose to go to his study, he stumbled over his own feet. Once within he locked the door, seated himself at his desk, studied his scarified hands, and picked delicately at the scabs. No use! It would be a week before they would cease to be noticeable, glaringly, damningly noticeable. Whereas if Cash Barlow were conveniently hanged, the case would be safely buried with him and nothing else would be considered. The conscience-tortured man bent his face on the desk-top and wept. When he lifted it, it had taken on a look of resignation and, at the same time, resolution. From a secret drawer he took a sheet of paper, formally drafted. It was headed:

ALERTE HALCYONS

There followed a list of twenty-five names, segregated in groups of five. They comprised the town's lustiest young Corinthians. Across the foot of the sheet was inscribed the motto:

Once a Halcyon; Ever a Halcyon

and below that the rallying-cry, filched from Aristophane's raucous comedy:

Brek-kek-kek-kex.
Co-ax! Co-ax!

He copied the lists, divided them into five sections with his shears, and sat back to wait.

Troy seethed. The tale of the river gypsy had become, by evening, town gossip, having been embellished and distorted in its passage along towpath, turnpike and river. Now it took the form that a man's voice had been heard from the dark island, threatening murder; a woman's begging mercy. Tipsy Turner revised his account to accommodate the public taste. The apparition on the waters, he now recalled, was of this earth. She had been picking her way along the ford. At the far edge she was met by a man. The man was short and stocky and wore a slouch hat.

As the purveyor of what everyone wanted to hear, Tipsy was a hero. Strangers stood him drinks. He passed in glory from tap-room to taproom, waxing ever more dramatic, ever more specific. At the Eagle he was hoisted to the bar. His memory being stimulated with punch, he rose to his climax of sensation. He had recognized the man who met the woman at water-edge by his limp. Swear to it? He'd swear on a stack of Bibles.

The man was Cash Barlow.

A blood-roar rose from the crowd and welled out into the night. "Get him! Hang him! To the jail! The jail!"

Mrs. Stockwell, going to summon her husband to supper, found the door still locked. A voice she hardly knew for his said: "Let be. I am busy."

Busy—she thought—with no light showing? What could such business be? She withdrew.

He sat there in dumb travail, waiting for the message that must call him to the test. When he heard Amos Goodwilly's shuffling approach along the gravelled walk, he threw open the window.

"Well?"

"It was Barlow, sir. The court's forming. You can see the torches in the square."

"Can the authorities not defend the jail?"

"The jailer's evaded already. Nobody knows where the sheriff is."

"The constables . . ."

"Two of 'em are locked in the Eagle cellar and glad enough to be there out of harm's way."

Gurdon Stockwell drummed nervously upon the window ledge. "Has he no friends, no supporters?"

"They say the unioneers will fight. What can they do, a handful? The mob'll rush them into the river."

Stockwell's hope died within him. "Where is the mob now?"

"In the square, listening to the speeches. Oh, it'll all be done orderly, Mr. Stockwell, sir. At the signal, they'll move on the jail. Court will hold at Ten Eyck's wharf, they say. They'll hang him to the big linden at the water's edge. Is there anything more, sir?"

"No. Go away."

He waited for the footsteps to die out, then dropped to his knees in prayer. God would always be a partner in any enterprise of Gurdon Stockwell's—such was the Stockwell faith—whether for good or evil. Of course, he would firmly believe that whatever he prayed for must be good.

He wrote several single-sentence notes which he addressed to former associates in the bonds of Halcyon, called black Jeshurun and sent him out with them. He then stood, flexed his powerful muscles, not without a thrill of unholy anticipation, and, catching up his Halcyon cane, made his way to the stables.

Guy Roy was yawning himself to bed at eleven o'clock after a dull evening over his accounts, when the outer door of his lodgings shook to a thunderous assault. He thrust his head from the front window. A dearborn stood at the curb with a span of restless blacks between the thills.

"Who's there? What the devil do you want?"

Gurdon Stockwell's face twisted upward. "Halcyons out!"

Guy jumped for boots and coat. This was a call which permitted no delay. He returned to the window for one question, "Ropples?"[1]

"Yes, ropples."

With his loaded cane leashed to his wrist, Guy took the stairs at a run.

"Where?" he asked.

"The jail."

"Barlow?" He had heard the flying rumours.

"Yes. We have to reach there before the mob."

"There's been no alarum."

"There will be. Any moment now." He consulted a list in his hand. "You're to alert Miller and Urena. Howland is with me on the box. I've sent out five notes; all I dared take time for. We'll need every hoplite we can get. Even that may not be enough." His words rattled forth. "Rendezvous at the jail—the Third Street side. Who's archon for this month?"

"You seem to be."

"I'm emeritus," the other said impatiently. "I'll turn over to the regular command."

"Doc Armitage," Guy said.

"He's on my list. If he's at home the note will have reached him by now. Get in. I'll drop you at . . ."

A brazen clangour rent the silence. The firebell was pealing out its message with a madman on the rope.

---

[1] Presumably from ropalon, a fighting-club. The Halcyons prided themselves on their Attic jargon.

They plunged into the wagon. The horses galloped. Guy leapt out at the bachelor rooms of young Urena and hammered at the door. When his battering brought no response, he kicked and shouted, still without result.

"Drive on," he shouted to Howland at the reins. "I'll join you at Miller's."

Prying a cobble loose, he flung it through the upstairs chamber window. This was no time for temporizing.

A head, swathed in a wet white bandage, appeared. From it issued a stream of appropriate and defamatory verbiage.

"Out!" Guy called. "Halcyons out!"

Young Urena moaned piteously. "My head! That punch . . . Zat you, Roy?"

Guy dandled a second rock. "D'you want another?"

"I'll come. What's up?"

"Lynch's Court."

The sufferer brightened. "Who we hanging?"

"Shut up and get dressed. Rally at the jail." He bethought himself. "Ropples," he added.

"Ah!" said young Urena. "It's a real turn-up."

"Too damned real," Guy answered grimly. "Are you fit to fight?"

"I can always fight."

Guy knew this to be true. The stocky Dutchman was a ready and redoubtable fisticuffer.

When he rejoined the equipage, Ralph Miller was coming down his steps. The fire-alarum, designed to rally the mob, was rousing an anti-element as well, hardly less lawless but, for this time, on the side of law and order. Dr. Saul Armitage, the Halcyon leader, came running round the corner, drawing his neck-piece into place, for he was a neat dresser. He conferred hastily with the others.

"You take deputy," he instructed Guy.

"How many can we muster?"

"Not more than ten, thus far," Stockwell answered.

"Not enough to defend the jail."

"Not if there were twice as many," Armitage decided.

"Then our best chance is to run him off and secrete him," Guy said.

"Our only chance," the leader said gravely.

Urena came panting up. "I've alerted Miles Tiggett and

Lucky Chance Wrench," he announced. A burly form appeared
from an alley. The irrepressible Urena sniffed the air. "Tim
Freegle, if my faithful nose don't deceive me."

The mackerel inspector joined the group. Like Tiggett and
Wrench, he was emeritus. But—"Once a Halcyon; Ever a Halcyon". Loving memories of past combat lingered. The archon
welcomed the newcomers.

"Thirteen," he said approvingly. "If we had a little more
time . . ."

"We haven't," Guy broke in as a dull roar sounded below.
"They're on the move."

How is a mob born? In what dark womb of fury is it nurtured?
What obscure lust, what deep-buried thirst for slaughter, drives
it to its work?

The component figures, dim and impersonal, welled from the
wharves and basins of the waterfront, from farm-byre and dank
alley, from the verminous huts of the outskirts and the crowded
and foul inns of the turnpike, crawled up out of the river slime,
scum of the shifting, irresponsible populace of turnpike and
towpath, raftsmen, vagrant tinkers and advertised apprentices
with a price of one cent and a bucket of ashes on their heads,
shifting, small clots of humanity which in time merged and
flowed, following the blood scent. The reek of slaughter was in
their nostrils, the thrill of base excitations in their nerves. "Flux
from the devil's privy," Ralph Miller described them in his un-
published report. All of them, as by some foul magnetism of lust,
were drawn to the square where the bellows-lunged inciters to
violence spent their rhetoric on the air.

Three hundred swelled to five hundred; five hundred to seven
and eight, milling below the inn balcony where the self-appointed
orators held forth, and blocking the square and the streets
adjoining. Some bore chance weapons: bottles, staves, implements
of household and field. The canallers brandished their fending-
poles. The mass weaved and muttered as the leaders worked
them towards the pitch of murder.

Tipsy Turner, barely able to enunciate, hiccoughed his
imaginative tale of what he had witnessed. Now he had reached
the flight of fancy where he all but saw the miscreant hurl his
victim into the death-pit. Martha Mull, the little "natural", had
been bullied and persuaded to the spot. Thrust upon the balcony,
she gibbered and drooled and provided her avid hearers with

Q

what sufficed them as identification of the cloaked figure in the boat. To every prodding inquiry she returned her assent.

"Yes . . . It was him. . . . Yes, Cash Barlow . . . Yes, I seen his face. . . . Now, lemme be. Lemme *be*!"

A foreman at the pin mill, the same who had instigated Barlow's latest arrest, recapitulated the garbled version of the river-gypsy's account. It was convincingly performed. A terrified work-girl from the Eureka told of the accused man's unsuccessful wooing of Prissy. "He said he'd kill her, so he did." The crowd roared:

"Get him! Hang him! String him up!"

A burly figure stepped into the light of the balcony, lifting a hand. Josh Loach, he who with his companion had entered his protest against the Montague & Roy Company before the Mill Owners meeting, was a tap-room orator of parts. He had a presence, a command of phrase, and a large and musical voice.

"All in order, my friends, all in order. This is not the only crime to the miscreant Barlow's account. He is a fomenter of discord in our midst. He would procure laws to snatch the bread of honest industry from the mouths of worthy mechanics. Such as he were better dead and buried."

"Kill him! Hang him! Hooray!"

"Give him his way and he would prevent our children from earning an honest livelihood. By his short-hour day he would cast our pure and spotless womanhood to the lure of the public streets. He is the enemy of God and man."

"Where is he?"

"Show him to us!"

"Ropes, ropes!"

"Hang the vermin!"

"Vermin he is and vermin he will remain until the earth is well rid of him. But, vermin though he is, he shall have his hearing, full and free, before Judge Lynch. Fair play. That's the American way of it, that's the Troy way of it. We will take Barlow from his cell, peaceful and orderly. We will hale him under guard to Ten Eyck's Wharf. There Judge Lynch's court will duly hear his case. He shall have his say. The witnesses will have theirs. And at the end, we will hang him to the linden tree at the water's edge and leave him there to swing. To the jail, my friends and fellow Trojans."

Yelling, whooping, howling, the mob surged from the square and up the slope to Third Street, avid for its prey.

The Halcyons were before them, though by little enough. Sixteen strong, they had approached from the rear. A shrill, thin cry of defiance met them from a straggling little contingent of labourers gathered to do what they might in defence of their fellow.

Gurdon Stockwell jumped from the dearborn. "We want Cassius Barlow."

"You can't have him," Silas Harris, the highboy driver and leader of the forlorn hope, said stoutly.

"Not while there's a one of us left," Yankee Bond, the furnace man, seconded him.

Guy Roy hurried up from the other side. "It's us or Judge Lynch," he called. "Take your choice."

"You, Mr. Roy!" the blackie gaped. "Whatcha going to do with him?"

"Take him to Castle Hill for safety."

"I am a magistrate," Stockwell announced. "I represent here the majesty of the law. Its protection will be thrown about the prisoner."

There was a quick conference among the group. "He's locked in a cell. What do you want us to do?" the spokesman said.

Doc Armitage flourished a fireman's axe in his hand. "We'll get him out."

"Go and meet the mob," Guy directed the labourers. "Hold 'em the best you can. If it's only two minutes it'll help."

The jail was dark. Freed from surveillance, most of the inmates had vanished gratefully into the night and freedom. But a few of the supposedly desperate characters were locked into the lower cells. Armitage entered and demolished the guardian bars without difficulty.

"Cash Barlow!" he called urgently.

The prisoner, huddled into a far corner, cried out lamentably, "You want to kill me because I'm the working man's friend."

Armitage hauled him into the half-light and pressed the axe into his hand. "We're going to save you. Take hold of that."

The hunted man grabbed and swung it. "There'll be lives to pay before they get me in a noose," he declared.

But outside, at the sight of Gurdon Stockwell, he recoiled. "What's this? A trap?" he snarled.

Guy Roy blocked the half-lifted weapon. "We're your friends. We're taking you to Castle Hill where we can form a defence. Get in. Or stay here and wait for the mob to get you."

A not-too-far-distant roar lent force to his words. Barlow bundled into the equipage.

A returned emissary from the embattled workers ran up. He was bleeding from a gash above his eye.

"They'll be on us any minute," he yelled. "Every street's filling up."

"Which way is the crowd thinnest? Quick!" Guy Roy demanded.

"I dunno. Ferry Street, I guess."

"Gurdon, you and two more in the carriage for guard," he snapped out his orders. "We'll make a diversion and join you. Whip up your horses, Howland. Lay into 'em. Stop for nothing." To the unioneer he said, "Fetch what men you can to Castle Hill."

"There won't be much left of us," the man said and hobbled back to the mêlée.

Put to full pace, the great Stockwell horses plunged into Ferry Street, the Halcyons streaming after, canes at the ready. In that block were perhaps seventy to eighty potential lynchers, who scattered with yelps of dismay.

"Runaway! Runaway!"

Unluckily someone caught sight of Cash Barlow. The yells turned to fury. The swiftly running, carefully deployed followers of the dearborn were cursed, threatened and presently attacked. But the whirling ropples did their work. The runners broke through the loose line of obstruction. It was only a skirmish, but when they had fought their way to open space, two of them were lacking. The odoriferous mackerel inspector lay stunned in the gutter, and sturdy Burton Van Liew reeled into a basement with a broken arm.

Several of the hotter heads were for returning with a view to vengeance. Guy Roy vetoed it.

"Keep on! Keep on! No fighting unless you're blocked off."

The Halcyon discipline was rigid. The little force sped along and were joined by three late recruits, Orlando Montague, Harmon Teale and Charles Veazie, all of the reserve. Gurdon

Stockwell and his companions had rallied two of the active band, Elias Plum and Taylor Paulding. They could count on a round twenty for the main fight.

Council of war was held before the mansion, among Guy, Doc Armitage and Gurdon Stockwell while the hard-breathed runners straggled in and threw themselves, panting, on the restful earth. To defend the house was manifestly impracticable; there were too many opportunities for ingress. The brick coach-house, backed by the cliff and fronting an open space surrounded with thick shrubbery, afforded the best chance. There was but one door, and the windows were small and difficult. Three Halcyons, plus Barlow, were posted inside to man these possible points of access. It was decided that Stockwell, in his dual capacity as magistrate and owner of the property, should take his stand outside the door and hold the invaders in parley. If and when he was attacked, the forces concealed in the shrubbery would converge on him, canes swinging. At best, however, the defenders would be desperately overmatched.

The first gobbet of the man-hunt swarmed over the stone wall of the garden, three or four dozen of them, led by Simmy Cobb, the hulking, dribble-lipped Cockney indentured to Butcher Carmody. They were the hobbledehoys of the city, out for a good time. Presently there straggled through the gate a long stream of rioters which spread and thinned through the garden. The invaders paused, uncertain, a little daunted by the implicit threat of darkness and silence. Reinforcements piled up. Plump Josh Loach toiled and puffed in the rear. At the same time, the battered remnants of the working-men contingent, half of them crippled or wounded, arrived by the longer route, having been piloted by Sam Blunt, who had once been a Stockwell gardener. They gathered at the toolshed for a last desperate sally when the time should come.

The mansion loomed, lofty, dim, forbidding. Confused clamour broke from the continually increasing mass of people.

"There's no lights."

"They've jicked us, the sonsabitches."

"Who saw the wagon?"

Loach shouted: "This's the place. Look! Fresh hoofmarks in the gravel. The coach-house. That's where he is."

As at a signal, a light flickered in the second storey of the smaller building, steadied to a flame, and the great tavern lanthorn, its four-square glass sheltering the bright flare, ran out smoothly upon its bracket of wrought-iron artistry.

"Thanks for the handy gallows!" a voice shouted, and a crackle of mirth greeted the ominous jest.

Gurdon Stockwell stepped forth from the door. He was empty-handed. His face was set in harsh lines. His powerful voice overbore the scattered rumour of the mobsters.

"Stand where you are."

The mass became immovable, except for an uncertain wavering. No man could tell what threat of violent death the silent walls might harbour.

"In the name of the law, I call upon you to disperse. This is private property. You are trespassers. Off!"

"Give us the murderer!"

"There is no murderer here."

"He's lyin'. Look at his face."

"Give us Cash Barlow!"

"Hang him!"

"Burn him!"

"Down with the door, boys!"

From a rear rank came a warning in a tone of would-be reasonableness. "Better give him up, Mr. Stockwell, and save bloodshed."

The magistrate identified the speaker. "I know you, Josh Loach," came in his measured speech. "If a life is lost tonight, you shall hang for it."

Loach whined a protest, but the steady and powerful voice cut him short, picking out and listing the familiar faces.

"Stacy Smith! Is that you? Stand forth like a man. Darrow, it is too late to hide your face. Corporal Simpson, when did you turn lawbreaker? George Collins! George Sylva! Each and every man of you shall be held responsible."

"He's taking the heart out of 'em," Guy Roy whispered into Doc Armitage's ear.

The older and more experienced Trojan answered: "Those are only the townfolk. It's the wharfers and canallers that won't be scared so easily. Like this one," he added, as a gangling, hardwood lath of a man pushed to the front.

"Come on, lads!" he shouted. "What the hell's a magistrate! Judge Lynch is good enough for us."

"Ain't we goin' to have any fun?" The appeal, rising in a

pathetic whine from the safe rear, won instant and savage response from the close-packed mass.

"Hi-yi-yi-yi-yi!" There was a ferocious gaiety and anticipation in the shrill staccato. The muscles of the Halcyons tensed for action. They had heard it before.

By that sound Gurdon Stockwell knew that the hope of a peaceful solution was past. The rush would come at any moment now. Stepping back, he reached within the entrance and brought forth a fowling-piece, which he hung in the curve of his arm. At low growl ran along the line facing him. When he spoke, it might have been as a judge on the bench, so level and quiet was his utterance.

"I wish no man's life on my conscience, however justified I may be in defending my homestead. This weapon carries a double charge of rock salt. If anyone is blinded, his be the blame."

"A stale trick!" someone bellowed. "Heads down and your elbows over your eyes."

Still the line hesitated.

"C'mon, boys!"

"Wotter we waitin' for?"

"Toss him a rock."

" 'Oo's afride!" yammered the Cockney lummox, resisting frantically as his companions thrust him forward.

The guardian of the door raised the weapon to settle it solidly against his shoulder. The far edges of the human crescent began to edge in for the rush.

"Harda back and stop her way!"

The call had in it an element of the jovial. The inching advance was checked. Into the full light of the swaying lanthorn the interrupter strode with a jaunty swagger. He was arrayed in the full splendour of an Erie packet captain's outfit: blue coat with brass buttons, flare pantaloons, sea boots and a costly beaver painted with a dashing representation of billows on a lee shore. Stockwell at once covered him with the muzzle.

"Halt!"

"Avast, my hearty!" the captain protested. "Hold your broadside." No deep-sea mariner could be quite as nautical as a seasoned canaller. This one took off his castor and swept Stockwell a mock bow. "Captain Trigg of the *Western Wave*, at your service."

"Trigg! Bull Trigg!" The words passed through the crowd, accented with respect.

The man was built like a bull: vast chest, bulky shoulders, neck like a tree-bole supporting a craggy head. He stood above Stockwell's six feet by a good three inches and looked to outweigh him two stone or more. Solid and uncompromising, the man with the gun said, "What do you do on my premises, Captain Trigg?"

"Will you put down that gun and run me off?"

"No. I am no brawler."

"I'll lay you a test."

"State it."

"You have the murderer, Barlow, secreted."

"I hear you say so.'

"Will you fight me for him?"

A hush spread over the assemblage.

Gurdon Stockwell said coldly: "Let me be sure that I understand you. If I fight and best you, will this mob disperse peacefully to their homes?"

The answer came in a roar from the crowd.

"No!"

"Not without Barlow."

"Give us the murderer and we'll go."

"We'll get him and we'll get you, too, if you meddle with us."

"Hemp for both of 'em."

"You see?" Stockwell said contemptuously to his challenger.

Trigg, somewhat discomfited, rubbed his nose. "Tell you what, brother, I'll make a bargain with you just the same."

"Speak up."

"I can't vouch for this crowd of blacklegs and guttermuck. But we got thirty-forty rough-and-tumble Erie men here."

"Well?"

"You best me, and they're yours. That kee-rect, boys?"

The response came from all sides.

"Right-o, Cap!"

"We're with you, Bully."

"The Ee-rye-ee for ever!"

Little did the canallers care on which side they fought, just so the battle was a good one.

Gurdon Stockwell thought swiftly. As matters stood, the defenders, comprising only the Halcyons and the few feeble labourers, were hopelessly outmanned. Joined by the Erie contingent, they must still face odds of three to one. But the canallers were practiced in combat and, if not as disciplined and expert as the younger Corinthians, could always be counted upon for last-ditch resistance.

"Very good," he said. "If I best you in fair fight——"

"Nixie-no!" Capt. Trigg bellowed. "None o' your fine-gentleman fighting for Bull Trigg. Nothing barred and may the best man win. That's my style."

Stockwell understood. It would be tooth, claw and boot, a rough-and-tumble from which no conquered man could hope to emerge unmaimed. His bearing was still unperturbed as he continued, "Then, if I win, your fellows will help man the door?"

"As long as one of us can stand on his feet. Done?"

"Done."

"Good-bye, poor Hurdy-Gurdy Stockwell!" mourned an exaggerated treble, and again the hard, crackling laughter rose.

"Form a ring."

"Hands round."

"Close in, there."

"Leave an open way," the jovial Trigg called. "I'm going to truss and drown him in his own founting."

"That's the gab!"

"Thumb his eyes out."

"Gouge out his gullet."

"Give 'im the knee."

With other suggestions for mayhem more specific and unpleasant.

Capt. Trigg stripped off his elegant broadcoat, folded it neatly, placed upon it his sarsanet waistcoat appropriately embroidered in anchors, and topped the heap with his artistic beaver. Rolling his fine linen shirt-sleeves above the elbow, he held up his mighty arms for the admiration of the crowd, making the corded muscles ripple.

Moving with deliberation, Gurdon Stockwell leaned his gun against the lintel and stripped off his Taglioni. A wharf-rat darted from the side, seized upon the weapon and was swallowed back into the mass. At this trickery, which he attributed to his opponent, Stockwell went berserk.

"You damned, treacherous bastard!" he yelled, and launched himself at Trigg's throat.

Against that insane fury, the canaller never had a chance. Before his hands were up he was battered into helplessness, staggering under the hail of blows until he went down.

Painfully he struggled to hands and knees. Stockwell stepped back, took a short run, and the awed crowd grunted as they heard ribs crunch on the impact of the heavy riding-boot. The stricken man toppled and rolled while the canallers howled in dismay. One of them, the steersman of the *Western Wave*, leapt to his chief's aid, but was grabbed and hauled away. The code was rigid.

Now the assailant was booting at the face which the victim was striving to protect between huddled arms.

"My God! He'll kill him!" Guy Roy cried to Armitage, forgetting the orders of silence and concealment.

They moved out, shoulder to shoulder. From a thicket, a figure plunged at Armitage, clubbed him down and scuttled away.

"Take over," he muttered to Guy as two Halcyons dragged him back into shelter.

Guy ran upon the maddened Stockwell from behind and pinioned his arms.

"Let me go!" the fighter raved. "Let me go! I'll kick his brains out!"

"Steady, Gurdon!" Guy's quiet voice was at his ear. "He's done. You don't want murder on your soul."

Stockwell went limp. In a dazed voice he mumbled, "Take me away." The madness had gone out of him.

Like a wounded animal the canaller was crawling blindly along the gravel. He lifted a face, hideously battered. He spat white and red, teeth and blood. The cries of his fellows stimulated him to a last mechanical attempt to get to his feet. With a pitiful effort he pushed himself to his knees. It was the end. He crumpled and rolled.

A squat gnome, carrying a steel-tipped fending-pole, jumped out, took one look at Stockwell's still dazed face, and addressed Guy.

"I'm Mogridge of the *Spray*. He's licked. Where can we take him?"

"Inside."

Three of the Erie men bore the twitching form through the door. Mogridge said: "We're your men. What's orders?"

"How many have you?"

"Close on two score."

"We might be able to hold 'em in the open."

It was, at any rate, a fighting chance, as against the forlorn hope which a rush from concealment had held out.

"You're the boss," the mate answered.

A lull in activity had followed the single combat. It was a fortunate respite for the defenders. Guy blew a short toot on his whistle. The Halcyons sifted out from the shrubbery. Under his direction they formed to the right of the door while the canal forces spread to the left. What remained of the working men's group fell in back of Guy's contingent. There were about equal numbers on either flank of Stockwell whose back was to the door. Hoots and yells greeted the manœuvre. Guy stepped forward.

"Why don't you people go home to your beds?" he inquired, in a tone of sweet reasonableness.

"We'll go 'ome awfter we've 'anged Barlow," Simmy Cobb bumbled. "Out the wye unless yer wanter get bashed."

"All you'll get is a broken head, Simmy," retorted Guy with unabated good-humour.

"It's gettin' late," came a grim reminder from the heart of the mass.

There was an almost imperceptible nervous quivering along the front line, an edging forward. A stone hurtled through the air, narrowly missing Guy's head. Scattering missiles followed. Grunts of pain and curses from the line-up testified that some of them found their marks.

"Give 'em rocks!" a rioter shouted.

This was bad. Strung out as they were in full light of the lanthorn, the defenders were only too vulnerable.

"Douse that light," Guy commanded.

A high-flight clod did the work for him. He blew a long blast on his whistle.

The Halcyons charged with weapons swinging. This, the main battle, was joined under such dim illumination as was provided by a watery moon filtered through murky clouds.

The besieging forces were all but disrupted by the savageness of the first and unexpected onslaught. There was a chance that they might dissolve in panic. But the weight of numbers was too great. Though the canallers backed up the drive with fervour, it was absorbed and dissipated as it pressed on. Individual combats isolated the young fighters.

Many of the Halcyons battered their way back across the
gravelled space, but several were beaten down and put out of
action. Out of the whole triple force there were soon barely two
dozen fit to put up effectual resistance. Gurdon Stockwell had
been downed by a rock, and though he was up again, he was
too dizzy to do more than swing blindly. Guy, Armitage, Taylor
and the nucleus of the best combat troops were all damaged.
The triumphant cry went up:

"We got 'em, boys!"

"Scatter 'em!"

"Bust in the door."

The opaque darkness of massed bodies opened up. A dozen
men staggered forward under the weight of an oak balk. They
poised the battering-ram. One of those inexplicable pauses to
which mobs are prone imposed its hush.

The silence was shattered by a gunshot. A dreadful shriek
split the darkness. Out into the open bounded a figure. It was
Sim Cobb. His hands clutched at the wound. He whirled and
leapt and shrieked in a horrid death-dance.

"I'm shot in the awse! I'm shot in the awse!" he screeched
and, tripping over his own feet, tumbled and rolled before the
staring eyes of the multitude.

The laughter burst like an explosion. It rose, it swelled, it
roared, it thundered. It washed out the lust of murder from
the mutable human hearts. Men hammered one another on the
back, howling, squalling, gagging and choking in uncontrollable
merriment. They cast themselves to earth, rolling and squirming.
Fresh paroxysms of glee, imposed by the mad contagion, convulsed their helpless bodies, their eyes streaming, their lungs
bursting under the stress. There was left in them no vice. They
were as harmless as little woolly lambs.

So the event, destined for tragedy, was neutralized by the
solvent of healthy, ribald mirth.

SIXTEEN

THE mob had melted away, bound for bed or the all-night taverns. The interior of the coach-house had become an impromptu surgical station. Forms were huddled or curled or laid flat on floor and bench. The roster of injuries was a varied one, ranging from the superficial to the serious. An unidentified apprentice sprawled in a chair with one eye gone. The hostler at the Eagle was senseless in a corner, a hideous dent in his forehead. Two minor outlaws busied themselves with amateurish splints for broken legs. Willson Taylor had a dislocated shoulder. Franklin Wrench and Charles Veazie had helped one another in from where they had been felled in the middle of the battle. Mate Mogridge sucked at three disjointed fingers. One of his chief aides exhibited a badly bitten jaw. Battered faces were on all sides. Grunts and wheezes testified to broken or bent ribs. A dribble of blood descended from a table on which had been deposited a towny with a hole in his thigh from a pole thrust.

Doc Armitage was being ably seconded by squat little Dr. Brockway, who was not of the fraternity but had been commandeered to help as he was returning from a country call. Armitage was engaged with the unconscious Trigg. Gurdon Stockwell touched his elbow.

"How is he?"

"Pretty bad." The physician did not look up.

"Will he die?"

"Can't say yet."

"Fetch him to the mansion."

"Can't risk moving him."

"Stockwell turned away, impassive. Guy Roy was hobbling across the floor.

"Are you hurt, Guy?"

"Not to amount to anything."

"Armitage! Here! Attend to my cousin."

The absorbed physician paid no heed. Brockway, trailing a bandage, paused peering, into Guy's white face.

"Let's have a look at that leg."

He stripped up the pantaloon, prodded and kneaded, and

performed a quick binding job. "No great damage. You'll do. Get some air."

Guy's wobbly progress towards the door was blocked by Cassius Barlow, still gripping the fireman's axe. He put his mouth close to Guy's ears.

"I want a word with you."

"Make it short."

"Come aside." At a safe distance from the workers he halted. "How's Stockwell so sure I didn't kill her?" he growled.

Guy said coolly, "Did you?"

"No. And well he knows it." He glared. "You ask him this: where was he that night? Where was he when the fireball fell?"

"What are you getting at, Barlow?"

"You know what I'm getting at. You know why Stockwell's so certain it wasn't me."

"Why, you damned ingrate! He saved your life tonight."

"Maybe he did," the other admitted. "But where was he? That's what I want to know."

(Yes, thought Guy, seeing again that seamed hand—where was he, indeed?) He said curtly: "In his study, working at his accounts, as can be proven." (Well for Gurdon Stockwell if it could!) "Will that serve to keep your foulmouth shut?"

Shaken but still obsessed with his suspicion, Barlow said, "I'll keep it shut till I find out."

Air was what Guy craved; air and relief from the close room which stank of sweat and blood. He pushed the door ajar and wandered aimlessly out, taking in huge, grateful gulps of the night's freshness. The white glimmer of an ornamental bench set amid frost-faded greenery tempted him. He relaxed upon it and at once fell asleep.

"Guy! Oh, Guy!"

If it had been the loudest thunder of heaven it could not have roused him to a tenser awareness, that soft, anxious murmur. Becky Stockwell leaned over him.

She had cast a robe hastily over her nightdress. Her feet showed a gleam of white above the low slippers. Her loveliness and fear caught at his heart.

"Why did you come out?" he muttered.

"The gunshot woke me."

"It's all over."

"Are you hurt, Guy? You look so—so strange."

"Not I. Others are."

"Could I help?"

"Yes," he said. "Later. Stay here with me now."

"I will," she said simply, and began to weep. Her nerves had been under a harsher strain than they could well withstand.

At that, his self-restraint, so long and bitterly mastered, broke. The fever engendered by the fighting pulsed again in his blood. The warrior, worn with battle, seeks the arms of his beloved. They were together, tight-clasped. She gave one small, muffled moan as she pressed closer to him, body throbbing against body, mouth merged with mouth.

Only when the breath failed her did she lean back, panting hard. She said in a lost whisper, "Anywhere, any time, my darling."

"Now?"

"Where could we go?"

"The house. Isn't there a safe room?"

"Not safe. Not from him . . . I don't care. Let him find us. Let him kill us!" she cried in the exaltation of her passion.

"Come," he said.

With his arm still circling her, he guided her along the narrow path to the dark doorway. It opened, flooding them with light. Gurdon Stockwell stood there. He set down the pail of water he had been carrying. The pair sprang apart. It was too late. Both knew that. Becky seized Guy's hand and set it round her again, pressing it defiantly to her breast.

"Now you know," she said.

"Yes," Gurdon Stockwell said dully. He turned his grave regard upon Guy. "You, my kinsman. You are the betrayer."

Guy's heavy conscience found no retort to that quiet and melancholy reproach. Guy gently put his companion behind him and moved a step forward in watchful protectiveness. But Stockwell only shook his head, as in response to an unuttered question.

"You need not fear for her or for yourself," he said. "I may well have killed one fellow-being tonight. There is no wrath left in me for further killing, adulterers though you be."

"No," the wife said. "Not yet."

"No more killing," he went on as if he had not heard her. The lust of murder had ebbed from that cold visage, leaving upon it the stamp of an inhuman, implacable rigidity. Guy addressed him for the first time.

"What are you going to do?"

"That will be decided as I see fit. Meantime, I put both of you upon honour." He paused doubtfully. "Is there honour left in you?"

"No," answered his wife softly. "Only love."

"Lust," he corrected. "Unhallowed lust. Is it true, then, your assignations upon the island? Is it?"

"They were innocent," Guy said.

"You expect me to believe that?"

"Why should he?" Becky put in. "How could he understand?"

Her quiet contempt did not even bring her husband's eyes round to her. He stared at the ground between his feet. Guy wondered what obscure motive inspired her baiting of Stockwell. Did it derive from sheer hatred? Or did she hope to force an immediate solution of destiny's ravelled pattern?

The great door had swung to behind Stockwell. He threw it open.

"Enter," he directed.

He herded them to his study where he busied himself meaninglessly with the lights, with the papers on his desk, with the placement of the chairs. Alert for any dangerous motion, Guy kept intent watch upon him. Becky leaned against the wall. The exaltation of love and of imminent peril had waned, leaving her stilled and passive. Guy moved over to stand beside her. She reached out a hand to him. Stockwell's lips twitched.

"Do not touch her," he warned. With the restored tensity of his calm, he added, "I impose seemly behaviour upon both of you."

"You are within your rights," Guy admitted.

Becky spoke up quietly and bravely. "Mr. Stockwell, will you divorce me?"

"No."

"You believe me guilty. I shall make no denial if you wish to divorce me."

"Cherish no such hope. I have other designs for your future." A thin smile flattened his lips.

Guy roused himself. "I play a futile part here. Let us try to reach some composition."

"You suggest to me a composition with a man—a kinsman—who has corrupted and stolen my wife?"

"That is a lie. Oh, I make no defence for myself! But for her —for your wife . . ."

"My wife will account to me in due time."

". . . I can only give you my sacred word as a gentleman and a fellow Halcyon that we are guiltless of any criminal relationship."

"Guy, you waste breath," Becky said.

Stockwell's bearing when he resumed was characterized by the chill, implacable precision of a magistrate on the bench.

"You, Guy Roy, will at once take steps to close up your business and will leave Troy, never to return."

"Don't think it," Guy retorted.

"Reasonable time will be allowed to you," the self-appointed arbiter pursued. "Six months should be ample. You, Obedience Stockwell, will, within the same period, return to your wifely duties, responsibilities, and submissions in full. In full, I say."

"Never," she said. "Never in my life."

"Pending that time," he went on, unheeding, "you will both give me your word of honour, for what it may be worth, not to attempt any rendezvous, and, if you should encounter by chance, to exchange no speech or sign."

"No," said Guy.

"No," said Becky.

Bending slightly forward, the husband sat with hands clasped between his knees. In a slow drone that was more affrighting because of its passionless monotony, he recited the penalties of a wife's unfaithfulness.

"I will make your name a hissing and a byword. I will blazon you on the public hoardings as an adulteress and a strumpet. I will declare you a common prostitute and, in my capacity as magistrate, commit you as such. I will——"

"Wait!" Guy Roy was struggling for mastery of himself against the fear and rage that swelled his heart. "Accusation is not proof. You cannot prove what is a damnable lie."

"The trysts on the remote island," Stockwell took him up. "Were those nothing? Secret rendezvous in town, I doubt not. For what licit purpose? The shameless embrace I have just witnessed. What more would be required to convince any bench?"

R

Guy moved forward. "I'll kill you if you do this to her. You must know that."

Stockwell's smile was coldly contemptuous. "Do you think to intimidate me from my duty, Cousin?"

"No," Guy answered despondently.

"Then you will carry out my directions."

"If he goes, I go with him," Becky declared.

"Not beyond reach of the law," Gurdon retorted, turning his thin, chill smile upon her. "A warrant will issue in *futuribus*. One furtive move, and you will be clapped in jail."

Guy turned white. "No," he said. "No, Becky. I can't stand that."

"I can," she said. "I'd rather go to jail than back to him."

"The choice is yours," the inexorable voice pronounced.

"No," Guy said, brokenly this time. "Not jail, my darling, not for you."

"Then are you going to give him your pledge?"

"What else is there to do?" The words were barely audible.

She whirled upon her husband. "I won't go back to your bed. Never! No matter what happens. Never, never, never!" She burst into a passion of tears and fled from the room.

SEVENTEEN

To restore Cash Barlow to jail that night would have been a needless risk. Though the mob had dispersed, casual bands still roamed the streets, whose sporting instincts might revive at sight of the prisoner. Barlow was presented with an armful of sacking, and slept out the night in the corner of the coach-house, guarded by Halcyon volunteers.

Hospitable drinks were served to the victorious defenders. Dr. Saul Armitage did not partake. He was too busy fighting for the life of the battered canal captain, with Gurdon Stockwell as aide.

With sunrise came the welcome verdict: Capt. Trigg would recover. His opponent in the duel uttered a prayer of thanksgiving and went to his study to enter a memorandum: one set of artificial teeth for Capt. Israel Trigg to be charged to Eureka Mills. Gurdon Stockwell could be a good winner.

Morning brought other important tidings, complete exculpation of Cassius Barlow. Mr. Claudius Kent, engineer of the locomotivator on the Schenectady line, produced evidence not to be doubted from a man of his high estate. On 13 October, as his recorded time-sheet showed, his train had pulled into Troy five hours later. Half a mile from the bridge, Mr. Kent, leaning from his cab window, had seen and identified a man between track and forest, stoning an owl in a dead tree. The man was Cassius Barlow. The time was verifiably 9.53. This was demonstrably before the meteor flamed, and after the death-shriek was heard from the island.

The owl, Mr. Kent added, had flown away unharmed. Cash Barlow had playfully menaced the locomotivator with an unflung rock, and turned in the direction of the river.

Anonymous missives began to turn up in windows and beneath doors.

It was presently noted that the great majority of these were addressed to members of the First Methodist Church, though a few prominent outsiders were included. Scriptural passages cropped up in several of the messages, dark references to Sodom, Gomorrah, and camp-ground immoralities. Others advised inquiry into the behaviour of "one high in the councils of piety". All ended with the stark query:

WHO KILLED MISS PRISCILLA STAMM AND WHY?

No stimulus was needed to keep that question stirring in the minds of the Trojans. After the exoneration of Cassius Barlow, surmise ran wild in the city. Among the dead girl's associates at the Eureka there was endless discussion as to the man that "got Prissy in the family way and then murdered her". Her male associates were few; her conduct with them, so far as was known, circumspect. Everyone was cognizant of her pious leanings; her assiduity in churchly activities. Was she not Gurdon Stockwell's chosen aide in his good works?

What's more—the girls repeated old suspicions—had she not been in love with him? The question passed from guarded whispers to open debate.

The light gusts of gossip became a steady wind, rose to a formidable gale. It blew about the ears of Gurdon Stockwell. He was not unprepared for it. People had been looking at him queerly on the streets. A pair of daring urchins had hooted at him before taking to their heels and scurrying away like young hares. A week before, he had received a cryptic message, with the ominous ending:

WHO KILLED MISS PRISCILLA STAMM AND WHY?

Nor was he unready when the Rev. Amos Cocroft paid him an official and agitated visit. The clergyman was a good and simple man, committed to a most distasteful errand.

". . . and so, Brother Stockwell, I deemed it my duty—gone so far—good name of our beloved church—your own repute— all believe in your uprightness and innocence—deeply concerned —the question is, can we longer ignore . . . ?"

Gurdon Stockwell interrupted him short of a breakdown.

"Ignore what, Brother Cocroft?"

The good dominie made a gesture of helplessness. "There is the difficulty. We walk in the darkness of evil rumour."

"Is there nothing concrete to fasten upon?"

"Yes," the clergyman admitted reluctantly. "There is talk of a letter or letters bearing upon the matter."

"Letters?" Stockwell frowned in concentration. "From me? To Sister Stamm?"

"The gossip is vague. Are there such letters in existence, Brother?" he asked timidly.

"It is quite probable. If so, they deal with Church matters purely."

Gurdon Stockwell was easy in his mind on this point. Any letter of a personal nature which he had sent to the girl, he had instructed her to return at once. She had obeyed. Every one had been destroyed by him. He now had cause to felicitate himself upon his methodical habits.

"I should be glad to explain any such communications which may be brought to me," Stockwell continued. "But first I must ask you to be quite plain with me. All this vagrant talk—does it connect me with the death of Sister Stamm? Is it an accusation of murder?"

"Oh, my dear brother! Do not utter the word. Not accusation. Wild rumours. Mean hints . . ."

"Of immoral conduct, then?"

"We—ell, vile minds are always avid to impute ill-conduct to the most blameless associations."

"Then," Gurdon Stockwell said firmly, "I see my way clear. I shall demand a full and free hearing before the Church Consistory, with access to all accusers and witnesses."

The light of a great relief illumined the gentle, clerical countenance.

"It is what I would have ventured to suggest," he cried joyfully. "With a clear conscience before man and God, you will meet and confound your traducers."

"I thank you for your confidence," the other said. "My conscience is clear. My traducers—who are they?"

"Indeed, I know of no one audacious enough to bring open charges against a Christian gentleman so notorious for piety as you except—except——"

"Except?" his parishioner prompted.

"Old Miss Stamm, our departed sister's aunt."

Stockwell's thin smile failed to warm his expression. "She has changed her tune. It was she who denounced Cassius Barlow."

"Whom you so magnanimously defended," the pastor said admiringly.

"A worthless scoundrel. But entitled to his presumption of

innocence. This Stamm female—is she, as I have heard it bruited, the writer of the scurrile and anonymous notes now in circulation?''

"There is talk to that effect, Brother Stockwell.''

"Good! We may have occasion to deal with her case later.''

"Shall I summon the Consistory?''

"Next week—no later,'' Gurdon Stockwell said decisively. "This slander must be checked without delay.''

Cassius Barlow wrote to Luther Simms:

Our man has asked for a Church trile. Next Wensday. It will be open. Any body can come. Will you be here. Please advise by return post prepaid.

The reply came back with unexampled speed, in three days:

Will arrive by Champion coach on Monday. Will try to get hearing from G.S. before church proceedings. Tell no one beforehand of my coming.

Late at his work in the gaunt and cheerless house of the Quaker, Guy Roy was startled by a rap at the door. He opened it and faced Cassius Barlow and another man who stood back in the shadows. Barlow motioned the other forward.

"It's all right.'' To Guy he said, "You know Luther Simms.''

"I do. Come in.''

They entered, but not before Barlow had peered up and down the dark hall.

"Anybody around?'' he queried.

"No. Sit down.''

They did so. Guy pushed aside the papers on his desk and faced them.

"You work late, Mr. Roy,'' Luther Simms said in his quietly courteous manner.

"Of necessity.''

"Is it true that the Montague & Roy Company is about to close its doors?''

The young proprietor frowned. "What is the purpose of your question?''

"I ask in all friendliness,'' the big man replied gently.

"It is not yet announced, but it is true.''

"This will throw many unfortunates on the street in a time of need."

Guy's shrug expressed not indifference, but fatalism.

"Can it not be avoided? Or, at worst, postponed?"

"I know of no way."

"If money is needed to tide over . . ."

"Useless," Guy said curtly. His habitual courtesy asserted itself. "You will pardon my shortness," he said. "I am somewhat overpressed."

Simms inclined his head. "I must ask your indulgenge, in turn. Is this necessity due to pressure on the part of the Mill Owners Association?"

Guy hesitated before answering. "No."

"Or of Mr. Gurdon Stockwell?"

Guy was silent.

"We can handle Stockwell," Cash Barlow put in confidently. "That's what we're here for."

His companion motioned him to silence. "As you doubtless know," he said to Guy, "Mr. Stockwell has demanded a hearing before the Methodist Consistory."

"No! Has he? On what?"

"The rumours associating his name with the Stamm girl. He brands them as baseless."

"Which they assuredly are," Guy said loyally.

"I make no charge," Simms said. "But there are certain matters which may not be known to you. I have recently visited Lawrence, Mass."

"Why Lawrence?"

"Priscilla Stamm's absence was spent there, working in the Happy Toiler mills."

"I know nothing of it."

"No? Not that, while there, she consulted a physician?"

Guy shook his head.

"Doctress Emmaline Howe confirmed Priscilla's fears. The girl dated her pregnancy from the Thompson Camp Ground meeting early in June."

"Did she name the man?" Guy strove to keep his voice steady. Was it relief or disappointment that loosened his taut muscles when Luther Simms returned a negative?

"Doctress Howe stated that her patient was amply supplied with money but greatly depressed in spirit."

"Why are you telling me all this, Mr. Simms?" Guy asked.

The labour man sighed. "You have nothing to add to our information?"

"Nothing."

"You will, I assume, attend the hearing."

"If I have time," Guy answered with assumed indifference.

He took to bed a teeming brain. The call from the two visitors had effectually roused him from the torpor into which the loss of Becky had plunged him. He could not sleep for the surmises that criss-crossed in his mind. What had been developing in those days of his self-isolation?

Gypsy Vilas was always a likely source of information. He summoned her to his office in the morning. After a quick, shrewd scrutiny, Gypsy said, "Something's happened." She eyed him. "You haven't been trystin' again with You-Know-Who?"

"No. Gypsy, is there something new in the Stamm case?"

"Plenty. Where you *been*?"

"Busy. I've heard almost nothing."

Gypsy curled comfortably into her chair. "Luther Simms is here."

"So I hear."

"Did you hear that he's tryin' to tie that psalm-singin' cousin of yours into the Stamm case?"

"Is he? How?" His astonishment was well-feigned.

"For one thing he found out that somebody sent Prissy a bottle of castlings."

"Castlings? What's that?"

Gypsy stared. "Doncha know what castlings is? Girlsease. God-be-thanked medicine. Tansy and seven-sisters-root and such."

"Oh! An abortifacient."

"If queer speakin' is your fancy. Question is, who sent it?"

"Well, who did?"

"Nobody knows yet. But some knows who bought a book about it at Heartt's."

"About medicines?"

"Well, about females in that kind of a fix and how to get out of it. Mr. Gurdon Stockwell," she declared triumphantly.

"He's a family man," Guy pointed out. "I dare say that would explain the book. See here, Gypsy, has Priscilla ever told any of her friends who was responsible for her condition?"

"Not knowin', can't say."

"I suspect that you can say more than you have."

"Mary Haynes has got a coupla cousins up-river. They were raftin' that night."

"And they witnessed something?"

Again the girl was elusive. "Not knowin', can't say."

"Has Luther Simms been talking with Mary?"

"He's been talkin' with all of us. Every girl that ever knew Prissy."

"And you think he got important information?"

"Not knowin', can't say," answered Gypsy in her exasperating singsong.

"Gypsy, is it old Miss Stamm who has been writing anonymous letters?"

"Not know . . . ." Gypsy broke off. "She says snap out it was Gurdon Stockwell."

"She'd better be careful or she'll let herself in for slander."

"Well, it's no skin off my behind. Or yours either. I don't know why you're stickin' up for old Hurdy-Gurdy," she went on resentfully.

"I'm not. I'm only thinking that there is no proof against him. And it strikes me, Miss Gypsy, that you're dealing in pretty flimsy articles of moonshine."

She said with apparent irrelevancy, "That Luther Simms, he's an old he-devil."

"I thought he was considered a saint."

"That's as you look at it. I wouldn't want him on my trail."

"Then you do think he has something definite."

"I'll tell you this much, lad. The County Prosecutor does. He'll be at the meetin'. You'd better go."

"I wouldn't miss it," Guy said.

EIGHTEEN

THE great church was packed with humanity, floor, gallery and choir-loft. Not Hellfire Hoadley himself, at his most fervent, had ever gathered a crowd more representative of Troy's best citizenry. From his seat in the front row of the gallery, between his fellow-Halcyons, Elias Plum and Jans Urena, Guy Roy could estimate how powerful was the Stockwell support. Not only was the cream of Methodism there, but the leading spirits of the other denominations, Baptist, Congregational, Presbyterian, Episcopalian, and Dutch Reformed, were present to lend countenance to the aspersed churchman.

The gallery was of a different and more various complexion. Scattered about were representatives of the incipient labour movement, John Grimes, Barlow, Harris Bond and a score more. Opposite the three Halcyons, Pliny Gregg, the County Prosecutor, unostentatiously slipped a notebook from his pocket to his knee.

A few rows back, a bevy of female mechanics rustled and giggled. Guy identified Clorinda Burgo, Mildred Hute, and, of course, Gypsy Vilas and Mary Haynes. Behind him, two men conversed quietly in thick, Palatinate German. These would be the Wember brothers from up-river, of whom there had been much talk.

On the rostrum were seated the Consistory's commission of three, appointed for the hearing. The Presiding Elder, Rev. Elihu Goss, D.D., in the centre, was a smallish, trim man with a bilious cast. At his right sat the Rev. Miles Parker, gaunt, shabby and with the light of devotion in his tired eyes. The third member was Deacon Daniel G. Stopes of Albany, the potent exhorter; tall, bulky, with a dreamy look which belied his energetic character. All were known as men of approved piety, upright, honourable and conscientious. Whether they were free of bias was another matter. Guy Roy took leave to doubt it inwardly. His misgivings were shared by the young lawyer. Plum whispered to him, "Packed jury."

As Presiding Elder, Dr. Goss opened the proceedings with a moving prayer for divine guidance, pleading for God's eternal

truth to be made manifest before all men. The congregation rose
and sang the five stanzas of the hymn:

> "Oh, gracious Lord, vouchsafe to us
> Thy wisdom and Thy peace."

As the words of the final verse rose and swelled in harmony,

> "Before Thine august judgments
> Our humble thoughts subside,"

Guy felt himself awed by a strange and alien solemnity.

The gathering was tense, but it had in it nothing of cheap
and vulgar curiosity. These good folk consciously embodied the
dedicated spirit of duty towards their God and the city of their
pride. They were there in defence of all that they held good:
their religion, the fair repute of an honoured fellow, the loyalty
of Church and class to one of themselves whose character justly
claimed it. If they had forejudged him guiltless, it was from high
and indignant conviction.

The Presiding Elder rose and said in his incisive yet curiously
gentle tones:

"My brothers and sisters and friends in Christ, we are met here
to make official inquiry concerning injurious innuendoes against a
member of this parish. Brother Stockwell, come forward."

Gurdon Stockwell rose from his accustomed pew, walked
firmly down the aisle, and mounted the four steps to the platform. He bowed with grave courtesy to the committee. Dr. Goss
motioned him to a high-backed, ecclesiastical chair, half-facing
the trio. He seated himself and folded his hands in his lap.

From the far distance of the centre balcony, Guy could
discern the deep hollows beneath the eyes. Stockwell's face was
rigid, the skin over the jutting cheekbones of a bluish pallor. But
his expression was calm and confident.

"Brother Stockwell is here upon his own initiative and at his
own intrinsic request," the Chairman announced. "I will now call
upon Brother Stopes."

The eloquent deacon came forward. For a moment he stood
with closed eyes and bent head in silent prayer for guidance. He
spoke quietly, sadly.

"The painful but necessary duty devolves upon me of stating
the issue. Charges against Brother Stockwell have been bruited
abroad. I shall not characterize his accusers other than to state

that they are now reluctant to appear, whether from conscience, fear or shame. These same mouths, now dumb, have uttered grave accusations. Brother Stockwell stands in the shadow of a double inculpation. It is whispered that he maintained carnal relations with our deceased sister, Priscilla Stamm. It is further hinted that he had guilty knowledge of and perhaps a hand in her tragical demise.''

A mutter, irresolute and wordless, thrilled in the air like the hum of bees at swarm. It had started in the gallery. The deacon faced the spot.

"If any among you has aught of evidence, I adjure you, speak out.''

No one responded. With a gesture of dismissal he sat down. The Presiding Elder Rose.

"To clarify the instance and to silence once and for all these malign tongues, I shall briefly question our falsely accused brother. With his consent,'' he added, with a deferential smile at the witness.

"I will answer to the best of my ability and conscience, sir,'' Gurdon Stockwell said.

Dr. Goss raised his voice in spaced and solemn words. "Gurdon Stockwell, I charge you before God and this assemblage to answer truly. Have you had carnal relations with the late Priscilla Stamm?''

"Never, so help me God!''

"Have you personal knowledge of the circumstances of her death?''

"None whatsoever.''

The inquisitor turned to his hushed audience. "Can any here present speak to the contrary?''

None spoke. The examiner's manner became more brisk and businesslike.

"Brother Stockwell, where were you between the hours of nine and eleven o'clock on the evening of October thirteenth?''

"I was walking abroad.''

"On what errand?''

"No errand, sir. I sought weariness.''

"You had no destination?''

"He's leading him,'' Elias Plum said in Guy's ear.

"No, sir. I sleep ill. Walking aids me to sleep. My physician will bear me out.''

Dr. Armitage rose from his place on the floor. "I confirm it, gentlemen. *Solvitur ambulando*. Exercise is recommended."

"Thank you, Doctor. Brother Stockwell, did you in the course of your peregrinations meet and recognize any person?"

"Yes, sir. Mr. Orlando Montague. In front of the whitesmith's on Madison Street."

The dandified ironmonger stood. "That is true, sir. I gave Brother Stockwell a good evening."

"What was the hour, Brother Montague?"

"A little before nine o'clock."

The chair again addressed the witness. "Had you any further encounter, Brother Stockwell?"

"Yes, sir. A block further along I saw Constable Brownlee."

"Did you accost him?"

"No, sir. He was asleep." (Titters were promptly suppressed by the chair, who reminded his hearers that they were in the House of God.)

"And thereafter?"

"I met no one but a tipsy woodcutter. I was then on the outskirts. When these accesses afflict me, I seek solitude. At times I become dazed with weariness and hardly know my whereabouts."

"Clever. Clever!" Lawyer Plum commented under his voice. "Gives himself an outlet."

"One more question, Brother Stockwell. Did you at any time in the evening see the deceased, Priscilla Stamm?"

"No, sir." The reply was quietly firm.

Guy's attention had been momentarily diverted by a curious bit of action just below the rostrum. A paper was being passed from hand to hand and was presently delivered to Deacon Stopes. After a glance, he folded it and put it in his pocket. Dr. Goss was now directing his attention to the mass below.

"Is there any here who desires to question Brother Stockwell further? If not——"

Some sort of commotion was evident in the near curve of the gallery. An angry female voice protested, "Lemme be!"

"Order!" the Presiding Elder called. "Stand and address the chair if you have aught to say."

Nobody stood. The voice, still angry, shrilled, "Ask him what he and Prissy Stamm was doin' in camp-ground bushes."

"Out of order!"

"Put her out!"

"Arrest her!"

Protests rose on all sides.

The chairman motioned for silence. "Who speaks?" he said.

"Gypsy Vilas." The reply came in a feminine chorus.

The red hair and redder face of the forewoman were projected upward after a struggle which suggested the use of force.

"The Chair is not prepared to recognize a request so improperly advanced," Dr. Goss said.

"With the permission of the committee," Stockwell interposed, "I will answer the insinuation."

"As you will, Brother."

Stockwell lifted his face towards the gallery. "Does the young person refer to Thompson Camp Ground meeting last July?"

"Certes." Gypsy was gathering assurance. "She rode over with the girls in the carryall. She didn't come back with 'em."

"That is true."

"You took her into the bushes. What was you two doin'? Sayin' your prayers?"

Angry exclamations mingled with cries of, "Shame!" "Stop her!" in the body of the church.

Stockwell called out: "Quiet, please, my friends! I welcome the opportunity of clearing up the point." He turned to the congregation. "Many will recognize that obloquy has been unjustly cast upon our Church by reason of infringements upon camp-ground worship by drink and lewdness."

"Yes, yes!

"Shame!"

"Minions of Satan!"

"There was a moot question of boundaries. An infamous rum-booth had been erected upon the doubtful ground. The duty of establishing certain measurements devolved upon me. Though the enterprise was not without danger from the ruffianly element present, Sister Stamm volunteered her aid. Together we made the survey. Afterward I drove her back to Troy. The den of infamy, I regret to state, proved to be outside our control."

"And that," Elias Plum remarked, "will put Miss Gypsy's red head in the bag."

The next instant that impious disturber was being plucked urgently from her place and hustled down the stairs. Before the door closed upon her enforced exit, she made another contribution to discord that rang through the auditorium.

"Ask Bookseller Heartt about the last book he sold him," she shouted.

The chairman frowned. "This seems far afield," he said doubtfuly.

Gurdon Stockwell spoke up with calm good humour. "To the best of my recollection, my latest purchase was Buck's *Theological Dictionary.*"

"A most edifying choice," the Rev. Mr. Parker said warmly.

Among the factory group there was a stir and confused mutterings. The chairman asked patiently, "Is there further matter?"

A man near the group spoke up. "She wishes to know, sir, whether she will be chucked out like the Vilas girl if she puts a question."

"Certainly not, if she maintains decorum. Who is it?"

"Mary Haynes," from several contributors.

"Speak freely, Mary Haynes."

Projected into the public eye as her predecessor had been, the reluctant witness panted out something indistinguishable.

"She is trying to tell you," the obliging mouthpiece announced, "that Mr. Heartt sold him a medical book."

"About ladies having babies," Mary added, with cheeks aflame.

Jans Urena poked a thumb into Guy's waistcoat. "Look at Gurdon Stockwell's wife."

"Where?" Guy said so eagerly that his friend stared.

"To the left. Half behind that pillar."

Now Guy saw Becky. She was leaning forward, her eyes wide upon her husband, her lips parted in the intensity of her watchfulness.

"Looks as if the Haynes gal had started a fox, huh?" Urena snickered.

The chair now addressed a question to Mr. Heartt. Yes, the bookseller answered, he had ordered such a volume for Mr. Stockwell. Why not? It was in considerable demand by family men. He smiled.

Mr. Stockwell, heavy with dignified disapproval put in his word.

"May I point out, sir, that this discussion infringes a subject of family privacy and delicacy?"

"The Chair finds the point well taken."

"Lovely Becky looks queasy," Urena said. "Think she's going to spew?"

"Don't be a double-damned fool," Guy bade him angrily.

Pliny Gregg was on his feet. "May I ask the committee's indulgence?"

Deacon Stopes anticipated the Chair's response. "Is this official, Mr. District Attorney?"

"Possibly pre-official, Brother Stopes." He accentuated the title.

"Then I shall advise the Chair not to entertain it."

"Very well." The tone was amiable. "I shall not seek to interrogate the witness. Unofficially, then, and as a member in good standing of this congregation, may I put a question to Mr. Heartt?"

"The Brother is within his privileges," the Chair decided reluctantly. "Brother Heartt may reply or not, as he chooses."

Little Dr. Brockway stood up. "Is this inquiry an attempt to disclose the truth or to conceal it?" he demanded.

A brief tumult rose and subsided. There was a note of savagery in it.

"We are confused by unwarrantable interruptions," said the Presiding Elder severely. "Put your question, Brother Gregg."

"Does not the volume which Brother Stockwell bespoke from Brother Heartt contain passages which, however respectable their intent, might guide the layman to procure an abortion?"

The bookseller looked uncomfortable. "I have not perused it with sufficient attention to form an opinion."

"Have you another copy?"

"No."

"Perhaps Brother Stockwell would permit an examination of his copy."

There was a perceptible pause before the witness said, "Certainly, if I can find it." Guy thought he had lost something of his self-confidence. Why shouldn't he be able to find it? Unless, indeed, he had loaned it to Priscilla.

"You could produce another copy if necessary?" the official asked Mr. Heartt.

"Certainly. Upon order. Dr. Codrick's book is a standard work highly esteemed by the medical profession."

"One last question, Brother Heartt. Was the book as delivered to Brother Stockwell, wrapped up specially for posting?"

"It was not. It was delivered direct to his hand."

"Thank you, Brother Heartt. And thank you and the committee, Dr. Goss, for your indulgence."

The District Attorney sat down.

A member of the congregation signalled for recognition. The chair recognized Brother Hoag, the railwayman.

"A note has been handed to the committee," he said. "Will it receive consideration?"

"I have the communication here," Deacon Stopes said.

Taking the paper from his pocket, he passed it across to the Rev. Mr. Parker. That gentleman fumbled for his spectacle-case, adjusted his glasses, unfolded the letter and smoothed it out on his knee for easier reading. As he read, his fingers went to his lips in perplexity. He cast an anxious glance at the witness-chair. Re-folding the note, he handed it to the Presiding Elder.

Dr. Goss read it once and again. Sharply watchful, Guy strove to interpret the expression of his face. Was it shock? Pity? Reluctance? Indecision? There was a slight quaver in the gentle tones as he asked, "From whence does this come?"

"Miss Elvira Stamm," several informants hastened to say.

From the fourth pew on the right of the centre aisle, the ageing spinster raised her uncertain pipe.

"I found it in my poor niece's box among her laid-away garments."

"When was the discovery made?" Committeeman Parker inquired hollowly.

"Three days since. I did not know what to do. I laid it before the Lord in prayer and was led to fetch it here." She burst into sobs. "Oh, my poor Prissy! My unhappy girl!"

"You were guided by His grace, Sister Stamm," the chairman assured her. He raised his voice. "The committee will take a ten-minute recess to consider this in private session," he announced.

"Look at Gurdon Stockwell!" Elias Plum muttered to Guy Roy.

NINETEEN

SITTING there, waiting, he kept saying it over and over to himself.

"I am guiltless of the death of that woman. I did not kill her. She killed herself. My conscience is clear. I am guiltless of her death."

It fortified his confidence, the repetition. It was a charm, an exorcism.

In the clarity of his conviction he found strength to endure the test. The people who crowded the pews felt it in him. Their faces were sympathetic, friendly. They knew him. They knew that a man of his character, of his standing, could not be a criminal. He had been wise to demand this hearing. It would confirm him as the man they had always believed him. His truth would be unassailable after this.

That message over which the three reverend brothers were now poring—what could it be? He racked his brains. Something serious, so much was certain. All three had been startled. Dr. Goss, after reading, had turned upon him a queer, dimmed look. What did it signify? Pity? Consternation? Distrust? Had that saintly man of gentle heart lost faith in him?

They had referred to it as a letter. What letter? Every one of any significance that he had written to the girl was accounted for. A forgery? Possibly something perpetrated by old Miss Stamm.

That withered spinster! What could she produce for the committee that would carry weight against his word? Let her bring as many accusations as she chose. He could handle them . . . Wait, though. Could Priscilla have confessed to her? He was pretty sure not. That last night she had sworn to him that she had kept their secret. He believed her. Priscilla had never lied to him.

Whatever the mystery behind that closed committee door, he had resolved upon his course. He would deny and deny and deny. They should never pry from him the smallest admission.

The congregation was abuzz with growing impatience. He bent his head on his propped hand to shut out the rustle and hum. He was determined that nothing should undermine his composure. He could rely upon his ingenuity to meet any foreseeable emergency.

"I am guiltless of the death of that woman. Guiltless in heart and deed."

But in God's name, when would they be done, back of that silent door!

The better to defend his innocence, he reconstructed the events of the dreadful night. All had gone according to plan until the end. Priscilla had faithfully obeyed instructions. She had met nobody she knew on the way to the river.

He had been less fortunate. The encounters in town were innocuous. But it was a mischief to have been seen by the halfwit at the riverside. Still, there was not much to fear in that. Martha Whatever-her-name had already publicly identified the nightfarer who embarked in the shallop once as Satan and once as Cassius Barlow. Her testimony would not imperil him.

Priscilla had been awaiting him on the island. It was dark, too dark for the carrying out of his design. So he had brought along a boxed candle in the fustian sack together with the book and the instrument. They picked their way upward by its light. He stopped her in a hollow of the grassland and fended the taper against the breeze.

"What are you going to do?" she asked faintly.

He told her in gentle, reassuring words what must be done. She wept a little. He put his arm around her.

She must not be afraid, he said. He had studied the matter. He knew what to do as well as any doctor. There would be no danger and very little pain. She cried a little more.

"Must I lose my child—our child?" she said.

He was prepared for this. "You will marry and have other children," he told her. "I will give you a generous dowry so that you can make an advantageous marriage."

He meant it. He owed her that much. When she still hesitated, he argued forcefully. He put his whole heart into it; he was persuasive and eloquent. She yielded. He had known all along that she would. When had she ever been able to say no to him?

She refused the whisky he offered. No, she said; she could bear it at his hands. She bore it at first without a sound. Something went wrong. He did not know what. He never would know. Suddenly she was writhing and moaning under his grip. He rose to his knees to consult the book again. It must have been the

animal instinct to escape from agony that lent her the unexpected strength. Before he could check her, she was up and
darting towards the pit mouth.

To overtake her would have been simple, had he not fatally
tripped and tumbled over the sack. He shouted to her in command,
in appeal. He heard the whitethorn crash and crackle against her
blind pressure. She shrieked once, loud and high. A startled
halloo from the black level of the water answered. Too late he
remembered the betraying light. He doused it and crept into the
nearest thicket.

Was someone rowing in to investigate? Or was it only the
ripples on the shore? Breathless and trembling, he crouched.
Nothing happened. Nobody came.

Time boomed out from the Baptist bell-tower, was blown
downwind to him. He had been too confused to count the strokes,
but the sound roused him to action. He crept out of his retreat.
He must find Priscilla. Yet he dared not relight the candle in
view of the river. As best he could he pushed through the brush,
guarding his eyes with outthrust hands, stumbled and staggered
down the declivity to the bottom of the pit. In that shelter he
could light up.

He saw the girl at once. She lay prone beside a great rock. She
was motionless when he bent over to examine. No pulse, not the
quiver of a muscle, not a flutter of the breath.

He recalled with astonished admiration how calm and reasonable he had been. He saw at once how providential the outcome
was. It was the happy—no, he must not think that—but the
ready, the heaven-sent, solution of his dreadful problem. And it
left him with a clear conscience. He had tried to do what was
best for both of them. The tragic result was no fault of his. She
had suffered the penalty of her own folly and stubbornness. It
comforted him now to remember that he had knelt and said a
prayer beside the broken body.

Carefully reviewing the subsequent course of events, he could
see no avoidable error on his part. He had conducted himself
with exemplary prudence. After pushing off the boat he had
waded ashore to scuff out the keel mark in the sand. The sack,
loaded with stones and bearing candle-box, book and instrument,
he had sunk in the safe depths of the stream.

He was well over towards the shore and pulling strongly when
the meteor flared. It lighted up two figures, standing erect on the

surface of the water—or so it seemed to his dazed eyes. One of them hailed him gruffly. He did not recall answering. But involuntarily he half-turned before he awoke to his danger and threw his arm across his face. The fireball had kept alive for not more than three or four seconds. He doubted whether it was possible for him to be identified in that short space. It was unlikely that any characters using the river at such an hour—on some illicit trade assuredly—would know him personally.

He rowed strongly to shore. From then to his re-entry into the mansion he met no one close enough for speech.

Should he have mentioned being on the river in accounting to the committee for his evening? He had considered it, but decided against it as coming too close. Anyway, he had not denied having been there.

Was the committee *never* coming out? It was unfair, inhuman, this suspense. Give him his chance to prove his innocence. Guiltless of the death of that woman. It rang like a refrain in his mind. He had questioned his own conscience in agony and prayer and it had given him answer—guiltless. Guiltless of the death of that woman.

Not wholly blameless, but guiltless of her death. He had erred. His relations with her had been sinful. Abortion was wrong, he admitted that. But, faced with such a problem, what would any sensible man do? Would he not take steps to save the woman from the consequences of her folly? Perjury? But he had not really perjured himself. He was not under oath. Surely an innocent man had the right, the duty, to defend himself? And he *was* innocent. If they hanged him, he would still maintain it on the gallows.

Back swung his mind to the resumed sin with Priscilla. That was less his fault than that of the wife who contumaciously denied him. That cold little demon! Cold to him, not to his cousin. *There* was a murder he would rejoice to commit. Murder? No! Simple justice upon both those wicked fornicators. Yes, Obedience had been the true agency of his lapse into sin. Priscilla had not been blameless either. If she had not been so yielding, so willing . . .

He came back to the present with a jerk. The door had opened. The three clergymen—his judges—those dire Fates in long black coats were filing slowly in. Ready! A firm mind. A composed front. A steady will. Guiltless—guiltless—guiltless; he was guiltless of the death of that woman.

The committee took their places, looking, Guy thought, perturbed. Dr. Goss advanced to the edge of the rostrum.

"A matter of grave moment has come up," he announced, "which, in the best judgment of your committee, requires more time for investigation. Before we adjourn, I will ask Brother Parker——" The remainder of the sentence, "to pronounce the benediction", was lost in angry clamour.

The gallery started it, but it was quickly swelled to a roar from all parts of the church. Protests, demands, accusations, even threats, blended in a shocking outburst against adjournment. The gathering was suddenly out of hand.

Guy saw old Miss Stamm rise above the heads of the surrounding mass as if by some magic propulsion. She had been hoisted upon the pew and was now crying out: "Read it! Read it!" The congregation took it up in a repetition like a sledge beat. "Read it! Read it! Read it!" Others shouted, "No adjournment!" and, "Let's have the facts!"

Dr. Goss thrust his hand protectively into his pocket. Silence fell, the hush of a dread expectancy. The Chairman faltered miserably.

"In justice to our accused brother . . . this is not the place or time . . . serious implications . . . unverified suspicions——"

The cool, incisive accents of Gurdon Stockwell cut in.

"I ask that the document should be read."

A roar of assent supported him.

"He's got grist," Jans Urena breathed.

Deacon Stopes stepped forward and, with a decisive gesture, plucked the moot paper from his confrere's pocket. Silence fell instantly.

"The missive," he said, "is alleged to have been found by Miss Elvira Stamm among her deceased niece's belongings. I will read it." He read:

"If I should be missing inquire of Gurdon Stockwell of the Eureka Mills. He will know where I am.

"It purports to be signed by Priscilla Stamm," he said quietly.

A long, soft, steamy exhalation sighed forth from the concourse.

"May I examine that letter, sir?" Gurdon Stockwell's demeanour was still calm. Guy had the feeling that beneath that composure, every nerve and muscle was taut to the breaking-point; that at any moment the man in the chair—on the rack!—might hurl himself from his seat in a mad rush to escape.

Stockwell read the few words. The tension passed from his limbs. Colour returned to his face. He sat at ease. Deacon Stopes took the sheet and stood in thought, fronting the witness.

At that moment Guy identified the crisp speech of Pliny Gregg close to him. The County Prosecutor was summoning the two Germans back of Guy to join him. The three met at the stair-top and left the building.

Deacon Stopes was again addressing Gurdon Stockwell.

"Brother Stockwell, are you familiar with that handwriting?"

"I am, sir. I have seen it on many Sunday School reports."

"Is it that of the late Priscilla Stamm?"

"I am sure of it."

Stopes re-examined the note. "It is undated."

"It is." Guy felt in the affirmation a sub-accent of relief, almost of triumph. The lack of date—did that account for Stockwell's swift relaxation upon seeing the note?

"Can you account for the communication?" the Examiner asked.

"I can."

"Do so."

"Two months or more ago, Sister Stamm left home to seek employment in Lawrence. She did not, I believe, apprise her aunt of her whereabouts."

"Is that true, Miss Stamm?" the Chairman inquired.

The spinster returned a quavering affirmative.

"It was desirable that someone be informed regarding Sister Stamm. She selected me as her medium," Stockwell concluded.

The Presiding Elder had his cue. "Naturally," he said. "You were, in a manner, her spiritual mentor."

"To the best of my humble and unworthy capacity, I was."

"So that her choice of you as repository of her secret was logical."

"I so deemed it."

"You did not know of the existence of this note?"

"Not until it was produced here."

"But you were cognizant at all times during her absence of the young woman's whereabouts?"

"During her sojourn in Lawrence, yes, sir."

"This covers the point fully and satisfactorily, Brother Stockwell." The Deacon now resumed his role. "If there are no further questions——"

"I rise to a point of information." Dr. Fitch Brockway was on his feet.

The Chairman peered at him. "State it."

"The Stamm letter forecasts that the writer might be missing. Can Mr. Stockwell explain this, since he was in her confidence?"

"There were painful circumstances which I had hoped to avoid." The reply came slowly. The speaker gazed with commiseration at the pew where the old aunt sat.

"Slick as a mink!" Urena said admiringly. "They won't catch our Hurdy-Gurdy."

"We all appreciate the delicacy of your feelings," the questioner said dryly, "but that doesn't answer me."

Mutterings of disapproval did not deter him. He stood, expectant and obstinate.

"I will ask the Chair to repress this individual," Deacon Stopes growled.

"The witness had professed himself ready to answer any reasonable question," the little doctor pointed out. "I submit that my question is reasonable."

"Will the brother put the question more concretely?" Gurdon Stockwell said with quiet courtesy.

"Did you know of the girl's condition?"

"I suspected it."

"Did you know or suspect the identity of the man in the case?"

Stockwell hesitated. "I should not be justified in naming any names without more evidence than is presently at my command."

"By Jove, he's good!" Elias Plum exclaimed. "And yet . . ." He shook his head.

"Yet what?" Guy asked.

"I wouldn't be satisfied in Pliny Gregg's place."

"Here's Pliny back again," Guy said.

"Officially this time, or I miss my guess," the lawyer said.

The District Attorney had appeared on the rostrum with a legal-looking document in his hand. He showed it to the committee. There was a brief consultation.

Priscilla Stamm's note was transferred to the custody of the law. Pliny Gregg left, taking it with him.

The Rev. Mr. Parker spread wide his arms. The people bowed their heads. The benediction was pronounced. The meeting adjourned.

TWENTY

IT was no surprise to Troy, but a matter for general congratulation, when the Methodist Consistory unanimously found the Hon. Gurdon Stockwell guiltless on all counts. Not only guiltless, but blameless, spotless.

> Through his Christian solicitude for the soul of an erring sister in the faith, his pious and cordial actions were misconstrued and his motives perverted by the report of evil tongues. Being cleared of all offence, Brother Stockwell has the right to demand of the constituted authorities that they detect the author of the infamous crime and bring him to justice. It is the sense of this body that failure so to do will constitute a dereliction of official duty.

The *Atlas* backed up the demand in a spirited editorial:

> . . . let the District Attorney act promptly or confess his incapacity for high office and resign the same.

District Attorney Gregg did not act, nor did he resign. He waited and watched. Something would turn up. It did.

Miles Tiggett came to him late one night, bringing a coat. The Learned Tailor was pale and tremulous. He had wrestled in prayer with his problem all the night before, and had been brought to see the light. His duty as a citizen and as a God-fearing member of the First Particular Baptist Church had impelled him to the grave decision. He had evidence which he must lay before the law.

The coat was Gurdon Stockwell's, brought in for cleaning by the family blackamoor, Jeshurun. It was scuffed and stiff with old mud. Deep embedded in the fabric were several thorns. The Learned Tailor, who was erudite in natural history as well as the classics, recognized the peculiar species. Gregg questioned him closely.

"Will you testify to this on oath, if required?"

Tiggett drew a long, unhappy breath. "I shall have to."

282

"Does anyone else know of it?"

"Not through me."

"I bind you to absolute silence and secrecy under penalty until I release you."

The Learned Tailor shambled out with drooping head.

It was Pliny Gregg's intention to proceed slowly and with caution, hoping for further evidence to clinch his case. But in the February first issue of the *Atlas*, Clarkson Crolius printed an editorial taunt which got under the official's skin. The blood of the innocent, the article pointed out, was unavenged after all these months. Justice cried aloud and was unappeased.

This time the official did act, and to an effect which jarred the city to its respectable foundations. He convened the Grand Jury and presented his evidence. The citizens could hardly credit the eyes with which they read, on the following morning, the words of the consequent indictment:

> . . . that the said Gurdon Stockwell, not having the fear of God before his eyes, and being seduced by the instigation of the Devil, did enter into carnal intercourse with the said Priscilla Stamm, whereby she lost her pucellage and became procreant;
>
> And further that the said Gurdon Stockwell, having vainly attempted to procure an abortion upon the body of the said Priscilla Stamm, did hurl and precipitate her from a height on Sadler's Island into the depths of the pit beneath, thereby causing her decease.

Around town it was whispered that the Grand Jury had received information too damaging for confutation. By most people, however, Prosecutor Pliny Gregg was roundly criticized for defamation of an honoured citizen. Pressure was brought to have the indictment quashed. Gurdon Stockwell entered a firm protest. His friends, he averred, were doing him an ill-service in their attempt. Let the trial proceed. He welcomed the opportunity—a manly attitude which was commented upon favourably in the press.

Taken into custody and released on his own recognizance, the accused bore himself with exemplary dignity. He went about his appointed occasions without interruption, punctual at mill, bank and committee.

He saw no reason for deviating by an inch from his position of one hundred per centum innocence in his statement to his lawyer, the lanky and grim old giant Phineas Dorr of the highly respected firm of P. Dorr & Son.

"All this gossip is a tissue of false assumptions and reckless fabrications," he assented.

The old lawyer, who was both shrewd and forthright, answered, "Am I to proceed upon that basis?"

"You are."

"Priscilla Stamm was not your light-o'-love?"

"You heard my statement before the Consistory committee. She was not."

"Who was her lover?"

"I make no accusation. It might have been Cassius Barlow. It might have been another."

"Do you wish us to direct suspicion of the murder upon Barlow?"

"No. His alibi is proofworthy."

"I wish ours were as sound."

Stockwell said, with cold anger, "If you are unconvinced of your client's innocence, you can always withdraw from the case."

"At your wish," the lawyer retorted imperturbably. "You have doubtless considered whether your cause will be prejudiced in the public eye by the displacement of P. Dorr & Son at this time."

"I spoke over-hastily," Stockwell said grudgingly. "But I must insist upon your acceptance of my position."

"Very well, Mr. Stockwell."

"You employed the term 'murder'," Stockwell continued. "As a matter of interest, and wholly dissociating myself from any connection with the tragedy, is it not a reasonable assumption that the unfortunate young woman either leapt into the pit or, in her blind flight, stumbled over the brink?"

The old gentleman set his finger-tips together and contemplated his client over the arch. "Mr. Stockwell, are you aware that an attempt had been made to perform an abortion upon the deceased?"

"So I understand."

"And that abortion is a felony?"

"I—I—yes, I suppose so."

"Then let me reconstruct the case for you. John Doe seduces Rachel Roe. She becomes pregnant. He arranges a tryst with her and undertakes to perform an operation. A criminal operation, be it noted. Rachel Roe, in her endeavour to escape the operation forced upon her by her lover, meets her death. Whether or not John Doe is the direct agent of her demise is now beside the point. The law holds that he who, in the commission of a felony causes the death of another, whether with direct intent or not, is guilty of first-degree murder. Is that clear to you, sir?"

"It is," the other answered in a lifeless tone.

"We will then consider another point. Have you by chance the habit of marking passages or dogs'-earing pages in your reading?"

"Sometimes."

"Did you do either or both with the medical volume purchased from Mr. Heartt?"

"I think it unlikely."

"I suggest that you ascertain." There was a suggestion of grimness in Lawyer Dorr's manner. "Are you, in fact, able to? Where is the book?"

"I don't know," Stockwell answered testily. "It may have been abstracted."

"Who would have motive to abstract it?"

"If I knew that, I should be able to point you to the murderer."

"Could the District Attorney have been the abstractor?"

"No. That, at least, I can be sure of." He bit his lip as the other glanced sharply at him. "Mr. Pliny Gregg does not frequent my house."

After meditation, the lawyer said, "Is your wife pregnant?"

Stockwell reddened. "She is not."

"Then your possession of Dr. Codrick's treatise is hardly referable to a family prospect."

Again the client flushed. "In a normal household there is always probability of increase."

Mr. Dorr refrained from inquiring whether the Stockwell household was normal, though he would well have liked to know. "Should the volume come to light, sir, I should like to examine it. Does anything further occur to you which should be communicated to your counsel?"

"Nothing, sir."

"Then I will take under advisement what you have told me, Mr. Stockwell."

"Good day, Mr. Dorr." The client left, still heavy-faced with secrecy.

Behind the heavy door of his inner office Phineas Dorr said to his son and partner: "God preserve us, Thomas, from the client who tries to conceal the truth from his counsel. Stockwell is lying like a bounetter. I think him guilty as hell. But unless the State can identify him with the time and place, we shall bring him off scatheless."

The trial was set for the March term.

A week before the date, Gypsy Vilas approached her employer. "Got anything on for tonight?"

"Yes. An appointment with a factor from Utica."

"What time?"

"Seven-thirty."

"Be through in an hour?"

Guy looked at her hard. "I can be."

"Meet me in the tool-shed on Castle Hill. Ha'past eight."

His voice shook as he asked, "Is it safe—for her?"

"He's goin' to be at his lawyers'. Fixin' up lies. D'you wanta see her or doncha?"

"Did she send you to me?"

"Whadd'you think? That we're playin' mumble-peg?"

"Eight-thirty," he said. "At the tool-shed."

Becky was waiting in the darkness.

"Guy!" she called tremulously.

"My darling!" He groped for her, but she held him back with a hand that was cold and tense against his cheek.

"I'm frightened, Guy."

"What is it, my love?"

"Gypsy, go out. I don't want anyone to hear this but Guy."

"Nobody ever caught Gypsy Vilas pokin' her nose where it ain't wanted," that young person declared in virtuous offence.

Nevertheless, after Gypsy had left (though not to a far distance), Becky lowered her voice to a half-whisper.

"I've found some—something has been found."

"The book?" he said quickly. "The medical book?"

"No. His coat," she said with an effort.

"Gurdon's?"

"Yes. Old Jeshurun found it. He was cleaning swifts' nests

out of the coach-house. The coat was all wadded up and jammed behind a baulk high in the corner. Jeshurun brought it to me."

"Well? I don't believe I quite see . . ."

"This was caught in the sleeve." She held out an object to him.

"I can't see it."

"You can feel it. Be careful of the thorns."

Guy jumped. "Thorns!"

"Yes. Like the ones on the island. Oh, Guy! What was he doing there?"

Guy thought rapidly. "Trying to spy on us, perhaps."

"Then why did he hide the coat?"

"It may have been so badly torn as to be of no further use," Guy said. It was feeble, but the best he could do offhand.

"It was torn. And muddied. There was something else I didn't tell you. I didn't want even to think of it. That morning—the day after Prissy Stamm disappeared—Mr. Stockwell's hands were terribly scratched, and after that he wore gloves for quite a while. Oh, Guy, you don't think . . ."

"No," he lied stoutly.

"I don't know *what* to do."

"Where is the coat?"

"That's what terrifies me. I told Jeshurun to burn it."

"A wise precaution."

"Guy, he didn't. I suppose he thought it was too good to destroy. He is a stupid fellow. He took it to Mr. Tiggett. The District Attorney has it now. There were probably other thorns left in it. Pliny Gregg sent for Jesh and scared him out of his poor wits. Jesh came back in tears and asked me what to do. That's how I know about it."

Guy stood thinking hard. He had lied to Becky in instinctive protectiveness as well as in obedience to the dictates of honour. But did she believe his lie? He doubted it.

"Becky," he said at length, "those thorns might hang Gurdon."

He heard her gasp. The spray fell from her nerveless fingers.

"Then you do believe that he did it!" He could barely catch the faint whisper.

"What I believe is of little importance. What the jury will believe is the point to consider. This is what will happen. Gurdon will take the stand and swear that he has not visited the island.

Then, if the evidence of the hidden coat and the thorns is produced, it will look black for him."

"Couldn't he claim that he had gone to Sadler's Island at some earlier time?"

"He could. But the scratches were on his hands the morning after the murder."

"Who saw them?"

"You did. And a few days later, I did."

A half-strangled sob broke from her. "Guy, he is my husband."

"Yes, he's your husband."

"We can't do it," she said desperately. "You *know* we can't do it!"

"No, we can't do it," he agreed dully.

Belly flat as a snake on the grass outside the shed's open window, Gypsy Vilas swallowed a bad word. The little fools! With the game right in their hands. Conscience huh? Well, that was their concern. Gypsy was not one to let *her* conscience interfere with the advantages which a kind Providence, abetted by her skilled eavesdropping, had provided for her. Cautiously she wriggled away. In the soft darkness of the shed, Becky pressed close to her companion.

He said with an effort, "You reminded me that he is your husband." She moved uneasily. "Becky, is he? Again? Now?"

"Oh, that!" she said, and groped for his hand. "There's nothing, darling. He's strange. He's changed. He's a man living in another world. He doesn't come into my world any more or even try."

She heard his sigh of relief.

"That night in the garden," she murmured, "when he stopped us. I'm glad he did, Guy. Do you know what I mean? I'm glad that we—that we didn't."

"I'm not," he said morosely. "I'm sorry. I shall be sorry all my life."

"No, it's better this way," she insisted softly. "Everything is coming out right for us. I know it is."

"How can it? We're throwing away our only chance. Here, tonight."

"Would you have it the other way? Would there be any happiness for us with his death between us? Or with our own guilt between us?"

He was silent.

"It's going to come right," she whispered vehemently. "It's got to! I couldn't live if I hadn't that to hold to." She kissed him softly. "Good night my only love."

"Time!" Gypsy called.

The news of the indictment had brought Luther Simms back to town. Gypsy sought him out without delay and revealed the fruits of her eavesdropping.

"I can go back there and find that sprig of thorn on the floor," she said triumphantly. "Let Pliny Gregg stick that under the jury's nose—that and what I can tell 'em—and I'll trouble you for the Hon. Gurdon Stockwell in a rope's end. Higher'n Haman's flutterin' shirt-tail, that'll hang him."

"Who wants to hang Gurdon Stockwell?" Simms said gently.

"I do. Don't you?"

"Would that bring the twelve-hour day to Troy?"

"It'd help. With old Hurdy-Gurdy out of the way, the other mills would come to time."

"On the contrary, if he's hanged, the Mill Owners junta will make a martyr of him. I've got a better use for him."

"Better alive than dead? I don't believe it," Gypsy said.

"You've done a good day's work for the cause, Gypsy. Now forget all about it. From here on, I will handle it."

"You mean keep my damn' mouth closed?"

"Precisely."

"So said, so done," Gypsy said despondently.

T

An exchange of notes passed between the Eagle Tavern and the Eureka Mills three days before the date set for the trial of the People *v.* Gurdon Stockwell. The outcome was an evening appointment for Luther Simms to call at Mr. Gurdon Stockwell's office.

The reverberations of the nine o'clock bell had died away; the last female mechanic had staggered, unsteady from exhaustion, through the mill yard to the dormitory when there was a knock at the outer door of the Eureka. Gurdon Stockwell, himself, opened. He looked stern and weary.

Two figures stood before him.

"What's this?" he demanded sharply upon sight of Gypsy Vilas.

"My witness, sir," Simms answered mildly. "I wrote you."

"I wish no dealings with my discharged help."

"Not me," Gypsy retorted. "You never gave me the boot. I quit."

With a harsh gesture Stockwell turned and led the way to the office. Closing the door after them, he stood with his back to it. Gypsy perched herself upon the desk and swung her legs. Luther Simms took a chair uninvited. The mill-owner addressed him.

"Say your say."

Simms ignored the discourtesy of the tone. "May I put some questions in your own interest?"

"Put them."

"What was your errand on the river the night of Priscilla Stamm's death?"

"Who says that I was on the river?"

"You were seen by two raftsmen."

The other smiled sourly. "Who would credit a raftsman?"

"These were not river trash but honest landholders, the Wember brothers. They were rafting their sheep to market. Would any jury dismiss the testimony of such respectable folk as negligible?"

"That would depend upon the nature of the testimony."

"Identifying you as the occupant of a craft which crossed their course."

"In the darkness of night?"

"You forget the meteor."

Stockwell had not forgotten the meteor nor the startling hail from the heart of the night. He pondered briefly.

"Suppose for the sake of argument that I was on the river. As I told the committee, after these fits of insomnia I am not always cognizant of where I am or what I do."

"Mr. Stockwell " the other said slowly, "is your defence to be that you slew Prsicilla Stamm without cognizance of what you were doing?"

"No, damn you!" Stockell shouted. He commanded himself instantly. "Assuming that the Wember testimony is acceptable. it does not follow that Sadler's Island was my goal."

"Agreed. Agreed further that your boat trip, however suspicious, is not in itself conclusive. The essential for the prosecution would be to establish your presence on the island. Mr. Stockwell, that proof is in our possession."

"Trumped-up testimony, doubtless. Have a care, Simms."

Simms said softly, "Mr. Stockwell, why did you wear gloves after but not before that night?"

"Because of painful scratches on my hands," he replied curtly.

"Inflicted by the thorns of the maybush."

Gurdon Stockwell managed a contemptuous laugh. "Now, this is pressing absurdity to the limits of the risible. Does this wonderful shrub impart a wound distinctive from any other scratch, such as a cat's? Come, Simms! I weary of this attempt to entrap me. Let us have done with it." He leaned to the door and held it open significantly. Simms did not move.

"Is that your last word?"

"It is."

"Then I am to go to the District Attorney?"

"As you choose."

"Taking with me a small branch of the maythorn found adhering to the coat which you wore when you went to your last tryst with Priscilla Stamm and which you subsequently concealed in the coach-house?"

"So whaddaya say to that?" Gypsy broke in malevolently.

"It is notorious that I am a habitual pedestrian. I walk much in the woods where wild growth is common."

Simms handed him a small brochure bearing the title, "Phe-

nomenal Manifestation of the Long-Thorned Maybush on a
Mohawk River Islet". Stockwell brushed it aside after a glance.

"I am not interested."

"You should be. The author—an eminent botanical authority,
Mr. Stockwell—points out that nowhere in the vicinity, except
on Sadler's Island, does the species occur."

Stockwell walked slowly across the room, seated himself at his
desk, brushing Gypsy aside as if she were not there, and leaned
his chin upon his hand. When his head rose, his expression was
thoughtful, wary and hard, that of the businessman faced with a
major issue.

"How much?"

"What?"

"I am asking what your price is."

"I am not concerned with money, Mr. Stockwell."

"Then what is the purpose of this inquisition?" Stockwell
began to twitch. "Before I throw you through the window," he
concluded in a choked mutter.

Unperturbed, the visitor said, "I offer you escape."

"By what means?"

"An alibi."

"Proving that I was not on the island?"

"Proving that you were."

"Do you think me a safe man to play with, you fool?"

"Gypsy, leave us."

She rose obediently, whispering as she passed: "Watch out!
Danger."

Simms asked, "Do you know of a cave on Sadler's Island?"

"I have heard of it. A resort of outlaws."

"Of fugitives from the inhumanity of you employers," the
other corrected. "Let us suppose that on the night of October
thirteenth you paid a visit to that cave."

"Why should I?"

The other raised his hand. "Kindly permit me to finish. There
you remained in conclave for the hours covering the time of
Priscilla Stamm's arrival on the island and her death. Three
witnesses would be prepared to take oath to your presence."

"Why should they?"

"In consideration of certain action we expect from you."

"Which is?"

"I shall come to that. Your witnesses are Barker Green . . ."

"The Syracuse inciter to strikes."

". . . Samuel Stillman . ' '

"A name familiar in the inflammatory Press."

". . . and myself."

"You would take the stand and supply an alibi?"

"A watertight one."

"By perjury."

"More than that," the other returned imperturbably. "We should become accessories after the fact—to murder."

"It was not murder!" Stockwell cried.

"Could a jury be persuaded of that?"

"Mind you, I admit nothing," Stockwell muttered.

"It is not necessary. In fact, it is undesirable."

"Why should I entrust myself to men of your type?" the other demanded. "Confessed members of a criminal junta."

"A group of us are joined in the work of protecting the interests of the mechanics. Is that criminal?"

"Perjury is criminal. Participation to conceal crime and abort justice is criminal."

"Agreed. And observe how safely you are shielded by the fact. We could not afterward betray you without rendering ourselves into the hands of the law."

"That is true." Stockwell pondered. "I recall your saying at our former meeting that to bring about what you call reforms, you would balk at nothing."

"Nothing," the visitor echoed gently.

"Not crime itself, it now appears."

"We are bonded to act in common concert at whatever risk or cost to ourselves."

"Again I ask you—what is your price?"

"The twelve-hour day in the Eureka."

Stockwell said hoarsely: "I might have known it! I'll burn the mills down first."

"And yourself in them?"

The tortured man stared.

"Make no mistake, Gurdon Stockwell," the labour man warned. "It is that or the gallows."

"Get out before I do you a mischief!"

Luther Simms rose. "Sleep over it, Mr. Stockwell," he said persuasively.

"Sleep!" The groan seemed wrung from tortured depths.

"Believe me, we have no wish to persecute you," the visitor went on earnestly. "What we ask is no great thing. It will come inevitably. You and the Eureka are but a temporary blockade."

"My life's principle," said Gurdon Stockwell. "My life's mission. To repel the encroachments of your vicious and revolutionary proletariat. If I abandon the cause, who is there to stand firm?"

"No one in Troy, God be thanked!"

"And you ask me—you blackmail me—to betray my friends and associates, my country, my faith in the stability of society," he cried wildly. "Do you think me any less a man of principle than yourself?"

"No." Luther Simms spoke with a touch of sadness. "I know your fidelity and honour it, even though it be to false gods. But I have no alternative in this matter. If your neck pays the price of your creed, yours is the responsibility. I shall await your answer up to tomorrow noon."

"And then?" He spoke dispiritedly.

"I shall go to Pliny Gregg."

Rejoined by her companion in the outer air, Gypsy said:
"We got him."

"Do you think so?"

"I know so. Did you see what he was doodlin' on that paper?"

"No. What was it?"

"Hangman's knots," Gypsy said.

TWENTY-TWO

It was the fifth day of Gurdon Stockwell's trial. Evidence had piled up as to his actions on the evening of the girl's death. It was indicated, if not proven, that he had appropriated a boat from its moorings at a dock. It was proven apparently beyond reasonable doubt, through the identification of the Wembler brothers, that he had been on the river, headed away from Sadler's Island after the hour set as that of the murder. He had been seen shortly before midnight on a street leading from the waterfront to his home.

The coat was produced, identified, offered in evidence. The thorns were identified as of the bush peculiar to the island. This might be regarded as proof that the accused had been on the island, but the element of time was still lacking. Elias Plum, in court with Guy Roy and Jans Urena, pointed this out. He further mentioned that the boat rowed by Stockwell might have come from the far shore and not from the island.

"They've got to place him on the island that night," he stated, with legalistic precision, "or it's no faggots for the woodpile."

Several witnesses swore to having seen the accused in company with the Stamm girl on various occasions covering a period of more than two years. Under Dr. Dorr's sharp probing, each deponent admitted that such association might well be explained by a common interest in Church work.

Charges became more specific when the Thompson Camp Ground meeting was taken up, through two witnesses, Long Gib Darrow and a fellow loafer named Cox, two of the gang of roughs whom Gurdon Stockwell had faced down. Darrow's description of what he had seen while concealed in the underbrush, after the meeting, was such that Judge Lang ordered the courtroom cleared of female spectators. Cox backed up his fellow in terms no less explicit. Though the adverse testimony of the pair was weakened by Lawyer Dorr's cross-examination, it built up at least a premise of illicit relations between the elder and the pious girl.

The doubt was bolstered by the reluctant deposition of Mr. Heartt, the bookseller. Questioned upon the Dr. Codrick opus, he was forced to admit that the prisoner had ordered a copy late in August. Passages of impressive implication as applied to

Priscilla Stamm's condition were read to the jury. Wiseacres among the spectators whispered that Gurdon Stockwell would have a hole to darn *there*, since his legally wedded wife, even this long after, exhibited no signs of pregnancy. What did he want the book for, anyway?

There followed on the stand a figure strange to Troy. The female was of middle age, gaunt, uncomely, serious and primly clad. Octagonal glasses on a silver chain aided her peering eyes. She identified herself as Doctress Emmaline Howe, specialist in female derangements, tetter, cancer, tumour, the evil, and all ailments of the skin and flesh.

Q   You itinerate in the pursuit of your profession?

A   Yes, sir; mainly in the New England States.

Q   Were you during the month of September last practicing in Lawrence, Massachusetts?

A   Yes, sir.

Q   Were you consulted by a young lady from the Happy Toiler mill calling herself Priscilla Stamm?

A   Yes, sir.

Q   You examined her?

A   I did.

Q   What was her condition?

A   That of pregnancy.

Q   Of what duration?

A   I judged it to be about three months.

Q   Did you understand her to be a married woman?

A   No, sir.

Q   Did she mention any man in connection with her condition?

A   She mentioned a gentleman from the city where she lived. She said he was rich and pious and owned a mill and a bank.

Q   Did she state his name?

A   No, sir.

Q   Doctress, pay careful heed to this question: did she further identify this gentleman in any way?

A   She sometimes spoke of him as Mr. S.

THE JUDGE: Order in the court!

Q   Did you attempt to relieve the pregnancy of the patient?

A   No, sir. I guess I know my business too well to get mixed up with the law.

Q   Very proper, Doctress. Did the said patient importune you for relief?

A (hesitantly) She asked my advice about a drug.

Q What was the drug?

A Oil of tansy.

Q A known abortive, if it please the Court. What did she ask you about this drug?

A She said that a phial of it had been sent to her with specifications for a certain dosage. I advised her that the dosage was excessive and might have produced fatal results.

Q Then she had not taken it?

A No, sir. She destroyed the phial in my presence.

Q Therefore you cannot produce it. Your witness, Brother Dorr.

Q (On cross-examination) Did the deceased, Priscilla Stamm, ever state or in any manner indicate that the Mr. S. referred to was responsible for her condition?

A Well, he was sending her money.

Q So that she might have the benefit of your professional care?

A Yes, sir.

Q Did she ever indicate in any manner that this unknown Mr. S. was the father of her unborn child?

A Now that you mention it, she didn't.

Q Were you aware that they were fellow church-members?

A She said something about a camp meeting.

Q A camp meeting in which she was affiliated in good works with Mr. S.?

A Well, yes; I guess so. She said he was pious and they worked together in the church.

Q Just so, Doctress. So that, for all you know to the contrary, Mr. S. may have been actuated by a wholly impersonal kindness toward and interest in an unfortunate fellow-member of his church.

A Well, so far as I've seen, gentlemen ain't so interested in other gentlemen's bast——

Q Never mind that, Doctress. Did she ever say anything to indicate that Mr. S. was anything more than her Christian benefactor?

A No, I don't know as she ever.

"That is all."

"I'd rather Squire Dorr had this case than me," Elias Plum commented to his fellow Halcyons as the prosecution closed after reverting to the gloves worn by Stockwell for a period after 13

October. Several witnesses testified on this point. Court then adjourned.

Mrs. Gurdon Stockwell made a point of going at once to her husband with a bright, wifely smile. One would have supposed her to be loyally rejoicing that all was going well with their cause.

Stockwell's staunchest supporters did not take this roseate view. They were disturbed and depressed. Some even felt that the defendant's counsel was not doing all that could have been done. An impromptu delegation from the Mill Owners Association, Messrs. Fosmire, Howland and Paulding, waited upon Mr. Dorr to express their anxiety. The gangling lawyer treated them to a derisive smile.

"Be on hand when court re-convenes," he said. "I think I can promise you a bellyful. Whether your digestion can handle it is your own affair. I bid you good day, gentlemen."

Rumours of sensational developments brought a record throng to the building when court resumed in the morning. The three Halcyons had to fight their way through the blockade at the entrance. There was some delay before Lawyer Dorr rose to open his case with one of the shortest outlines on record.

"Gentlemen of the jury, I shall put my client on the stand and elicit from him his own account. Four witnesses will support his testimony. Our case will then be submitted to you with perfect confidence in the outcome. Gurdon Stockwell, take the stand."

The prisoner passed within a yard of Guy Roy on his way. His face was a cast of grey immobility. His eyes were fixed and level. But as he walked, Guy saw his mouth twitch once and settle back into the thin line of suffering and resolution. A light froth of spittle gathered at one corner of the down-drawn lips. Guy's first thought was—He's going to have a cachetic stroke; his second—My God! Is he going to confess?

The prisoner made his affirmation with calm. The hand that held the Bible was rigid. The voice in which he answered his counsel's questions was expressionless and controlled. It never varied in cadence during the brief ordeal of his examination.

Lawyer Door began: "Mr. Stockwell, before entering upon the vital phase of our inquiry, I shall, upon your own specification, afford you opportunity of clearing your moral character from the aspersions cast upon it. Have you at any time had illicit or immoral relations with Miss Priscilla Stamm?

A   Never.

Q You have heard the testimony of the witnesses, Darrow and Cox, regarding commerce between you and Miss Stamm at Thompson's Camp Ground. Was that testimony true or false?

A False in every particular.

Q Did you write to Miss Stamm in Lawrence?

A I did.

Q Did you send her money?

A I did.

Q Why did you do this?

A As a Christian duty toward a fellow worshipper in dire need of aid. Deeply though I deplored her sin, I could not leave a sister in the Church alone and unfriended.

"Old man Dorr looks as if he was swallowing raw rhubarb," Jan Urena chuckled under his breath. "I don't believe he believes a word of it, and I know damn' well he don't like it."

Q We shall now approach the matter of the major accusation. Mr. Stockwell, you have heard the testimony of sundry witnesses who saw you in the early evening of October thirteenth. What was your destination?

A Sadler's Island.

Q Have you ever under oath denied visiting Sadler's Island that evening?

A I have not.

Q Neither have you admitted your presence on the island hitherto?

A No.

Q Why not?

A I was bound by an oath of secrecy.

Q To whom?

A To Mr. Luther Simms and Messrs. Stillman and Greene.

THE JUDGE If there is further disorder in the court, I will have the room cleared. (To Messrs. Fosmire, Howland and Paulding) Gentlemen, resume your seats or leave the court.

Q You went secretly to the island to meet the said Messrs. Simms, Stillman and Greene?

A I did.

Q For what purpose?

A To consult and confer upon certain problems of labour affecting the conduct of the Eureka Mills.

Q How long did the meeting last?

A From about nine to nearly eleven p.m.

Q   Between which hours, if the Court please, it is established beyond doubt that the deceased girl met her death. Was anyone else present at your rendezvous?

A   Cassius Barlow, the latter part of the evening.

Q   Where did the consultation take place?

A   In a cave at the south-west corner of the island.

Q   Part way up the bluff?

A   Yes.

Q   Did you have difficulty reaching the cave?

A   I did. I lost my footing on the declivity and fell into a thicket of maythorn.

Q   Did you scarify your hands?

A   Yes.

Q   And thereafter for a time wore gloves?

A   Gloves containing a healing medication.

Q   One more question, Mr. Stockwell. Did you at any time between your arrival at and departure from the cave—the period in which the deceased lost her life—absent yourself from your companions?

A   No. I did not leave the cave.
"Your witness, Brother Gregg."

Q   (By the District Attorney) Mr. Stockwell, I note that your attorney did not go into the matter of the subject of the conferment between you and your cave companions. Do you plead privilege in the matter of secrecy?

A   No. In defence of my life and character I have been released from my oath.

Q   What was the object of your meeting?

A   To arrange for the establishment of the twelve-hour day in the Eureka Mills.
Uproar in the court—gavel-pounding by the Judge—threats and dissuasions by bailiffs and constables—hisses—order restored with difficulty.
(After comparative silence was established.) Was this motion of the twelve-hour day imposed upon you by the said Simms, Stillman and Greene one or several?

A   No. It was my own intrinsic motion.

Q   (savagely) Can you give this court any explanation for this sudden and fundamental change of attitude on your part?

A   (almost indistinguishable) Changing order . . . other cities already . . . keep pace with trend of commerce . . .

Q Speak up, Mr. Stockwell.

A (loudly and mechanically) I take this measure as a matter of principle. The welfare of my labourers has ever been close to my sentiments. We must recognize the demands and rights of those who look to us for support. The Eureka has always been and, I trust in God, always will be in the fore-front of improvement.

"He doesn't believe a damned word of what he's saying," Elias Plum whispered, and Guy answered:

"This is the end of sunrise to sunset in Troy."

Re-direct examination brought out that there had been a solemn oath of secrecy between Gurdon Stockwell on the one side, and Luther Simms and his aides on the other.

Q And that is your reason for your previous silence regarding your movements on the night of October thirteenth last?

A It is.

Q Your sole and only reason?

A Yes.

One after the other, Luther Simms, Stillman, Greene and finally Cassius Barlow variously supported the statements of the prisoner. Their accounts tallied perfectly, as they should have done, having been minutely rehearsed and re-rehearsed by the careful Luther Simms. On the stand he explained the under-lying reasons for the strategy of secrecy. Gurdon Stockwell wished for time to cushion the shock to the commercial structure. Simms had prepared a plan of campaign calling for a demand upon every cotton factory in Troy under threat of strike. When the demands were rejected, as he knew they would be, the Eureka announcement would be the heavy artillery that would breach the walls of the cottonocracy. May 1 was the date set. Only when it became evident that the prisoner's fate hung upon the evidence connecting him with Sadler's Island did the labour leader release him from his oath.

The evidence was determinative, particularly that of Luther Simms. The other witnesses might be of dubious reliability in the view of conservative folk. But Simms, apostle of labour's rights though he was, was a man of piety and—more convincing —property. Why should he risk his liberty and his reputation by committing perjury for one who had always been his unremitting enemy? The outcome of the trial was inevitable.

Gurdon Stockwell was acquitted.

TWENTY-THREE

ONE week after the acquittal, the Mill Owners Association met to consider its course in regard to Gurdon Stockwell.

Horace Howland, the ironmaster, was in the chair.

Sylvester Fosmire stood up. "I move you, Mr. Chairman, that we call for the resignation of Mr. Gurdon Stockwell."

"On what ground?"

"Treason to the principles of our Association."

"Has anyone here seen him since the verdict?" Le Grand Cannon inquired.

"He's keeping himself very private," Independence Stark said. "Hasn't stuck his head outside his own door, so I am advised."

"Do you think that he will refuse to resign?" Banker Paulding inquired of the Chair.

"Vy give um a chanz?" grunted Sweer Van Velsen of the pearl ashery. "Vire um, I say."

The suggestion met with some favour. Expulsion was the fitting answer to Stockwell's base betrayal of the cause, in the minds of many.

Pinmaker Beebe claimed attention. "Ridding ourselves of Mr. Stockwell is not enough, Mr. Chairman. This honourable body should record itself as repudiating the abominable heresy which he fosters and supporting the retention of the natural work-day."

"I'll go that one better," Sylvester Fosmire declared. "The day that the Eureka initiates the twelve-hour day, let every other factory in Troy post a sixteen-hour notice."

"And throw its lever." The harsh voice of Lawyer Dorr was an unpleasing interruption to the growing unity of thought. "There won't a wheel turn in all Troy except in the Eureka, one hour after the notices go up," the realistic old lawyer prophesied.

"With the streets full of unemployed?" said Beebe.

Fosmire glared at the prophet of ill. "We all know where Lawyer Dorr stands and why. It's the old saw, 'Whose bread I eat, his song I sing.'" He delivered the quotation with equal relish and malice.

"I am in no man's pay except for legal services," Dorr said

equably. "But I will give you gentlemen some free counsel. Go down to the water's edge and throw stones at the fish."

"Explain your reference, Mr. Dorr," the Chairman bade him austerely.

"You waste your time in idle boasts of what you would like to do," the lawyer retorted. "How many hands does the Eureka employ? More than any two other mills in Troy. Already we have the ten-hour day in one industry. On the day when the Eureka goes to the twelve-hour schedule, you may adjust yourselves to it, willy-nilly, or close your doors."

Ellis Miller, who had something of the diplomat in his make-up, rose. "I am loath to think that Lawyer Dorr advocates these reprehensible measures——"

"I advocate nothing," the old man interrupted vigorously. "I merely point out facts."

"Therefore I appeal to him. Could not Mr. Stockwell be prevailed upon by reasoning to reconsider his rash measure?"

"In my opinion, no."

The Chairman put it to the gathering. "Did any man here present ever know Gurdon Stockwell to reconsider anything to which he had made up his mind?"

Blank and unhopeful silence followed.

"I will be one of ten to swear a bond never to reduce the Lark at Morn to twelve hours," Fosmire offered. "Who will join me?"

The hush that followed was painful. Three voices presently assented. But they were those of Carey (lumber), Van Velsen (pearl-ash) and Corey Smith (shot tower). Not a factory man in the weaving or spinning category responded. Stout though their words had been in denunciation of the renegade among their number, when it came to bond-and-forfeit, their vision beheld the writing on the wall.

"We have a suggestion, but no motion before the meeting," Chairman Howland pointed out. "Does anyone wish to offer a motion regarding Mr. Gurdon Stockwell?"

"I move," said Ellis Miller, "that the Association officially request Mr. Stockwell's resignation both of his presidency and his membership."

"Second that," Independence Stark said, adding uneasily: "No use stirring up extra trouble with a man like Gurdon Stockwell."

Debate became lively, and presently acrimonious. While no one defended the absent president, opinion as to the proper procedure against him was sharply divided. In the midst of the discussion, Peter Osband, who had the floor, noticed a concentration of interest on the part of the Chairman quite alien to his own well-chosen remarks. He followed Mr. Howland's intent gaze to the rear door and fell silent. Gurdon Stockwell stood in the doorway. A slow, surprised buzz died away.

"Good day, gentlemen," he said.

Not a man answered. He walked the length of the room without haste, mounted the platform and took the gavel from the hand of the pro tem. Chairman. Horace Howland offered no resistance.

"This meeting is now officially in session," the President announced briskly. He swept the uneasy assemblage with his calm gaze. "I believe there was a motion before the rump session," he said. "If repeated, I shall be glad to entertain it."

"Motion to request your resignation as president and member," Banker Paulding said hastily to forestall Van Velsen who was lumbering to his feet.

"Any remarks?"

There was none. Mr. Stockwell permitted himself a frugal smile. "All in favour signify by saying aye." The ayes were general and strong.

"Contrary, no."

The noes were less so.

"The motion seems to be carried in. It *is* carried. I accept the will of this body and gladly relinquish my membership in a coalition which I always suspected to be fools and now perceive to be cowards as well. You will live to rue this action. Gentlemen, I bid you good day."

He took up hat, stick and gloves and left. The members straggled after him without formality of adjournment.

The perturbation and uncertainty in the minds of his former associates occasioned by Gurdon Stockwell's unaccountable behaviour were repeated in his household. His wife did not know what to make of him.

"I might as well be a faggot of wood these days," she told Gypsy Vilas, though on no note of complaint. "He's living in a daze. Gives me good morning and good night, and I doubt that he sees me when he speaks. I could come and go as I please, I do believe, without his taking note of it."

"And meet Guy Roy?"

Becky quivered all over. "I haven't set eyes on him," she said dolorously. "What can I do, Gypsy?" Becky appealed to her friend. "What can I do?"

"I damn' well don't know," the other admitted.

"I wonder if my husband is going crazy. He sits up in that den of his to unearthly hours. After midnight, night after night, writing, writing, writing. Then he'll sit and think with his big chin propped in his hand. Sometimes he reads over what he's written and smiles to himself. I don't like that smile, Gypsy. It's—it's got shivers in it."

"What's he write about?"

"I've only seen it once. Then it was a legal paper. He called me in one evening to sign it. But he didn't want me to read what was in it."

"Couldn't you make out anything?"

The wife hesitated before answering. "Gypsy, I think he's going to sell the Eureka."

The visitor bounced in her chair. "*Sell* it? What for?"

"Or give it away. Get rid of it, anyway."

Gypsy had the flash of an idea. "So's not to have to put in the twelve-hour day?"

"That's what I think."

"Can't you get a peek at them papers?"

"He keeps them under lock in his desk. I only got the chance to see them Saturday evening when he jumped up and went to the window. Somebody was outside."

"Spyin', huh? Who was it?"

"Mr. Stockwell thought it was Guy. He accused me of a rendezvous."

"Was it?"

"No. I think it was Cash Barlow. I looked for footprints this morning. They were uneven. Cash is peg-legged, you know."

"Smart gal! I wonder if he had—never mind. I'm goin' to have a palaver with Cash."

She got Barlow aside from his cleaning job in the collar works the next noon.

"What are you doin' nights on Castle Hill, Cash? And don't lie to me."

U

"Nothing," he said surlily. "Watching."

"What for? What can you find out?"

"That son-of-a-bitch killed her."

"Twelve men on a jury say not."

"And I'm going to prove it on him," he continued doggedly.

"So said, so done, and then what? They can't try him again."

"I'll tend to that."

"*You'll* tend to it! How?" She stared hard at him.

"That's my affair."

"Is it your affair to be scramblin' on him nights?"

"What's he writing all the time? That's what I want to know."

"What d'you figure it might be, Cash?"

"His confession."

"Nah," the girl said. "He'd never be one to confess." She reflected. "I dunno, though. He could be figurin' out excuses for himself. Get it off his mind, like."

"I've seen him crying over it."

"Huh?" said Gypsy, unpleasantly startled. "Old Hurdy-Gurdy? Wouldn't have thought he had a tear in him. Have you told Luther Simms?"

"Yes."

"What's he say?"

"He wants to see you as soon as he gets back. We'll meet him Thursday after closin' hour."

The agitator listened to Gypsy's account with a face that became more and more shadowed. He agreed with her interpretation of the document signed by the wife.

"Undoubtedly a transfer, requiring the wife's signature," he said. "He is going to forswear his agreement. Cassius, can't you get those papers?"

"Not me," his henchman said. "I'm no picklock."

"You want a picklock?" Gypsy asked quickly. "A good one?"

Luther Simms asked, "Is he trustworthy?"

" 'Djever hear of Four Skate Pilkington?"

"Everybody's heard of Four Skate," Cash said.

It was true that everybody in Barlow's world knew of the tough little adventurer's classic escape by ice, with skates attached to both hands and feet, from a Pennsylvania sheriff and his posse.

"He's hereabouts," she said.

"In jail?"

"No. But keepin' kinda private."

"Another little job of body-snatching?" Cash grinned.

"He was never in on that," Gypsy returned. "He's an owler, not a resurrectioner."

"What's an owler doing in Troy?" Luther Simms asked. "There is no smuggling across the Mohawk, so far as I have heard."

"No. Pilk got into kinda low company. A canal-boat bogus gang. They turned out a five-dollar note that I wouldn't use to patch baby's di'pers with. He's layin' doggo, but I can find him."

"Do you think he would serve our purpose?"

"I wouldn't want to say that Pilk is regularly on that lay," Gypsy said. "But I never saw the door he couldn't go through like grass through a goose. And a desk is easier than a door."

"Yay-ah. But why should he be in on this?" Cash demanded.

"I done him a favour once when he needed help bad. Pilk ain't one to forget a friend."

They discussed plans for the housebreaking. Cash would act as guide.

"And leave that militia musket of yours at home," Luther Simms said with his quiet emphasis.

Fox-eared Gypsy caught it, and gave Cash an estimating glance, but said nothing.

Saturday night was set for the attempt. There remained only to pray for propitious darkness.

TWENTY-FOUR

THE reek of sperm oil from two betty lamps was heavy in the air of the office which Guy Roy had loaned to his forewoman for her private and late nocturnal purposes. Three sober-faced men bent over the sheaf of ruled stationery which the expert Pilkington had duly delivered on the stroke of midnight. Gypsy Vilas sat, intent, in a corner.

The sheets were evenly inscribed in the strong and precise writing of Gurdon Stockwell. There was not a single erasure or correction. The manuscript stood, fair copy for perpetuation.

"Read that again, will you?" Gypsy requested.

Luther Simms set his finger to the first page and reread, " 'I am guiltless in heart and conscience of the death of that woman.' "

Cassius Barlow muttered something unintelligible.

"He can't believe that," Samuel Stillman said incredulously. The prolific contributor to *The Man* and other proletarian publications had accompanied Simms to Troy.

"He can believe anything he wishes to believe," Simms said. "You don't know Gurdon Stockwell."

"*I* know him," Cash Barlow said. There was menace in his tone.

"This first part seems to be a full confession of everything but intent," Simms went on.

"Intent be damned!" Barlow said. "Prissy's dead, ain't she? And he's her murderer."

"Morally, I believe that to be true," the leader said.

"And legally they can't do a thing to him," Stillman put in.

"No. A man cannot be twice put in capital jeopardy for the same crime. Legally he is in the clear," Simms said. "I have a lawyer's opinion on that point."

"More than we are," Stillman said gloomily. He struck the paper with open hand. "This might mean Auburn for us. Perjury."

"Chuck it in the river with a horse-shoe tied to it for luck," Barlow said, and laughed.

"To what avail?" Simms asked in his gentle voice. "Stockwell need but write it all over again."

"What's he writin' it at all for?" Gypsy propounded. "That's what gravels me."

"To prepare the way for his principal thesis. This is comparatively unimportant."

"Ay-ah, unimportant. To you, maybe," Cash Barlow said.

Luther Simms ran rapidly through the main points of Stockwell's laborious self-exculpation.

"Mere preface," he said. "By unimportant, I mean that Priscilla Stamm's is but one life among the thousands yearly sacrificed to the brutalism of the factory system. You and I, and Green and Stillman, may go to prison for our part in Stockwell's crime. That, too, is unimportant. What matters is the Cause." He was speaking now with the intensity and absorption of the fanatic. "We have saved Gurdon Stockwell's neck, and he has betrayed us for *his* cause. If this, his plan, be fulfilled, labour in Troy is doomed to the indefinite perpetuation of the long work-day."

"It's all double Dutch to me," the girl complained. "What's in there besides Prissy Stamm?"

"Total repudiation of his agreement with us. He revokes his covenant to establish the twelve-hour day on the ground that he was forced into it."

"We'd ought've let him hang," Barlow growled.

"To assure his design," Simms went on, "he turns over the Eureka Mills to the Mill Owners Association to be managed by trustees with the explicit proviso that the factory maintain God's Natural Day in perpetuo. 'God's Natural Day!'" he repeated bitterly. "Sunrise to sunset, and may dividends prosper."

"What'll old Hurdy-Gurdy be without his mills?" Gypsy asked. "What's he goin' to do? Cut his throat?"

"His design seems to be to go away and make a new life where he is unknown," Simms answered. He resumed his reading.

" 'I go with a conscience clear and purged. For my crime of unchastity I have been cruelly punished. Of the worse crime of murder, I absolve myself. Again I declare it: I am guiltless of the death of that woman.' "

" 'That woman!' " muttered Cash Barlow, and flexed his fingers as if they gripped a throat.

" 'There hangs over me,' " the reader resumed, " 'the blacker offence against the community of which I have long been an honoured member. Through the perjury of evil and

310 SUNRISE TO SUNSET

conspiratorial men I have been forced into an impious compact. Even as I entered into the agreement which I now denounce and repudiate, I knew to what fate I would have doomed my city. Through the opening wedge of the twelve-hour day, the tyrant forces of the proletary would have taken over control. Who can say what excesses might have supervened? The ten-hour day is already in force, though waning. Even such a monstrous measure as the eight-hour day is not impossible, should we set audacious labour in the saddle and commit our fair city to the ravening wolves of the mechanics class. Never let it be said that an act of Gurdon Stockwell helped to bring this about. Rather would I sacrifice my life, as well as my reputation.' ''

"Sounds as if he were exhibiting an oration," Stillman commented.

Simms went on:

" 'Now as I depart from all that I held dear and honorific to essay a new and obscure life in the fastnesses of the Great West, I can humbly ask the prayers of my fellow citizens who have signalized me with their confidence and esteem.' ''

The reader looked up from the neat black script. "Here it is again," he said. " 'I am guiltless of the death of that woman.' ''

"Kinda has it on his mind, ain't he!" Gypsy commented.

"There follows a passage commending us to the attention of the Grand Jury as perjurers. I shall not trouble to read it," Simms concluded, laying the manuscript aside.

"Where does that leave us?" Stillman asked blankly.

"Facin' clinkety-clink," Gypsy said.

"Not me!" Cash Barlow growled, and made as if to seize the document.

Luther Simms interposed a massive arm. "This goes back to Stockwell's secret drawer."

"What for?"

The leader made an impatient gesture. "We don't want to force the issue. Stockwell has not completed his work. There are marginal notes for addenda. Several days' leeway are still probable. If, tomorrow—today, I should say—he finds this gone, he will act at once. Let us avail ourselves of all the time possible."

"What for?" Cash Barlow demanded again. "To cut sticks and run?"

"I shall not evade," was the quiet rejoinder.

"I will," Stillman said. "What good can I do in jail? They don't even allow you quill and ink."

"There'll be no jail," Barlow muttered. Gypsy caught her breath and shot him a swift glance.

Simms brought out his great silver watch and consulted it. "Two-thirty," he said. "Barlow, are you sure that you and Mr. Pilkington can gain re-entrance?"

"Pilk's gone. I can do it myself. I left the window unbarred."

"Replace everything exactly as it was. See that you leave no marks. Report back to me here." The henchman nodded, carefully tucked the papers into his shirt-front, and left. Simms said to the others, "Gurdon Stockwell has notified the mill-owners that he will have a statement to present through his counsel at the next regular Association meeting."

"You think this is the statement?"

"I have no doubt of it."

"When's the meetin'?" from Gypsy.

"The first of the month."

"That gives us ten days," Stillman reckoned.

"I don't reckon it'll be that long," the girl said.

"What d'you mean by that?" the labour-writer demanded. "What won't?"

"Never mind," she said.

Conversation faded. They sat in thoughtful silence until Cash Barlow was with them again, having entered with a startling quietness.

"All clear?" Simms asked.

Barlow said: "Yes. He'll never know anyone was there. Damn his black soul to hell." he added. He reached for his cap. "I'm off," he said.

He left with the same uncanny stillness that had marked his arrival. Stillman, with a brusque good night, followed him.

Gypsy sat, nibbling at her lip. "Mr. Simms," she said, very low.

"Well?"

"You know what's liable to happen, don't you?"

There followed a long silence. Then he said, "Cassius Barlow?"

"Yes."

"He didn't have his musket with him."

"Not tonight."

"When, then?" the leader asked fearfully.

"How can I tell? Maybe tomorrow. Maybe not for two-three days. Accordin' as he gets his chance."

Luther Simms heaved his bulk half out of the chair, then slumped back with a half-groan.

"Ain't you goin' to do anything?" the girl asked curiously.

"No," he said. "God forgive me, no."

Gurdon Stockwell allowed himself two more sessions of work on his statement before it should be completed. He reflected with a bitter relish upon the discomfiture of the Mill Owners Association when their accusations of betrayal should be thrown back in their teeth. Let them retract! Let them humbly apologize. He would spurn the pusillanimous advances towards a composition with him which, he doubted not, they would proffer.

It was a wild, uneasy night outside. A noisy wind had set in out of the north-east, stripping the wet spring snow from the twigs. Was there someone prowling again in the garden? He went twice to the window, but could see nothing. His veracious account of the death of Priscilla Stamm with its convincing exculpation, would be left under seal with Lawyer Dorr, to be opened only after the fastnesses of the Boundless West should have taken the writer into their oblivion.

Wakeful and waiting for her husband's foot-drag in passage past her door, Gurdon Stockwell's wife fell into a light sleep as eleven o'clock stuck, Presbyterian time. The report and the splintering of glass only half-awakened her. It might have been part of a restless dream. She craned her neck and blinked at the dull lustre of the downstairs light against shaken branches. Mr. Stockwell sat late. She slept again, secure in her domestic aloofness.

Thudding impact on her barred door roused her. She burrowed her way out of her down pillow. Half-light was greying the window panes.

"Becky! Becky! For God's sake, Becky!"

She leapt to the floor and raised the bar. Gypsy Vilas staggered in.

"He's dead."

Becky's hands clutched at her breasts. "Guy? Gypsy! Not Guy," she wailed.

"Clam up! Your husband."

"Mr. Stockwell?" She gasped, staring half-dazed. "Mr. Stockwell?" she repeated. "How?"

"Killed. Shot."

"Yes, I heard it," the wife said stupidly.

"You heard it? And you lyin' there dossin'!"

"I didn't know what it was." The tender mouth set in firmness. "Where is he?"

Gypsy put her back to the door. "No," she said. "You mustn't."

"Who did it? How do you come here? Gypsy! Tell me."

Gypsy had no intention of telling her. "I don't know," she said.

Becky's mind was levelling out. "If you don't know, why are you here?"

This, also, the visitor designed to keep to herself. Cash Barlow had come to her after the successful shot, to leave certain directions. He had paid out for Prissy's murder, he boasted. Let 'em try to catch him! He'd join the shifting armies of the towpath and be lost in them. Troy would never see him again.

"I had an early errand at the Eureka," Gypsy lied.

Unlikely though the story was, Becky took no exception to it.

"Dead!" she murmured. "I *must* go to him, Gypsy."

Gypsy yielded. "I'll go with you."

At the closed study door she stopped and gulped air. "No! I can't do it."

"You needn't. I will."

"Wait," the working girl said. "There's papers."

"What papers? Where?"

"On his desk. The ones he was writin' on."

"I don't know what you're talking about, Gypsy. Let me go."

"We gotta have 'em. Will you fetch 'em with you?"

Becky broke the hold of the other's hands. "Gypsy, tell me the truth," she commanded. "Did you have a hand in this?"

"Not me, so help me God!"

Becky entered. Gurdon Stockwell sat almost upright in his chair. The musket bullet, truly aimed, had gone through his heart. His face was peaceful. It bore a look of satisfaction, of the self-approval of the man who has acquitted himself worthily of an onerous duty. Becky could not quite believe him dead.

"Mr. Stockwell!" she said softly.

The papers which were the object of Gypsy's solicitude lay gathered on the desk. A sentence printed out in strong capitals caught Becky's eye:

I AM GUILTLESS OF THAT WOMAN'S DEATH

It was lightly splotched with blood.

Beneath was the deed with its provisions for trusteeship. With spirit and hand under rigid control, Becky gathered the sheets. She stepped out of the room and handed them to her friend.

"That's them," Gypsy said. She bore them to the big fireplace, found a box of matches on the mantelpiece, struck a light and burned them one by one.

"So said, so done," she muttered.

"The law," Becky said. "We must tell them."

"No," Gypsy said. She had thought it out while Becky was in the room with the dead man. "That can wait. Listen. I ain't been here. You ain't seen me. You don't know anything about it yet. You go back up to your bed and let be. Jeshurun'll find him." She looked about her with a contemplative and wondering eye. "Just think! This is all yours. Little Becky, Fortune's Factory Gal."

Becky began to shake. "I don't want it. I hate it, everything about it." She made a gesture of repudiation. "It's an unchancy house. There's no happiness in it. I want to go away from it and never come back—never, never, never!"

She climbed the stairs to her chamber and lay in the broad bed, staring at the ceiling until the weeping and trembling Jeshurun brought her the news.

A month after the tragedy, Gypsy Vilas said to the widow, "What are you waitin' for?"

"There are decencies to be considered," Becky said. "One year. It's not respectable for a widow to be married sooner."

"Fah-doodle!" said her friend. "How long since you been *really* married?"

"Oh, that!" Becky answered. "That's more than a year."

"And there you are!" Gypsy said. "Look, wench! If you want *me* at your weddin', you better hurry it up. I hear there's jobs out westward, and my foot is itchin'. What does Mr. Guy Roy say?"

"Oh!" said Becky, dimpling. "He says tomorrow if not today."

"Make it August," Gypsy said, "and I'll stay for it."

December morning. Four months after the quiet wedding that made Becky Mrs. Guy Roy. One lone pre-sunrise bell sent out its summons, sole survivor of a passing age, and that was too far away from the new house of the Roys to waken them.

Only a handful of the Lark at Morn workers stirred in their beds. The rest were on turn-out.

The inauguration of the twelve-hour day by the Eureka Mills, now the inherited property of Obedience Roy, had been followed by the most tumultuous days in Troy's by no means placid history. Turn-out, strike and riot turned the mill yards into battlefields. *"Non sine sanguine,"* Gurdon Stockwell had threatened Luther Simms. Blood did indeed flow from cracked heads, bashed noses and bitten necks. With the Eureka paying full hire for the shorter day, rival after rival gave in and accepted the inevitable. First came the New Enterprise, then the Arbia, and, month after month, King Cotton, the Paragon and the Double Eagle. The contagion spread to other industries: to Gideon Beebe's Sixty-Perfect-Pins-per-Hour, to the Smith shot-tower and Sweer Van Velsen's pearl ashery. Alone of the once-invincible Association, Sylvester Fosmire continued to defy the inexorable gods of progress until in a final burst of profanity directed at recalcitrant labour and cowardly employers, he nailed shut the Lark's front door, and drowned himself in his millrace.

Now the booming bell of the Eureka was sounding across the ruinous garden and abandoned mansion of the Stockwell property, and dinning in the resentful ears of an ex-factory girl asleep luxuriously on the second floor of a new house of Haverstraw brick. Becky yawned and shrank and threw a bare arm across her eyes.

"Don't douse me," she muttered.

She came fully awake to the sound of her husband's laughter.

"Oh, dee-ar!" she sighed. "I thought I was back in Dorm Four."

"And that I was the Widow Devroo?"

"You look like it in that nightcap." She tweaked it off. "Listen to that bell. Seven o'clock and we don't have to get up yet. D'you believe it, Guy?"

"I've always believed it," he said. "But not that we'd be listening to it like this."

"You did it," she chuckled. "You and your pesky ten-hour day. And respectable Troy will contemn you for ever for it."

"No," he denied. "I didn't do it. Not alone. I never could have."

"What was it, then?" she asked more soberly. "Chance? Fate? God?"

"See, now, how queerly things work out," Guy said. "We've got the short day in Troy, and why? Good men and women suffered persecution for it, and nothing happened. Workers starved. Fomenters went to jail. And we were no nearer it. Then a man who hated the cause and opposed it to his last breath, gives way to his hot blood and the battle is won. And how? Virtue and courage and unselfish endeavour couldn't do it. It took trickery and crime. It's a perilous world, wife of mine."

"It's a grand world," Becky retorted with deep contentment. "Bad deeds fetch good in their trail, and God moves in a mysterious way His wonders to perform, and we make the finest collars in the trade, and I love my husband, and you can just *be* the Widow Devroo for I'm going to get up and write a long letter to Gypsy in way-off Syracuse and tell her all about it."

"Save your ink. She couldn't read it."

"So I post it to Penmaster Robinson at Van Tromp's tavern with sixpence fee for reading it to her."

She sharpened her nib, thickened her ink, set her sand-box at her elbow and wrote in the beautifully shaded script of fashionable instruction:

It is mortal reprehensible to be so enamoured of one's husband as I and I am much reprehended for it by the respectables of Troy. And what care I! Not a tinker's damn, as my wicked Gypsy would say. One day there will be a little Factory Girl in the Roy household—Heaven only knows why there is no news of her yet!—and you shall be her Godmother. Gypsy Roy. Isn't that a cruel pretty name?

Do you hear aught of Cash Barlow? There was a dead man dug up from the snow by bears and some said it was Cash, but

I believe he's in the West, if the Wild Aborigines have not scalped him. Luther Simms had a mysterious post some time since.

Our commerce prospers mightily and I have invented an improvement to the product. Mrs. Orlando Montague says it is an excellent device. But my dear husband is an old Stodgers-Stick-in-the-Mire and says that my beautiful collar-stud would be always falling out and losing itself. It is patterned like a sandglass to fit into the neckband hole and button down the collar fore and aft, snug and fit. But my husband says that men have always tied their collars on and always will. Men are such fools!

Nobody but his doting wife knows how queer Mr. Guy Roy is and how wonderful. When they moved the mortal remains of my late husband—I cannot bear to set down the name that I once bore—to the mansion gardens as his will devised, not one member of the Mill Owners Assoc'n attended the service. But Mr. Guy Roy was present in his blacks as family. I send you a drawing of the stone. And who do you think wrote the epitaph? My sweet and foolish Guy.

Your ever loving,
Becky.

The inscription on the plain stone was in three lines:

Hereunder Lies
Gurdon Stockwell, Esq.
A Man of Principle.

APPENDIX

RULES & REGULATIONS

TO BE OBSERVED BY ALL PERSONS

EMPLOYED IN THE FACTORY OF ·

AMASA WHITNEY

Rule 1 The Mill will be put into operation 10 minutes before sunrise at all seasons of the year. The gate will be shut 10 minutes past sunset from the 20th of March to the 20th of September, at 30 minutes past 8 from the 20th of September to the 20th of March. Saturdays at sunset.

2nd It will be required of every person employed, that they be in the room in which they are employed, at the time mentioned above for the mill to be in operation.

3rd Hands are not allowed to leave the factory in working hours without the consent of their Overseer. If they do, they will be liable to have their time set off.

4th Anyone who by negligence or misconduct causes damage to the machinery, or impedes the progress of the work, will be liable to make good the damage for the same.

5th Anyone employed for a certain length of time, will be expected to make up their lost time, if required, before they will be entitled to their pay.

6th Any person employed for no certain length of time, will be required to give at least 4 weeks' notice of their intention to leave (sickness excepted) or forfeit 4 weeks' pay, unless by particular agreement.

7th Anyone wishing to be absent any length of time, must get permission of the Overseer.

8th All who have leave of absence for any length of time will be expected to return in that time; and, in case they do not return in that time and do not give satisfactory reason, they will be liable to forfeit one week's work or less, if they commence work again. If they do not, they will be considered as one who leaves without giving any notice.

9th   Anything tending to impede the progress of manufacturing in working hours, such as unnecessary conversation, reading, eating fruit, &c., &c., must be avoided.

10th   While I shall endeavour to employ a judicious Overseer, the help will follow his direction in all cases.

11th   No smoking will be allowed in the factory, as it is considered very unsafe, and particularly specified in the Insurance.

12th   In order to forward the work, job hands will follow the above regulations as well as those otherwise employed.

13th   It is intended that the bell be rung 5 minutes before the gate is hoisted, so that all persons may be ready to start their machines precisely at the time mentioned.

14th   All persons who cause damage to the machinery, break glass out of the windows, &c., will immediately inform the Overseer of the same.

15th   The hands will take breakfast, from the 1st of November to the last of March, before going to work—they will take supper from the 1st of May to the last of August, 30 minutes past 5 o'clock p.m.—from the 20th of September to the 20th of March between sundown and dark—25 minutes will be allowed for breakfast, 30 minutes for dinner, and 25 minutes for supper, and no more from the time the gate is shut till started again.

16th   The hands will leave the Factory so that the doors may be fastened within 10 minutes from the time of leaving off work.

AMASA WHITNEY.

Winchendon, Mass. July 5, 1830.

EXPLANATORY NOTES

"Gate" means the water-gate or sluice-gate, the raising of which started the wheel which transmitted the power for the mill operation.

The earliest start of the working day was about 4.15 a.m. The latest closing-time was about four hours after sunset, in December, except in case of emergency orders when the gate might not be dropped before ten. There is a record case of a female weaver earning nearly thirty-seven dollars in one month. This was pointed to with pride by factory owners as a conclusive retort to labour agitators. The average wage of a skilled female weaver was about $3.50 a week; of a child under ten, about $1.25. An intelligent girl of six was considered competent to run a Baxter loom.

Breakfast was served in the mill in all but four months—November to March; supper, the year around.

The original notice in the form of a broadside for posting, from which this copy is made, is in the possession of the Slater Mill Museum at Slaterville, R.I.